A WINTER WONDERLAND

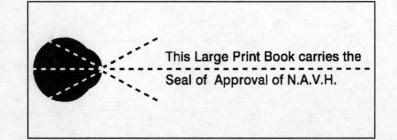

A WINTER WONDERLAND

FERN MICHAELS
HOLLY CHAMBERLIN
LESLIE MEIER
KRISTINA MCMORRIS

WHEELER PUBLISHING
A part of Gale, Cengage Learning

GALE
CENGAGE Learning·

Detroit • New York • San Francisco • New Haven, Conn • Waterville, Maine • London

GALE
CENGAGE Learning®

LIBRARY OF CONGRESS CATALOGING-IN-PUBLICATION DATA

Michaels, Fern.
  A winter wonderland / by Fern Michaels . . . [et al.]. — Large print ed.
    p. cm. — (Wheeler Publishing large print hardcover)
  ISBN 978-1-4104-4367-0 (hardcover) — ISBN 1-4104-4367-1 (hardcover)
  1. Christmas stories. 2. Large type books. I. Chamberlin, Holly, 1962–
II. Meier, Leslie. III. McMorris, Kristina. IV. Title.
  PS3563.I27W55 2012
  813'.54—dc23   2012028653

Published in 2012 by arrangement with Zebra Books, an imprint of Kensington Publishing Corp.

Printed in the United States of America
1 2 3 4 5 6 7 17 16 15 14 13

CONTENTS

■ ■ ■ ■

A WINTER
WONDERLAND
FERN MICHAELS

■ ■ ■ ■

CHAPTER 1

December 2012

Angelica Shepard tossed aside the script she'd been reading. It was beyond her skills as an actress even to begin to get into character for a part in yet another off-*off-*Broadway play under financial duress, and most likely — and this is only if she was lucky — it would have a short run, and the reviews would be atrocious.

When she began to study acting right out of high school, she'd given herself ten years to "make it" to the top. Meaning, she would be able to support herself and, if the gods smiled on her, she'd be able to quit her second job. At eighteen, ten years had seemed like a lifetime. Now at thirty-two, four years past her self-imposed deadline, she was still searching for the role that would catapult her to stardom.

She glanced at the script, then told herself to forget it. Something better was sure to come along.

A cup of tea would be nice right now, she decided as she walked three feet from her living room/bedroom to the small kitchen — if you could even call it a kitchen. It consisted of one small counter, four cabinets that hung above the countertop, a mini-stove, and a refrigerator. She'd made the best of the limited space, calling it home for more than ten years. It was a small studio, even by New York standards, but Angelica couldn't help feeling a wee bit of pride. Purchasing the place on her own, and in the city, was quite an accomplishment. Yes, she had to supplement her acting career with a part-time job bartending at one of New York's hottest nightspots, but without that job, she would never have been able to pay the mortgage, much less continue to pursue an acting career. Many times, Angelica had wanted to throw in the towel and just work at the club full-time, but she was determined to pursue an acting career a while longer. Maybe after six months, she would once again reevaluate her career choice.

She filled the white ceramic teakettle from the tap and placed it on top of the burner. Walking the few feet back into the living room/bedroom, she caught a glimpse of herself in the mirror above the small chest of drawers that held her entire wardrobe. She had medium-length coffee-colored hair and hazel eyes, which were just beginning to reveal the first signs of crow's-feet. Her skin was still smooth, her lips full, her teeth perfectly aligned, but she could see the beginning signs of aging. Maybe she should consider having Botox injections. Her friends swore by the stuff. But the thought of injecting botulism in her system was a bit too much.

She'd had high hopes for a part she'd auditioned for just last week. The role had called for an actress in her mid to late twenties who could sing reasonably well, dance, and, of course, act. Her agent, Al Greenberg, a kindly old guy who'd been in the business forever, had promised her he would call and tell her if she'd gotten the part. No sooner had the thought crossed her mind than her cell phone's musical ring filled the small studio apartment at the same time the teakettle began its low whistle. She grabbed her cell phone, leapt to the stove, and removed the kettle.

"Hello," she said anxiously.

"Angelica, my dear, how is my favorite client?"

She took a deep breath. "It depends on

11

why you're calling," she said, hoping to sound light and silly rather than dark and desperate.

Al laughed before responding. "Now, now, don't hold me responsible for your moods, kiddo." He paused.

Angelica heard his intake of breath and knew then that his reason for calling was not to impart the news she'd hoped for. A heavy sigh escaped her before she spoke. "Go ahead, Al. Shoot."

"I couldn't believe it when I heard it myself. Ross called." Ross was the director and producer of the play Angelica had auditioned for. "He wants Waverly Costas for the part."

Silence.

Al did not need to explain to her what that meant. Waverly Costas was twenty-three, with beautiful ash brown hair and a body to match. The sad thing was, and Angelica couldn't help but acknowledge the fact, the younger woman was actually a gifted actress. Her stomach instantly knotted, and her eyes pooled.

Darn, dang, and double darn! She'd *really* wanted the part! Inhaling, then slowly exhaling as she'd been taught in her yoga class, Angelica chewed her bottom lip, then plunked down on the cream-colored sofa.

"It's okay, Al. As you always say, it must not be the right part for me."

She heard Al's heavy sigh. "That's true. It takes time. Everyone wants to star on Broadway. You know the competition is tough, but your time will come, Angie." He used the pet name that he'd given her years ago.

"Sure, Al. You've been telling me that for how long now?" Of course, she knew exactly how long. He'd been her agent for twelve years. Yes, she'd had a number of good roles, all supporting, but never a lead.

"Ahh, come on, Angie, don't be discouraged. I hear that Johnny Jones has something in the works. It'll be the perfect role for you. Rumor is that Morgan Freeman has accepted the leading male role."

How many times had she missed out on "the perfect role"? And this one was with *Morgan Freeman*? Her favorite male actor in the world. Al knew it, too. She could just see it now. Her name beneath his on the playbill. Blotting her eyes with a corner of the dark green throw tossed on the back of the sofa, Angelica took another deep breath. "Listen, Al. We both know I'm not getting any younger. Maybe it's time to call it quits. We know youth rules the business these days. The younger, the better. I really appreciate everything you've done for me, truly I do. Maybe I'll take some time off during the holidays, rethink my career choice."

Al's robust laughter filled her ears. "I think that's an excellent idea, Angie, best I've heard all day. Why don't you head out West? I know how much you enjoy skiing. Hell, who knows, you might even meet some lucky ski bum."

Her spirits sank even further. Al sure had a way of making her feel good about herself today. "Yeah, that's what I'll do. As a matter of fact, I'll call the travel agency now. I'll get in touch when I return."

"See? That's the attitude! You have a Merry Christmas, kid, and I'll see you when you come home. Who knows what'll be waiting for you?"

"Yeah, who knows? Merry Christmas, Al." Angelica disconnected. She suddenly felt as though she were about to say a final good-bye to her dreams.

Fourteen years of hard work.

Down the drain.

CHAPTER 2

Dr. Parker North, trauma surgeon at Denver's Angel of Mercy Hospital for the past eight years, dropped the bloodsoaked bluish-green scrubs into a disposal bin. The coppery smell of blood filled his nostrils as he removed the paper covers from his Nike cross trainers. Inside the physicians' changing room, he took from his assigned locker his favorite pair of faded Levi's and a worn-out gray T-shirt that read HARVARD MEDICAL in faded black letters, and tossed both articles of clothing on a metal chair. Catching a glimpse of himself in the mirror, he saw that his dark hair was in need of a trim. Gray half-moons rimmed his dark eyes. He couldn't remember the last time he'd had a good night's sleep, but apparently his eyes had another story to tell, looking like he'd just woken up.

He stepped inside the stall, hoping to wash away the day's memories. Under the shower's warm, pelting spray, Dr. North mentally relived every last detail of the patient he'd spent the last three hours trying to save. Eight years old. It sickened him to think of the loss, the heartache the family felt. Seeing the young girl's parents break down had more of an effect on him than anything he had ever experienced before. Sadly, patients dying was part of the job, and Parker knew it. But seeing a perfectly healthy child die senselessly was not a part of his job that he relished. And knowing that the child's death could have been prevented, it was hard to accept. He truly sympathized with the parents, but he was also very angry. The little girl's death was the result of a total lack of parental responsibility.

Vigorously, he lathered up with the harsh antimicrobial soap the hospital provided. He scrubbed his skin until it hurt, but he knew that no matter how much he tried, he could not erase from his memory the image of the little girl's lifeless body.

She had been airlifted from Aurora, the third largest city in Colorado, just eight air miles away. Parker had been informed of her arrival minutes before the life chopper had landed in its designated area. He and his trauma team were prepared for the patient's arrival. Knowing it was a child put the team on high alert, not that an adult elicited any less of a response. They'd been informed by the paramedics that their patient had been hit by a vehicle while riding her bicycle on the street where she lived. They were also told the child had not been wearing a helmet. There were massive head injuries and severe blood loss.

Parker knew the statistics. The survival rate among children with head injuries was not good. Not at all. How could parents allow their children to ride bicycles without the proper headgear? A twenty-dollar helmet could prevent an extraordinarily large amount of traumatic brain injuries, especially in children. And donor blood could drastically improve one's chances when a significant amount was lost. This accident could've been prevented.

The swish of the trauma center's entrance doors and the thundering footsteps of the paramedics jolted him into the present. There was no time for what-ifs. He had a life to save.

Flashes of dark blue whizzed past Parker as he raced toward the gurney that held the victim. Quickly, Parker assessed the girl's visible wounds. Her left arm was almost detached from her shoulder, her right foot was shattered, the bones haphazardly resembling a set of pickup sticks. Most concerning, she did not appear to feel any pain. After a hasty examination of the still child, Parker said, "Let's get a CT scan, stat."

Within seconds, a portable computed tomography — CT unit — was quickly wheeled into the trauma unit next to the gurney. The technicians made fast work of performing the CT and getting the results to radiology.

Parker did what was required of him but knew at this point that his efforts might not save this little girl's life. She'd lost way too much blood and was completely unresponsive. When the tech returned with the CT results, Parker's heart plunged to his feet and back. The parents needed to be told of her condition immediately.

"Where are the parents?" Dr. North barked.

"They're on their way," a nurse offered.

Dr. North nodded, probed the child's neck. "We don't have much time. Let's get this child to surgery. There is intracranial pressure." He looked at the machine, which beeped with the child's vitals. Her oxygen level was dropping. Fast.

"Let's get moving! We don't have much time." Knowing the little girl's chances were slim to none, Dr. Parker North was going to do everything within his power to see that she survived.

Two and half hours later, he knew it was time to inform the parents of their loss.

Parker turned the water off and stood inside the shower, mindless of the cold water dripping off him as he remembered his unsuccessful efforts to save the patient. A child was dead, two parents were devastated, and his skill as a trauma neurosurgeon was not up to standards, at least not *his* standards. He should have been able to save the girl. He had tried every medical procedure he knew, but sadly, her injuries were just too severe.

Knowing it was useless to continue to mentally flagellate himself, he reached for the white towel that hung limply on a rusting steel rod.

Fifteen minutes later, he was dressed and in his rusted Ford pickup truck heading to his apartment just blocks away from the hospital. He was a trauma surgeon and part of the job was being there when he was needed. He could make it from bed to the hospital in nine minutes flat. Faster if he ran the two traffic lights between his apartment and the hospital.

After today's loss, Parker North had decided to do something he hadn't done since he'd begun his residency. He was taking some much-needed time away from his duties as a doctor. What had happened today made him realize the true value of life and his role as a doctor in saving precious lives. He'd never suffered from the God complex that some doctors did, but at that moment he wished for any other profession than that of a doctor. Seeing the looks on the faces of the parents when he had told them he hadn't been able to save their daughter had made him cringe.

He'd wanted to be a doctor his entire life. His father had been a cardiologist, but, sadly, he'd died from a heart attack before Parker had graduated from high school. His mother was still alive and well but spent most of her time hopping from one cruise ship to another, so it was only very occasionally that he saw her. After his father's unexpected death, his mother hadn't been the same. And if he was honest with himself, he hadn't been either. His father's death had led him to this very moment in time. And right now, he did not want to be a doctor. He did not want the responsibility of holding another human being's life in his hands.

Maybe it was time to consider a career change.

CHAPTER 3

Angelica headed for the car-rental agency at Denver International Airport just as she had numerous times in the past. She never tired of seeing the extensive art collection as she made her way through the airport, where she'd reserved a four-wheel-drive vehicle. Sculptures, murals, and dozens of paintings rivaled those in many of New York City's museums.

She located the rental booth quickly, placing her carry-on beside her as she joined the other travelers in the lengthy line. She'd never seen the line quite so long but remembered it was the Christmas season. Like New York City during the holidays, the Colorado city was transformed into a shiny magical land of dreams and never-ending cheer. This was her first trip away from the city during the holiday season. Suddenly, she doubted her decision to leave, to ski and pretend her life was as it should be.

It could be worse, she thought, as she viewed the long lines at the other car-rental counters. She had her health, a decent amount of savings, and a home of her own. Sort of. Hers and the bank who held the mortgage. For now, Angelica figured this was as good as it was going to get. She decided she would enjoy the next two weeks and forget about her acting career and anything connected to New York. Or at least she would try.

As she waited in the ever-growing line, she observed the scene around her. Tourists from all over the world occupied every available inch of space. Some carried gigantic pieces of luggage. Others, like herself, pulled a small carry-on behind them, while some, mostly people with families, pushed fancy strollers as small children lugged mini-suitcases with their favorite superhero characters emblazoned on them. Backpacks of every shape, size, and color perched on the backs of many. Businessmen in Brooks Brothers suits carried their iPads in soft leather cases. Angelica couldn't help but smile. Technology. She hadn't upgraded to the latest and greatest in the technological field since her profession didn't require much more than a telephone, but someday she'd investigate the high-tech world and decide if the leap was worth it.

Slowly, the line inched forward. She continued to peruse her surroundings while she waited. The voices of children could be heard throughout the airport, their shouts of welcome and cries of good-bye suddenly making her homesick for the familiar sights and sounds of New York City. The scents from street-side vendors hawking roasted chestnuts, skewers of overcooked meat, and soggy hot dogs permeated the city. The acrid odor from the subway, and the exhaust from hundreds of taxis that traversed the city, were as familiar and comforting to her as a child's favorite blanket — which brought to mind the red and green afghan she'd knitted years ago and had kept in her tiny dressing room at the Forty-seventh Street Playhouse. She'd left it there after her last performance and had never gone back to retrieve it. Maybe another young actor could use it. The backstage at the theater was always too cold anyway. Her last conversation with Al let her know she was on the downside of her career. There wouldn't be time to knit backstage while waiting for her call. At her age, she'd be lucky to get an acting job in a dinner theater. The kind where the actors and actresses waited tables in between acts.

She should've gone to college. Studied literature. She'd bet the bank she wouldn't be out of a job if that were the case. The line started to move, jarring her from her negative thoughts. 'Tis the season, she thought, and forced a smile. For the next two weeks, she was not going to think about her career or lack of one.

She'd said that twice to herself already.

No, she was going to ski until she dropped, drink hot toddies by the fireplace, curl up with a good book at the end of the day. Do whatever she pleased, and all by herself.

Another wave of sadness overwhelmed her.

"Stop!" she whispered harshly. When she saw several people glance at her, she did what she knew best. She plastered a huge grin on her face and acted as though she hadn't a clue why they were staring at her.

When it was her turn at the counter, Angelica removed the required driver's license and credit card from her wallet, signed on the dotted line, and listened carefully to the agent's instructions. She'd asked for a vehicle equipped with a GPS just in case. The last thing she wanted was to get lost in the Colorado mountains. Not that she planned on leaving Maximum Glide, the ski resort where she planned to ski and sip all those hot toddies. She had splurged and rented a small cabin located midway up the mountain. She could've stayed in Telluride itself, but Angelica wanted time to reflect and come to a decision. Being isolated would force her to focus on her choice of careers.

With the keys to her rental in hand, she found the automatic doors leading to the parking garage. Instantly, they swished open, allowing the frigid wintry air into the overly warm airport for the briefest of seconds. Angelica shivered, glad that she'd worn her heavy parka. New York was cold, yes, but she thought Denver downright bone-chilling as she searched the giant lot for her vehicle's designated parking space.

After walking for what felt like a mile, Angelica spied the white Lincoln Navigator. A male attendant wearing olive khakis and a rich brown jacket greeted her, asking her to wait while he inspected the vehicle for scratches and dents. He walked around the SUV twice, then handed her a pink slip of paper attached to a clipboard. She signed the slip.

"We're supposed to get some nasty weather tonight," he said as he inspected her signature. "Be careful."

Having spent her entire adult life in New

York City, she wasn't the most experienced driver in the world. Too bad there wasn't a taxi or a subway to deliver her to her destination. "Uh, what do you mean by 'nasty'?"

The young guy gave her a quick once-over. "Blizzard nasty. The interstate closes in bad weather. If you're heading to the mountains, you'd best be on your way."

Angelica thanked him. Using the key fob to unlock the hatch, she placed her luggage in the back before sliding into the driver's seat.

Knowing she had several hours of driving ahead of her, it suddenly occurred to her that it would be very late by the time she reached her cabin. As she adjusted her seat belt and rearview mirror she remembered that she had to program the GPS. She located the Post-it note crumpled inside her denim bag that had the address on it. It took several minutes for her to become at ease with the GPS before she tapped the address on the touch screen. When she saw the travel time and mileage displayed on the flat screen and realized she had a six-and-a-half-hour road trip ahead of her, she became weak in the knees.

"Darn, what was I thinking?" she asked out loud.

"I wasn't," she answered herself as she drove out of the underground parking lot.

Realizing it was too late to rectify her mistake, she looked at the time. Just after four thirty. She'd be lucky to make it to her rental cabin by midnight. If the car-rental attendant was right, and the weather took a nosedive, she was in trouble. Big-time. She didn't know her way around Colorado and wasn't as well traveled as one would expect for a woman her age. Living in New York City, she had everything one could possibly need without benefit of an automobile. There was no need to learn how to navigate through a blizzard. That's what taxis and subways were for. And if those were not available in a really bad snowstorm, then one just stayed home.

As she piloted her way through the congested roads around the airport, she focused on the task of driving, paying close attention to the animated female voice coming from the GPS. She should have booked a flight directly to Telluride and saved herself the aggravation of the long drive. She'd been in such a rush to leave after her phone call with Al, she hadn't really cared where she was headed as long as it was away from New York. Now that she had calmed down a bit, she saw the stupidity of her actions.

The drive was going to take longer than the flight had.

An hour later, Angelica was cruising along on Colorado's I-70. So far, so good. Traffic wasn't too bad, and she found a radio station that played nothing but Christmas music. The weather was holding its own, too.

Maybe the trip wasn't going to be so bad after all.

CHAPTER 4

Dr. Parker North hated leaving at the last minute, but he felt that he had no other choice. He needed time away, time to reflect on his future as a medical professional. When his father died, he'd decided to become a doctor, a trauma surgeon. He wanted to see and heal up close. Never once had he questioned his choice of careers. It was in his blood. Both his father and grandfather had been doctors. But, for the first time in his life, he wondered if he'd made the right decision. Losing that little girl had left its mark on him. She should be alive now. But she wasn't because he hadn't been able to save her.

Briefly, he thought that her parents should be charged with neglect. If they'd used their brains, this would never have happened. Parents should always provide helmets for their kids. In his profession, he saw head injuries daily. Seeing the devastation, the regret, the sorrow on the faces of the little girl's parents, he knew they had to know they were responsible for their child's death. Quite the burden, he thought. If only they'd been more aware.

He could "if only" all day. It would get him nowhere.

Parker couldn't put it off any longer. He'd taken an indeterminate leave of absence. He wasn't going to sit around his apartment and mope. He'd hear the ambulances anyway; he lived that close to the hospital. No, he had to leave, go somewhere to relax, clear his head, and decide if he wanted to continue practicing medicine. So, he was about to do what he'd promised an old college buddy he would do years ago.

Parker North was going to call Max Jorgensen and take him up on his offer to spend some time at Maximum Glide, his ski resort in Telluride, Colorado. Then he remembered Leon, his ten-year-old black and white tuxedo cat. He'd have to bring him along or hire someone to sit for him. It was too late to find someone, so that decision was made. Leon, who absolutely hated riding in his truck, was going on vacation with him. He knew that Max had dogs, was an avid animal lover, so he wasn't worried about Leon being unwelcome.

Once Parker had made up his mind, there was no stopping him. He found his ancient suitcase stuck in the front closet, along with his old skis and boots. He examined them and decided he could always replace them once he tested them on the slopes. It'd been almost twenty years since he'd skied, and he was a native.

He yanked jeans and sweatshirts from his single dresser, warm wool socks, and several T-shirts. In the bathroom, he stuffed his shaving gear and toothbrush in a Ziploc bag. He found Leon's carrier, grabbed several cans of cat food, then, since Leon was an indoor cat, he emptied the litter box, rinsed it out, and tucked a thirty-pound sack of litter next to the front door so he wouldn't forget.

Once he finished, he checked his e-mail, responded to a few that were important, then figured he might as well make the call to Max.

He'd met Max when they were both students at the University of Colorado in Boulder. Max had gone on to achieve Olympic fame, winning several gold medals. The last Parker had heard, he'd married, and his wife, a police officer, had been shot and killed in the line of duty. That'd been three or four years ago. Hopefully Max had healed and moved on, but Parker knew it couldn't have been easy.

He himself had been involved in a serious relationship while attending Harvard. Jacqueline Bersch. A knockout. Tiny, with large brown eyes and chocolate hair, she had a smile that would've made Scrooge grin. He'd fallen for her hard and fast. They'd been inseparable through medical school and during their residency. After graduation they'd both accepted positions in Denver. Dr. Jac, as he'd referred to her, went into private practice a year after they returned to Denver. Sadly, she'd fallen for her partner, Dr. Jonathan Flaherty. She broke Parker's heart, and he hadn't been in a serious relationship since. Too much effort anyway.

He flipped through the contact list on his cell phone, found Max's number, and hit Send.

Max answered on the third ring. "I hope my caller ID is working," he said. "It says that this call is from Parker North, but I know that can't be right."

Parker grinned. "It's working just fine, my friend. I called to see if that offer still stands."

Max chuckled. "I thought you had forgotten. It's been what — ten, fifteen years?"

"I don't think it's been that long," Parker

answered, then did a quick mental count. Close to fifteen. Where had the years gone? It seemed like yesterday he and Max had shared a dorm and spent many late nights kicking up their heels and suffering for it the next day. The memory made him grin. "It's been a while. Hey, I heard about your wife. It's probably too late, but for what it's worth, I'm sorry."

"Thanks. It was a tough time in my life. I remarried a few years ago. I have a daughter now. Her name is Ella. She's two. Life is good right now."

At the mention of a child, Parker clammed up. It took him a couple of seconds to get his bearings.

"Congratulations, Max. I've let too much time pass. I've missed a lot of life. I just took a leave of absence, which is my reason for calling. Would it be too forward of me to think that offer you made me after you purchased that big resort still stands?"

"Hell no, it wouldn't be too forward. Just give me a time and date, and I'll make sure you're taken care of. I'd like to get you on the slopes again, my friend, and I'd like you to meet Grace and Ella."

Parker wasn't up for kids just then, but he wasn't going to tell that to Max after all these years. He'd perfected avoidance after

Jac dumped him. There was no avoiding the occasional bumping into one another as they both spent most of their days and some nights at Angel of Mercy. "Actually, I'm leaving now. I need to relax a bit, take some time for myself. I haven't taken any time off since I started practicing. And I'm bringing Leon, my cat — that is if it's okay with you." He could not bring himself to explain the real reason why he needed a break.

"You know what they say about all work and no play," Max said, then added, "It's crazy busy this time of year, but I'll hook you up. I'll reserve one of my best condos for you. You're more than welcome to bring Leon; hell, you know I love dogs and cats."

"Yep, just me and the fur ball. You sure this is a good time? I don't want to mess up anyone's holiday plans."

"Any time is good, Parker. We always leave a few condos vacant. Just in case, you know, the president or the secretary of state decides at the last minute to come for some time on the slopes. I can't wait to introduce you to Grace and Ella. I'll tell Grace to set an extra plate for dinner tomorrow night. She can cook better than anyone, and her mother cooks, too. And she's the sweetest old gal you'd ever want to meet. The mother, of course. Grace is definitely not old."

Parker couldn't help but smile. Max had it bad for his wife *and* mother-in-law. He was happy for him. "I'll look forward to meeting them both," he said.

"I promise you won't be disappointed," Max said. "When you arrive, just come to the main building, you can't miss it. You'll see the signs that lead to the registration office. I'll have everything set up for you. Drive safe. The forecast is calling for massive amounts of snow once you're on the continental divide side."

"I'm leaving now. If the weather gets too bad, I'll call you and drive in tomorrow morning. Max, I really do appreciate this, especially since it's last minute. I owe you, big-time."

Max chuckled. "Not to worry. It's my pleasure. Now get your ass on the road before that storm hits."

"I'll see you tomorrow." Parker was about to hang up when he realized he had no clue where Max lived. "Where can I find that dinner you promised?"

"I'll pick you up tomorrow evening around seven," Max said.

"Good, then I'm out of here. And, Max, thanks for this. I really need to get the hell out of Dodge for a while."

After hanging up, Parker looked around at

his apartment to make sure everything was as it should be. There were no plants to water, no mail to hold, as he had most of his bills paid electronically now. No one in the complex would miss him, that's for sure. He did set the automatic timer, so his single lamp in the living room would come on for three hours every evening, but that was it. He took one last glance around, then locked the door behind him.

It took twenty minutes to force Leon into the carrier. Another ten for him to stop howling. "Look, it'll be nice for both of us. We need a change of pace, and you, my friend, are coming along no matter what, so give it up and get over it." He placed all of Leon's necessities in the back of the old Ford, then tossed the skis and boots in the back, too. He placed his suitcase on the passenger's side, below Leon's carrier.

After programming the radio station to his favorite rock station, he checked his gas gauge, then pulled out of his assigned parking space. He'd devoted his entire life to medicine and hadn't bothered with much of a personal life since Jac. It was a sad testimony for a man nearing forty years of age.

As he turned onto the street, Parker focused on nothing but his driving. The last thing he needed was to wind up at Angel of Mercy as a patient. Hearing a favorite tune on the radio, he cranked up the volume and headed north. Fortunately, Leon didn't seem to mind the loud music.

CHAPTER 5

Angelica checked the bright blue numbers on the dashboard and saw it was 11:36. She'd accomplished her goal by arriving at her cabin before midnight. The snow hadn't been as heavy as predicted, and she'd only stopped once for gas and coffee. She'd listened to Christmas music, singing along to several songs she'd known since childhood and focusing her attention on arriving safely. Once she was ensconced in her cabin, then she would contemplate the real reason behind her sudden trip.

She found the registration building without too much trouble. Not only was the area well lit, but there were hundreds of colorful Christmas lights strung throughout the small ski village. Tall pines were decked out in sparkling white lights from top to bottom. Freshly fallen snow resting on the tree branches reminded her of a scene directly out of a Norman Rockwell painting.

A piercing night wind sent up flurries of snow throughout the parking area. Shivering, Angelica carefully made her way across the icy asphalt. The last thing she needed was to fall. She'd been there, done that, in the city more than once. With that in mind, she practically tiptoed to the office.

An engraved wooden sign indicated she should ring the doorbell when arriving after hours. Sure that midnight qualified as after hours, she placed a gloved finger on the bell and pushed. Hearing a dim buzzing from inside, Angelica hoped she hadn't gotten anyone out of a warm bed, but if she did, she assumed this was part of their job requirements, and they were used to waking at odd hours. When no one answered her buzz, she pushed the lighted dial again. In seconds, she heard heavy footsteps leading toward the door. "I'm coming, I'm coming. . . . Keep your britches on," said a male voice from inside.

Britches? Angelica couldn't help but smile. She could hear little beeps coming from inside. Probably deactivating an alarm. After hearing of several burglaries in her area, she had had one of her own installed in her apartment just last year and recognized the familiar beeps.

A bearded older man opened the door.

"Come on in, you're letting the cold inside. You must be that actress from New York. Max told me you'd be coming today. He didn't mention it'd be this late."

Stepping inside the warm office, she spoke. "I'm sorry. I flew in from Denver. It was a much longer drive than I remembered. I hate to get you out of bed."

The old man, probably in his mid to late seventies, brushed a bearlike hand in the air. "Who says I was in bed? I was checkin' my Facebook page and got to talkin' to an old pal from high school."

Angelica couldn't help but grin. Seniors were certainly keeping up to date with technology these days. "I hear a lot of people say they've found old friends through the social media. I'm afraid I'm behind the rest of the world as I don't even own a computer. Just a cell phone." And an extremely old one, too, but she didn't say that.

He gazed at her, then turned, motioning for her to follow him. She'd bet anything that this old guy, when he was not behind the counter pecking away at the keyboard, dressed up as Santa. He had the requisite white hair and matching beard. Crystal-clear blue eyes sparkled behind rimless, round glasses. The belly was perfect, too. Not that she would mention that. She grinned as she imagined him all decked out in red.

Behind the counter, he clicked a few keys, then, without looking up, said, "I know, I know, I hear it all the time. And just so you know, I only dress up because Amanda and Ashley expect me to."

A mind reader, too? She had no clue who Amanda and Ashley were, but figured if he wanted her to know, he'd tell her.

"I would've never guessed," she added. "But you do look the part. The Santa at Macy's in New York City doesn't look quite as realistic."

"So they say. Now" — he stared at the monitor — "Ms. Shepard, it says here you've reserved the Gracie's Way cabin. You'll love the view."

"Uh, yes." She didn't realize the cabin had a name. "I want to spend the days skiing and the nights relaxing."

"Then you've come to the right place. Gracie's Way is smack-dab in the center of the mountain. Has its own lift, too, but I assume you already knew that." He turned his back to her.

No, I didn't, she thought, *but he doesn't need to know just how unprepared I am.* If she'd been thinking straight, she would have booked her flight directly into Telluride, but she'd had other things on her mind.

"Of course, it's just what I wanted," she said, winging it and filling the silence while the old guy removed several sheets from the printer behind him.

While he busied himself with the paperwork, Angelica took the time to view her surroundings. On the wall to her right was a giant rock fireplace. A log chose that moment to fall from the top of a large stack. Red, yellow, and orange sparks shot out like a miniature shower of fireworks. She took a deep breath, loving the heady scent of wood smoke.

A roomy dark brown sofa was placed directly across from the massive structure. A table made out of logs was covered with magazines and a few paperback novels, inviting one to sit and relax. Angelica imagined that during business hours, guests took advantage of the charming arrangement while they enjoyed the warmth from the fire. Floor-to-ceiling windows flanked the fireplace. She guessed that, during the day, the view of the mountains was out of this world. But she wasn't here to stay in the registration area and knew her view would certainly rival this one, or so the travel agent said when she'd made the booking.

The old man fanned the white sheets of paper across the counter, reminding Angelica of the snow angels she used to make in the snow when she was a kid. The memory made her grin.

"If you'll just sign here, here, and here," he said, adding, "and we'll need a credit card and your driver's license."

He turned the papers around for her signature. She scribbled her name, removed a credit card and her license from her wallet. He took them, then turned away from her. She observed him as he made copies of her identification. Soft tan khakis and a black and gold flannel shirt looked to be well worn, comfortable. On his feet were a pair of snakeskin cowboy boots. *Well, I am out West,* she thought.

He placed a single-page map in front of her. "Okay, young lady, it looks like you're all set. If you'll just follow this road" — he traced a single black line with a bright yellow highlighter pen — "all the way to this intersection, then turn right. You can't miss the cabin. The lights are on, and there's coffee fixins, but no food. You'll want to get down to the market first thing in the morning if you want eggs and milk and the like. Food sells out fast, just so you know." He nodded at the exit, his way of dismissing her.

So focused on arriving safely, she hadn't given the first thought to food. She should have bought a few basic necessities when she'd stopped for gas, but again shoulda, coulda, woulda didn't cut it.

"I'll keep that in mind," she said before stepping out into the bracing night air. She gave a half wave to the old man, then trekked back across the parking lot.

Tiny snowflakes swirled beneath the amber glow from the lights. An old beat-up pickup truck pulled into the lot, blocking further viewing of the snowflakes' late-night performance. Probably works here, she thought as she walked carefully across the lot. No one in his right mind would be out in this kind of weather unless he absolutely had to.

A loud meowlike sound startled her. As she turned around to see where the noise was coming from, she lost her footing. Flailing about as she searched for something to hold on to in order to break her fall, she suddenly found two large hands wrapped around her waist. Stunned at the speed of her rescuer, she turned around to look and see who'd saved her from total humiliation — sort of.

Describing her rescuer as tall, dark, and handsome in no way did justice to the stranger who gently helped her to regain her footing. Stunned by the sudden turn of events, Angelica took a moment to gather herself, to recover from whatever it was she needed to recover from. Never one to be at a loss for words, she couldn't come up with a single syllable as she stared at . . . this . . . *classic Greek god* who was still holding onto her arm.

"Miss, are you all right?"

All she could manage was a slight nod as she stood there, blank, amazed, and very shaken. Finally she found her voice. "Uh, yes, I'm okay, just . . . well, I'm fine," she said, her tone almost defiant. *Why does this strange man make me feel defenseless, and totally aware that I'm a woman?* It was entirely out of character for her, but she was out of character. She was completely out of her element there in that . . . ice palace. *I should have stayed in the city.*

"If you're sure?" the man said, his voice sounding impatient.

Who is this guy? And why the attitude? Angelica wondered. Blinking rapidly to clear her vision, she turned to face her rescuer. What she saw momentarily threw her off guard again. She'd spent plenty of time

45

around some of the sexiest men alive — she was an actress, after all, and it was part of the job. But this . . . this guy defied the rules. He didn't own a sports car if that rusted old truck was his. His clothing didn't appear to be custom made, and Angelica couldn't forget the fact that he was there so late. More than likely, he worked at the resort and had been on his way inside the registration building when he'd rescued her.

Lucky for me.

Forcing herself to step away from him, Angelica tossed her hair over her shoulder, something she'd learned from improv, then she put her hands on her hips. If that didn't reek of confidence, she didn't know what would.

"Actually, I am more than all right. I am on vacation, and I plan to enjoy every single minute of it. It's gotten off to a bad start, but I'm sure it can only go uphill from here."

She was about to walk to her SUV when the man placed a strong hand on her forearm. She shivered, and it wasn't from the outside temperature. "You're sure you can drive? You look a bit rough."

Had she heard him right? Did he say she looked *rough*? Taking a minute to absorb his words, her first response was to tell him to kiss off and mind his own business. Her second response was to tell him to take a flying leap, but gazing at the giant mountains that surrounded her, that might not be such a good idea. Especially if the guy had issues.

Knowing she couldn't continue to stand there and stare, she found her voice. "I'm quite capable of driving, thank you very much. I was simply startled by that noise. I'm sure I heard a wild cat or something. Did you hear anything?" she asked, and gazed at his hand, which still lingered on her forearm. Apparently, he realized he was still touching her and quickly removed his hand, stuffing it in his pocket. *He appears to be uncomfortable,* Angelica thought. *Good. Let him stew for a bit. He would probably look a bit rough himself if he had just driven for almost seven hours in not so perfect conditions.*

He nodded. "It was Leon. My cat. He hates riding in the truck. Sorry he scared you. Watch your step, this ice can be treacherous," he added before proceeding to walk toward the registration building.

What does he think I am, she wondered as she watched him walk away. *A kid?*

No, she was definitely not a kid. A kid

would not be looking at a man's rear view
with such blatant lust.

CHAPTER 6

Parker pressed the doorbell and waited. He'd left the truck running, with the heater cranked up to high for Leon, but cracked the window an inch, just in case. He hated arriving at such a late hour, but it couldn't be helped. The old Ford pickup truck maxed out at fifty-five miles an hour. After stopping for gas and a quick bite, he'd taken his time, and it had gotten away from him. It had been almost midnight when he'd pulled into the deserted parking lot at Maximum Glide.

He'd only just stepped out of his truck when he'd seen the woman slip when she heard Leon's cry of misery. Lucky for them both, instinct kicked in, and he'd caught her in the nick of time. Another second and she would've smacked her head against the icy asphalt. The last thing he wanted to do on his self-imposed sabbatical was step back into the role of medical doctor. Hell, he wasn't sure if he even wanted to return to Angel of Mercy at all. Maybe he'd just enjoy being a ski bum for a while. He and Leon could hang tight on the slopes indefinitely. He wondered if they made skis for cats. Something to look into later.

Before he could pursue the thought of life without the responsibilities of being a doctor, the door opened. A heavyset man with a white beard and rosy cheeks stood to the side. "You must be Dr. North. Max said you were coming this evening. I figured you'd be late, too. The weather and such."

Parker smiled, then stepped inside out of the cold. The old man held out a hand to him. "Thanks for waiting," Parker said. I just took my time; I guess I should have phoned ahead."

"Not to worry. I'm up. Just checked in that actress from New York City. Poor girl drove all the way from Denver."

"She must be the woman I saw in the parking lot," Parker said out loud.

"I would suspect she is. Now, I have instructions to personally drive you to your condo. Max said you would probably be arriving in a beat-up old truck that wouldn't make the climb."

Parker laughed. Figures. Max remembered everything. "Yeah, I still have the old truck, but I'm sure she can make it up the mountain. There's no need for you to bother. It's late and cold. If you'll just give me the directions, I'm sure I can find my way." He didn't add that he had an angry feline in the truck. No, he'd keep that tidbit of info to himself. As long as Max was okay with it, then that's all that mattered.

The old man, unnamed at that point, pondered his words. "If you're sure. I'd hate for you to get lost. The weather gets mighty cold at high altitudes. You sure your truck can make it?"

No, he wasn't. He wasn't sure of anything other than that he was dead tired and wanted to lie down and forget about the day, but Parker wasn't totally without social skills. "I'm sure. She's in the best shape ever. Just had a new transmission installed last winter."

The old man nodded. "Yep, that'll make it up the mountain, no doubt. Now, if you'll just look at this." He produced a single sheet of paper. "If you follow this road" — he traced a thin white line with a yellow highlighter pen — "then turn here. The condo unit Max has reserved for you is the best. The penthouse. It's smack-dab in the middle of the mountain. You'll have access to the private ski lift. There are skis and boots of every size waiting for you. Max wasn't sure you'd have them, so he took a few guesses and had Candy Lee pick out several pairs. She works at the Snow Zone — that's the ski shop around the corner. The kid picked out the best of the best and left them next to the fireplace. There's a boot warmer inside, too. Make sure and use it. Most people don't and then don't find out until it's too late that it's lots of work puttin' on a cold boot. Boots slide right on when they're warm. Remember that."

"I will, thanks," Parker said. Somewhere in the back of his mind he knew that but was glad for the reminder.

"Well, then you'd better get goin' while you can. I'll let Max know you arrived first thing in the mornin'. He said he was coming to pick you up for supper tomorrow. I'm sure Grace and Ella will be with him, too. Probably the other girls, as well."

Parker stopped.

Other girls?

It would be just like Max to try and fix him up without giving him a chance to explain that the last thing on his mind was women. No, he'd better give the old man a message for Max. "Tell Max I'm flying solo now and prefer to keep it that way. I don't want to see any girls," he said, a bit abruptly, but he wanted the man to understand that when he relayed his message to Max, he was serious. He was there to relax and reevaluate his future, not entangle himself in a winter romance.

The old guy chuckled, hearty and warm. He shook his big head from side to side. "He didn't tell you about the girls, did he?"

"No, he neglected to tell me about the girls."

"They're Stephanie's kids. She's the manager at Snow Zone. They usually ride up with Max and Grace when they get the chance. Ashley and Amanda. Both smart as a whip. Max'll want you to ski with them while you're here, too."

Parker felt as though he'd been poked with a pin, and all the life drained from him.

Kids? The girls were kids!

Maybe Max had changed after all.

"Sure, I guess I'm up for meeting a couple of kids," he said when he couldn't think of anything else to say. Relief flowed like oxygen throughout his veins.

"You best get started. It takes about forty-five minutes to make it up the mountain in the daylight, a little longer at night."

Parker nodded, took the sheet of paper with the map off the counter. He turned for the door, then stopped. "You never told me your name."

The older man shifted his eyes up, then down. "No, I reckon I didn't."

Suspicious, Parker waited. The man shoved his large hands inside his pants pockets. "Aww, you'll just laugh like everyone else does. The name's Nick. Nicholas Star."

For a second, Parker thought the old guy was teasing him, but when he saw the red flush creep across his face, he knew he was serious. Having a somewhat unusual name himself, Parker just nodded, then spoke. "It was nice meeting you, Mr. Star. I'll see you around."

Blue eyes sparkled, and Parker would've sworn Mr. Star's belly shook just like Clement C. Moore described in " 'Twas the Night Before Christmas."

CHAPTER 7

Angelica pulled off to the side of the road, allowing a semitruck to get in front of her. It had been virtually blinding her, its glowing headlights shining in her rearview mirror. Pulling back onto the winding road, she crept up the mountain, careful to keep her speed low in case she hit a patch of ice. Though the SUV had four-wheel drive, she was not anxious to use it. No, she would take her time. It wasn't as if she had a schedule to keep. She glanced at the clock on the dash. Almost one in the morning. Smiling, Angelica mused that if she were in the city, she would be going out for breakfast with friends right now. They'd be lucky to get to bed before sunrise. She'd kept up this routine for so many years, she wondered if she would be able to adjust her internal clock. Given the time difference, it shouldn't be too hard, but again, she had no curtain call, no one to make any demands on her time. She was totally on her own, without responsibilities, for the first time in her adult life.

Grinning, she shifted the SUV into low gear. She could get used to this, but if anything, despite her chosen career, Angelica was a realist. Being an adult in and of itself was a responsibility. A couple of weeks of snow and fun was her due. She'd worked hard. At thirty-two, she wasn't about to shuck all responsibilities and give up completely. Give up her career? She might not have a choice. Youth was everything in her business, but there were other areas in her profession to explore.

She adjusted her rearview mirror and focused her attention on the road. It wasn't the time to mull over her professional life. The satellite radio station she'd been listening to since she'd left the airport turned to static. "You'd think the reception would be better at this elevation," she observed out loud. Adjusting the dial to another station, she turned up the volume, singing along as Bing Crosby crooned "White Christmas." It was her all-time favorite Christmas song.

A flash of light coming from behind made her take a glance in her rearview mirror. Whoever was behind her had the bright lights on. "Idiot," she muttered before tapping on her brakes several times in a row, hoping the driver would notice and realize that the lights were blinding her. Careful to watch the road ahead but aware of the vehicle trailing her, she slowed down. Then she realized the car was stopping when she saw the driver pull to the side of the road. Whoever it was flashed the bright lights several times.

Not wanting to, but fearing the passenger or passengers in the vehicle might be a mother with children, or someone with a health issue, Angelica did what anyone else in her position would do. She stopped, made a three-point turn, then pulled alongside the other vehicle but kept her cell phone in her hand and did not put the SUV into park. If she had to hightail it back to the registration office, at least she would be heading in the right direction. She hit the button to lower the window.

When she realized that this was the same old beat-up pickup truck she'd encountered in the parking lot, she wasn't sure if she should be happy that at least the man wasn't a total stranger to her. He *had* prevented her from smacking the asphalt and injuring herself after being startled by that noisy cat of his.

Angelica watched as he struggled to lower

the driver's window. What she knew about trucks could fill a thimble, but it was enough to judge that this one was probably close to her age. *Poor guy,* she thought, *it must be all he can afford.*

"Hi," was all she could come up with when she saw his face. She was glad for the darkness.

"Yeah, hi. I'm thinking this old gal just decided to take a rest. Could you give me a lift to the office?" He smiled at her, and Angelica's heart rate quickened.

I'll take you anywhere, she thought, then mentally smacked herself.

"Sure, I'd be happy to, but I don't know if it will do you any good. That old guy in the office wasn't too thrilled when I took him away from his social networking." She smiled, hoping she'd licked all the chocolate from her teeth. She had a sweet tooth and rarely went anywhere without a few chocolate bites. Lucky for her, it didn't take much to satisfy her craving.

"I think he enjoys every minute of his job; he's just slightly embarrassed by his name," Parker informed her.

Angelica realized the old guy had never told her his name. "And what would that be?" she asked, still allowing the blistering cold air inside.

"Nicholas Star."

Laughing, she understood. "He does look somewhat like the man in red, with that white beard and big belly," she said. "Do you work here?" she asked brazenly. What else would he be doing out this early in this kind of weather?

"No, I'm here to ski for a couple of weeks," he said. "It's not getting any warmer inside this old gal, so how about I lock up, and you can drive me down the mountain? I'm sure they have one of those all-night towing services in a place like this."

Angelica was surprised that he was a guest but didn't say so to him. He'd probably scrimped and saved all year for this trip. "If you're sure that's what you want. I could drive you to wherever you're staying and bring you back in the morning." Before the words were out of her mouth, she regretted saying them. She didn't know this guy, didn't know if he was a weirdo or what, though she had to admit he appeared normal and was certainly easy on the eyes.

"That's probably a good idea. I'll just leave a note on the windshield and call Max first thing in the morning. I'm sure he wouldn't mind."

She wanted to ask who Max was, but by that time she was so cold, her teeth were chattering, and she really didn't need to know. "Okay, let me turn this vehicle around while you lock up and write your note, but hey," she called out before rolling up her window, "you didn't tell me your name."

"Oh, sure. Parker North." He nodded, gave a brief, sexy smile, then removed his personal items from his truck, along with the whiny cat inside its carrier. "Mind taking him? He hates the cold."

"Angelica Shepard, nice to meet you, Mr. North," she said, as he walked around to the driver's side of the SUV, opened the rear door and placed the carrier on the seat. As an extra precaution, he adjusted the seat belt so that the carrier wouldn't fall off the seat. One never knew in this kind of weather.

She settled back in her seat before turning the heat to the highest setting. It was bitterly cold that night.

Angelica suddenly remembered how snippy and rude she'd been to him after he'd referred to her as rough, but it wasn't the most flattering comment she'd ever received. It wasn't a compliment at all, she reminded herself.

She watched as he pulled the old rattletrap as far off the narrow mountain road as possible, grabbed an outdated suitcase, an ancient pair of skis and ski boots, and what must have been a litter box. He waited next to the old truck. She hit the electric button to open the hatch. He tossed his things in the back before coming around to the passenger side. Angelica hit the automatic lock, praying she wasn't making a mistake by allowing a complete stranger to accompany her on a deserted mountain road in the wee hours of the morning. If her mother were still alive, she could just imagine what she would say to her. But she *had* lived in New York City for most of her life and was a fairly good judge of character. Though he appeared to be a bit unrefined, that didn't make him a bad person.

He slid into the passenger seat and held his hands against the heater vents. "It's much colder at this high elevation," he said before turning around to check on Leon. His accent remained neutral, giving no indication about what part of the country he was from. And she wasn't going to ask either.

Angelica put the SUV in low gear and slowly retraced the short distance she'd made before turning around. "I'm staying at Gracie's Way — that's what they're calling my cabin. How about you? Does your place have a name?"

Parker North seemed to be contemplating

her question. "No, I don't believe there was a name. It's the penthouse apartment at the main condos mid-mountain."

Penthouse apartment? I have totally misjudged this man. Of course, he might've won the trip. Given his mode of dress and transportation, he does not look as though he is financially equipped to foot the bill for an extravagant penthouse condo at a luxury ski resort.

Her surprise must've been obvious because Mr. North apparently felt the need to explain. "I went to college with Max Jorgensen. He owns Maximum Glide. He won several gold medals in the Olympics several years ago. He invited me for a complimentary stay, and I decided to take him up on his offer."

College? With the owner of the resort? Wow. Of course she'd heard of Max Jorgensen. Who hadn't? She had to admit, she was a wee bit impressed.

He produced the same map Mr. Nicholas Star had given her. Removing a penlight from his pocket, he shined it across the map. "According to the map, we're about four miles from our turnoff."

"Okay, I'll watch for the turn, but I don't want to drive too fast. I'm not used to driving." She felt the need to explain her reason for barely going thirty miles per hour.

"Would you feel more comfortable if I were to drive?" he asked. "I've lived in the area most of my life, and I'm used to driving in snow and ice. Actually, I can drive in just about any condition."

Wondering why he was so experienced, it occurred to her that he probably worked on one of Colorado's road crews. He said he'd gone to college with the owner, but it didn't appear that he was as successful as his friend.

"No, but thanks, I'm fine as long as I focus my attention on my driving," she explained.

"Well, if you're sure," he said.

This insignificant conversation could go on and on. Angelica just wanted to make it to her cabin, take a long, hot bath, and spend the day on the slopes.

"Thanks, but I can handle it. I need the practice. Just relax. You look like you could use a nap."

He didn't really, but she had to say something to his remark that she looked rough.

"Thanks, I think I will do just that." He closed his eyes and leaned back against the headrest.

Angelica was more curious about her passenger now than ever. He seemed to be capable of relaxing at a moment's notice.

Fifteen minutes later, she made the turn as indicated on the map. She saw the lights from the high-rise and knew it was her passenger's destination. Not bothering to wake him just yet, she drove through the parking lot to an underground garage. She'd give him a few more minutes to rest. He certainly appeared to be sound asleep.

When she found a parking spot, she turned off the engine, which immediately awakened her passenger.

"That was fast," he said. "Thanks for the lift."

She hit the electronic switch to open the hatch. A burst of frigid air filled the vehicle.

He removed his skis and suitcase, then came around to her side of the SUV for Leon. "Again, Leon and I appreciate the ride. I really am tired and want to call it a night."

Angelica gave him her best smile. "Anytime. Maybe we'll bump into one another on the slopes."

"Just so you know, I didn't come here to make friends." A sudden chill hung on the edge of his words.

Glad of the semidarkness that hid the flush in her cheeks, she punched the electronic window, raising it as fast as she could.

With nothing but glass and harsh words between them, not to mention her humiliation at his total rebuff when she mentioned meeting on the slopes, Angelica had nothing more to say. This guy was an ass. Before she changed her mind, she lowered the window once again. "For the record, I didn't either. I felt sorry for you and was just trying to be polite. I wouldn't ski with you if my life depended on it."

Before he had another chance to humiliate her, she tromped down on the accelerator, hoping the ice and snow that blew in her wake smacked him right upside the head.

CHAPTER 8

Angelica found the turnoff to Gracie's Way without any trouble. Just as Mr. Star had said, the lights were on, both inside and out. A warm greeting, but this only reminded her of the cold send-off she'd received from her . . . travel partner, for lack of better words. She pulled the Navigator into the long drive, still somewhat miffed over the remarks made by Mr. North.

As she unloaded the SUV, she thought about the two men she'd met in the past hour. Mr. Star and Mr. North. Made her think of the North Star. Was there any significance between the two names, some kind of divine message that someone was trying to give her? She didn't think so, but one could never be too sure.

Dragging her carry-on up the wooden steps, she found the key just where Mr. Star said it would be. Unlocking the door, she stepped inside, surprised at the cabin's luxuriousness.

A giant fireplace, an exact replica of the fireplace in the registration office, dominated the great room. A cherry red plush sofa and two forest green chairs were strategically placed. A fire crackled in the fireplace, popping embers filling the large room with inviting sounds and the enticing scent of wood burning.

As she dropped her luggage next to the fireplace, a log fell, sending blazing orange, red, and yellow embers upward. Deciding that she had better add another log so as not to lose the warmth from the fire, she found a fully stocked supply next to the hearth. She placed two large logs on top of the others, found the fire poker, and nudged the logs until she was satisfied they were positioned properly in order to continue to burn. Satisfied that the fire would burn for another hour or two, she located the kitchen around the corner from the great room.

She was shocked at its size — she could have placed her entire apartment inside and had room to spare. It had a full-size range, two ovens, and more counter space than she'd ever seen in one kitchen. She continued to explore, finding a Sub-Zero refrigerator that could hold enough food for an entire winter. Maybe that's what it was used for, she thought, as she opened it to look inside. Mr. Star, of course, was right — it was as empty as her stomach was beginning to feel. She should have prepared a bit better. She'd have to make a trip tomorrow down the mountain for supplies. She found the makings for coffee exactly where he said they would be and decided to make a small pot for herself. She wasn't ready for bed yet. Her New York habits were not going to be as easy to put aside as she'd thought.

Walking through the cabin, she saw that the walls were made from honey-colored logs, as was the staircase that led upstairs to the two bedrooms and a loft. Why she'd felt the need for so much space, she didn't know. After spending fourteen years in New York City, she had gotten used to living in minimal space. But she was *not* going to focus on what brought her to Colorado, at least not that first night. She was there to ski, think about her life, and decide if it was time for a career change. But her first night was for her to do nothing but explore her new digs for the next two weeks. Later, there would be plenty of time for deep thoughts, but not immediately.

Inside the master bedroom was a king-sized bed, also made of giant honey-colored logs. A navy and red quilt covered it. Several pillows were scattered about, making the bed as inviting as the rest of the cabin. She had a sudden flash of what Parker North would look like sprawled across the bed but quickly focused her attention on anything but him. He was a rude, overbearing jerk as far as she was concerned.

Angelica realized she'd come to that conclusion very quickly, which wasn't her usual style. She was the least judgmental person in the world, but this man had gotten under her skin, and she did not like that at all. Clearing his handsome face from her mind, she found the second bedroom. It was much smaller than the master but just as warm and inviting. It also had a bed made out of logs, with a hunter green quilt and several matching pillows. It would be a shame not to use the room, but hey, she could if she wanted. This was *her* place for two weeks, and she would sleep in each room. Between the two bedrooms was yet another surprise. A bathroom the size of her apartment had a giant glassed-in shower that looked as though it could hold at least a dozen people, and in the center of the room was a giant Jacuzzi tub that would hold at least half that many people. Plush towels hung from a warmer, bars of scented soaps and creams were artfully arranged on a dark green marble countertop flanked by two long mirrors, their frames made from branches. The outdoorsy theme dominated the cabin, and she thought it perfect.

It was exactly what she needed. Space, time, and a bit of fun on the slopes.

The smell of coffee lured her back downstairs. She searched through the cabinets, finding a bright red mug. Pouring herself a cup, she walked back into the great room, where she spied a giant box marked clearly with the words "Christmas Tree and Decorations."

She hadn't really thought of trimming a tree, figuring there would be trees all over the resort for her to enjoy, but instantly decided that setting it up and decorating it might be a fun way to spend the next couple of hours since she was wide awake.

Placing her coffee on the hearth to keep it warm, she dragged the artificial tree from the box. It was at least six feet high if her judgment was correct. It only took her a few minutes to put the tree together, as there was just a bottom, a middle, and the top, and all she had to do was insert one on top of the other. Once she had the tree together, she placed it next to the fireplace, careful that it was far enough away that there would be no fear of its catching fire.

With that out of the way, she strung colorful bright twinkle lights from top to bottom, then began opening the boxes of decorations. The first box held several glass angels. She hoped that what she was doing was okay, and that the owner of the cabin didn't mind her taking the liberty of using their decorations, but they were there, and she assumed they were hers to use as well. They were delicate, and Angelica made sure to handle each carefully. The second box held more angels, but those were department-store varieties. After an hour, she had a beautifully decorated angel tree. She went to the kitchen for one last cup of coffee, bringing it to the great room, where she sat on the sofa, admiring her handiwork.

As the fireplace warmed the room, combined with the comfort of the sofa, and her general contentment with how her vacation was turning out to be much more than she'd hoped for — minus Parker North — she relaxed and fell into a deep sleep.

CHAPTER 9

Parker didn't bother with a walk through the condo. There would be time for that later. At the moment, all he wanted to do was take a hot shower and crawl into bed. It would be the first time since he'd been working in the trauma unit that he would not have to worry about being awakened in the middle of the night by a phone call. The thought brought a smile to his face. He might sleep until noon, but then remembered he had to call Max and make arrangements for his truck to get towed off the mountain. That old guy, Nicholas Star, would be sure to say "I told you so" when he learned that the pickup truck hadn't made it up the mountain as Parker had assured him it would.

After a hot shower, he dressed in sweats and a worn-out T-shirt, yet another from his college days. He let Leon out of his carrier, opened a can of smelly Chicken Delight, and filled a small cup with water. Leon had it made and didn't even know it. Maybe Parker would come back as a cat in another life.

Right. If you believed in such garbage.

"Meow," Leon offered after he'd finished his dinner.

"Yep, I'm tired, too," Parker said absently.

The black and white ball of fluff pounced from the floor to the countertop. "Meow, meow!"

"Hey, I said I was tired. And I don't think so," he said as he scooped Leon from the countertop. "This should meet your needs." Parker set Leon in the black leather recliner situated next to the fireplace. "Warm and comfy. What more could a guy ask for?"

Leon's fluffy tail flapped slowly from side to side, letting Parker know he was being dismissed. Cats, he thought as he reached down to scratch his buddy between the ears. Can't live with them, and he personally couldn't imagine life without a feisty feline. Sort of like women. Couldn't live with them, or without them. Though if he were honest, he'd lived just fine without one. And this brought to mind that gorgeous actress. She was sexy, easy on the eyes.

And he was *not* going to even think about her. Not now. Tomorrow he planned to shop for a new wardrobe in the Snow Zone, or at least something warmer than what he had on. He didn't think the college T-shirts were going to cut it in the weather at Maximum Glide. He spent so much of his time in scrubs, he'd never given too much thought to what he wore beneath them. He'd have to at least consider making a few purchases out of necessity. Remembering that Mr. Star had said that someone with a funny name, Candy something or other, had taken care of this, he'd take a look at her selection before calling it a night.

He went in search of the ski supplies the girl had delivered. Leave it to Max. He knew him well even though it had been years since they'd seen one another. Max knew that his old friend wouldn't have bothered replacing his skis or boots. When had there been time? he wondered, as he spied several items of heavy-duty clothing on the sofa. A red and black Spyder jacket, with matching ski pants and wool socks that promised to keep one's feet warm in subzero temperatures. Boots that weighed as much as a small child were sure to support his ankles and keep his feet warm in the iciest conditions, too. And there were several fleece shirts and a pair of mountain boots. From the looks of it, Max's employee hadn't missed a bit.

Three pairs of what he knew had to be top-of-the-line skis leaned against the wall. He chuckled, as he viewed the windfall. Christmas was going to be good this year. No more holidays spent caring for people who were either ill, injured, or incapacitated by their own hand — or their parents', he couldn't help but add, as he recalled the reason he'd needed to get away in the first place. He shook his head, thankful for Max's generosity. The first full day there, he'd ski until he dropped and try to forget the real reason he was at Maximum Glide in the first place.

Satisfied that he'd be properly outfitted when he hit the slopes, he returned to the master suite, dropped his sweats and T-shirt on the floor, and crawled beneath the heavy comforter. Leon had situated himself on the pillow next to Parker's the same way he did at the apartment. So much for the soft leather chair.

It had been forever since he'd slept in the nude, and he could not recall ever having slept on sheets as soft. The thread count must be up there in the thousands. Again, Max spared no expense when it came to his guests.

Guests. He couldn't help but remember the woman who'd given him a lift up the mountain, a total stranger. Then he'd had the audacity to tell her he wasn't out to make friends. Damn, it'd been too long since he'd been with a woman, in an intimate setting, or any setting, for that matter. If he ran into her, he would apologize, and if she didn't tell him to go to hell, he might even ask her out for a drink. It would take his mind off that little girl who wasn't going to be celebrating Christmas this year or any other, opening presents and screaming and shouting her delight.

With an even heavier heart, Parker slid farther beneath the plush bedding, willing himself to go to sleep and forget about events of the dreadful day.

Tossing and turning, Parker concluded sleep was not his friend that night. Normally, he could fall asleep instantly; given his profession, he had to catch a few winks when the opportunity arose. Now, there he was in that luxurious condo, nothing to keep him from doing whatever he wanted, and he could not force himself to fall asleep. Unwilling to lie in bed any longer, Parker found his sweats on the floor where he'd left them. He slipped them on and went to the kitchen in search of a late night, or in this case, an early morning snack.

Upon hearing his feet hit the floor, Leon

stretched, arching his back into a V, then had the audacity to crawl into the warm spot Parker had just vacated.

Laughing as he found the kitchen, Parker realized Max had outdone himself yet again. The kitchen was all black and chrome; a man's kitchen, Parker thought. He found a giant refrigerator filled with so much food, he had a hard time choosing.

Between fresh meats, fruit, and a variety of cheeses, he finally settled on slicing a Granny Smith apple and a few wedges of sharp cheddar. Some gourmet he was. He poured himself a large glass of milk and took everything to the living room, where he found a giant-sized television mounted on the wall. It had to be at least sixty inches if his estimate were correct. He found a remote on the table by a long, sleek, black leather couch. While the leather was a nice touch, it wasn't him, he thought, as he sat down with his plate of food and his milk. As he munched, he surfed through hundreds of channels yet saw nothing that would grab his attention.

Without knowing or understanding why, his thoughts returned to the woman who'd driven him up the mountain to the condo. Hadn't old Nick Star, as he was now going to refer to him, said she was an actress from

New York City? *What in the world is she doing out West? Or is she simply taking a vacation, like me? And alone, too.*

It surprised him that someone with her good looks would be alone. *Maybe she isn't,* he thought. *Maybe she has a lover, boyfriend, beau, however they referred to them now, coming to meet her tomorrow.* She had said she'd be on the slopes, but she really hadn't indicated if she would be skiing solo. And, of course, he'd had to put his foot in his big-ass mouth and let her know he would not welcome any new friendships. On or off the slopes. Period. So, just like everything else in his life, he'd screwed that up before he'd even had a chance to start anything.

Normally, Parker was not one to wallow in self-pity. As a doctor, he knew you couldn't allow your emotions to get the best of you, knew that there was a risk with all patients, even those with nothing more than a runny nose. *It is what it is,* he'd told himself. But in all his years as a trauma surgeon, he had never lost a child. This event had marred his vision of himself as a professional.

Then he reminded himself, before that day, he'd never had a child die on his table.

Never.

CHAPTER 10

Angelica jolted awake, disoriented. Seeing her surroundings brought it all back to her. She was in Colorado to ski. She'd fallen asleep on the sofa, her cup of coffee still sitting on the hearth, the Christmas tree lights still twinkling. She rubbed the sleep from her eyes, tossed another log in the fireplace, then went to the dream kitchen, where she made another pot of coffee.

Excitement tingled in her veins for the first time in a very long time, even more so than her first time walking on stage in a semi-big production. She'd spent so many years trying to "make it" in the theater that she hadn't focused on life's simple pleasures as much as she should have. As she waited for the coffee to brew, she peered out the kitchen window.

A clear blue sky shone on glistening ivory snow on the mountain. Giant spruce trees, cedars, and firs of what must be every variety in the world dotted the mountainside like individual Christmas trees, their branches full and heavy with recent snow. Snow that sparkled like diamonds instead of the brown slush she was used to. Yes, the first real snowfall in the city gave Manhattan an added purity, but once it melted, the beauty became nothing more than a hassle to get through. Angelica didn't see that where she was now. What she saw boggled the mind, the great majestic mountains serving as a protector of Mother Nature's bounty.

Not wanting to waste another minute looking out the window, she gulped her coffee down, poured a second cup, and brought it to the master bath. She would have loved to sink into the large Jacuzzi tub but knew she would appreciate it much more when her muscles ached from a day of hard skiing. She opted for the giant shower and was mildly surprised to see there were eight showerheads, each placed at a different level, so that no part of her would be without the shower's warm spray. Ingenious, she thought as she lathered with a grassy-smelling body wash provided by someone who knew the business. All she was lacking were a few groceries. She scrubbed and washed her hair, then dried off with a warm towel from the heating rack. She could get used to this lifestyle. Afford it, no; used to it, most definitely.

From her luggage, she removed a pair of old jeans she'd had since high school, which, fortunately, still fit. She pulled a white tank top on, then topped it with a bright yellow wool sweater. Layers always worked in the city; she didn't know why they wouldn't work at the ski resort. She pulled on red wool socks, then slid her feet into her worn black Uggs. She wouldn't trade her Uggs for anything. Well, maybe a new pair, she thought as she saw that the heels were low and worn.

She piled her wet hair on top of her head, then thought better of it. The temperature was due to drop into the single digits. She found a blow-dryer in the bathroom cabinet, dried her hair, then placed it in a ponytail. It was nice not to wear a wig, or have her own hair styled in such a way that it actually hurt. No, this was perfect. Clean hair and nothing more. Again, one of the simple things in life that she'd been somewhat deprived of. Then she thought about the makeup. No wonder she was starting to see early signs of aging. She'd allowed her skin to take a brutal beating daily with stage makeup. Other than sunscreen, she was not going to put anything on her skin either. It was time to go au naturel.

Angelica finished her coffee, then turned off the pot and Christmas tree lights before heading out to her rental. Though the air was cold, it was dry, making it much more tolerable than what she was used to. She hadn't bothered to wear her gloves or hat, deciding she wouldn't need them since she would be inside the car except when she'd make a fast run inside the mini-market. She cranked the heat to max and was greeted with an icy blast of cool air. She clicked the fan off, allowing the engine to warm up before turning it on again. Just showed her lack of driving experience. Once she adjusted the heat control and her rearview mirror, she backed out of the narrow drive and steered the SUV downhill toward the main village at Maximum Glide.

Angelica drove carefully down the mountain. Though there was snow piled at least five feet high on either side of the road, salt covered the road itself, assuring her that someone was watching out for those slick patches of ice she did not want to become acquainted with.

She'd traveled approximately two miles when she almost ran off the road. Not from a patch of ice, but from what she saw. Slowing down to a crawl, she lowered the passenger window, straining to make sure she was seeing what she thought she was seeing, that her mind wasn't playing tricks on her. Squinting against the bright Colorado morning sun, Angelica checked her rearview mirror for traffic, then, seeing there wasn't any, she stopped right in the middle of the road.

"Hey," she called out to the guy she'd taken to the penthouse condo last night.

Parker North.

He stopped and turned to look at her. When he saw her, he shook his head and stepped up to the passenger side. "We've got to stop meeting like this," he said, his voice and attitude the complete opposite of last night's.

"I take it you must've had a visit from old Scrooge himself," she added, trying not to smile. She was not going to make this easy on him. He'd told her she looked *rough,* and he'd been incredibly rude to her after she'd driven him all the way to his condo.

In the early morning sun, Angelica thought him much more handsome than she had last night. His dark hair flipped up at the ends, and his eyes were a deep chocolate brown with gold flakes, making them appear as though a fire radiated from within.

He wasn't tan at all, so she could safely assume he didn't spend too much time on the slopes. She guessed he did most of his work inside, though she had no clue exactly what kind of work he did and didn't really care. As he'd said last night, he really wasn't there to make friends. Well, she wasn't either. Not really. She reminded herself she was in Colorado to relax, enjoying life's simple pleasures while she debated her future as an actress.

He leaned against the door, peering inside the open window. Angelica was sure he was blushing. Or maybe he was about to have a heart attack from walking in this thin air and at such a high altitude. "Oh my gosh, are you okay? Get inside, quick!" Without further thought, she leaned across the bucket seats and opened the passenger door. "Hurry!"

He did as instructed but didn't appear to be in any kind of physical distress. "Thanks, I guess I deserved that." He hit the button to raise the window.

Angelica glanced at him. "What are you talking about?" She put the car in gear and cautiously drove down the mountain, trying to watch the road and her passenger at the same time.

"I was rude last night. I'm usually not so

quick to snap a pretty girl's head off."

She slowed down, then stopped. "You're not having a heart attack?" she inquired, suddenly unsure of everything that had passed between them in the past minute.

"Why would you think I'm having a heart attack? I'm not in the best of shape, but I do work out when my job allows me to."

Angelica felt like the idiot of the month. She wasn't sure what to say but knew she needed to say something, anything, that would get her out of the hole she worked her way into. "Uh . . . your face was red. I just thought . . . the high elevation, you know, some people have trouble with it." If ever she sounded airheaded, it was then.

Parker North smiled, and when he smiled, Angelica thought a second sun chose that moment to shine exclusively for her. This guy had a smile that truly lit up the world, or at least her portion of it. He adjusted the heater's vent so that it was aimed directly at his face. "Lucky for me, I don't have any trouble. I've lived here most of my life."

Yes, he'd told her something to that effect last night, but it escaped her just now.

"I need to get my truck. I tried using my cell phone to call Max but couldn't get a signal. I figured I'd keep walking until this piece of electronic magic decided to do its thing."

She never would've thought about that; her cell phone was so old, she was sure it still used the old analog system if it still existed, but he didn't need to know this. Was he into all the new electronic gizmos? And if he was, how did he afford the stuff? You would think he would invest in a new vehicle. She knew the latest models of cell phones were quite pricey, and it hadn't been something she'd been willing to pay outrageous sums of money for because she had a phone that worked just fine, thank you very much. She did not need all the extras. She'd learned to live in a small space and on an even smaller budget all those years ago when she'd migrated from Texas to New York.

Taking a deep breath, hoping to clear the air of her idiocy, she said, "I was just on my way to the mini-market, and you're welcome to ride with me." She couldn't come up with another intelligent word. She would have sworn he was looking her over in a . . . a *seductive* way?

Maybe the high altitude was getting to *her*?

CHAPTER 11

Focusing her attention on the road, Angelica did her best to ignore her passenger. He was charming, witty, and sexy as hell. She didn't need his attention any more than he'd needed to make friends, but she wasn't going to tell this to him, at least not now.

"So why aren't you on the slopes?" Parker questioned. "I figured you'd be up with the chickens."

She laughed. She hadn't heard anyone use that expression since she was a kid in Texas. "My stomach is telling me it has issues to deal with. Like starvation." Suddenly, her stomach growled, and she busted out laughing. She couldn't help herself.

"I wish I would've known. I made pancakes, eggs, and sausage this morning. Had a ton of leftovers, too. Left a plate out for Leon, but he hadn't touched it when I left. He's peculiar."

Was he trying to tell her something? That

he'd cooked too much or that someone had cooked for him? Or was he simply making small talk? She wasn't about to ask but hoped it wasn't the latter — yet didn't know why it would even matter to her as he was practically a stranger. But for some unknown reason, it did matter.

"Max filled the refrigerator with every kind of food imaginable. It's been a while since I cooked a meal for myself. It's harder to cook for one person than a crowd, don't you agree?"

Again, Angelica wondered if there was an underlying meaning to his question. Was he asking her in a roundabout way if she was involved, or committed? Or was he simply making small talk until they reached the bottom of the mountain? It didn't matter either way, she thought as she stepped hard on the brake, finding that the road practically nosedived for a few feet before leveling out. She was no more in the market for a relationship than he was. He could be married with ten children for all she knew.

"I don't cook much. The theater usually orders takeout, so there's really no need," she explained.

"So you really are that actress from New York?"

Has he actually seen me in a play? Or

maybe he recognized me as that piece of dirt in that floor-cleaning commercial currently airing!

"After you left the registration office last night, Nicholas — *Mr. Star* — told me you were an actress."

He'd answered her question, and she hadn't even had to ask. What a relief! It suddenly occurred to her that she'd felt a bit embarrassed when he'd asked her if she was an actress! Her entire career suddenly had the power to make her feel nothing but . . . *shame*? Did Meryl Streep and the late Elizabeth Taylor feel shame at their chosen careers? She doubted it. They were two of the greatest actresses of all time, in her opinion. She'd aspired for so many years to be just like them. Stage, film, television, she wanted it all, yet when a stranger asked her about her career, she found that she didn't want to discuss her profession. As though she'd been struck by a bolt of lightning, Angelica had just answered the question she'd mentally asked, but she pushed it aside. It wasn't the time to make a career choice or change. She was driving in snow and ice, and was just distracted.

"An actress with nothing to say," Parker added. "That seems a bit unusual."

"Like you, I'm not here to make friends

or discuss my career." She knew that she sounded terribly juvenile, but she didn't care. She'd just had an epiphany and did not want to deal with the significance behind it, or at least not with a stranger in the car. This trip down the mountain was becoming way more than a quick trip to the market.

"I guess I deserved that," he said, turning away.

Lucky for her, she spied the turnoff for the registration building just then. She assumed that was where he wanted to be dropped off, so she found an empty spot close to the entrance and parked. Part of her felt a tiny bit of sadness and a sense of loss. She had never had these kinds of feelings about a stranger, and it bothered her. She wasn't sure if it was a good thing or not. Most likely not.

She turned to face him. "So," she said, struggling to fight her sudden confusion, "I guess you can use the phone in the office if you can't get a signal on yours." Angelica said the words quickly as she tried to still her rapidly beating heart.

Lame, lame, lame, she thought as she felt an unwanted warmth flow through her. *This is* not *happening! What is wrong with me?*

"I'm sure of it," he agreed. Then he

continued, "Are you going to be on the slopes later? Maybe we can meet at the lift."

Unexpectedly, Angelica didn't know what to say. One minute, he was telling her he wasn't there to make friends; the next, he alluded to a possible relationship with someone — well, not really, but she wasn't going to assume anything where this man was concerned — and now, he was asking her to meet him. Confused, and surprised at his change of heart, all she could manage was a quick nod.

"I take it that's a yes," Parker stated.

Again, she'd made an idiot out of herself. "I'd planned to ski all day anyway. If we see each other at the lifts, then sure, I can ride up with you, race you downhill." She didn't want to appear too anxious, but she didn't want to brush him off, either. She kinda liked this guy she'd known for less than twenty-four hours.

What does this mean? she wondered.

Is this *love at first sight?*

CHAPTER 12

"Ouch! That hurt, but I see where you're going," Parker said, obviously chagrined by her comment.

Angelica offered up a mischievous grin but said not a word.

"I owe you an apology. I was tired." He held up a gloved hand. "And I know that's not an excuse for being so crabby, but I'd like to start over." He gave her his dazzling smile again, and her heart did another flip-flop.

She liked that he'd used the word *crabby.* A regular guy, not the suave sophisticated GQ type she normally dated. Angelica was getting way ahead of herself, though. First, he'd only asked her to ski with him, and she didn't really believe that qualified as a date. Second, she lived on the East Coast. What happened if she really liked the guy? No way would she commute from coast to coast for a date.

"Earth to driver," Parker said, jolting her back to the present.

Looking at him as though he had two heads, she wasn't sure if he was insulting her while trying to apologize.

A driver? Am I being oversensitive? Yes, I am. It was so unlike her to be so offended by comments that were simply *comments.* The critics had been beyond hard on her many times throughout her career. It went with the territory. *So why him and why now? Why am I so defensive with this man?*

"Apology accepted," she said before she changed her mind. It *had* been late when he'd rescued her. She could be a tiger herself when she didn't get enough sleep. Maybe Parker was telling the truth. He had fallen asleep last night in the car, after all. So maybe he *had* been overly tired. Besides, she had no real reason not to trust him. She'd met and made friends on the slopes many times before. No harm in hanging around with the guy for a few hours.

He opened the door and climbed out of the car, then smacked his gloved hand against the roof. "So I'll meet you at the private lift in a couple of hours. If you agree," he added, offering her his drop-dead killer smile.

Two hours would be more than enough

93

time to go to the market, make breakfast, and prepare herself to spend the day skiing with a really hot guy. She smiled. "I'll be there."

Parker closed the door, winked at her through the window, then turned away and walked toward the registration office.

She gave a half wave and backed out of the parking lot onto the main road that led to the center of Maximum Glide. Angelica slowed the SUV to a crawl, searching for another parking spot, when she spied a black Hummer leaving. She whipped the Navigator into the spot before someone beat her to it. Grabbing her purse and keys, she opened the door and, once again, was greeted by bitter cold, but the kind of cold that didn't make you cringe and race back inside. After New York, where the cold was damp from the ocean, she found the sharp coolness refreshing.

The sidewalks in the village were clear of all traces of ice and slush. Angelica observed several maintenance men working hard to keep the streets and pathways clear. Briefly, she wondered if Parker was part of this crew, but he really didn't look like he spent too much time in the sun. Maybe he was a supervisor and spent his time behind a desk. It didn't really matter what his profession was. In two weeks, he would be nothing more than a memory. A pleasant one, she hoped.

She found the village market around the corner from the Snow Zone, a ski supply shop she planned to visit later. Her old ski jacket wasn't quite as warm as some of the new-fangled ones she'd seen in the catalogues; it was time to replace it.

Entering the market, Angelica was greeted by the scent of fresh-baked bread, reminding her that she hadn't eaten since her last bite of chocolate yesterday. With the warm yeasty smell guiding her, she found the bakery at the back of the store. As expected, the line was long, and she could see plenty of baked goods displayed for those waiting in line. Several young women wore white coats, with their hair matted against their heads with the required hairnet. Each performed her task with a smile on her face. Angelica thought that she might like to learn how to bake someday.

As the line inched closer to the front, she made a mental list of the supplies she would need for the next two weeks. She added a bottle of wine and a nice pair of filets, thinking if the opportunity arose, she would invite Parker to her cabin for dinner.

Greeted by a friendly blonde, Angelica

selected a loaf of freshly baked sourdough bread, three poppy seed bagels, four red velvet cupcakes, and a loaf of French bread. With both arms loaded, she headed to the front of the market, where she found a small shopping cart. In New York, she usually just grabbed a few things and never required a shopping cart, only buying as much as she could carry home on foot She walked up and down the narrow aisles, picking items that she normally wouldn't even consider and placing them in her cart. Two bags of potato chips, something she never indulged in as her profession didn't encourage weight gain. A large hunk of dark chocolate because she simply could not go a day without it. She filled the cart with cans of soup, milk, eggs, and two packages of precooked bacon. In the produce section, she filled bags with apples, oranges, and grapefruit. At least some of her purchases were healthful, she observed, while waiting at the checkout counter.

Ten minutes later, she had the Navigator loaded with groceries. As she pulled out of the parking place, she glanced at the clock on the dash. She had more than an hour before it was time to meet Parker at the lift.

Angelica felt blissfully happy, totally alive.

Did this have anything to do with Parker,

or was it simply the fact she was on vacation and had shucked all responsibilities for the next two weeks? It didn't matter. Whatever the reason, she was boundlessly happy, and didn't care why.

CHAPTER 13

Angelica found her way around the kitchen and decided she enjoyed the simple act of preparing breakfast for herself. She microwaved the bacon, scrambled eggs, and had three slices of toast. If this wasn't enough carbs and protein to see her through her ski run, then she was in big trouble. She was not going to count calories on this trip, no way, no how.

After a quick cleanup, she began the laborious task of dressing for a day on the slopes. Because her jacket was so old, she made sure to wear several layers of T-shirts and a warm sweater. She put on two pair of tights before topping them off with her old ski pants. First thing tomorrow, she would visit Snow Zone and update her ski gear.

She planned to rent skis when she'd originally made her vacation plans, but was told by the travel agent that the cabin provided skis as well. All she had to do was give them her height and weight, then visit the repair shop, where they would make sure the fit was right for her. As she shoved her foot inside the cold ski boot, she was surprised when her foot slid in comfortably without all the hassle that she usually encountered. Tromping outside in the heavy boots, she found the skis and poles inside the storage shed, just where the agent told her they would be. She should have brought them with her in the morning, when she'd made her trip to the village, but she figured she would just ski to the repair shop, where they could make any adjustments.

Kicking the toe end of her boot, then pushing down on the heel, she found that the boots fit perfectly in the ski's bindings. Same with the other foot. There was no need for a trip to the repair shop, she thought as she poled her way several yards away to the private lift.

Her skis cut through the snow, leaving tracks in her wake. She took a deep breath, reveling in the pure scent of pine and fresh powder. Her part of the mountain was still and calm, except for the soft whir from the wind that blew gently through the tops of the tall pines. She could get used to this, especially after the city.

Remembering the directions she had read

that morning while eating breakfast, she found the private chairlift without any trouble. The operating instructions were easy, so no worries there. It gave her enough time to smooth her hair and add an extra layer of lip balm. As soon as she tucked the tube inside her pocket, she looked up to see Parker, all decked out in Spyder's latest red and black ski attire. He poled his way across the small expanse to the lift, then turned sharply, spraying her with snow.

Winded, but smiling, he said, "I still have it."

Angelica's heart raced at the sight of this incredibly sexy man, but she did nothing to reveal this. "You thought you'd lost it," she commented wryly.

"Never, but it has been a long time since I've skied. Work has kept me occupied, and there really hasn't been time for a vacation," he explained.

Of course, she wondered what he did for a living and why there wasn't time for a vacation, but she was not going to ask. If he wanted her to know, she guessed that he would tell her. For the moment, she was happy to be accompanying him.

"Well, we're here now. Let's take the lift to the top of the mountain," Angelica said. "Or is that too much for a first run?"

Parker gave her a look that sent a warm glow throughout her body. Yes, she was in trouble, she thought, as they poled across to the chairlift. This guy was definitely worth pursuing.

"Of course I'm up to it. I wouldn't be here if I wasn't. What about you?"

"I'm ready. It's been a couple of years, but I think I can handle a run down the mountain. Though I have to admit, I am a bit leery of this lift. I have never used this kind before." She had read the instructions just a while ago and hoped the timer was set to allow them enough time to get seated comfortably before shooting up the side of the mountain.

Angelica punched in the number of seconds required for the lift to come to life, then poled over to the entrance area with Parker by her side. In fifteen seconds, the chair, squeaking but moving at a slow pace, swung from the heavy cable, stopping when it crossed the line where they waited. As soon as the chair stopped and touched the back of their legs, they dropped down onto the icy seat, and Parker pulled the safety bar into position.

With a squeal and whine, the chairlift began its climb up to the top of the thirteen-thousand-foot mountain.

Angelica inched into a comfortable position, or as comfortable as one could be on a ski lift, carefully placing her skis on the bar provided directly below the chair. Sitting on the left side, she held her poles in her right hand over her left shoulder. Parker did the opposite. Once they were settled for the slow climb, the wind in their faces and the sun almost blinding in its intensity, Parker turned to look at her.

Glad that her face was covered by her scarf, her eyes hidden behind the amber lenses of her ski goggles, she knew she was blushing.

Damn, I am thirty-two years old! This stuff only happens in those terrific little romance novels I used to read back when I was in high school.

As was becoming the norm for her when she was with Parker, her heart beat so fast, she wondered if it would pound right out of her chest.

His words were muffled when he spoke, but she clearly understood him. "Are you nervous?"

Darn! Am I that transparent?

Shaking her head from side to side, she adjusted her scarf so she could speak. "Not at all, just cold."

Before she knew what was happening,

with his free arm, he pulled her closer to him. Their heavily clothed thighs rubbed against one another, and her shoulder was hard against his. Trying to inch away was not possible as Parker now used his free hand to tilt her chin up. Again, he surprised her when his lips lightly touched her own.

For a few seconds, again, she was at a total loss for words. When she found her voice, all she could manage was a low, "Wow!"

CHAPTER 14

"I'll take that as a compliment," Parker said, mere inches away from her face. He smelled like freshly washed skin and shaving cream.

She wasn't sure what to say or if she should say anything at all. She decided on not saying anything simply because she was shocked by her reaction to such a . . . chaste kiss! Mentally ticking back the clock, she realized it'd been almost a year since she'd gone out on a real date. Yes, that had to be the reason she was reacting like a lovesick teenager.

Angelica felt Parker's gaze on her. It wasn't like she could turn around and leave. Nope, she was stuck. Deciding to make the best of her situation, as there really wasn't another choice, she looked him squarely in the eye. "What do you want from me? If you're looking for a . . . cheap fling, look elsewhere. I certainly hope I haven't done anything that would make you think I was that kind of woman."

Did I actually say that? I must have sounded like an old spinster right out of the nineteenth century!

Parker laughed, and Angelica couldn't help but smile behind her scarf. Once again, she came across as an idiot.

They were more than halfway up the mountain when Parker spoke. "Trust me, a fling, cheap or otherwise, is the last thing on my mind." His voice became more serious, as though an unpleasant memory had surfaced.

Angelica wished she had kept quiet. Why couldn't she just accept that a nice, handsome man kissed her for no reason other than that he wanted to? Did there have to be an answer for every move a man made toward her? Yes, yes, and yes, she told herself. It was probably the reason why she'd had so many dates, most of them disastrous in one way or another.

She pulled her goggles on top of her head, then wiped her eyes. The air was so cold, her eyes were watering. She knew without looking in a mirror that her nose was probably as red as Rudolph's.

"Look, I shouldn't have said that. I do that a lot," she said as a way of explaining herself.

Parker still looked serious, all traces of

that fantastically sexy smile gone. "No, I shouldn't have kissed you. I don't know what came over me. Look, I don't normally do that either. Hell, I can't remember the last time I kissed a woman. It's been too long. I'm sorry," he said.

Wanting to ask him to explain further, she stopped herself before she put her foot in her mouth again. "Hey, it was just a kiss. As long as you don't expect anything else, then we're okay. And if it makes you feel any better, it's been a long time since I went out on a date myself. I work odd hours. Broadway being Broadway and all." She didn't dare tell him that, in point of fact, she worked off-*off* Broadway. She'd already gotten the impression he thought her profession was unprofessional.

And why did I just tell him I haven't had a date in a long time? What is wrong with me? Surely, I must be oxygen deprived!

The cable whined, then came to a complete stop. Knowing this was a private lift, it seemed odd, but Angelica was sure the lift was used by other guests, too. Hanging in mid-air, the wind whistling through the trees, snow swirling beneath them, she couldn't have asked for a more vulnerable position to be in, but again, her heart beat double time when she looked at the man

106

seated next to her.

"I guess someone fell," he said.

"I'm sure," she answered, then turned away. She didn't understand why she was feeling the way she was. It had never happened to her before. Ever. Zilch. *Why now?* And she didn't know squat about the man! He could be a pervert or . . . well, she was sure he was decent and upstanding. She trusted her instincts on things like that. But her reaction to him was just not normal, of that she was sure.

With a clunk and groan, the lift slowly came to life, transporting them to the top of the mountain. Feeling as though she had to fill the silence between them, Angelica spoke the first words that came to mind. "Look, I didn't mean what I just said. I mean, I haven't had a date in a while, that's true, but the other." She turned away again, feeling a tiny bit ashamed of her chosen profession. "I don't work *on* Broadway. Only once, and that was a very long time ago. I've been bartending and working in off-*off*-Broadway plays. Don't get me wrong, they're very successful in their own right, but still they *are* off Broadway."

She could actually feel Parker's gaze. It was as though he were trying to penetrate through all the layers of heavy clothing and see what lay beneath.

"You don't have to explain your choices to me," Parker said. "To each his own."

That was not the answer she was hoping for, but it was what it was, she thought, as they dangled once again in midair. "I wonder why they keep stopping," she said.

"People fall, and it takes a few minutes to get them up and out of the way. If they're inexperienced, it takes longer."

She knew all of that. It was not her first time on the slopes. Wishing she'd skied downhill to the public lift, Angelica felt very confused as a tumble of thoughts and feelings assailed her. One moment, she wanted to throw herself at this handsome man seated next to her, and in the next, she wanted to run, or rather ski away from him as fast as she could. She'd heard her friends talk, and she wasn't so unsophisticated that she did not know what was happening to her. The question was — why now? Why this man, who lived across the country? Why not one of the actors she worked with? Someone she knew and could see whenever she chose? She hadn't come halfway across the country just to fall in love with a stranger. She came to meditate on her chosen profession.

The lift returned to life, jolting her back

to the present. Though they were stopped for a couple of minutes, it seemed much longer. She could not sit next to this man and say nothing. She felt too exposed, and somewhat puzzled at this new turn of events. But, she remembered she was an actress, and acting she could do. She only had to pretend that she was onstage and that this situation was staged just for her.

The only difference was that she did not have a script, so she did not know her partner's lines.

CHAPTER 15

Finally reaching the top of the mountain, Angelica couldn't wait to ski downhill, where she knew there would be hundreds of other skiers to take her mind off Parker North. Quickly, as though they did this together daily, both she and Parker moved effortlessly off the chairlift and toward the right, where they both zoomed downhill.

Angelica felt free of all negative emotions as she surged downhill, Parker at her side. When they reached the middle of the mountain, Parker skied off the trail to an area where he could rest if he so desired. She slid into the sectioned-off area but not without a little snow pluming of her own. Before she could stop herself, she quickly whipped her skis around so that she showered Parker with snow.

Blissfully happy to be alive, Angelica dropped to the snow-covered ground, where she proceeded to laugh loudly and uncontrollably. Parker dropped down beside her. "Want to tell me what's so funny?" he asked, all traces of his earlier stuffiness gone.

Saying the first thing that came to mind, Angelica spoke. "This sounds stupid, but I can't remember being so . . . happy!" There, she'd said it, and the world hadn't swallowed her up. So what if she came off as nerdy or silly. She *was* blissfully happy to be there, glad to be alive, and more than thrilled to be sitting in a deep pile of snow with this man who'd unknowingly captured her heart.

A shadow dimmed the otherwise golden sparkle in Parker's eyes. Clearly, Angelica's words had upset him. She didn't want to do or say anything that would interfere with this moment, so she clammed up, keeping her joy to herself.

"It's good to see you so cheerful, happy. In my line of work, it's not always the outcome," Parker said as plumes of cold air spilled from his mouth.

Her heart quickened with anticipation. Finally, she thought, as she turned to look at him. He'd removed his goggles, and she did not like what she saw. Yes, he was the sexiest guy she'd encountered in a very long time, mostly, she thought, because he wasn't trying to be sexy like the guys she was used to. But there was such a look of loss and sadness about him that she reached out and placed a cold, gloved hand on his cheek. "Tell me. You look as though you've lost your best friend. Why so sad?"

She could see that he struggled with his thoughts, as if he was contemplating whether to reveal them or not. He shook his head, his dark hair damp from the wet snowflakes that had begun to fall. He removed his gloves and placed them on his lap. "What makes you think I'm sad?" he asked.

She hesitated a moment before answering. "You look sad, Parker. No mystery there. Are you having problems at work?" Angelica watched Parker's expression change from sad to ticked off.

"Who told you I was having problems at work? Was it Max or Grace? Because I didn't say anything to them," he said vehemently.

"Good grief, you don't have to bite my head off! And for your information, I have never so much as spoken to Max or Grace. I don't even know who they are." She stopped and backtracked. "Yes, I do know who Max Jorgensen is. Who doesn't? But Grace, no, I don't know her, and no one told me a thing about your work situation.

Whatever it is you do." She mumble last words.

He reached for the gloves in his lap, pushed himself up off the snow. After adjusting his goggles, he grabbed his poles and wrapped a leather band around each wrist, then skied out of the sectioned-off area straight to a trail that led to a black run.

"Hey," she shouted, but all she saw was his black and red Spyder jacket flash around the catwalk.

Wanting to catch up with him, needing to know what in the hell she'd said to send him racing off like some spastic skier, she poled out of their resting spot and across the large bowl area to the catwalk that led to some of the toughest black runs on the mountain. He must be one hell of a skier, she thought, as she approached the top of the slope. She was a decent skier, blue runs her most challenging. He must be expert, she thought, as she pushed off down the steep mountainside, traversing back and forth so as to slow her descent. There were some icy patches that could be tricky. Away in the distance, she saw his dark silhouette as he zigzagged through the unplowed snow. Hurrying to catch up with him, she used her poles to push forward, then lowered her lips and knees to a position that afforded her a bit of speed. She would be damned before she would let him beat her to the bottom of the hill.

As she careened around the moguls, she saw a lone skier in her peripheral vision. Wondering how he just so happened to appear out of the blue, she saw he was flying, and didn't seem to see she was directly in his path. As he got closer, she realized he was on a snowboard. She began to make her way to the side of the mountain even though she had the right of way. She heard him coming closer, the edge of his snowboard slicing across an icy patch.

She whipped away from the kamikaze boarder, felt herself careening as she lost her balance . . .

Then everything went black.

Parker looked up just in time to see a flurry of snow and a body as it was tossed in the air.

"Son of a bitch," he shouted as he saw the skier slam against the icy ground. Without another thought, he kicked off his skis, tossed his goggles aside, and poled his way back up the hill. Several spots were crusted over with ice, and he slipped. "Damn! I shouldn't have taken the black run, dammit!" Hurrying as best as he could given the circumstances, he gasped for air as he made his way uphill.

Out of breath, Parker managed to drop to his feet when he reached the injured skier. And lo and behold if it wasn't his new friend, Angelica Shepard.

Knowing he shouldn't move her, yet not sure where the nearest first-aid unit was located on the mountain, he did what all skiers knew to do in such a situation. Quickly, he placed his ski poles in an X position. With any luck, someone would see them and send for help. Until help arrived, he would do what needed to be done to ensure that Angelica survived the accident.

He leaned over her and felt for a pulse. Strong and steady. Always a good sign, he thought to himself. With exaggerated carefulness, he felt her head, searching for a lump or a cut. When he found nothing, he breathed a little sigh of relief but knew there could still be spinal injuries. Not wanting to move her, he straddled her waist and so very, very gently, probed the back of her neck and spine as much as he could given the heavy ski clothes she wore.

The moment he leaned up and looked down at this striking woman, her eyes fluttered open. "What happened?" she asked in a whisper.

Parker North felt like shouting to the world but knew it wasn't the time or the place. Angelica was speaking, and that was a very good sign.

"You were hit, sweetie. It's going to be all right. I promise you," he said, vowing he would not lose this woman to a head injury. Not now. Not when he was just beginning to feel something that he hadn't felt in a very long time. Or ever.

"You're an angel, right?" Angelica said softly.

He shook his head. "I am anything but, trust me."

The sound of snowmobiles provided a much-needed reprieve. As they flew across the snow and ice, Parker could see that there were four emergency techs, two on each snowmobile. "Over here," he shouted. They jumped off the machines, carrying a backboard.

"She was knocked down by some out of control snowboarder. I don't know where the guy wound up, but she was knocked out for at least five minutes. It took me that long to get to her," Parker explained to the medics.

They quickly shifted her onto the backboard, then carefully secured her neck and mouth with medical tape so she couldn't move.

One of the medics leaned over her and asked her a question. "Do you know what your name is?"

"Yes. Angelica."

The paramedic gave a thumbs-up sign to the others. "Do you know what today's date is?"

"No," she said.

"Okay, that's good. Now, I am going to give you a number, and each time I ask, I want you to repeat it for me. Think you can do that?"

"Sure," she muttered.

"Number eight," he said. "Now, can you tell me where you live?"

"New York."

"This is good. Now can you tell me the number I just told you?"

Angelica frowned and tried to shake her head. "I can't seem to remember. Why can't I move?" she asked, her voice a bit louder than before.

Parker watched from behind her and knew she was frightened. It was always the same. Once people knew they were injured and couldn't move certain parts of their body, they instantly freaked out. Not that he expected anything less.

"You're going to be fine, ma'am. We have your head taped to the board as a precaution." The medics' radio came to life then. "Have a chopper ready. We need to get her to Denver, to Angel of Mercy. They've got the best neurological unit in the state."

"What?" Angelica asked. "I have a head injury?"

"We don't know. This is just a precautionary move on our part. Please, relax," the technician said.

"Wait!" Parker shouted. "Let me go down with her. She's all alone."

"Are you . . . Hey, I know who you are!" the second tech said. "You work at Angel of Mercy, right?"

Parker nodded, then placed a finger over his lips. "Shhh. Let's just get her out of here before she freezes."

Parker looked up just in time to see the helicopter swirling above them. "Where will they land?" he asked.

"We have to bring her down to the station. There is no place to land here."

"Then let's move it! Time is of the essence here!" Parker shouted as though he were right back in the trauma unit that had driven him to Maximum Glide in the first place.

Once a doctor, always a doctor.

Two of the paramedics hoisted Angelica inside what appeared to be a plastic canoe of sorts. They covered her face with plastic, then he saw her hand move slightly — another very good sign.

"Please, don't put that thing over my face," she said in an almost normal voice. "I'm a little claustrophobic."

"Of course," the tech said, then arranged the plastic so that it didn't cover her entire face. "Ma'am, we are going to take you down now. Sit tight, okay?"

In a broken voice, she replied, "It's not like I have a choice, do I?"

"That's my girl," Parker said. "We'll have you back to normal in no time."

He noted she was speaking coherently, and that was very good under the circumstances. She tried to turn her head to see him, but couldn't. "You're going for a ride, hang on," Parker said, as the two medic/skiers each grabbed an end of the boatlike plastic contraption that would carry her to safety.

Trees whizzed by, and the pure blue sky was all she could see as they hustled to get her to the hospital. Her last thought before things went black again was that she'd been saved by an angel.

CHAPTER 16

Angelica opened her eyes only to discover that she was in the back of an ambulance. "What happened?" The words were no sooner out of her mouth than she remembered being knocked down by that lone snowboarder she'd seen just as she'd tried to get out of his path.

"We're taking you to Angel of Mercy in Denver. You're getting the best medical care in the state," someone said to her.

"Why can't I move my neck?"

"You're secured to the backboard as a safety precaution. Once the doctor examines you, they'll decide what to do."

Angelica was not going to remain on this stupid board. Her feet were freezing off, and her hands felt like two blocks of ice. "Look, I am cold here. And what happened to my ski boots? My feet are cold."

Low voices came from behind but she couldn't make out what they were saying. "I want to know where my boots are! My toes are going to freeze off!"

"Here," someone said as he began to rub her cold feet. "Does this help?"

She could feel a slight tingling sensation in her toes. "Yes, but I still want to know where those boots are."

Laughter came from all those in the back of the ambulance.

"I don't think this is funny, not even a little bit," she said firmly and in a much louder voice than before.

"No, ma'am, it isn't funny. We're just happy to see that you're getting back to normal," the man who rubbed her feet said. "We'll be arriving at the hospital any minute now. They'll have heated blankets waiting for you."

"I don't hear a siren," Angelica said out of the blue. "Why isn't there a siren?"

"We turned it off as soon as you came around. Your vitals are good, and it appears, now mind you I am saying it *appears,* as though you have no trauma to the head, so we're simply following protocol."

It was then the vehicle came to a stop. The two rear doors opened, letting in a blast of bitterly cold air. Angelica had never been so cold in her life. Her insides shook with tremors as they removed her from the ambulance. Seconds later, she was whisked through automatic doors and, thankfully, was greeted by a gush of warm air. She smiled for the first time since she'd been plowed over.

"What is so funny?" Parker asked her.

"What are *you* doing here? If not for you, this wouldn't have happened! Go away! I don't want you near me!"

"Hey, calm down. I rode in the chopper and the ambulance because I didn't want to leave you all alone."

"You didn't seem to have a problem leaving me alone on that mountain, now, did you?" she asked, as a nurse checked her blood pressure. She wouldn't be surprised if it didn't register. She was beyond pissed at this . . . idiot who'd forced her to chase him down a trail that was meant for experts only. She would never forgive him for that. Never.

Parker took her cold, limp hand in his. "I didn't know you couldn't keep up. I thought you said you were a good skier. I thought . . . Well, it doesn't really matter what I think, does it?" he asked, more to himself than her.

Angelica jumped when the nurse placed the cold stethoscope under her clothing.

"Sorry, this is a little cold," the nurse said,

apologetically.

"Tell me now," Angelica muttered between clenched teeth.

"Sorry," the nurse said.

"No, it does not matter what you think," Angelica said to Parker, "so please leave before I ask the nurse to call security." What nerve he had! It was partially his fault she was here in the first place.

"Doctor?" the nurse asked.

"You can leave now. I'll wait with her until the . . . *doctor* on call arrives," Parker said in a hushed voice.

"No, you won't! I asked you to leave. Now go away!" Angelica said as she tried to lift her head from the gurney.

"Please, don't move. You might injure yourself more," the nurse soothed. "Dr. Mahoney should be here any minute. One of our on-staff trauma doctors decided to take an indeterminate leave of absence, so we're a bit shorthanded at the moment."

Angelica would swear the nurse was upset and directing her words to Parker. "That's not my problem," she said. "Anyway, what kind of doctor takes an 'indeterminate leave of absence'?"

"That's what I would like to know," the nurse replied. "You just try to remain still and relax. We'll remove the tape and the backboard as soon as Dr. Mahoney examines you."

"I hope he gets here soon. I need to go to the ladies' room," Angelica said, feeling a bit embarrassed by the call of nature that she soon would be unable to ignore.

"Let me call a nurse's aide. They can assist you with a bedpan."

"No!" Angelica shouted. "I don't have to go that bad. I can wait." She hoped. There was no way she would allow an aide to shove a cold bedpan under her. She was already half frozen as it was.

An attractive older man, probably in his mid to late fifties, entered the room then, saving her from further conversation about her bathroom habits with the nurse.

"A ski accident, I see," he said as he punched a few keys on the computer keyboard next to the examining table where she lay freezing and pissed off.

"Yes, and it was his fault." She tried to lift her arm to point at Parker, but it, too, was strapped to the board. She could barely move her hand.

"Parker North. Hmm. Yes, a lot of things are his fault," Dr. Mahoney replied as he placed his cold hands on her neck.

"You know him?" she asked in amazement.

"Quite well, I must say. Or I thought I did," he said to her.

"Either you do or you don't." The conversation was confusing her. *Maybe I do have a brain injury, and it is just beginning to show.*

"He works here," Dr. Mahoney explained to her as he continued his examination. "Lori, let's get this tape off her. Before we release her, I want an X-ray and an MRI done just to be on the safe side. I don't think we'll find anything, but I'd rather be safe than sorry."

"Does this mean I'm okay? I can leave?" she asked.

"Provided the tests come back negative, you're free to go. You've suffered a slight concussion, nothing more as far as I can see. But I want to make sure, so we'll do an X-ray and MRI first." He turned to the computer, where he clicked a few keys, then back to her. "Is there someone we can call? I don't think you should drive or ski for a few days. You're going to be one sore cookie tomorrow, and I can assure you that you'll have a killer headache, but other than that, I think you will be just fine."

"Some vacation this has turned out to be," she said. "And no, there isn't anyone to call. I'll hire someone to drive me back to Telluride, then I'm going to catch the next flight back to New York City. I should have stayed where I belong."

"Mahoney, I can drive her back to Maximum Glide," Parker said, his voice firm and commanding.

"Yes, you can. You seem to have a lot of time on your hands now. So, there, Ms. Shepard, you won't have to worry about hiring a driver. Mr. North has offered his services. For whatever that's worth," he added.

"He's the reason I'm here in the first place. He doesn't even have a decent vehicle to drive, even if I would let him take me back to the resort. And besides, that piece-of-junk truck he has is broken down on the side of the road. I'll take my chances with a driver."

"Parker, you mean to tell me you're still driving that beat-up pickup truck?" Dr. Mahoney shook his head, then handed Angelica a piece of paper. "This is for a higher dose of ibuprofen if you need it; otherwise, you can take the over-the-counter stuff."

She just nodded while the two men gave one another the evil eye. There was a story here, but right now all she wanted was to get these bindings off and make a quick trip to the ladies' room. Whatever the two men had between them would wait.

Another nurse entered the small examination room with scissors and a bottle of something liquid. Probably alcohol.

"Now, Miss" — she looked at Angelica's arm bracelet, which had been attached sometime during her visit — "Shepard, I'll try not to pull or get your hair caught, but I can't make any promises that this won't hurt."

"Just yank it off, I really want to get to the ladies' room," she said, as the nurse began to cut through the heavy layers of tape on her neck and head.

The nurse laughed. "Sorry, I can't do that, but I'll try to make this as quick and painless as possible." She snipped, clipped, and tugged, and in under five minutes, Angelica was free from the binding tape.

Thankful that she was able to move freely, she pushed herself into a sitting position, then flopped back on the pillow. "I'm so dizzy!" she said, surprised.

"That's why you can't drive," Parker stated from his position at the foot of her bed.

"No, I'm dizzy because you had to go skiing away from me, like that friend of yours, Max Jorgensen. If you hadn't been in such a hurry, this wouldn't have happened."

"Okay, it's my fault. Satisfied?" he asked

127

as she tried to push herself up a second time.

Angelica knew when enough was enough, and that time had arrived. Slowly, so as not to jar her head in any way, she pushed herself up. *So far, so good,* she thought as she scooted to the edge of the examining table. From there, she swung her feet to the floor, careful to keep a firm hold on the bed.

"Dr. Mahoney said you worked here. What are you, an orderly or something?" she asked Parker when her feet found the cool tile floor.

"Something like that. Now, let me help you. The ladies' room is just down the hall."

If she hadn't been so light-headed and unsure on her feet, she would have told him flat out *NO!* But she had a concussion, and she wasn't going to risk falling flat on her face. She'd done that once already and did not want to damage anything else unnecessarily.

Parker North wrapped one arm around her waist, and with the other he held her hand firmly in his own. While he knew he wasn't one hundred percent responsible for Angelica's injuries, he did hold himself responsible for skiing off without really knowing her skills as a skier; for the rest, she could thank the jerk who didn't know

how to come to a complete stop.

"So, what do you do here?" Angelica asked as she baby-stepped down the hall.

"Does it really matter?" he asked.

That made her think about her own situation. Did people always define themselves by their profession? She wasn't sure about Parker, but she knew that she'd lived her life *for* her profession. Not sure if that was good or bad, she was certain of one thing: she had *never* been this cold in her entire life. She'd pursue deeper thoughts when she was physically able. For the moment, the restroom was her goal.

Parker stopped when they reached the end of the hall. "You sure you don't need assistance? I can ask one of the nurses to go inside with you. Just in case," he said, a worried look on his handsome face.

"No, thanks. I'm fine. If you hear me fall, just call a doctor," she said before entering the restroom.

"And that would be me," he said to himself when she was out of earshot. That *was* him. Like his father and grandfather, he'd been destined to become a doctor. Why the realization came to him just then was beside the point. He was a trauma surgeon. He'd saved many lives, more than he could count. Yes, he had lost a young patient, but he knew the moment he'd laid eyes on her that it was too late. One child mattered, and he knew he would never forget her face, but he also knew that he had a job to do, and that was to save as many lives as possible for as long as he could.

The bathroom door opened, revealing a relieved-looking Angelica. "Okay, I want to see that doctor again. I need to ask him how long the tests are going to take. I don't want to spend the rest of the day lingering in the halls like an unwanted virus."

Parker laughed, deciding he'd kept her in the dark way too long even though he'd only known her for less than twenty-four hours. "It depends on how busy they are."

"And you know this because . . . ?" she interrupted.

"Because I am a doctor. A trauma neuro-surgeon, and I have asked for the same tests for patients of my own on many, many occasions."

There, it was out in the open. He was not ashamed of himself or his chosen profession. He'd worked his ass off to get to this point, and he knew, just as any other doctor knew, that there would be times when you couldn't save a patient. Those were the low times. Times he hoped he wouldn't have to experience too often, but if anything, he was

a realist. Though there would be more death and sadness, he wasn't going to let that prevent him from practicing medicine.

Angelica had stopped in the middle of the hall. She stared at him as though he had three eyeballs. "Yeah right," she said before turning around and heading back in the direction she'd come from.

Parker raced to her side. Curious, he asked, "Why did you say that?"

She rolled her large brown eyes and laughed. "Come on, give me a break. First of all, if you were a doctor, you wouldn't be driving such a hunk of junk. Secondly, if you were really a doctor, you would have saved —"

"I did," he said, her reaction suddenly amusing.

She flushed, but remained silent. "You . . . it was you! The angel I thought I saw!"

"Yes, it was me. When you opened your eyes, I can't tell you how relieved I was."

Angelica wasn't so sure she didn't have a brain injury. She did remember opening her eyes and seeing a bright burst of sun, a halo-like glow hovering above and behind him as he bent over her. In her state of semiconsciousness, she'd mistaken him for an angel!

"You really are the angel," she said, sounding like she'd just solved the biggest mystery on earth.

He led her back to the room. "I've been called a lot of names, but never an angel," he teased as he helped her get back up on the table before continuing. A low, buzzing noise coming from his pocket stopped him dead in his tracks.

"Now it decides to work," he said before answering the cell phone that he was going to replace as soon as possible. He was a doctor, and doctors needed to be contacted at all hours.

"Hello." He held up a hand, indicating he needed a minute. "Max, what gives?" A smile as wide as the mountain spread across his face.

"I can do that. Sure. Okay if I bring a guest? Great, I'll see you tonight. One more favor — could you send someone to check on Leon?" Parker turned to Angelica, his eyes filled with laughter. "Yeah, he's the cat I told you about." Parker spoke into the phone a few more seconds, then ended the call.

"That was Max Jorgensen — you remember him?"

Angelica rolled her eyes. "Yes, about like I recall you just said you were a doctor."

Frustrated, Parker picked up the phone and dialed a number. Less than a minute later a nurse entered the room pushing a wheelchair. "Hi, Dr. North. I thought you'd taken a leave of absence."

"I'm off for two weeks, skiing. My friend here, she needs an MRI and an X-ray, stat. Mahoney issued the order, but we're kind of in a rush. It seems I've, rather *we've,* been invited to see *Angels with Paper Wings.*"

"Well, then, let's not keep this girl waiting. Come on, honey, if Dr. North asks, we jump. He's the best trauma neurosurgeon in the area. Of course, I'm sure you already knew that. We've been dying, well not literally if you know what I mean, but most of us nurses have had our eye on Dr. North for a long time. Oh, not like that, but we've been waiting for him to meet someone . . . nice, not in this profession. The hours are terrible, the money isn't that good, or at least from what I hear. Me, personally, as an RN, I do just fine, but for a man of his caliber, well you would think he'd be a —"

"Ruthie, please take Ms. Shepard down for her X-rays. And please don't annoy her with all the details of my private life."

"Oh, Ruthie, I love details," Angelica said with a wicked grin. "All the dirt and gore, too," she added, as the nurse pushed her out of the room.

"Don't you dare," Parker said, his words

133

nothing more than an echo before he re-membered there really wasn't anything in his private life worth repeating.

EPILOGUE
EAGLE VALLEY HIGH SCHOOL
EAGLE, COLORADO

Angelica Shepard could not recall when she enjoyed a local production as much as that night's performance of *Angels with Paper Wings.* And they were high-school kids! Awed and overwhelmed with emotion, she didn't care when Parker saw the tears flow down her face like two shimmery Christmas ribbons.

The gymnasium was packed, standing room only. She could see why. These kids were better than some of the actors and actresses on Broadway! The actors returned to the small stage one last time for yet another standing ovation. Angelica clapped so hard her hands hurt, plus she was beginning to feel a slight headache just as Doctors Mahoney and North had promised. She'd taken three ibuprofen before she left the hospital just in case. All of her test results were perfectly normal, and for that she was grateful. But more than anything, she was so excited over the performance she'd just witnessed. Not because it was pure excellence, though that was part of it, but she knew what she wanted to do in her professional life. Now more than ever. Why she'd spent so many years wasting time on-stage didn't matter. She'd learned her craft, had been moderately successful, and she wouldn't trade the experience for all the tea in China. However, it was time to move on. Her reason for taking this strange trip. And now, here she was, barely a day into the trip, and she'd solved her career dilemma!

"Why are you crying?" Parker asked as he thumbed the tears from her face.

"Have you ever had an epiphany?" she asked, knowing he'd just had a rude awak-ening in the career department himself. On the drive from the hospital to the high school, he'd told her about his doubts when he'd lost the little girl who'd been hit while riding her bicycle. Doubts that had sent him into hiding. Doubts that had led them straight to one another, she'd thought then and still did. This was not going to be easy, but they would make it work.

"I've had a few in my day. I take it this is the reason behind your tears?" he asked.

Never in her life had she ever been in such sync with another human being, and especially one of the opposite sex. "Yes and no. When I left New York, my agent had just told me that a younger actress had gotten the role I'd been dying for. If I'm honest with myself, she is the best actress for the part. Al said he'd find another part for me, but just now, here in this gymnasium filled with normal people, I realized I don't want to be onstage. I want to direct, to lead and guide and show and . . ."

She didn't get the chance to finish. Parker wrapped his arms around her and pulled her next to him. As though they'd been a couple forever, he leaned down and kissed her fully on the mouth. It took a minute for Angelica to break away. "Hey, we're at a high school! What will all these kids think? And their parents?" she asked, not really caring about anything except the moment.

"They'll think a sexy hot actress from New York City just kissed a handsome prince." He kissed her again, only this time it was deeper, more passionate. He drew in a deep breath. "Maybe this isn't the place, but I promise you, I won't forget where we left off. Now." He turned to a group of people who were waiting by the foot of the stage.

Angelica realized that they were waiting for Parker. Without another word, Parker introduced Max Jorgensen, and he, in turn, was introduced to Max Jorgensen's wife, Grace Landry, and their daughter, Ella. Not to be outdone, next came Patrick and Stephanie.

Then came the girls and Mr. Nicholas Star.

"Now, these are those girls I was tellin' you about," Nicholas said. "I think they're just about as pretty as this little actress you've hooked up with. What'd ya think?"

"They're beautiful," Parker said.

Two girls, around nine and twelve, held out their hands as though they were royalty and did this every day. "I'm Ashley, the oldest, and this is Amanda. She's three years younger than me. Are you and Dr. Parker going to get married?" the dark-haired oldest girl asked.

Normally, Angelica would've been mortified by such a question, and coming from a child, too. Not this time. She looked at Parker before answering. "Someday, I'm sure, we'll both get married. I don't know if we will marry one another if that's what you're asking." Pure and simple. No in between the cracks.

"Ashley! I can't believe you asked Ms. Shepard such a personal question. You know better," Stephanie said to her daughter

before turning to Angelica. "I'm sorry. I hope she didn't embarrass you too much. She is obsessed with weddings now. Ever since Patrick and I married, then it was Melanie and Bryce. He's Grace's younger brother. Well, I've said too much. Please, accept my apologies," Stephanie asked, then grabbed both girls by the hand and took them to a nearby corner.

"And to think I was going to catch the next flight back to New York," Angelica said, still in awe.

"You know, it is quite a leap from Colorado to New York. You have any suggestions?" Parker asked as they followed their new friends out of the gymnasium. "And there's Leon to consider. He hates flying."

"I hope you have a lot of frequent-flier miles," Angelica teased, before adding, "but if not, I kinda like this neck of the woods. And I'm sure Leon will fall madly in love with me when he gets to know me."

Parker leaned down to whisper in her ear, "Does that mean what I think it means?"

"What do you think it means?" she couldn't help but ask.

"I think it means this is the beginning of something new, maybe the best new beginning of my life. Would I be correct in my assumption?"

"Look, we hardly know one another. Plus, you owe me big-time for today's injury. But, I am willing to make you a deal," she stated before climbing back inside the limo Max had sent to the hospital.

"And what would that deal be?"

"I want free medical care for the next two weeks. If, and this is a very big *if,* you and I, well, if we are as good as we are right now . . ." She let her words trail off.

"Sweetie, you ain't seen nothing yet. This is only the beginning," Parker said before sliding in beside her.

"Something tells me this is going to be the merriest Christmas ever." Angelica finally relaxed. Her trip had started out on a sour note, but something told her this was just the beginning.

"And you have your very own personal angel to watch over you," Parker added, then kissed her.

Today was perfect, Angelica thought as she melted in his arms. Tomorrow would be even better.

■ ■ ■ ■

THE JOY OF
CHRISTMAS
HOLLY CHAMBERLIN

■ ■ ■ ■

As always, for Stephen
And this time, also for Julia

ACKNOWLEDGMENTS

Many thanks are due to John Scognamiglio for once again giving me an opportunity to tell a story.

Thanks also to Heather Nichols, owner and muse of Stones & Stuff, for the warm and fuzzy mittens! And thanks to jewelry designer Kate Hebold for her inspiration!

This is in memory of Torch.

"How simple a thing it seems to me that to know ourselves as we are, we must know our mothers' names."

— ALICE WALKER

CHAPTER 1

"Aren't you glad I told you to wear a hat that covers your ears?" Bess Wallis asked from the depths of her heavy wool coat and red and black plaid hunter's cap.

Her friend, Iris Karr, from the depths of her own heavy wool, nodded. "Yeah, and I'm still freezing. I forgot just how cold you could get standing still."

"You could stomp your feet."

"I would," Iris said, "if I could feel them."

"Ha! Maybe now you'll come over to the SmartWool set."

"I'll take it under consideration."

It was Friday, the second of December. The two women had come to the annual lighting of the copper beech tree at the Portland Museum of Art. Everyone gathered in the small side yard outside the McLellan House had been given a slim white taper to hold against the early December darkness. The tapers were a nice idea,

149

Iris thought, even though the little flames were snuffed out with even the tiniest movement of air. Relighting a taper from the flame of a neighbor's taper brought people together. It united the crowd in the spirit of community and love that was Christmas.

"Bah humbug," Iris muttered, then coughed to cover her words. Bess looked at her curiously, then turned away.

Iris's lack of holiday spirit had nothing to do with spending a Friday evening at a museum, or even with the presence of the tightly packed crowd. She had loved museums from the time she was small and her mother had begun to take her on cultural excursions. She had so many wonderful memories of visits to museums in Massachusetts, Connecticut, and New York.

And then the excursions had stopped. Iris and her mother had never made it to the Art Institute of Chicago or the Smithsonian in D.C. or the J. Paul Getty Museum in Los Angeles.

Iris squeezed her eyes shut against the darker memories, a futile effort but one that had become habit.

No, the museum wasn't the problem; the revelers weren't the problem; even the ridiculous cold wasn't the problem. Christmas was the problem. Christmas would always be the problem. Iris's mother, Bonnie Karr, had died on Christmas Eve three years earlier, two months after Iris's thirtieth birthday.

Not that Iris was sad. Not anymore. But still. The month of December definitely presented challenges the other eleven months did not, not even March, the month in which her mother had been born.

In short, December was the cruelest month. So as she had for the previous two years, Iris avoided the lighting of the giant pine tree in Monument Square right after Thanksgiving and had turned down a neighbor's invitation to the old-fashioned Holiday Fair at the Cathedral Church of St. Luke on State Street. And she would stay home when Bess and a few of her friends joined the crowds for Merry Madness in about two weeks' time, carrying glasses of wine from shop to shop, choosing locally made presents for a special few. No, Christmas and all the celebrations that led up to it were toxic for Iris. It hadn't always been that way but it was now, and as far as Iris could see, it probably always would be. Going to the museum this evening with Bess had been a huge concession to her friend, one prompted partly by guilt. Bess gave an awful lot in their friendship. The least Iris could do was sing a few carols with her.

Iris drew her bulky wool coat more closely around her and buried her neck further into her fluffy scarf. Under her faux fur hat her hair was thick, dark, and naturally curled into loose waves. It was her mother's hair, as her eyes were her mother's eyes, large and deep brown. From her father, whose forebears had been English, she had inherited very white skin, the primary reason she avoided the beach in summer. She was average height and average weight. She dressed in gray, black, tan, and taupe, reserving bright color for accessories like scarves and bags. Though Iris designed and crafted jewelry, she wore very little jewelry herself. At the moment, the only piece she wore was a narrow gold bangle bracelet set with three demantoid garnets.

"Marilyn could have joined us," Bess said, "if her new sous chef hadn't called in sick. Half the waitstaff is out, too, with some dreadful bug."

Iris made appropriate sounds of sympathy.

Bess, who taught poetry at the University of Southern Maine, was taller than Iris, and slimmer. She had recently celebrated her fifty-seventh birthday by treating herself and her partner to a few days in Paris. Her hair, once brown, hung down to her waist in a silver cascade, which made a striking contrast to her vivid blue eyes. At the moment she was wearing a heavy, Black Watch plaid wool skirt that came almost to her ankles, tights, black knee high boots, and under her coat, a cream-colored wool sweater she had bought on a long ago trip to Ireland. The large, antique gold and opal ring she always wore on her left hand, once her great-grandmother's, was hidden from sight by one of a pair of chunky knit mittens. Bess considered the ring a talisman of sorts, a good luck charm, though she hadn't shared with Iris just what specific good luck the ring tended to bring.

A tiny old man to Iris's right stumbled over the rough ground and jostled her as he tried to regain his footing. She stepped a bit to the left to allow him room to pass. Her altered position gave her a partially new perspective of those gathered across the yard. Iris blinked. The cold had been known to make her eyes water and sting. It had been known to blur her vision. She blinked again.

But there was no mistake. It was Ben.

Iris heard her own sharp intake of breath.

"Are you okay?" Bess asked.

"Yeah," Iris lied, faking a smile. She suspected it appeared more as a grimace.

"Just a shiver."

"A loud one."

"Sorry."

"Oh, good," Bess said, pointing to the chorus gathering on the steps of the building. "The singing's about to start."

The local choral group that had been hired to perform began a program of traditional songs. The crowd sang along to "Deck the Halls" and "Jingle Bells," booming baritones and thin sopranos, the old and the young, the talented and the tone deaf. Iris, however, was too stunned even to mouth the words. Let her neighbors think her a party pooper. She just couldn't care.

Iris bent her knees a bit, hoping to shrink to a point below notice. She couldn't be sure he had seen her. Ben Tresch. They hadn't made eye contact, of that she was certain, but maybe when she had so suddenly stepped to the side something of her movement had caught his attention. Maybe. She didn't want to stick around to find out.

But how to orchestrate an escape? She could tell Bess the cold was too fierce for her to tolerate and force her way through the tightly packed crowd, back into the museum and out the doors on Free Street. From there it was a brisk ten-minute walk back to her home on Neal Street. She would be safe there. Home was her haven, her sanctuary.

Iris sighed. Home would have to wait. She had promised to accompany Bess to the lighting and it would be rude to abandon her, especially for a lie. Her knees were aching now and Iris stood to her full height. It had been a ridiculous idea, anyway, attempting to hide in plain sight.

Beside her Bess's clear contralto voice rang out in the cold air. But Iris couldn't trust herself to open her mouth in a semblance of singing, and not only because she was still stunned at seeing her former love across the crowd, the man she had been poised to marry. Now the familiar music had worked its way into her heart, too. This is why I hate Christmas celebrations, she thought. I don't want to cry ever again and Christmas is all about crying. There were the sentimental songs and the cheesy television commercials where everyone was smiling and laughing and getting diamond engagement rings and charm bracelets.

And then there were the funerals. It was all — horrible.

After what seemed to Iris like an interminable amount of time the chorus ended their performance with a rendition of "Silent Night," and with fanfare, the sprawling,

155

majestic copper beech tree came to sparkling life amid cheers and applause.

"Come on, let's get out of here," Iris said
before the applause had entirely died down,
grabbing Bess's arm.

> " 'But now, beyond the things of sense,
> Beyond occasions and events,
> I know, through God's exceeding grace,
> Release from form and time and space.' "

"Who is that?" Iris asked, not really
interested in the answer.

"It's John Greenleaf Whittier, from his
poem 'The Mystic's Christmas.' So, you
didn't enjoy this occasion just a little bit?"

"The chorus was lovely," Iris admitted as
they moved toward the museum. "But I
don't want to get stuck behind the crowd."

"You've got an important appointment to
get to? Maybe even a hot date?"

Iris didn't answer.

Together they made their way back inside
the museum, past the Gillian Rotunda,
through the gift shop, past the information
desk and the great hall, and finally out again
into the clear, cold December darkness.

Once on the sidewalk, Iris felt the tension
in her body begin to drain away. She would
make her escape now and —

"Iris!"

The tension, all of it, was back. Stiffly, Iris turned to face the past in the form of Ben Tresch.

He was a very handsome man by almost anyone's standards, tall and broad-shouldered and slim. His features were strong but also fine and his hair, once bright blond, had mellowed to a warm gold. His eyes were very blue.

"What are you doing here?" she blurted. Portland was her city now, not his.

"Hello to you, too," he replied. "I've taken the job of curator of a new department at the museum. I started just yesterday."

"Oh," Iris said feebly. "Congratulations."

"Thanks," Ben said, a wry twist to his lips. He extended his hand to Bess. "I'm Ben Tresch."

"Bess Wallis. Nice to meet you."

Iris shook her head. "I'm sorry. I should have . . ." There was an awkward moment when none of the three seemed to know what else to say. Iris could feel Bess's eyes on her and looked down to her chunky winter boots.

"Well," Ben said into the big silence, "I should get back inside. I have a meeting. You know how it is when you start a new job."

Iris remained silent, though she did look up from her boots. Bess said, her voice pitched to make up for her friend's rudeness, "It was very good meeting you, Ben. I hope the job is all you want it to be."

Ben thanked her and with a look at Iris that Bess couldn't quite interpret, he turned and ran lightly up the museum's few front steps.

Iris, finding that she couldn't bear to watch him go off, had turned away from the building and was pretending to find something very interesting in the December sky.

"So, who was that?" Bess asked when Ben was out of earshot. "Why do you look as if you've seen a ghost?"

"Because I have," Iris mumbled.

"Oh. Do you want to come over for some hot cider? Marilyn's got a new recipe. It's amazing. It'll grow hair on your chest if that's your sort of thing."

Iris looked away from the sky and attempted a smile. "No, thanks," she said. "I think I'll just head home."

Bess shrugged. "Suit yourself. And, Iris? A word of advice?"

"Yeah?" Iris said warily.

"SmartWool."

CHAPTER 2

It was Saturday evening, December third, and Iris was at her home on Neal Street. She had bought the condo not long after moving to Portland a little less than three months after her mother's passing. It was on the third floor of an enormous house that had been built in the nineteenth century for one extended family. The building had charm to spare, as did most of the homes in the West End.

Iris had taken to the neighborhood immediately. The architecture of its private homes appealed to her sense of history and whimsy. The majority of them were massive, rambling structures, built in either brick or stone. Many featured enormous wraparound porches, fanciful turrets, and especially on the homes overlooking the water on the Western Promenade, widow's walks. Most homes had beautifully tended gardens, either walled or open, and lots of the streets spent a good deal of the day in shade because of the massive pines and sprawling oaks.

This evening Iris found herself staring out her living room window at the house across the street. On its front door was hung a big bunch of pine boughs tied together with bright red velvet ribbon. If Iris enjoyed the Christmas season, she would have found the West End at this time of the year a bit of heaven on earth. Almost every house displayed an elaborately decorated Christmas tree in the window of its front room, a pretty enough sight to make even the grinchiest of people smile.

Iris turned irritably from the window. It wasn't even seven thirty but she contemplated the idea of going to bed. What was the point of staying up when she felt at a loss as to what to do with the rest of the evening?

The whole day had been the same. She had spent the majority of it at work in her studio but every few moments her thoughts had turned to Ben Tresch. It seemed impossible but she had forgotten just how blue his eyes were and just how they seemed to see far more of you than you had decided to show.

Iris brushed her hand across her face, as if

chasing away the memories, and picked up a large, smooth chunk of charoite sitting on a tall, narrow stand in the front hall. She loved its marbled purple and white appearance. The stone was heavy and dense, yet she had the sensation that her fingers were ever so slightly making indentations in its surface. Holding the stone gave her a feeling of sensual satisfaction. It helped calm her.

After a moment she carefully returned the stone to its home. She really didn't know why she had been so surprised at Ben's appearance the night before. Portland and Boston were at best two hours apart. It wasn't inconceivable that she and Ben might run into each other, especially at a museum or gallery. They were both in the art world, which could be notoriously small, even incestuous. The real surprise was that their paths hadn't crossed before now.

Still, seeing Ben across the crowd and then face-to-face outside the museum had shocked Iris and rattled the still-fragile construct she had made of her life since moving so abruptly to Maine from her hometown of Wakefield, Massachusetts. For better or worse, Ben Tresch was too intimately associated in Iris's heart with her mother and the world Iris had purposely, even ruthlessly, left behind.

Iris went into the living room and over to the elaborately framed antique mirror hung above the maroon velvet couch. She saw there what she saw each time she looked, the undeniably strong resemblance to her mother. Still, even in the depths of Bonnie's illness, Iris never saw the look of defeat in her mother's eyes that she saw in her own at that moment. Well, maybe it had been there and she just hadn't wanted to see it. Iris turned away from the mirror.

Bonnie Karr had been a well-regarded sculptor who worked mostly in stone and then, later in her life, largely in wood. Eventually, a full eighteen months before her death from a recurring cancer, Bonnie had been forced to give up her work entirely. That was only one instance of how the disease had been unkind to her. It had gradually but sometimes in brutally large steps robbed her of all the little joys in her life, and then, finally, of the biggest joy — life itself. Bonnie Karr had passed away at the age of fifty-six, leaving behind a devoted and grieving husband and a loving and emotionally defeated daughter.

Iris drifted across the living room to a basket of small stones sitting on a long, low credenza. Some of the stones she had bought. Others she had found and some she had been given. She had so many stones now, there were literally hundreds around the apartment, but she would never forget buying her very first one.

She had been about five years old, vacationing with her parents on Cape Cod. One afternoon her father had taken her shopping. She remembered being overwhelmed by the endless shelves of what she later realized were cheap and tacky souvenirs — kitchen magnets, T-shirts with dubiously funny slogans splashed across the front, wind-up plastic lobsters. She had two whole dollars of her own to spend but nothing interested her and she remembered feeling pretty grumpy as she and her father made to leave the store. But then a jumble of polished rocks on the checkout counter caught her eye. Without hesitation she had snatched up a chunk of rose quartz as her prize.

Iris still had the stone; it was something she would never willingly part with because she believed it had signaled the birth of her creative life. Something inside her had responded to it. Something inside her had known she wanted to work with the materials of the earth, just as her mother did.

With a dramatic sigh Iris walked back

across the room and sank onto the couch. Her mother's illnesses had dominated Iris's life for close to twenty years. Even now, three years after her mother's passing, Iris remembered as if they had happened yesterday the landmark events her mother had missed out on. The sixth-grade holiday play in which Iris had had a speaking role as the Snow Queen. Iris's graduation from high school, at which she had been presented an award for top honors in art. Her graduation from college and the opening of her first studio in Boston's SOWA district a few years later.

Sometimes, Iris thought, picking at a loose thread on a pillow, her life read as a catalogue of loss. If that was being self-pitying, then so be it. Someone had to feel bad for her. Besides, she knew she couldn't bear pity from anyone else. She didn't deserve it. She had failed her mother in the end and nothing could relieve her from that burden of guilt.

Losing a parent was a very strange thing, Iris had learned. You didn't know any life without your parent. Life simply had never existed before her. And then . . . life did exist but it was a completely different one. It was an alien life. And for Iris, that alien life had to be lived on an alien stage, one far away from the vivid reminders of what once had been. Reminders like her father. Reminders like Ben.

Iris got up from the couch and went into the kitchen. She opened the fridge and stared inside. A few half-empty bottles of condiments. A lone egg. A head of broccoli she had no interest in cooking. She closed the fridge with a sigh of frustration.

Well, at least her father, Robert Karr, hadn't seemed to mind her defection, she thought now. He had remarried barely a year after his wife's death. Iris had already gone off to Portland so hadn't been on hand to — to what? To talk her father out of his mad idea that his first wife could be replaced?

The doorbell rang then, interrupting Iris's reluctant trip down memory lane.

"Thank God," she murmured, and hurried to answer it.

CHAPTER 3

It was Bess, dressed this evening in a floor-length sable coat. It had belonged to the same great-grandmother who had owned the opal ring, but somewhere along the line its care had been neglected. Moths had eaten tiny holes up and down the arms, and areas of fur were oddly flat and dull. Just looking at the coat made Iris feel itchy.

Bess held out a plastic food container. "I brought you some butternut squash soup. Marilyn's experimenting with a new recipe."

"Thanks." Iris said, accepting the gift. "I kind of forgot to go food shopping this week. I was facing peanut butter on pretzels for dinner."

Bess dropped the sable coat on the closest chair, a high-backed antique monstrosity (her term) upholstered in a pale green fabric printed with big pink cabbage roses. As was her habit she glanced quickly around the rooms. It never failed to puzzle Bess why

Iris, the daughter of a famous artist, had none of her mother's works on display in her home. There were no framed photographs of her mother or of her father, either, nothing on an end table or on the mantel of the fireplace in the living room.

What Bess didn't know was that Iris did keep a picture of her mother, hidden away in her college copy of *The Riverside Shakespeare.* It had been taken on the day Bonnie had graduated from art school. It had always been Iris's favorite picture of her mother, this smiling, hopeful young woman who had no idea of what awaited her in life, good or bad.

Bess also didn't know that there was no photo of Ben Tresch hidden away in a book, no letters at the bottom of a desk drawer, not one memory in tangible form. Even the antique locket he had given her on their first anniversary was in a box of neglected memorabilia somewhere in Robert Karr's basement.

"Peanut butter on pretzels?" Bess said, eyebrows rising. "Are you sure you aren't a guy?"

"Quite sure. A guy would eat the pretzels with ketchup."

"True. I once caught my older son chowing down on condensed soup right out of the can. He said it was too much of a hassle to add water and stir."

Iris pretended a look of sympathetic horror. She watched with some amusement as Bess surveyed her surroundings, as if she were seeing them for the first time.

The furniture was a jumble of styles, some distinctly Victorian, like the maroon velvet couch, others Danish modern, with a few slightly awful pieces from the sixties thrown in for fun. The overall atmosphere was one Iris liked to think of as "decayed elegance." Bess was inclined to describe the contents of Iris's home as "messy old stuff," from the mismatched furniture, to the worn velveteen curtains, to the rough rocks and polished stones scattered on pretty much every surface. Perhaps oddly for a professor of poetry, someone almost required by profession to be romantic and sentimental, Bess's own home was largely furnished with nondescript but clean-lined pieces from IKEA. She preferred, she said, to invest her limited money and vast creative resources in collecting old books and in practicing on her authentic Australian Aboriginal didgeridoo.

Which was one of the things, according to Bess, that had led to her divorce several years back. Frank had demanded Bess not play the instrument in the house. Not everyone, he argued, could tolerate its low-pitched drone without wanting to kill himself. Bess had declared she would play her didgeridoo wherever and whenever she pleased. Frank sold the didgeridoo. Bess filed for divorce, which, in Iris's opinion, was entirely understandable. You just didn't sell another person's stuff without express consent.

Soon after, Bess bought back her beloved instrument and Frank moved to Southern California to take a job at his brother's plumbing business. (What, Iris wondered, had led him to choose plumbing as a midlife career option, especially after a career in teaching Latin and Greek?) And as soon as their two sons had graduated from college, they had followed in his wake. Not long after learning about Bess's family situation, Iris had asked her if the boys had rejected her for having rejected their father.

"You throw the nasty reality of a divorce at a teenaged kid," Bess had explained, "and then you add on top of it the 'interesting' information that his mom has changed teams midgame, and let me tell you, there's bound to be dissatisfaction."

"But your sons got over the shock?" Iris asked hopefully. "I mean, it's not as if you left their father for another person. You didn't meet Marilyn until much later."

Marilyn Schwartz was a few years younger than Bess. She owned a small and very popular restaurant named Snug on Pine Street in the West End. Marilyn was long divorced from someone whom she once described as "an insult to Neanderthal man." Iris could only imagine. Perhaps luckily, they had had no children.

Bess had shrugged. "They tell me they're okay with it all. But they left the East Coast and they never mention Marilyn when we talk. They'll come around in their own time. Or, they won't."

Iris put the tub of soup into the fridge and offered her friend a glass of wine.

"Have I ever said no?"

"There's always a first time."

"Not until I'm on my deathbed," Bess said with a laugh. "And by then, who cares?"

Iris ignored Bess's careless reference to dying and poured them each a glass of Malbec. They sat at the kitchen table. It was an old pine piece, the only bit of decor with a distinctly country feel to it, but somehow, even Bess admitted that it worked with the "messy old stuff." Iris had a flair for bringing odd bits together into a coherent whole.

"I think there's something you're not telling me about that Ben fellow," Bess said, after taking an appreciative drink of the wine. "By the way, he's quite good-looking."

"Yes," Iris said, pretending absentmindedness, toying with her glass.

"Yes, there's something you're not telling me or yes, he's good-looking?"

"What? Oh. Uh . . ."

"What's struck you with a case of the inarticulate?"

"Nothing. I'm just thinking about all I have to do for the holiday season. . . ."

Bess finished her wine and got up from her seat at the table. "I'll take the hint and get out of here. But you know I'm available to help at your open house. Ring up your massive sales and all."

Iris laughed. "From your mouth to God's ears."

Bess looked at her curiously. "That's an odd thing for someone who doesn't believe in God to say."

"I never said I don't believe. I just said that I'm not sure."

"Well, you're not alone there. I should be off."

Bess put on the ancient sable and let herself out. When she was gone, Iris took Marilyn's soup from the fridge and a spoon from the drawer next to the stove and began to eat the soup cold.

CHAPTER 4

Iris's studio was on the tenth floor of a large old brick building on Congress Street just off High Street. Close to forty artists rented space in the building, and more than a handful lived illegally in their studios. From the windows of her studio Iris could see a good deal of the PMA, and in the winter when the trees were bare, if she leaned up against the far most window at a certain angle she could make out the curving back of the *Rising Cairn* in the museum's side yard.

The work was by an artist named Celeste Roberge. It was one of the most beautiful pieces of sculpture Iris had ever seen. It bothered her that she had no idea what her mother had thought of it. Iris had never asked her.

Iris's neighbors in the building were a motley crew. Down the hall was a young woman who worked with encaustic and to

Iris's immediate left was a guy who built kinetic sculptures out of discarded pieces of old cast-iron furniture. A woman on the fourth floor specialized in assemblage and on the ninth floor a very popular photographer of children and pets had set up camp. Iris knew these fellow artists as acquaintances but not as friends. That was fine with her.

This late Sunday morning, the fourth of December, found Iris in her studio preparing to work. The room was about three hundred square feet. The bank of windows was the studio's best feature. They were seven feet tall and ran almost the entire length of the wall facing the street. The other walls of the studio were bare but for some sturdy racks from which Iris had hung tools of her trade.

The room was stocked with the usual things one would find in a jewelry designer's studio. There were two worktables and various pieces of equipment, from an all-purpose flex shaft (a big machine you worked with a foot pedal), to a mandrel, steel hammers, pumice blocks, and a fan. There were her soldering tools, including an acetylene tank, a torch, and clamps, and the items needed for the steps following, including a tumbler. There was a punch stamp for identifying a piece as authentic sterling silver, and one for adding her initials to a finished piece. From the largest wall rack hung a variety of metal tongs, including some made of copper, and a collection of pliers, from needle-nose to flathead, to those covered in nylon so as not to gouge silver. Iris didn't cast her own metal; she bought metal in sheets from a wholesale online source. Coils of round, flat, and square gold, silver, and pewter wire, in a variety of gauges, were neatly piled on one of the tables.

Against the left wall stood an enormous safe — it had been in place when she rented the studio — where Iris housed her stones. She bought the stones, most of them cut and calibrated and many but not all of them polished, from reputable Web sites, as well as at wholesale gem and jewelry shows. On occasion she found wonderful, odd pieces at a store called Stones & Stuff on Congress Street. The owner, Heather, kept an eye out for particular gems she thought might be of interest to Iris, like a stunning fire opal from Mexico, and a faceted chunk of garnet that flashed a burgundy red, reminding Iris of medieval stained glass.

The work of a jewelry designer and crafter might sound glamorous to some, but the reality was it could be very dangerous. It took not only skill but also a fair amount of natural talent and a good dose of sheer luck not to ruin a piece of jewelry in progress, or, worse, to get seriously burned. Mostly, Iris loved every minute of it.

Except this morning she just couldn't seem to get started and that worried her. She couldn't afford to be distracted, especially not at this time of the year. What had her mother told her about those times when inspiration just wasn't visiting? Right. Just go ahead and work. You can always toss the results and start over the next day. The important part was to keep in motion.

From when she was a little girl Iris had loved visiting her mother's studio. For years Bonnie had rented a space about an hour from their house. Over time, when the daily trip became too wearying, Bonnie had moved her studio closer to home. But then, the marble and wood dust began to exacerbate her already compromised ability to breathe, and eventually, Bonnie had been forced to stop working.

Iris assumed her father had taken care of the contents of Bonnie's studio after her death. Robert had been Bonnie's true partner in life, her professional manager, her husband, the father of her child, her friend.

Just as Ben had been Iris's true partner . . . Iris picked up a short length of silver wire and idly twisted it between her fingers. Ben had always been supportive of her work. He was the academic to her practitioner, the theorist to her craftswoman. They had both gone to Hollander College of Art though Ben was a few years ahead of her and they hadn't met until Iris was in her senior year.

After college, while Ben was finishing graduate work, Iris had taken a job as an apprentice to a local jewelry designer. After a time she was able to set up her own small workshop in her parents' basement until, with a loan from her father and a few steady clients, she was finally able to afford a studio in Boston's arts district. Eventually, she was earning enough to get a tiny apartment in the South End. Ben shared an apartment in Charlestown with a friend from school.

Iris dropped the length of wire onto a table and picked up one of the sketching pencils she preferred. She tapped the pencil on the table as her thoughts turned to Ben's parents. Hanna and Jim Tresch had supported her burgeoning career as firmly as they had their son's. Hanna had bought a piece from Iris's very first complete collection, an eighteen-karat gold pendant set with a cabochon peridot. She had purchased several more pieces over the years and had introduced a few of her friends to Iris's work. She had even provided the wine and cheese for a few openings, and helped Iris to ring up sales.

Iris dropped the pencil and glanced out at the colorless December sky. She doubted that Mrs. Tresch still wore those bracelets and earrings and pendants she had bought. Not after what Iris had done to her son.

Iris turned from the window, put her hands over her eyes, and pressed her fingers into her forehead. For a brief and insane moment she thought that she might call Ben and . . . And what? Apologize?

Well, she had a lot for which to apologize. Everybody had known that Ben and Iris would marry. They would have. They should have. By leaving Ben, especially in the way that she had, she had destroyed the rightful assumptions of two good families. She had broken a verbal contract. She had betrayed an emotional promise to Ben, her parents, his parents, and finally, to herself.

She hadn't set out to damage so many lives. If it hadn't been for that fatal conversation, the conversation no one knew about but for Iris and her mother . . .

A few months before Bonnie had gone into hospice she had asked Iris into her bedroom for a private talk. "I want you to be happy," Bonnie had said, without preamble. "And it would make me happy, too, to see you and Ben married before I die."

Iris remembered standing there in shock. Her mother had never, ever mentioned her death. And when the shock had passed, the forces of superstition and avoidance reared their formidable heads.

"I'm not wasting time planning a wedding when you need me," she had said firmly. "Besides, you'll be fine, Mom. You're not dying. You always come through."

Her mother had begun to protest but Iris had cut her off. "But nothing, Mom. No more talk of dying."

Iris had practically run from the room and her mother never mentioned a wedding again. And even when Bonnie had gone into hospice, a sure indicator of the impending finality, Iris had refused to believe the evidence staring her right in the face. No matter that death was inevitable. Let the Grim Reaper work alone. Iris would not prepare his way. If there was no wedding, there would be no dying, at least for a long, long time.

It was foolish and delusional thinking. And then, Bonnie hadn't survived and it was too late for Iris to give her mother that one final gift she had desired.

Iris walked over to the window and looked out at the *Rising Cairn,* so beautiful in its simplicity, so monumental and weighty. It consisted of a welded steel grid shaped like an oversized human crouched on one knee on the ground, head bent. Inside the grid the artist had packed rocks collected locally, gray and brown, smooth and round, large and small. Since Iris had first come under its spell she had found herself imagining the figure one day rising from its crouching position and standing tall, its limbs stretched, its head raised to look out at whatever challenge came ahead.

Iris turned away from the window. The day the sculpture rose would be the day she would forgive herself for failing her mother. And that day would never come.

CHAPTER 5

"Knock, knock."

Iris looked up to see Alec Todd standing in the open doorway.

"You in?" he asked, loping into the studio, his footsteps loud on the old and slightly bouncy wood floor.

"I guess I am."

Alec and Iris had dated desultorily for close to two years. The desultory part was her doing. Alec had finally left her because he wanted more of a commitment and found her position on relationships to be frivolous. That was his word, *frivolous.* Iris had almost laughed the first time he had accused her of this, but out of consideration for his feelings, which were genuine, she had not.

Iris's former boyfriend was a "brilliant computer guy," a successful thirty-eight-year-old man wrestling with the spirit of the nerdy eleven-year-old boy he had once been. He was medium height and stocky. His light brown hair was thinning in the classic horseshoe pattern, about which he wasn't happy because he was a little vain. For some reason Iris couldn't understand he refused to shave his head, as if clinging to the sad stray strands was any more attractive than a naked skull. He wore funky glasses (his eyesight was awful) and a virtual uniform of jeans, black mock turtlenecks (in honor of Steve Jobs), and black work boots (those even in summer). Once in a while a frayed flannel shirt made an appearance, but only on special occasions, like when one of his favorite bands was playing in town.

Alec hadn't spent many weeks mourning the death of his relationship with Iris. His new girlfriend, Tricia, was twenty-five, pretty, happy, and a wee bit dense. Not dumb, really, but not bright, either. At least, that was Iris's opinion of her. Tricia worked in one of the high-priced clothing shops on Exchange Street. Iris didn't know which one and she didn't really care to know. The less she knew about Tricia, she decided, the better. She just couldn't see Alec and Tricia as a serious or successful couple.

As if reading her mind, Alec said, "Did I tell you that Tricia got a bonus at work? She thinks she might make manager before long if she really tries."

"That's nice." Iris could think of nothing more to say.

"Yeah, she's really happy about how things are going at the boutique. About a month ago she suggested the buyer stock up on some cool leather bracelets from Thailand and they sold out immediately. Tricia really has her finger on the pulse of what women want."

"That's nice," Iris said again.

Alec frowned at her. "What's up with you? You might show a little enthusiasm. Dude, you might even feign some."

"Nothing's up," Iris lied. And then, she couldn't lie again. "Except that I don't know how you can be involved with her."

"Excuse me?"

"It's just that . . . Oh, never mind."

"No, it's just that what?" Alec pushed. "Tricia's too young for me? Too pretty, too nice, too fun to be with?"

"No, no. It's just that . . . Come on, Alec. You're a lot smarter than she is."

Alec shrugged. "Maybe in some ways. But not in others."

"So, what are you saying? She completes you? You balance each other out?"

"Yeah. That's exactly what I'm saying.

And pardon me, Iris, but you're not exactly one who should be giving relationship advice."

Iris sighed. "I know," she said. "I'm sorry. It's just that the last time we were all together, when she didn't know who Rauschenberg was, well . . ."

"Hey, not everyone is into modern American art. And she can make pancakes exactly the way I like them and she calls her parents every Sunday no matter what and she gives money to every homeless person she passes on the street. And there are a lot of homeless people in this town."

"Yes, I suppose that is all something."

"It is," Alec said emphatically. "It's a big something. Especially the pancake part."

"Sorry. Really."

"You're forgiven." Alec turned away and began to browse through a stack of Iris's more recent sketches.

Iris had the good grace to feel ashamed. Deep down she could admit that her biggest problem with Tricia was that she took up so much of Alec's time. Not that Iris wanted Alec back — she didn't — but she had come to rely on his being around when she needed him to hang out watching movies with her or to fix the kitchen sink's food disposal when she dropped something in it she shouldn't have.

Iris watched as Alec handled the sketches gently and with care. He had respect for her work. He was a good man. Still, she had never really been attracted to him, not in a romantic way. But part of the moving on process, she had told herself when she had come to Portland, was to get a new boy-friend. Not a Ben. Not a soul mate. Not even someone with whom she could be truly happy. Just . . . someone.

Poor Alec. Iris had strung him along for the two years they were a sort-of couple. Maybe she should have come right out in the beginning of their relationship and told him that she had no intention of ever get-ting serious. But she hadn't. For that she was sorry. Luckily, her less than honest behavior didn't seem to have badly affected him. Alec was nothing if not his usual resilient and rational self.

"Why did you come by, anyway?" she asked now.

Alec turned back toward her. "Oh, I almost forgot. I wanted to know if you're interested in hearing a band this Thursday night at One Longfellow Square."

"Depends. What are they like?"

"They're excellent. You can take my word."

"I'm sure I can. But I'll pass. I have a lot of work to get done by Christmas. You know, I'm hoping all those rich husbands out there will want to buy their wives a one-of-a-kind Iris Karr piece."

"That's a pretty old-fashioned — nay, downright sexist, and might I add cynical — view of relations between husbands and wives."

Iris shrugged. "You know what I mean. I have no sentimentality about who buys my work. I have bills to pay. I can't afford to care where the pieces go when they leave my studio."

"Be that as it may — meaning, I don't really believe you — are you sure you don't want to hear the band?"

"Yes. But thanks."

"Your loss. I'm told the drummer is really cute."

"Who told you that?" Iris asked, stifling a smile.

"One of Tricia's friends. You think I would know? Guys are gross. I don't know what you women see in us. Anyway, I'm off. I have to clean my car. Tricia gets off work at two and I promised her we'd take a drive to the outlets in Freeport. Did you know she's really good at hunting down bargains?"

Alec didn't wait for an answer but left as

abruptly as he had arrived. Suddenly, the studio felt very big and very empty and Iris felt very alone. Half of the city was busy having brunch with friends, including Bess and a few other women who were enjoying a meal at Snug, Marilyn's restaurant. She could have joined them — they had asked her along — but she had said no, which now seemed like a pretty foolish thing to have done. No thanks. I'd rather suffer my own lousy company than share a yummy meal with a group of nice, interesting, and intelligent people.

Iris busied herself straightening the stack of sketches through which Alec had been browsing.

When she and Ben were together she had never felt lonely, even when he was out of town or simply too mired in graduate work to spend time with her. It was true. Loneliness had little if anything to do with the presence of someone you cared about. It had everything to do with how you felt about your own company.

"And I," Iris announced to the walls, "am pretty lousy company."

CHAPTER 6

It was Monday, the fifth of December, around ten thirty in the morning. Iris was coming out of the Maine College of Art's store on Congress Street, a recycled shopping bag filled with new sketch pads in her arms. Ben was coming in.

Ben smiled and stepped aside. "Imagine running into you here."

"It's a small city," Iris said, perhaps a bit too sharply.

"Exactly. Which is why I really think we need to clear the air, Iris. Especially if we don't want to be afraid of an unhappy encounter every time we leave our houses. I hear from my assistant that we both live in the West End. Like you said, it's a small city."

Iris hesitated. Certainly, Ben had a point, but the last thing she wanted was a collision with the past. She had left her home, her entire life, to avoid such a thing.

"I could argue," Ben said into the silence, his voice pitched low, "that you owe me that much, a chance to clear the air."

"I . . ." Iris began, but she had no real idea what it was she wanted to say.

Three scruffy art students dressed in a collection of old combat boots, funky hats, and various massive tattoos, and wrapped in the odor of filterless cigarettes, bustled their way into the store.

"I said I could argue it," Ben said when the students had gone. "But I won't."

Iris repressed a sigh. This confrontation would have to happen at some point; she had been dodging it in one way or another since she had first announced her intention of moving to Maine. Common sense told her she couldn't outrun the inevitable forever. "Okay," she said. "Tomorrow night?"

"Good. You decide where we should meet. I don't know much about the city yet."

Iris thought. It should be a place where she would be unlikely to run into anyone she knew. The fewer people who associated her with the new curator at the PMA, the better. The fewer people there would be to sniff out the past and learn of her shame.

"DiMillo's," she said. No one she knew even vaguely ate there. But the food was good and the staff was pleasant and in the daytime the views were wonderful. "It's on Commercial Street. Is seven o'clock okay?"

Ben nodded. "Sure. I'll see you there."

With a small, halfhearted wave, Iris walked on to her studio. Once there she went over to the bank of windows and stared down mindlessly at the passersby on Congress Street. Though the temperature had been below freezing several times since Thanksgiving, there had been no snow yet, unlike the year her mother had died. That winter the entire Northeast had been buried under feet of snow from November through February, a grim, cold blanket under which her mother's body was "put to rest." How could the idea of one's mother abandoned to lie alone beneath frozen ground be of any comfort?

Bonnie Karr had wanted to be buried, not cremated, though she had requested that the casket be closed at the wake. Iris remembered staring down at the highly polished casket the day of the funeral. She remembered wondering if her father had removed her mother's wedding ring and the ring Iris had made for her when she was first getting started as a professional jeweler. She had found that the answer didn't matter.

People had patted Iris's arm and taken

her hand and some had even kissed her on the cheek. She had tried not to flinch at their touch. She supposed she nodded and maybe even managed to say "thank you" or "you're very kind" but she had no recollection of saying anything to anyone.

She did remember, though, the limousine ride from the church to the cemetery, with Ben and her father beside her. For the entire five-mile ride she had been plagued by the macabre thought that the hearse driving her mother's casket to the cemetery would spin off the icy road and crash into a tree, dumping its precious cargo. The images of this spectacularly gruesome disaster played before her mind's eye as if on a giant movie screen, loud and horrifying. She had suffered these images in silence.

The weeks following Bonnie's death were bleak. The snow turned dirty where it was lumped against the curbs. The world sunk into a mess of bland gray and oily black. A romantic might have said that nature was in mourning for Bonnie Karr. A romantic might also have said that the outer world was a reflection of Iris's state of mind. Colorless. Empty. Cold.

Iris turned away from the window. Grief, she had long ago realized, was often raging red and pulsating purple. It was often

190

crowded and it was mostly noisy. And it was usually as hot and searing as a lit charcoal grill.

But when grief ran away, it left behind a bland and chilly and deserted space.

She had refused to go to counseling after her mother's passing. She had, she argued, been preparing for the death for years. She was fine. Why should she waste a counselor's time and her own hard-earned money?

And if by moving abruptly to Portland, where she knew no one at all, she had rejected the experts' suggestions to make no major decisions while grieving and to surround herself with loved ones, then it was because she was not in fact grieving. She was not stuck in the numbness and isolation stages of grief because there was no real grief. Not anymore.

She hadn't thought about it for a long time but now, Iris remembered how when she was a little girl and her mother was first sick, she would lie in bed each night and attempt to make a bargain with a God she wasn't even sure she believed in. "If you make Mommy better, I'll never complain about making my bed."

But nothing ever changed for the better, at least not for long. She had half known all along that it was futile to try to make a deal with a being she could barely imagine. And yet, even at the end of her mother's life she had still been indulging in magical thinking. If I don't marry Ben, Mom won't die. Foolish. And irresponsible. She should have left those emotional and psychological habits in her past.

A loud crash from the hallway, followed by a string of inventive curses, startled her back to the moment. Iris walked briskly to one of the worktables. No more wallowing in the grim past. It was time to get down to work.

CHAPTER 7

Later that afternoon, Iris and Bess were having coffee at Arabica on the corner of Free Street and Corner Street.

"So, have you run into that old friend of yours again?" Bess asked when they had settled at a table with their steaming drinks. There were only a handful of other people in the shop at this time, and each one of them was intently engaged with a laptop or iPhone or iPad. "The handsome blond ghost."

"As a matter of fact," Iris said, hoping to sound nonchalant, "I ran into him at the MECA art store this morning."

"And?" Bess prompted.

"And we're going to get together for dinner tomorrow. You know, just to catch up." And, Iris added to herself, to clear the air. To answer the questions Ben clearly still needed answered.

"So, you knew each other well?" Bess asked.

Iris shrugged. "Fairly well. You know."

"No, I don't know. That's why I was asking."

"We used to be close," Iris admitted, but would be no more specific than that.

Bess sighed dramatically and put her hand over her heart. " 'Ah, how good it feels! The hand of an old friend.' "

"And who was that?" Iris asked, smiling in spite of herself.

"It might have been a Bess Wallis, but in fact it was our own dear Mr. Longfellow."

"Well, I haven't shaken Ben's hand so I don't know if it feels good or not. Besides, I'm not out to reestablish a relationship." Certainly not the one we used to have, she added silently, even if that were possible.

Bess broke in half the raspberry scone she had bought. "Here," she said, handing a half to Iris. "Now, I'll take half of yours."

They exchanged halves of Iris's pastry, and Iris nibbled without really tasting. Sometimes, she thought, like right now, in this warm and quiet coffee shop in the middle of a cold and sunny December afternoon, she wanted to tell Bess every little detail, both the good and the bad, about her relationship with her mother, about what it had been like being the only child of a talented and passionate woman. Sometimes she wanted to share with Bess the myriad memories, both the good and the bad, the time when Bonnie had taught Iris how to bake sugar cookies from scratch, and the time when her mother had to be rushed to the hospital in the middle of the night, leaving Iris at a neighbor's, clutching her stuffed rabbit and terrified. She wanted someone in her new life to know how she had resented her mother's illness, but how she had also always admired the courage her mother had showed while battling it. And sometimes, but not often, she wanted to confess how she had failed her mother in the end.

"Marilyn has decided to cook a goose for Christmas," Bess suddenly announced.

Iris choked on a crumb of scone, startled. "Oh," she said. "Okay."

"There'll be plenty for everyone, you know. I'm just offering an invitation. Again. And one of my poet friends will be reading from her new collection. She's quite good."

"All right."

"All right you'll come for Christmas dinner?"

"No. All right I'll think about it."

"You have to eat. Consider it just another

everyday meal."

"With a poet in residence?" Iris laughed. "Nice try."

Although the truth was that for the young Iris, meals in the company of poets and painters and musicians had been the norm. She wondered now with whom her father and Jean would spend their Christmas this year. She wondered how Jean felt about socializing with her father's artist friends and clients. She wondered how her father felt about spending time with Jean's nursing colleagues. She had no clear idea of their relationship. On the surface they seemed a mismatched couple but maybe when the door was closed behind them, they suited each other just fine. She did hope so, even though she had little desire to find out for certain.

"Look at my ring," Bess suddenly commanded. Iris did. The opal was throwing off colors in a fantastic display — orange, yellow, green, purple.

"That's pretty amazing," Iris admitted. "It looks like the aurora borealis. Or like something you might see in a hallucination. Not that I would know anything about that."

Bess held up her hand and regarded the stone in another angle of sunlight. "It shoots out color like that sometimes, even when it seems to me there's not the right kind of light, or maybe not enough light. It has a life of its own, this stone."

"Who will you leave it to when you die?" Iris asked.

Bess dropped her hand onto the table. "That's a grim thought."

"Sorry." Yes, Iris thought. It was a grim thought. But it's December and this is when I think about dying.

"Well, to tell the truth, I hadn't thought about it," Bess went on. "I suppose I don't plan on dying for quite some time."

Iris smiled. "Good. Sorry I'm such a downer."

Bess reached across the table and patted Iris's hand. "It's all right. I know this time of the year is hard for you."

Iris looked down at her half-empty cup of coffee. She had only told Bess that her mother had died on Christmas Eve. Nothing more.

" 'The dead are always with us,
mocking.
They have the time in space
And the space in time
To console
But not the inclination,
Or the conscience to compel it.' "

197

Iris looked up at her friend. "Wow," she said. "That's harsh."

"What did you expect from Joan Throckmorton? But maybe you don't know her work."

"Oh."

"I wouldn't advise you to read much of Throckmorton's poetry unless you're in a particularly sunny mood. The results could be — bad."

"I'll keep that in mind. Well, I guess I should get back to the studio." Iris began to gather her scarf and hat and mittens.

"And I should get back to preparing the end-of-term exams."

"How do you test someone's understanding of poetry?" Iris asked as she finished buttoning her coat. "How do you know they're not just repeating what you've told them? How do you know they really get a poem?"

Bess tugged her hat over her ears. It was a bright blue felt with a dark green brim and a fingerlike appendage sticking up about two inches from the dead center. "Those are questions," she said with a sigh, "that I've been asking myself for years."

CHAPTER 8

DiMillo's Floating Restaurant had been a family business since 1954 and in its present location at Twenty-five Long Wharf — in an old car ferry first commissioned in 1941 — since 1982.

It wasn't hip or trendy, there was no loud and thumping music, and the food wasn't experimental or skimpy, all of which made it a favorite with families. It wasn't unusual to see several generations sitting around a table, from great-grandma in a wheelchair to her great-grandchild in a highchair.

In short, DiMillo's was a cheering place and the thought of going there for dinner, even with an old love abandoned in less than ideal circumstances, should have boosted Iris's spirits a teeny bit, but it did not. Since morning she had been thinking about the lines of poetry Bess had quoted her at the coffee shop. The dead sat around mocking the living. Talk about depressing.

If Bess were right about Joan Throckmorton's poetry Iris would have no trouble avoiding it, at least at this time of the year.

Now it was evening and Iris was walking through the doors of DiMillo's. And there was Ben, waiting for her. Iris's heart ached. Had she really forgotten how wonderful it was to be greeted with a warm and welcoming smile? God, what a thing to have given up!

"Hi," Ben said when she was a few feet away. "Thanks for coming."

Iris nodded. She realized he was wearing a coat she had never seen before. Why should I have seen it? she asked herself. I've known nothing at all of his life these past three years. Nothing.

They were shown to a table immediately and took seats across from one another.

"In summer it's almost impossible to get a table on one of the decks," Iris said.

Ben nodded. "I can imagine."

"Yes. Sorry there's not much of a view on a late autumn night."

"That's okay. I wasn't expecting a view. So, did you walk here?" Ben asked.

"Yes," Iris said. "I don't have a car at the moment."

"Oh."

"How are you settling in to your place?"

she asked.

"Just fine. I'm renting until I find something right to buy."

"Oh. That's good. I mean, I'm sure you'll find something."

Iris managed a small, anemic smile. She didn't think she could stand making insipid small talk all evening, not with Ben of all people. And yet, the thought of his opening a brutally honest conversation terrified her. She remembered what Ben had said outside the art store. "I could argue that you owe me that much, a chance to clear the air."

"That old diving suit by the hostess desk really freaked me out," Ben said suddenly.

Iris managed a genuine smile. "I know. The first time I saw it I literally jumped. And I might have yelped."

"Imagine the courage it took to go down into the depths of the ocean in that thing."

"The courage or the sheer stupidity."

"There is that," Ben admitted. "I've always considered people who take extreme physical risks a different species of human from the rest of us. I don't care if it's for the sake of a sport or science or for the thrill alone."

"I remember when one of the students who worked with you at that tiny gallery off

Boylston Street asked you to go hang gliding."

Ben laughed. "Yeah, like that was ever going to happen."

He looked down at his menu then. Iris watched him surreptitiously. It felt odd to be admitting to memories. It was as if she still somehow possessed a part of Ben, though of course, she didn't. She had relinquished intimacy and maybe even the right to the memory of it.

"Is it terribly clichéd of me to order lobster?" Ben asked, looking up from his menu.

Iris smiled. "Probably. But I won't tell anyone."

"If I'm going to be a Mainer I suppose I should at least attempt to fit in."

"No, you shouldn't," Iris told him, "because you won't succeed. You'll always be from away. But don't despair. There are a lot of strangers. And some of them have lived here for twenty years or more."

Ben raised an eyebrow. "Thanks for the advice."

Their waiter, a skinny young man with a crew cut, took their order then and it was a long moment after he had gone off before Ben spoke. "I saw some of your recent work for sale in the museum's gift shop," he said.

"The pieces are beautiful. I recognized the work as yours before I saw the identification card. It's evolved since when I last saw it, but it's still uniquely yours."

"Yes. I mean, thanks. If you're not busy changing you're busy dying. Someone famous said that. I think." And why, Iris wondered, did I have to mention dying again?

"Where else do you sell?" Ben asked after another moment of silence that was beginning to feel uncomfortable.

Iris shrugged. "In a few places around town. Also, at a store in Ogunquit and at a gallery in Portsmouth and one in South Portland. Sometimes I sell from my studio. I'm having an open house on the sixteenth. You know, for holiday shoppers."

"Who does your marketing these days?" Ben asked. "Did you finally hire a manager?"

Iris laughed. "With what money? No, I do my own marketing, such as it is. I have a Web site, of course. I really should be more proactive about the whole thing. Maybe in the new year."

"It's not easy to promote yourself. Some people have the knack for it and some just don't. Which is why they hire someone like your father to manage their careers."

"Yes," Iris said. "He had such amazing patience with the clients who were socially — awkward. Well, I suppose he still does."

"He certainly did a wonderful job managing and promoting your mother's career. Not that she was, as you put it, socially awkward."

"Yes. I mean, no, she wasn't." She was anything but, Iris thought. Everyone had liked her. Everyone.

"You know," Ben said, "my mother still wears the pendant she bought at your first show."

Iris was stunned. "Oh," was all she managed to say. And then, "Where were you working before coming to the PMA?"

"I was cocurator of new works at the Harbor Museum," he told her. "It was a great place to learn the essentials of the process."

"Then why did you leave?" she asked carefully.

Ben shrugged. "The job in Portland came up. Frankly, it was too good an opportunity to ignore. The PMA is a bigger, more prestigious museum. And, they made me an offer."

So, Iris thought, his moving to Maine had nothing to do with my living here. She wondered if that were true.

"On an entirely different subject," Ben said suddenly, "I might as well tell you that I was married. Not for very long, less than a year, actually. But you probably know that."

Iris felt a stunning sense of betrayal. She knew she had no right to feel betrayed. But oh, this news hurt. "No," she said finally, mustering what she hoped was a normal voice. "I didn't know. I'm sorry. I mean, I'm sorry about the divorce."

"I'm surprised you hadn't heard," Ben said. "I thought there were no secrets these days. I assumed you must have read about it on Facebook. Not that I have a personal page. I don't care to share my life with thousands of virtual strangers. But Melinda did. Does. I'm afraid I come off pretty badly on her page. But she was hurt and disappointed. . . ."

"Oh," Iris said. She couldn't imagine what this Melinda person could have said about Ben. He was a genuinely good person. Then again, Melinda had been married to him. She had known Ben as a husband. Iris had not. "See," she went on, "I don't look at Facebook much. . . . Um, what happened? I'm sorry. I shouldn't pry. . . ."

"That's okay," Ben said. "I don't mind telling you. Briefly, it was a spectacularly unspectacular match. I thought it was about time I should get married. So did Melinda. And in the end, that was about all we had in common, though we each did a good job convincing ourselves otherwise. Amazing how stupid two educated and otherwise intelligent people can be, isn't it?"

Iris fiddled with the edge of the napkin she had yet to unfold and put on her lap. She wondered if Ben had married on the rebound, determined to move on and put the troublesome Iris Karr firmly in the past.

"I'm sure something good came of it all," she said lamely.

"Not really," Ben replied bluntly. "We each wasted almost eighteen months of our lives from start to finish, and we each lost a fair amount of money. Not to mention what we put our families through. No, the whole relationship was a disaster."

"Oh." Iris finally unfolded her napkin. Maybe Ben was accusing her in some way, wanting her to take responsibility for his disastrous marriage. Maybe he wanted her to feel sorry for him. Iris stifled a sigh and wondered how things had gotten to this sorry state, when she could no longer detect the real meaning behind his words. But she had the answer to that.

"So," Ben said heartily, as if (Iris hoped)

eager to close the subject for good, "what have you been up to these past few years? Besides working, of course."

Iris managed a smile of sorts. "Nothing, really," she said. "Work is pretty much my life. Not that I'm complaining. I'm lucky to love what pays my bills."

"I guess I could say the same right now," Ben said. "Though I'm sure that given time I'll find something to complain about. No job is without its challenges."

"True."

Their food arrived then, brought to the table by the skinny young waiter.

"How's your lobster?" she asked after Ben had made an initial attack.

"Lobstery. How's your pasta?"

"Good."

Silence descended as they ate. Iris realized that her entire body was tensed, as if for fight or flight. When was Ben going to bring up her dramatic defection from their relationship, and all those months of his ultimately futile pursuit? Why else ask her to dinner to "clear the air"? She had no idea how she was going to handle his questions — with deflection, outright refusal, lies, a tantrum, a dramatic exit? None of those options was right and each would be insulting to both of them, especially to Ben. She didn't know how the food was moving down her throat and actually staying in her stomach.

"You know," Ben said into the silence, "I run into your father on occasion. Well, when I still lived in Boston."

Iris took in that bit of information. She wondered if they talked about her when they met, her father and her former lover.

"He never mentioned that," she said. Not that she talked to her father all that often. Undoubtedly, there was a lot about his current life she didn't know, like how his second marriage was faring and how his business was doing in the terrible economy when buying art was a very low priority, even for those with disposable income.

Ben shrugged. "He probably didn't think you'd care."

That was harsh but what else was Ben — or her father — to think? When was the last time she had called her father or even sent him an e-mail? She thought of Tricia, who called her parents once a week, and felt a little bit ashamed.

The waiter came to clear their plates. Neither wanted dessert or coffee. Ben asked for the check and paid for their meals. "After all," he said lightly, not meeting her eye, "I pretty much insisted we meet to-night."

Together they walked back through the covered walkway lined with gift shops selling baseball caps, T-shirts, and snow globes, and then out into the parking lot.

"So, has the air been cleared?" Ben asked, his tone still light.

Had it? They had talked about a lot of things, even, briefly, her mother, but not about the one thing that most mattered: why Iris had abandoned Ben. "I don't know," she said, thinking that what she should have said was, "No. The air is as murky as ever. And it's my doing."

"Me, either," Ben said quietly. "But maybe it's been cleared enough for us to coexist peacefully in this small city."

Iris looked out over the water of Portland Harbor. It looked infinitely black and very, very cold. "Yes," she said after a moment. "Maybe."

"Can I offer you a ride home?" Ben said. "You won't believe this but I still have my old black Volvo."

The old black Volvo. How many times had she been in that car! Easily thousands of times over the six years of their relationship. If she got into the Volvo this night the sensory memories alone would rob her of what little reason she possessed.

None of this was supposed to happen. She and Ben were not supposed to be standing within inches of one another after having shared a meal. Ben was not supposed to be offering her a ride home and she was not supposed to be remembering how it felt to sit by his side in the warmth of his car on a dark December night.

"Oh, no, that's okay," she said weakly.

"Are you sure? It feels like it's going to snow."

"Yes, I'm sure. I like the cold air."

"Since when?" Ben held up a hand. "Sorry. I shouldn't presume that I . . . I shouldn't presume that I still know you."

Yes, Iris thought. Virtual strangers. That's what we've become. "It's okay," she said. "Well, good night."

She didn't put out her arms for a hug or her hand for Ben to shake. She just turned away and began to walk, quickly, out of the parking lot. She didn't see in what direction Ben walked, and if his car passed her as she made her way along Commercial Street she didn't know that, either. Before too many minutes she realized she was trembling and it wasn't entirely due to the cold.

CHAPTER 9

A pale sun filtered through the window shades Wednesday morning, the seventh of December. Iris peered over the covers at the clock on her bedside table. Eight o'clock. It was high time for her to be up and about. But she remained where she was.

She had been frozen to the bone by the time she got home the night before, her fingers red and swollen and stiff in spite of her mittens, eyes streaming tears, nose running. Ben had been right about the snow, though it hadn't started until she was home and tucked into bed. This morning there was probably only an inch or two on the ground. As Iris lay there in bed under blankets and comforters, she wondered if a thin layer of snow still sat on the back of the *Rising Cairn,* or if the weak morning sun had exerted itself enough to cause the snow to melt away through the gathered stones. Sometimes a foot or more of snow settled on the sculpture's back, a burden or a protective cloak, depending on how you looked at it.

Iris burrowed deeper. She was still surprised the evening had passed without Ben's having asked her why she had left him almost three years earlier with no explanation other than "the need for a change." Maybe, she thought, he was biding his time. But why? To torture her for having hurt him? Or, maybe he really didn't care any longer. Maybe he had gotten past the misery she had inflicted, recovered from the shock and pain to which she had subjected him, and just wanted to be friendly neighborhood acquaintances.

Friendly neighborhood acquaintances, indeed. Iris wondered what her mother would have thought of such a pathetic outcome to a once vital relationship.

Her parents had loved Ben and for all Iris knew her father still did. What was not to love about him? He was intelligent and kind, generous with his time, and respectful of others even when he had a good excuse not to be. He could be great fun. He was hardworking. He got along well with his own parents. On paper, he was impossible. In reality, he was, well, real.

In short, Ben Tresch had been a blessing

for the Karr family. Bonnie had even admitted to Iris that she regarded Ben as the son she had never had.

Iris sighed to the empty bedroom as she thought about how Ben Tresch, Bonnie Karr's surrogate son, had been the last person to see her alive. She had been unconscious during his visit as she had been for the better part of the day. But what might have happened if her mother had been conscious, even for a moment? What might she have said to Ben about the request Iris had denied her? What might Ben have felt?

Iris flinched as if in physical pain. She remembered how she had told Ben he needn't bother to come to her mother's funeral. It was an outrageous thing to have suggested to him — a part of her had known that even then — and he had been understandably appalled. Telling her own father that he didn't have to attend the services for his wife would have been no less bizarre.

She remembered, too, that not once during the services for her mother had she cried. In fact, she hadn't shed a tear since Christmas morning when a private nurse greeted Iris and her father with the news of Bonnie's passing in the night. She had cried then, intensely, for close to an hour and then, the tears had simply gone away.

Only weeks after the funeral the idea of moving to Maine had come to Iris like a flash of divine inspiration. That, or a bolt of madness, she thought now, rubbing her forehead. Only a month after the funeral she had announced her plans for departure. And in spite of Ben's pleading, she had packed her car and driven off, alone.

And that, as it is said, was that.

Iris looked again at the clock on her bedside table. It was almost nine. She would get out of bed. Soon.

Chapter 10

By midafternoon, Iris had finally made it out of the house and after a quick stop in Aurora Provisions on Pine Street for a sandwich and a cup of coffee to go, had walked on to her studio. There were orders for Christmas to complete and her open house was in days. She had been working for close to two hours when Bess stopped by with another culinary experiment for Iris to sample.

"It's kale and couscous," Bess explained, tossing her wildly colored knit hat onto one of the worktables. "Very hearty, very flavorful. And very good for you, I'm told."

"Thanks," Iris said, taking the square plastic container. "Are you sure Marilyn doesn't want some kind of payment for all the food she gives me? Sometimes I feel that I'm taking advantage of her."

"Don't be silly."

"Well, I appreciate it."

Bess seated herself on a stool Iris had salvaged from an abandoned studio. "So, how was dinner with your old friend?" she asked.

"It was fine," Iris said. She was aware that her voice was unnaturally high.

"Where did you guys go?"

"Um, DiMillo's."

"Huh. That's an unusual choice for you."

"Not really. It's very nice."

"I'm not denying that it's nice. Have you been to the happy hour? It's the best in town. Well, what did you talk about?"

"Stuff. General stuff. Work. The weather."

"I hope you weren't this boring at dinner."

Iris managed a small laugh. "I think I might have been. It was . . . It was kind of awkward. We used to date."

"Well, that much I figured out the night of the tree lighting."

"Oh," Iris said. "Well, we did more than just date. We were a couple for almost six years. We didn't actually live together, but we might as well have. We were pretty much inseparable."

Bess nodded. "Interesting. So, what happened?"

"I guess we just, I don't know, outgrew each other maybe."

"You guess? You don't know? Maybe?"

Iris looked toward the bank of windows facing Congress Street. "It was after my mother died," she said steadily. "Things were — different."

" 'There is no remedy for love but to love more.' "

"Who?" Iris asked, looking back to her friend.

"Henry David Thoreau."

"And what does that have to do with me?" Iris asked, slightly annoyed and not sure why.

Bess considered for a moment. "Maybe nothing. But the line just popped into my head so I thought I would share it."

"Thanks."

"So, how did you leave things last night?" Bess asked. "Will you see each other again?"

"Accidentally, I'm sure. I mean, he lives only a few blocks away from me, at least for the time being. And he works at the museum. But . . . No. I think . . ."

"You think what?" Bess pressed.

"The truth is I don't know what I think," Iris said finally, hearing the exasperation in her voice. "About Ben, about me, or about us. And that's pretty upsetting. I don't like uncertainty. Well, I suppose not many people do."

217

"Yes. When we don't quite understand our feelings about something or someone, life can be unusually tiring." Bess slid off the stool. "Well," she said, "when you're ready to tell me the whole story, I'll be there. For now, I've got papers to grade."

"The horror, the horror."

Bess rolled her eyes, retrieved her hat, and jammed it onto her head. "You have no idea," she said. "And nice quoting by the way."

When she had gone, Iris walked over to the windows and peered down to the sidewalk. Her eye was drawn to a couple strolling hand in hand on the other side of the street. There was something attractive about them, though Iris couldn't see their faces under their big winter hats. Maybe it was the ease with which they moved or the way the woman swung the man's hand. And for the first time since seeing Ben across the crowd at the tree lighting it occurred to Iris that he might have a girlfriend. He hadn't mentioned one at dinner but that didn't mean anything. Maybe he was involved with someone back in Boston. A long-distance relationship wasn't unheard of, especially between two professional people.

Or maybe he was single and eager to meet someone. Why wouldn't he be? He was young and attractive and had a good career. Lots of women would see him as the proverbial catch. And Ben was not a loner. Well, at least he hadn't been a loner when Iris had known and loved him.

And, significantly, she had known him before he had gotten married and divorced. The fact of marriage alone, for better or for worse, changed a lot of things about a person.

Iris turned away from the window. The thought of having to witness Ben in a romantic relationship with another woman made her feel a bit sick.

It wasn't hard to recall how she had longed for Ben upon first coming to Portland, in spite of her firm resolve to put aside the life she had so badly damaged. And his intent pursuit of her in those first few months had made her struggle even more difficult. She had fought fiercely against that longing, trying desperately to convince herself that her feelings were only nostalgia for a time that had never really existed.

Finally, worn out, Ben had ceased his efforts and Iris was left in what might pass for peace. Still, at random times the longing escaped the clutches of her lies and threatened to overwhelm her. Only weeks earlier, it had reared its powerful head, flooding her with sense memories of the man she had loved so completely and . . .

Stop! Iris told herself. She could not let Ben's being in town rattle the sense of command over her life she had worked so hard to establish. The sometimes wobbly command . . .

The ringing of her cell phone interrupted Iris's troubled thoughts. It was Clare, a customer from Cape Neddick, asking about the progress of her brother's Christmas gift. He was recently home from Iraq, Clare had explained at their first meeting, and his last tour of duty had been more emotionally draining than the earlier tours. He had always worn a cross on a chain around his neck; his grandfather had given it to him for his high school graduation. But somehow, it had been lost or stolen overseas. Clare wanted to replace it for him and had worked with Iris to design something special.

Iris ended the call with the assurance that the project was on schedule. How lucky this man Bill was, Iris thought, this soldier, to have a sister who cared so much about him. Some people were just blessed with good fortune. Iris sighed aloud. Unlike me, she thought, an only child, a partial orphan, a . . .

Iris stamped her foot against the floor. Oh, for God's sake, she scolded herself, mortified by the morbid turn her thoughts had taken. Drop the self-pity and get to work!

CHAPTER 11

This Thursday morning, the eighth of December, the *Rising Cairn* was blanketed with a sprinkling of frosty, winking crystals. The sculpture looked almost pretty, which was not a word Iris would use to describe it at any other time.

Iris shivered and turned away from the window. Heat in the studio was minimal at best, and appeals to the landlord routinely went unanswered. Iris often worked with fingerless gloves and a silk scarf tightly knotted around her neck. Today she was wearing three layers of sweaters, as well. She had taken Bess's advice and bought a few pairs of SmartWool socks. Over today's pair of socks she wore her black winter boots, lined with fleece. On her head was an unflattering but seriously warm knit cap.

"It's me."

Iris looked around to see Alec, standing just inside the studio. He had to be wearing five pounds of clothing above his waist alone. His hat, a monstrous, bumpy woolen thing in bright green, was jammed down low on his forehead. His legs were encased in what looked like snow pants for an overgrown child. He looked both ridiculous and adorable.

"So I see," Iris said with a smile. "Come in."

"Cold enough for you? Jeez, it's no better in here than it is outside."

"Hence my attire. And speaking of attire, how can you move in all that?"

Alec yanked off the hat and the outermost scarf. "With difficulty. So, how was dinner with your old buddy?"

Iris's stomach knotted. "How do you know about the dinner, or about the old buddy?" she demanded.

"I ran into Bess at the library. She told me some old friend of yours just moved to town."

"That's all she said?"

"Yeah, and that you'd had dinner at DiMillo's. Why? What else should I know?"

"Nothing." Because, Iris thought, there's nothing else that needs to be told.

Alec shrugged. "Speaking of dinner, you should come over some night. Tricia's been perfecting the omelet."

"Since when do you like eggs?"

"Since Tricia's been cooking them for me. Did you know eggs could be fluffy?"

"Amazing."

"It really is," Alec said, nodding rigorously. "The scrambled eggs you get in a diner are always kind of dry and flat."

"So, has she moved in with you or what?" Iris asked.

"No, she still has her own place. It's way nicer than mine, too. Well, at least it's way cleaner. And neater. And more comfortable. And way sunnier."

"So the plan is that you're moving in with her?"

"There's no plan yet," Alec admitted. "But if things keep going as well as they've been going . . . Hey, there's no need to tell you I'm a settling down kind of guy."

"After thirty-eight years!"

Alec looked a little bit hurt. "It isn't easy finding the right person, Iris. Look, for a while I thought you were the right person for me. No offense but, boy, was I wrong."

"Yes," Iris admitted. "Eternal romance wasn't in the cards for us. But you really think that Tricia is the one?"

"Could be. Yeah."

"And how does she feel about you?" Iris asked, though she wasn't entirely sure she

224

wanted to know the answer. "Has she said those three little words yet?"

Alec blushed, which made him look about ten years old. "Yeah. She has. And so have I."

"Well, then," she said now, trying for a note of sincerity, "I'm happy for you."

"No, you're not. But that's okay. I know you don't wish either of us active harm."

"Am I really that easy to read?" Iris said with an embarrassed laugh. "Let's put it this way. I'll be at the wedding, if it comes to that. And I'll never say or do anything to damage your relationship. I promise."

"I guess it will have to do. Oops. I'd better go. I promised Tricia I'd pick up some leaf lard for something she's cooking tonight. I never even knew there was such a thing as leaf lard. It can't be made out of leaves, right?"

"I doubt it. You're going to get fat with her."

Alec shrugged. "Fat and happy, that's my goal."

"So, why are you here, anyway?"

"Just on my way to work and thought I'd see how you were doing."

"And find out about my dinner with the old buddy."

"It's natural to be curious about these

things," he said as he jammed the hat back onto his head and rewound the scarf. "I'm off. Stay warm."

"Thanks for the advice."

When Alec's heavy footsteps had ceased to be heard, Iris said, "Blah, blah, blah," into the silence of the studio. Hearing about Alec's newly found domestic bliss had made her feel grumpy and sad and lonely. It wasn't that she begrudged Alec his happiness. She didn't. It was that she wasn't in the mood to bask in its rosy glow.

Which wasn't very nice of her. Her own choices had brought her to this place in her life, though leaving Ben and her father behind hadn't felt like a choice at the time. It had felt like a desperate but necessary attempt to salvage a remnant of her sanity. And it had felt like the only thing painful enough to be punishment for her having failed her mother.

Iris shivered. She considered putting her coat on over the sweaters, but decided her arms would probably be too constricted to move properly. And there was work to be done. For example, one of her repeat customers, a lawyer who worked in the Old Port, was proposing to his partner on Christmas Eve and had hired Iris to make a white gold band inlaid with a small round cut sapphire.

At first, Iris had found the project exciting. A one-of-a-kind piece was almost always fun. But in the last few days — well, since Ben's arrival in town — the project had come to feel like a bittersweet undertaking.

She had made engagement and wedding rings before now. But never had other people's domestic bliss — not only Alec's — thrown her own lonely status into stark contrast. It wasn't being single that made her feel so lonely. You could be single and not be in the least bit lonely. She knew that from her own past experience. Loneliness was that awful feeling that you should belong to a particular person but don't and that he should belong to you but doesn't. Loneliness was knowing that it was your own fault things were the way they were.

Iris glanced at the old-fashioned paper flip calendar taped to the front door of the safe. The eighth of December. John Lennon had been murdered on the eighth of December. If you believed such things, Mary, the mother of God, had been immaculately conceived on the eighth of December. What else? Oh, yes. My mother, Iris thought, Bonnie Karr, spent her last day in her own home. By the evening of the eighth, she had been moved to the hospice where she was to spend the final few weeks of her life.

The white gold band was waiting. Iris rubbed her hands together for warmth and got back to work.

CHAPTER 12

"We meet again."

Iris nodded. "Yes. It seems that way."

It was lunchtime on Friday, December ninth. Iris and Ben had just emerged from the Maine Historical Society. A professor from Southern Maine University had given a talk on social mores in Maine's larger cities in the mid-nineteenth century.

"What did you think of the lecture?" Ben asked.

"It was very interesting," Iris said truthfully. She was glad she hadn't seen Ben in the lecture hall. She suspected she wouldn't have been able to concentrate on the speaker if she had known he was in the audience.

"Yes, I thought so, too. Hey, remember the time we went to hear that woman speak at that school in Framingham?" Ben asked. "What was the topic? Oh, right. The fauvists."

Iris laughed. "Oh, my God, she was awful!

She was completely unprepared. We probably should have asked for our money back."

"She should have paid the audience for having to endure her verbal meandering."

"Yes."

They stood there then, the conversation exhausted. Ben checked his watch. Iris cleared her throat.

"Um," she said abruptly, "any progress on finding a house?"

"Not yet," Ben said. "But I'm in no hurry. There's a lot to occupy my time. And then there's Christmas. I'm thinking that next spring I'll really get busy looking."

Yes, Iris thought. And then there's Christmas. "Yes," she said. "That's probably a good idea, to wait until spring."

"I'd better get back to the museum," Ben said, a note of polite apology in his tone.

"Yes. And I'd better get back to my studio."

With a wave Ben was gone, dashing across the street during a lull in the traffic.

Iris walked on toward her studio. Say what you would about Congress Street, it was not a boring stretch of downtown Portland. Between Monument Square and Longfellow Square alone there was the main branch of the public library and a branch of the post office, two high-end jewelry shops, a

CVS, vintage clothing shops like Encore and Material Objects, quirky stores like Stones & Stuff where you could buy ancient fossils and have your tarot cards read, upscale gift shops like Emerald City, and the newest branch of Renys. Then there was the prestigious Maine College of Art, galleries featuring local artists, the Maine Historical Society, and the Longfellow House.

And if you were hungry, there were high-end restaurants like 555, and funky havens for the young foodie crowd like Nosh, business lunch places like David's, and Otto's, the insanely popular pizza place. There was the lovely Greek restaurant Emilitsa, and small, unpretentious Chinese, Indian, and Mexican restaurants, a Dunkin' Donuts, the ubiquitous Starbucks, and a specialty cheese shop.

There were at least three music venues that Iris knew of, and Space Gallery, where you could hear a band or attend a slow food event or watch a piece of performance art. There was no doubt about it. Portland was a vibrant city where no one had an excuse to be bored. A small stretch of Congress Street alone could keep an intelligent, interested person busy for weeks. An intelligent, interested person like Ben. Iris wondered what he would be doing that evening. It was the beginning of the weekend after all, when normal people went on dates or set out to find one or hung out with their friends, hoping to have an adventure. The next time she met Ben he might very well be with a woman. . . .

Iris drew her coat more closely around her, though she didn't feel particularly cold. She was an intelligent, interesting person, she told herself. At least, she had been, once. But she had no plans for the evening. Of course, she could pop by Snug, sit at the bar and have something to eat, maybe chat with the bartender or a fellow diner. It would be pleasant enough. But she knew that she wouldn't leave her apartment.

Iris pulled open the heavy door to the lobby of her studio building and immediately groaned. A handwritten cardboard sign taped to the elevator door announced that the elevator was broken again. With a sigh Iris grabbed the thick wooden banister and began the slow climb to her studio on the tenth floor.

When she had almost reached the third floor, two laughing young women jostled their way past her, arm in arm. One was dressed from head to toe in tattered black. Her clunky combat boots made her legs look like toothpicks. Her companion was easily three times her weight and about a head taller. She was dressed in 1950s vintage girly style, complete with ruffled skirt, pigtails, and cracked patent leather Mary Jane's. Iris had seen them in the building before. They were perfectly harmless, even nice when they wanted to be, but Iris suddenly found them supremely annoying.

And she knew why. It was the fact of their obvious friendship that bothered her. She stopped to let them get far ahead of her on the stairs. While she waited she suddenly remembered an afternoon three winters before her mother's death. Bonnie and Ben had gone to visit a gallery in Connecticut that was planning to mount a show of Bonnie's work. By the time they got back to the Karr house snow and temperatures had been falling for hours and no amount of salt was going to render the pavement safe going. Iris remembered standing at the living room window, watching her mother and her boyfriend laughingly negotiate their way up the icy driveway, arm in arm.

Ben and her mother had been friends. That was a fact. Why, Iris wondered, continuing her climb, had she never, until now, until it was too late, considered how much Ben had lost when Bonnie died?

233

Yes, in the depths of her grief she had failed to understand the loss of others who had loved her mother — Ben, her father, her mother's fellow artists, those who had continued to visit Bonnie and to love her until the bitter end.

When Iris finally reached the tenth floor, her knees were burning and her head was spinning. She walked shakily down the hall to her studio and unlocked the door. The moment she stepped inside a heavy pall of sadness descended upon her. She had a strong urge to crouch low to the wooden floor of her studio like the sculpture in the yard of the museum was crouched low to the frozen ground.

Only a supreme effort of will sent her back to work.

CHAPTER 13

"Make yourself at home," Bess suggested. "I'll get the wine."

It was Saturday, the tenth of December, around three in the afternoon. Iris hung her coat on a trim, steel rack in Bess's front hall and went into the living room. The infamous didgeridoo was propped against a wall. Three tall and wide bookcases were filled to capacity, with books stacked horizontally on top of those stacked vertically. More stacks of books climbed the sides of furniture. To sit in any chair required moving several volumes from the seat cushion and relocating them onto the floor.

Though the majority of Bess's collection was old, the room was miraculously breathable. Dust had a habit of settling and old books had a habit of crumbling. The care and maintenance alone must be exhausting, let alone the cataloging of each volume. And Bess was serious about cataloging.

"My mother would have looked at this room and seen a kinetic sculpture of sorts, a work of art in perpetual progress," Iris said, turning to accept a glass of wine from Bess.

"I often think of it that way as well," Bess said. "I have no idea how this room will look next year, or even next month."

"I do. More crowded."

Bess laughed. "Well, yeah."

Most of the apartment's decor was utilitarian and ordinary. Marilyn's presence was found mostly in the bedroom, where she had indulged her love of pillows. The bed was piled high with them, red and green at Christmas time, heart-shaped for Valentine's Day, pastels and flowery patterns in summer. "I tried to draw the line at turkey-shaped pillows," Bess had once told Iris, "but darn it if she didn't sneak them in somehow."

And, of course, the kitchen was also Marilyn's domain. She had given Bess careful instructions about how to wash the cast-iron pots and the expensive, perfectly balanced knives, and had told her to never, ever throw out any liquid in any pot before checking with Marilyn to be sure it wasn't a broth or a sauce in the making. For the resulting meals, Bess was willing to follow any and all instructions.

Bess settled in a chair across from Iris and looked at her closely. "What's on your mind?" she asked.

"Actually," Iris admitted, "I'm kind of surprised I said that about my mother before. I mean, about how she would have regarded this room."

"Why are you surprised?"

"I don't know. I don't talk about her very much. You know that."

Bess nodded. "Yes. I have noticed."

"It's not because she was a bad person, in any way," Iris said, hurriedly.

"Of course not. She was just a sick person. Or, a better way to put it would be, she was a person who was often sick. And that certainly wasn't her fault."

No, Iris thought. It wasn't her fault. "And your mother was?"

Bess laughed. "A harridan. But that doesn't mean I didn't love her. I still do, I guess, odd as that might be, given the fact that she's been dead for almost ten years."

"The cord that can never be entirely cut. Speaking of which, have you talked with Jason and Michael lately?" Iris asked.

Bess uncrossed her legs and then crossed them the other way. "With Jason," she said, "no. He's bad about returning e-mails or phone calls. At least, he's bad about returning my e-mails and phone calls. And you know I don't text. I can't participate in that sort of butchering of the language."

"And Michael?" Iris asked.

"We talked the other night, in fact." Bess smiled. "He's been going head to head with his father again. You should have heard the fights those two had when Michael was in high school. Anyway, he thinks he might want to train to be a chef. I had no idea he was interested in food. To be honest, my culinary skills are not the best. I doubt the meals I cooked for him ever made much of an impression."

"Maybe he wants to learn to cook well because his mother wasn't a good cook," Iris suggested. "Maybe it's a reaction against you in some way. Maybe he's trying to comfort himself with food in a way you never could. Maybe —"

" 'The terrible but inevitable sorrow that every woman must acknowledge as her right . . .' "

"Who?"

"Throckmorton again."

"I should have known. And how does that relate to what I was saying?" Iris asked with a smile.

"I looked up your mother's work online,

you know," Bess countered. "I see it's still in one of the best galleries in Boston."

Iris took a big sip of her wine. "Nice change of subject," she said then.

"Not really. We're still talking about mothers and their children. You never told me the Kleinman Museum in Los Angeles owns a piece of Bonnie Karr's work."

"Didn't I? Oh."

It was strange, Iris thought. Just the other day, when they were sitting in Arabica with coffee and scones, she had so wanted to talk to Bess about her mother, and now that the topic had been introduced, all she felt was skittish, uncomfortable, and ready to bolt.

"You know, Iris, you can't deny your mother's existence by ignoring it."

Iris felt her eyes widen. "Oh, my God, that's not at all what I'm doing!"

"All right. Then what is it you're doing?"

Iris hesitated. It was a good question. "Nothing," she said lamely. "I'm just living my life."

"Iris, please."

The silence that followed wasn't entirely awkward. Iris felt a bit lulled by the wine and what she had always felt to be the strong and comforting presence of old books. And then, there was Bess.

"I said an awful thing to her once," Iris

blurted. "My mother. I was only a kid, but still."

"What did you say?"

"I think I was about nine or ten, definitely still in grammar school. She was too sick to come to some mother-daughter thing at my school. I'd been so looking forward to it. Anyway, I told her that I hated her. I told her that I wished she was a normal mother."

Bess sighed, as if feeling the blow herself. "Did you apologize?" she asked after a moment.

"Of course. I felt terrible the moment the words were out of my mouth. I couldn't stop crying for hours."

"Did your mother tell you that she forgave you?"

"Yes. She did. But I'm not so sure she wasn't lying to get me to stop crying. How could she really forgive something so cruel?"

"Iris, I know that she forgave you."

"How can you know that?" Iris demanded, her voice rising.

"Because I'm a mother, twice over," Bess said. "We have an enormous capacity for forgiving our children. Sometimes that's a liability. Sometimes it's a blessing."

Iris took another sip of her wine and thought she would probably never know the truth of what Bess had told her. She and

Ben had talked about having children once they were married. But now . . . No. There would be no further heirs to Bonnie Karr's legacy.

A key being inserted into the lock on the front door alerted them to Marilyn's impending presence. A moment later Marilyn came into the front hall, tossed her keys onto the occasional table there, and dropped her coat on the floor.

At six foot tall with curly red hair and piercing blue eyes, Marilyn had a commanding presence. Iris had seen her at the restaurant with her staff. She spoke with a grace and cordiality just short of condescension that made it very clear that she was the queen of her kingdom and would tolerate no rebellion. Her personality when at home with friends was still strong but without a trace of dominance.

"Something the matter?" Bess asked.

"It's a good thing I have the patience of a saint," Marilyn said, "because otherwise I'd be behind bars right now for attempted murder."

Bess arched a brow. "Not full blown murder? I've never known you to do things by half."

"Well, murder, then. I had to let go another waiter today. Completely incompetent, even after a month under wing."

"I thought it was easy to find people to wait tables," Iris said. "College kids, actors, people who like their days off."

"Oh, it's easy enough to find them. It's the training and keeping of them that's a challenge."

"Well, have a drink with us," Bess suggested. "We've been talking about our mothers."

Iris got up, her foot accidentally knocking askew a small stack of old novels. "I should get going, actually," she said, bending to straighten the stack.

"If I were going to talk about my mother," Marilyn said, "especially with the day I've had so far, I would need a lot more than a drink, let me tell you. Anyway, I've got to get back to the restaurant. I just came home to change my shoes. These new clogs are killing me."

Marilyn went off to the bedroom and Iris began the process of bundling up against the weather. When Marilyn returned a moment later she said, "I'll walk out with you." Bess hugged them both good-bye and they trudged down to the first floor and out onto the sidewalk. Even though snowfall had been minimal in the past weeks, somehow the old red bricks remained treacherously slippery, the bane of every pedestrian in the city. Sometimes quaintness was a serious liability. The fiber artist who had her studio five floors below Iris's had cracked three ribs just last winter, falling on one of the cobbled streets in the Old Port.

"She worries about you, you know."

"Who, Bess?" Iris said, pulling her scarf more tightly around her neck.

"She worries that you're unhappy deep down."

Iris attempted a laugh. "But I'm just fine."

Marilyn shrugged. "You should come by the restaurant more often."

"Maybe," Iris said, remembering her halfhearted intentions of the day before.

"I'll see you around, Iris."

Iris watched for a moment as Marilyn carefully made her way up the block toward the restaurant. And then, she turned toward her own home, the knowledge of Bess's worry concerning her.

CHAPTER 14

"Are you warm enough?" Ben asked. "I could turn up the heat."

Iris shook her head. "I'm fine. Thanks."

It was Sunday, December eleventh, and Iris and Ben were on their way back to Portland from Portsmouth, New Hampshire. If that morning anyone had told Iris she would be spending the afternoon alone with Ben she would have rejected the idea as absurd. Or, she would have unplugged her computer, turned off her phone, closed the blinds, and ignored the doorbell.

What had happened was this. Iris had emerged from the women's clothing section at Renys that morning to come face-to-face with Ben in the crammed central aisle.

"Oh, hey," he had said brightly. "This place is amazing. I mean, look. I just got a jar of olives, a pair of winter boots, and a bath mat. All under the same roof."

Iris smiled. "There are some of us people

from away who can't seem to get over the thrill that is Renys. Now, you're one of them."

"What are you here for?"

"I have no idea," Iris admitted. "I like to browse and see what catches my eye."

Ben nodded toward the display just to his left. "Like a dish towel with a picture of a moose on it?"

Iris laughed. "I think I'm all set with moose-related accessories, thanks."

There had been a moment of silence as Iris decided how to slip away politely.

"Look," Ben said then, with the air of someone who had come to a difficult deci-sion, "I want to see the new show at the Bailey Gallery in Portsmouth. I was plan-ning on driving down today. Why not come with me? You mentioned at dinner the other night that you don't have a car at the mo-ment and frankly, I could use the company."

Iris's immediate instinct was to refuse. "Why not ask one of your colleagues at the museum?" she replied.

"I could," Ben said. "But I'd have to be on my best behavior. With you . . ."

Iris couldn't help but grin. "With me you can call idiot drivers creatively nasty names."

Ben laughed. "Exactly."

For another moment Iris hesitated. There was work to be done at the studio. And what if Ben took the opportunity of a long car ride to delve into their past? She didn't think she could handle that conversation while trapped in a moving vehicle. Would she lie? Would she tell the truth? Would she create some mix of falsehood and reality to explain away why she had abandoned him?

"Iris?"

"Okay," she blurted, stunned by her answer.

"Great. Well, how about we head out now?"

Iris nodded.

On the drive down to Portsmouth there was not much talk and most of it was small. Iris was still wondering what perverse impulse had led her to put herself in the path of the potential predator. Well, maybe that was being a bit dramatic. . . .

"So, the old girl is still driving well," she said after a while.

Ben fondly patted the steering wheel. "I don't want to think about having to replace her."

"But everything comes to an end." The moment the words left her mouth Iris cringed. What an idiotic thing to say, she scolded silently, especially to Ben!

Ben didn't respond. Iris tried to read his expression in profile, but could see nothing more than his concentration on the road.

They got to Portsmouth without further incident. As they passed through the doors of the Bailey Gallery on Hanover Street, Iris told herself that it was perfectly natural for her to be there with Ben. They were simply two colleagues seeking information and experience. There need not be anything personal about it.

On three of the room's four walls were hung two large canvases. On each canvas the artist had drawn (in what Iris thought was child's crayon) a depiction of a house (at least, Iris thought they were houses) with a maximum of five crooked lines. Each house was drawn in a different color. At the bottom right of each canvas was a dark, scrawled signature that Iris defied anyone but a hand writing expert to decipher.

Iris and Ben each made a slow circuit of the room, and then another, before meeting in the middle of the space to share their thoughts. Ben cleared his throat. Iris coughed a bit.

"It's . . . interesting," Iris said finally.

Ben clasped his hands behind his back. "Yes," he said. "You could say that."

"The artist's choice to . . ."

"Yes."

"I wonder if he . . ."

"Me, too."

Iris glanced around to see if the gallery owner or an employee was in sight. No one was. "Oh, my God," she whispered then, "they're awful, aren't they?"

"They're beyond awful," Ben whispered back. "What was Bailey thinking, mounting this show? His taste is usually pretty good."

"Come on, let's get out of here before —"

The voices of two men broke into the space as the gallery owner emerged from the back office with a companion.

"We're in for it," Ben breathed, turning his back on them. "That's the artist. His picture was in the paper the other day."

Iris glanced at the insanely skinny man in the preposterous feathered hat and paisley cape and stifled a desperate laugh. "If he comes over here, what are we going to say? I don't think I can lie well enough to —"

Ben turned around again just as the gallery owner was sticking out his hand. "Ben," he boomed, "good to see you. I hear you're at the PMA now!"

Ben shook Michael Bailey's hand. "Yes. Yes I am."

"Good, good! Well, this is a bit of luck. May I present Melchior von Offenberg du

Loire, the creator of the masterpieces you see around you!"

The second man bowed with a flourish of his emaciated hand.

"Nice to meet you," Ben said. "And this is Iris —"

"So, what do you think of my show?" the man interrupted, turning to block Iris from his line of sight. His voice was affectedly low and booming and seemed bizarre coming from his reedlike physique.

Ben scrunched up his face in an exaggerated expression of contemplation. Iris prayed she could control the laughter threatening to burst from her.

The artist stared boldly up at Ben, as if daring him to criticize. "Well?" he demanded.

Ben's face relaxed. He sighed and put his hand over his heart. "My good man," he said with great solemnity, "I stand in the presence of greatness."

Mr. von Offenberg du Loire smiled smugly and wandered off to contemplate his genius.

Ben made an excuse to Mr. Bailey and somehow he and Iris got out of the gallery without giving themselves away.

"That was hilarious," Iris said when they had reached the safety of the sidewalk. "I'd forgotten how good you are with egomaniacs."

Ben grinned. "You kind of have to be in this business. Just ask your father."

"So, you think his name was false?" Iris asked.

"Oh, yeah. Just like the rest of him."

Iris laughed. See, she thought, Bess was wrong. I'm not unhappy deep down. People who are unhappy deep down can't laugh at the absurd and be, well, almost happy for minutes on end.

Before leaving Portsmouth they stopped for a quick lunch at a pub. Iris ordered a roast beef sandwich. "Your usual," Ben commented.

"Well, I guess some things don't come to an end," Iris admitted, feeling her cheeks flame. "Like my love of roast beef. And your habit of putting two sugars in your coffee."

Ben looked down at his cup and smiled.

Once back on the road to Portland, Ben turned on a jazz music station, which precluded much talk. As they drove, Iris felt the anxiety of earlier in the day return. She was highly aware of Ben being just inches away. It was almost four o'clock and the sun was setting. It would be dark soon. Iris realized she felt as though she were a teen on a first date, scared and excited at the same time.

Where would we be right now, she wondered, if I had granted Mom her dying wish? Very likely we would be sitting side by side in this car but other than that, everything else would be different. Most likely, everything else would be better.

Time sped by and Iris was surprised to find that they were already passing into Portland. As Ben made a left on to Danforth Street she noticed a woman pushing a stroller and holding the hand of a bundled toddler. She remembered what Bess had said the other day about mothers forgiving their children even grievous emotional crimes. She stifled a sigh. If only there was a way to be sure that her mother hadn't died disappointed in her daughter's lack of fidelity. If only her mother could speak to her from wherever it is she was and reassure her!

"Penny for your thoughts?"

"I'm not sure they're worth that much," Iris said with a false lightness.

Ben just smiled. A few minutes later, he pulled up outside her house on Neal Street. In the odd light from the old-fashioned street lamp Ben looked older than his thirty-six years. For the first time Iris noticed the fine lines around his eyes. Of course, he must be under great strain, learning a new job, adjusting to life in a new city, and possibly still recovering from a failed marriage. And now, here he was confronted with his former love, the one who had abandoned him as casually as one would abandon a torn sock. Iris felt her heart leap in pity, concern, and affection. Love?

"Thank you for today," she said sincerely. "It was good to get out of town. I guess I should get around to buying that car."

"In the meantime, I can chauffeur you any time you need to be somewhere."

"I wouldn't want to impose on you."

"No imposition," Ben said easily. "I offered. Anyway, it would be a good way for me to get to know my new surroundings."

"Of course," Iris said. He'll chauffeur me around because he's a nice person. Nothing more. It's what you wanted. "Well, thanks again." Iris opened the door.

"I'll wait until you get inside," Ben called.

Iris made her way up the building's front steps and let herself into the tiny lobby. She turned and waved to Ben. He waved back and drove slowly off.

Iris watched him go and wondered why, why, why he was being so nice to her. Why wasn't he pressing her for the answers he richly deserved? She couldn't understand what, if anything, was happening between them. Was it more than just the healing of a rift between old friends? Maybe. But maybe not.

Whatever was going on between her and Ben could wait to be understood. If she didn't get upstairs to her apartment she was going to freeze to death. It was an old building, built around 1865, and full of drafts. First, she retrieved her mail from its box and quickly shuffled through it. There was a Christmas card from an old friend, a flyer for a Chinese restaurant, and a bill.

Clutching the mail, Iris climbed the stairs to the third floor. And on her way she repeated her wish that Ben had never moved to Portland. Then, she took the wish back.

CHAPTER 15

There was no sleep to be had that night.

Iris shifted in the bed. She crossed her legs beneath the covers and then uncrossed them. She felt anxious and her heart was racing just a bit. She turned on the bedside lamp and turned it off again. Whatever feeling of pleasure she had experienced on her outing with Ben had long flown — she should never have spent all that time with him! — leaving behind the bitter reality of what her life had become and would always be.

December was a ticking time bomb, each day leading inexorably to the next and the next and finally, to the day she had come to dread more than any other. December twenty-fourth. Christmas Eve. The anniversary of her mother's death.

Sometimes Iris wished she could be put into a controlled coma for the month of December. But then, when she woke in

January, what really would have changed? It was just more crazy thinking.

For the remainder of the month she would continue to go through the motions with those close to her. Her father had left her a voice mail, inviting her to join him and Jean for Christmas. Iris had e-mailed him a polite rejection. She had, however, bought them a card and would send that out the next morning. Bess and Marilyn should probably get one, too, though they would not be disappointed if they didn't. Alec wouldn't notice either way. He often left mail unopened for weeks at a time.

Besides, this Christmas his focus was on Tricia. Iris wondered what Tricia would give Alec on Christmas morning. A big, fluffy stuffed bear named Mr. Snuggly Pants? A gift certificate to hearty, healthy meals at her house?

These were uncharitable thoughts. Iris realized that. Who wouldn't want a big, fluffy stuffed animal? And Tricia supposedly was a whiz in the kitchen. Who wouldn't want to be fed by a pretty, sweet-natured young woman?

Iris stared up at the darkened ceiling and wondered what Tricia's family was like. They were probably very normal and very nice. Her own family was — or had been —

somewhat atypical.

Iris's father came from a well-to-do family, none of whom Iris had ever met. Her paternal grandparents were long gone by the time Iris was born, and though her father had an older sister, they had been estranged for years. Iris's mother was an only child and had also lost both of her parents long before Iris was born.

So, the Karr family had been small and self-sufficient, though not socially isolated. And there had been no lack of holiday traditions for all their lack of aunts and uncles and cousins. There were always batches of pfeffernusse, her father's favorite holiday cookie, and a standing rib roast for Christmas dinner, with Yorkshire pudding and green beans with slivered almonds. For dessert there would be homemade apple pie with cream whipped by hand and a fruitcake that was moist and sweet and oozing rich flavor, none of that brick-hard stuff made in a factory that people regifted for years until it finally shattered. Try as she might, Iris couldn't remember where they had gotten that fruitcake. Had they bought it from a local bakery? Had a neighbor given it as a gift?

Each Christmas some of her parents' friends would join them, artists without family locally or for whom family had become the enemy. A half-drunk aging painter might bring along his starving and brilliant musician friend or an innovative young graphic designer might bring along his most recent girlfriend, a reluctant and morbid poet. There was always a lot of laughter (except from the morbid poets) and a lot of loud and passionate argument. These were people to whom ideas truly mattered. Even when she had been too young to understand what it was her parents' guests were arguing about, Iris had drunk in the passion and knew that she was glimpsing her own future.

For Iris, life at home had seemed almost magical. Most of her classmates' parents were doctors or lawyers or teachers or financial people. Only Iris Karr had a mother whose work was written up not only in the local paper but also in serious, glossy art journals and, on occasion, in the *New York Times.* Only Iris Karr's father routinely hosted famous people in his home and attended big art openings as far south as Atlanta and as far west as California.

And then, things had begun to change. As her mother's cancer continued to roar back to life after increasingly shorter periods of dormancy, those wonderful Christmas dinners had ceased to become annual affairs. There had been none in the last few years of Bonnie's life. And there had been no celebration whatsoever the day after her death.

Iris yawned and rubbed her tired eyes. There really was nothing preventing her from re-creating those holiday traditions. But the idea struck her as bordering on sacriligious. Her mother had been the moving spirit of the gatherings, the central energy around which everyone had flocked. Iris was not her mother. At best she was a vague shadow of Bonnie Karr, and no one could convince her otherwise.

The bedroom faced east, allowing Iris to watch the first light of morning inch its way into existence. She tried to remember the last time she had spent the entire night awake and for a moment drew a blank. And then it came to her. It was the time she and Ben had first made love. Afterward, she was too happy to sleep, entirely content to keep watch over Ben as he slept. So many years ago . . .

Iris flung the heavy covers aside and steeled herself to greet another day.

CHAPTER 16

Iris spent Monday, December twelfth, buried in work, diligently restraining any thoughts of her outing with Ben the day before and fighting the fatigue that was the result of a fraught and sleepless night. Now it was six in the evening and all she wanted to do was to go home and fall into bed, but she had promised Alec that she would come for dinner. Alec and Tricia.

Alec lived in the East End. Some of the best restaurants in Portland were located in the neighborhood, like Hugo's and Duckfat and Blue Spoon and the Front Room. There was a popular bakery called Two Fat Cats, and a wonderful Italian market called Micucci's, and an increasing number of interesting retail stores, like the one owned by the designer Angela Adams and the Ember Grove Gallery and the shop called Ferdinand. Not that any of that much mattered to Alec. He didn't go in for shopping and would eat an old sock if presented to him as food. Well, Iris thought, maybe not now that Tricia was around to educate his palate.

Alec lived in a new condo development on Middle Street. His apartment was never exactly dirty, just messy and cluttered. Iris had never tried to organize him but it looked as if Tricia had and had met with some success. The pile of magazines that usually occupied half of the dining table had disappeared and there was nothing on the bathroom sink but a cup containing a tube of toothpaste and a brush. Where were the whiskers and scraps of soap and balled up tissues that Iris remembered doing battle with every time she wanted to wash her face? A quick peek into the bedroom revealed a bed almost made and no clothing strewn across the floor but for one dark sock in a corner.

"So this is what the place looks like," she said under her breath to Alec.

"What do you mean?" Alec asked, looking honestly perplexed. "You've been here a thousand times."

"Never mind."

Tricia came out of the kitchen then, bearing a plastic platter of shrimp wrapped in bacon. "I hope you're hungry," she said, in a mildly singsongy way.

She was taller than Alec by a full inch, and she was as slim as Alec was stocky. Her long blond hair — natural, from what Iris could tell — was pulled back into a sleek ponytail. That night she was wearing pencil jeans and a long, slim wool sweater that had a very expensive look about it. Iris wondered if it was from the boutique where Tricia worked. Tricia must have an employee's discount. Maybe knowing someone who worked in a store that sold beautiful sweaters like that wasn't a bad thing. . . . Iris was bothered by her sudden and atypical mercenary thoughts.

"I'm so glad you could come over," Tricia was saying. "I just love to cook and it's nice to have more than just Alec to feed. Practically all of my girlfriends are on these weird diets. It's very frustrating."

"Have you eaten at Snug?" Iris asked. "My friend's partner is the chef and owner."

"Oh, my God!" Tricia cried. "I love that place. I can't believe you know the chef. Wow. That is beyond cool."

Iris felt a smirk come to her lips. "Well, I don't know about beyond cool."

Alec shot her a warning look and Iris said quickly, "But it is cool to be able to get a table almost always."

Tricia smiled and went back into the

kitchen. Either she hadn't seen Iris's expression or she had chosen to ignore it. Iris felt like a jerk. "Sorry," she muttered in Alec's direction.

Alec just frowned.

A moment later Tricia was back. She sat in the one decent armchair that Alec owned. Iris felt an uncomfortable twinge of jealousy. She was not "the woman of the house," even though she never really had been and never really had wanted to be. But now she was most definitely a guest. She no longer had the right to open the fridge and rummage for a snack, or to flop into that one good armchair and kick off her shoes. Those rights now belonged to Tricia. I'm officially a third wheel, she thought gloomily.

Inevitably, she thought of Ben and remembered all the dinners and the parties they had hosted together. She remembered how they had each bought household items with the intention of everything living under one roof at some time in the not too distant future, dishes and flatware and handcrafted mugs from their potter friends.

But that had never happened. When Iris moved to Portland she had taken with her only the belongings she had bought prior to knowing Ben. She had even left behind the beautiful antique soup tureen they had used on the night of their first semiformal dinner party, a night that had ended in decidedly informal laughter and mishap.

Damn, Iris thought now, sitting there with Alec and Tricia. I miss that tureen.

The appearance of dinner was a welcome distraction. Tricia had made pork chops (bought at the winter farmers' market, she pointed out) with a sauce made from apples (also from the farmers' market) and reduced balsamic vinegar. She served the meat with sides of roasted beets and mashed turnips. She apologized for not having made the bread herself but as it was from Standard Bakery on Fore Street, Iris didn't think there was a need for an apology. The wine had been suggested by one of her friends who was studying to be a sommelier. Iris wanted to be less than thrilled with the meal but Tricia had made that impossible.

"This is amazing, Tricia," she said, helping herself to more beets. "Really."

Alec beamed. "I told you she could cook! Wait until you see what's for dessert!"

"Finish your vegetables first," Tricia said in a mock stern voice.

Alec beamed even more brightly. "See how she takes care of me?"

Tricia laughed. "When I first met him he was surviving on potato chips and pizza."

"Two of the major food groups," Alec argued.

Iris smiled lamely. When she had been Alec's girlfriend, she hadn't cared enough to urge him to improve his diet. Nor had she bothered to teach him how to fold and put away his clothes or how to throw away used tissues. It was all too clear that she had done Alec absolutely no good by "dating" him.

Dessert was a spectacular homemade apple tart served with vanilla ice cream.

"Did you make the ice cream, too?" Iris asked, wondering if it would be rude to ask for a second piece of tart before she had finished the first.

Tricia pouted adorably. "No, but I would have if I had an ice-cream maker."

Iris left soon after dessert, claiming work to attend to. Tricia put out her arms for a hug and Iris complied. Alec patted her on the back as she left the apartment.

Iris landed back on Middle Street infinitely more depressed than she had been a few hours earlier. She was missing Ben and the companionship they had shared and it bothered her more than she could express. She was hugely worried that the life she had structured here in Portland, a life of relative solitude, was not strong enough to carry her ahead into the future. But she had no idea how to shore up that life.

The walk home was long and cold, as Iris had known it would be. Wearily, she climbed the three flights of stairs to her condo. She wondered what Tricia was saying about her at that very moment. She had been entirely pleasant at dinner and had shown no jealousy whatsoever, which could only mean that she saw Iris as no threat to her own happiness with Alec. Which was indeed the case. What would any good man want with a woman who kept wriggling out of his grasp when he could be with someone warm and caring, someone who actually wanted to be with him?

Iris unlocked the door to her apartment and carefully locked it behind her. She removed her coat, hat, scarf, and mittens and tossed them onto the couch. Then she went into the bathroom, brushed her teeth, and removed what little makeup she wore before slipping into bed almost fully clothed. This was not unusual. There were many nights when she was just too cold to expose naked skin to the winter chill. But tonight, going to bed in her pants and turtleneck and big fuzzy socks made Iris feel pathetic and old and unlovable.

God, Iris thought, pulling the covers over her head. I am such a loser.

CHAPTER 17

Iris's studio was as cold as ever on Tuesday, the thirteenth of December, but Bess had brought a space heater with her and was roasting her feet under the worktable where she sat carefully printing descriptions of jewelry on small white cards, noting the metals used, the stones and their provenance, and the prices. The open house was in three days and there was still much to be done.

Iris was choosing and cleaning up the rough sketches of certain pieces that would be shown near the finished products. "I had dinner at Alec's house last night," she announced into the silence, putting aside one sketch and reaching for another.

Bess looked up from her work, reading glasses low on the bridge of her nose. "Oh. Did you have a good time?"

"It was okay. Tricia can really cook. And she's so nice! I really want to dislike her but she makes it very difficult."

"Yeah," Bess said, looking back to the card she was preparing. "She's the genuine article."

"I guess. Wait, how do you know her?"

"I bumped into the two of them in Arabica the other day."

"Oh."

"I hope you're happy for Alec," Bess said, in a pointed way.

"I'm coming around."

There was another silence as both women worked on. When Bess spoke, her tone was light. "So, how's 'the one that got away' adjusting to life in Portland?"

Iris dropped the pencil she had been using to mark some of her sketches. "What? How did you know?"

Bess rolled her eyes. "I'm a witch. Seriously, Iris, you're very easy to read. At least, I find it easy to read you. And you did tell me that you two were once inseparable."

Iris retrieved her pencil from the floor where it had rolled after falling off the table. "Oh," she said. "Right. I forgot. Anyway, he didn't actually get away." She paused for a moment before adding, "It's more like he was the one I tossed back."

Bess raised an eyebrow. "You might not want to do that again."

Iris shrugged noncommittally.

" 'But we loved with a love that was more than love . . .' "

"Even I know that," Iris interrupted. "It's from Poe's 'Annabel Lee.' "

" 'And neither the angels in heaven
   above,
Nor the demons down under the sea,
Can ever dissever my soul from the soul
Of the beautiful Annabel Lee.' "

"Anyway," Iris said when Bess had finished reciting, "you're assuming Ben would want to be with me again."

"Were you planning to marry?"

Iris toyed with the pencil. "We weren't formally engaged," she said quietly. "We didn't have a ring. But yes, we were going to be married."

"The jewelry designer without a ring."

"Whatever."

"So, in spite of what you told me the other day, you didn't just outgrow each other."

"No," Iris admitted.

"Did you take him by surprise when you broke things off?"

"Not entirely by surprise," Iris explained. "I think he knew that something was . . . wrong."

Like when I told him he didn't have to come to Mom's funeral. Like when I didn't shed one tear throughout the wake or funeral. Like when he tried to take my hand on the way back to the house afterward and I pulled it away.

"Yes," Bess said. "He didn't strike me as slow-witted."

"He's anything but slow-witted," Iris agreed.

They worked quietly for a time and then Iris found herself saying, "Ben knows me at my absolute best. And at my absolute worst."

"And?" Bess prompted.

"And that scares me."

"Are you saying you're afraid of intimacy? Real love means exposing the best of you and the worst, the strongest and the weakest, the beautiful and the ugly."

"Then yes, I'm afraid of intimacy." Rather, Iris corrected silently, I became afraid of intimacy. When my mother died.

Bess sighed. "Too bad. I feel sorry for you."

"Don't," Iris said, faking a laugh. "I feel sorry enough for myself."

" 'To pity oneself,
to cry out for justice from an improbable
   God

270

or an unfathomable universe,
is to invite the disdain of both.' "

"Well, now I feel even sorrier for myself than I did before."

"The lines belong to Jack Parish, a poet I know in Vermont," Bess said. "The sentiment is a bit harsh, but then again, so is Jack."

Iris nodded. "All right. I think I've had enough poetry for one day."

"There's no such thing as enough poetry, but I'll respect your wishes this one time."

They worked quietly again for a while until Iris found the words coming out of her mouth in spite of her strenuous mental attempts to drag them back in.

"Did you know," she said, in a falsely casual voice, "Ben was the last person to see my mother alive."

Bess put down her pen and looked intently at Iris. "Of course I didn't know."

Iris looked down at the worktable. "It was about nine o'clock at night. Christmas Eve. My father and I were sent home. I didn't want to go, I didn't want to leave my mother's side, but I was exhausted and so I allowed myself to be persuaded. Ben left with us. But he went back to the hospice, later that night. And he was there when she

271

died, just before midnight. Not me. Ben."

"Wow," Bess said softly. And then, after a moment, she asked, "Do you blame yourself or Ben?"

Iris's head shot up. "It wasn't Ben's fault that I left the hospice that night!"

"Then why have you been punishing him?"

"Is that what you think I've been doing?" Iris asked. She was stunned by the idea. Had she been punishing him? God, she thought now that she had.

Why had it never occurred to her that by punishing herself she had also been punishing Ben, and unfairly? She had assumed he would be glad to see her go so that he could be done with sickness and death. She had assumed when she had no right to assume.

"Do you still love him?" Bess asked now.

That was an important question. Ben had done nothing to make her fall out of love, dislike him, hate him. But Iris said nothing.

"Did you hear what I asked?"

"Yes," Iris said a bit testily. "But even if I did still love him, what would it matter?"

"It would matter," Bess pointed out, "if he also still loved you. And, you haven't answered my question."

No, Iris had not answered Bess's question but she had the answer at hand. Of course she still loved Ben. She had never stopped loving him. She had just stopped . . .

Iris sighed and rubbed her head vigorously with both of her hands. "Why is all this happening now?" she muttered.

" 'To every thing there is a season, and a time to every purpose under heaven.' "

Iris smiled. "So you're branching out from the Americans and the British."

"The ancient Israelites know how to write, my dear. Talk about powerful poetry."

"I thought you weren't going to quote at me anymore today."

"I lied. So, have you told Alec about Ben?"

"Not really."

"Why?"

"Oh, he's so into Tricia right now. . . ." Iris's words trailed off lamely.

"He's your friend. Get a male perspective. Granted he's not an average guy but that's a good thing. And he's certainly not going to be jealous."

"I'm not sure I want him to be telling Tricia my secrets."

"You could ask him not to tell her about Ben," Bess said. "But he might, anyway. He tells me he's in love."

"Since when are you and Alec such good friends?" Iris asked.

"I make it my business to know the friends

of my friends. Hey, did you know Alec likes seventeenth-century English poetry?"

"Honestly, I had no idea. God, what were Alec and I doing all that time together?"

"Not being together."

"Touché."

"This pen is running out," Bess announced. "Do you have another?"

Iris nodded. "There's a box of them on that shelf."

She watched as Bess retrieved a new pen. She was surprised she had revealed so much of herself to her friend, though she had stopped short of admitting that she still loved Ben. But she was pretty certain Bess knew that. There wasn't much that got by her. Maybe that opal ring she wore really did have some magical powers. . . . The thought made Iris smile.

"What's amusing?" Bess asked, returning to her work place.

"Nothing really. I was just thinking about your opal."

"Are you hoping I'll leave it to you in my will?"

"Bess!" Iris cried.

Bess grinned. "Just asking."

CHAPTER 18

Iris stood outside her studio building on Wednesday afternoon, the fourteenth of December, staring down at the large square appliance on the sidewalk, and wondering how she was ever going to get it into the lobby, in and out of the elevator, down the hall, and finally into her studio. The fact that she had gotten it this far amazed her.

"Need some help?"

Iris whirled around. "Oh, Ben." She laughed a bit wildly. "Uh, yeah, actually I do need some help."

She pointed down at the appliance. It was an ancient dorm room style fridge. Some of the enamel exterior was chipped away but the inside was perfectly clean.

"How did you manage to get it this far?" Ben asked, eyeing it dubiously.

"I took a cab from my house, of course. But the driver had no interest in helping me any farther than the curb."

"Smart man."

"But I offered him five dollars."

"That's not going to cover the cost of a torn hernia." Ben crouched, took a deep breath and lifted the fridge in his arms.

"At least the elevator is working," Iris said as she held the lobby door open for him. "It's been broken more often than not lately."

"It didn't occur to you to borrow a dolly?" he puffed. "Or a hand truck?"

"Obviously not."

They said nothing else until the elevator jolted to a stop on the tenth floor. "Wish me luck," Ben muttered. Then he wrangled the old fridge down the hall and into the studio with an admirable minimum of huffs and groans.

"You know," he said, straightening his back with a slightly pained expression, "a new one can't be that expensive and it's got to weigh less than this dinosaur."

"I know," Iris admitted. "But my downstairs neighbor seemed so pleased with herself for offering it to me I couldn't say no. She's got some sort of mental disability — she told me that once — but she's the nicest person and quite competent as far as I can tell."

"Does she live alone?"

"Yes. And I'm not sure she has any real friends. I mean, I never see anyone coming or going, except for her sister. The family owns the condo. The sister seems to be the one designated to keep an eye out for Maeve."

"At least she has family," Ben remarked.

"Sure. But it would be nice if she had some friends, as well."

Ben regarded her with interest. "Who are your friends here in Portland?" he asked. "I mean, besides that woman I saw you with the night of the tree lighting."

Iris laughed a nervous little laugh. She wondered if Ben had meant his question in a challenging way. "There isn't really anyone important besides Bess," she confessed.

"How did you two meet?"

"We were on line at the library not long after I came to town and we got to chatting. Actually, she approached me. Next thing, we were having coffee and our friendship took off from there."

"What about a boyfriend?" Ben asked. "I mean, are you seeing anyone?"

Iris felt her cheeks go red.

"Come on, Iris," Ben urged, his tone light. "I told you about my marriage. I haven't assumed you've been living an entirely celibate life since . . . since I last saw you."

"All right," she said. "There was someone for a bit. His name is Alec. We're still friends. Actually, that's really all we ever were. He's seeing someone else now. She's totally different from me and he's very happy."

Ben had the good grace to smile but to refrain from commenting. "You know," he said, "some of your old friends in Boston still ask about you."

"Oh. Who?"

"Herbie Taylor, from the Nightingale Gallery, for one. And just a few weeks ago I ran into John Morelli and he asked me if I knew how you were doing. He'd read something about your work in an online journal."

"Oh." Iris didn't know how she felt about this. She tried hard not to think about everyone she had left behind. Out of sight, out of mind. Mostly, it worked. "Well," she said, "I doubt they miss me. It's been almost three years."

Ben took a step closer to her, maybe casually, maybe with purpose. "Don't be so sure," he said. "You might be gone but you're not forgotten."

Iris felt her cheeks flush again. She wondered if he was talking about his own feelings. God, it was horrible not to know exactly what Ben's words meant. They had never dealt in anything but clear terms, but so much had happened. . . .

"Well, I should give you the grand tour, I guess," Iris said, her voice unnaturally high. She scooted a few feet away from Ben. "Over there is my safe. Well, obviously, what else could it be? And then there are my tools. And then there are the worktables and the shelves. And, well, that's about it."

Ben nodded. "It's a good-sized space. Are you happy with the light?"

"Oh, yes. The light's good."

"Good."

Oh, God, Iris thought, I wish he would leave! But she couldn't make the words, "Well, I have work to do," come out of her mouth.

And it seemed that Ben had no intention of leaving. "Iris," he said, his voice low and careful, "I know this must be a hard time for you, with your mother's anniversary in a few weeks. And then, I showed up unexpectedly. . . ."

Iris folded her arms across her chest. "You have no idea," she blurted.

"I think," he said, "that I might."

For the space of a moment Iris felt that to spill the secrets of her heart would be an enormously welcome relief. But what she whispered was, "I'm so sorry, Ben."

"For what, Iris?" he asked, his eyes pleading with her. "Tell me."

But no, she couldn't tell him the truth, not now, not here, not ever. Iris shook her head. "I'm just . . . I'm just sorry."

Ben stepped even closer and lightly laid a hand on her shoulder. Iris jumped back as if she had been stung.

"Did you know you can see the *Rising Cairn* from this window?" she said, her voice trembling.

"No." Ben slid his hands into the pockets of his coat.

"Well, you can. If you stand right here and lean just this way. . . ."

Ben smiled vaguely. "I should get back to work," he said.

Iris nodded. "Sure. And thanks for helping me with the fridge. I owe you a favor."

"No, Iris," Ben said. He was already walking purposefully toward the door. "You don't owe me any favors."

And then he was gone.

CHAPTER 19

It was Friday, the sixteenth of December, exactly two weeks since Iris had spotted Ben across the crowded museum yard, and exactly nine days until Christmas. It was also the day of Iris's holiday open house. Several other artists in the building were also holding open houses and the halls rang with laughter and conversation. It was better, Iris thought, than the noises one usually heard in the building — faulty plumbing, a creaking elevator, and the skittering of mice in the walls.

"You're doing nicely," Bess informed her sotto voce, two hours into the event. "And look who just walked in. The ghost."

Iris felt her stomach knot. She had so hoped that he wouldn't come, especially after their last, supremely uncomfortable encounter two days earlier. She had come perilously close to revealing all to Ben and if she were to live the new life that she had chosen, that must never happen again.

"We probably shouldn't keep calling him that," she said, hoping to sound casual. "He's become all too real."

"Who's become all too real?" Marilyn asked.

Bess nodded toward Ben. "Him. He's Iris's former beau. But don't say anything."

Marilyn looked puzzled. "What would I say? And to whom?" When neither Iris nor Bess answered, Marilyn shrugged and wandered off.

As Ben came toward her Iris remembered all the times he had supported her at shows and fairs and openings. He had been such a selfless, generous friend. . . .

"You didn't have to come," she blurted.

Ben raised an eyebrow. "I'm aware of that." He turned and extended his hand toward Bess. "Hello, Bess is it?"

"Yes. And, Ben, it's nice to see you again. How's the new job?"

"Pretty good, thanks."

A well-dressed woman of about fifty joined them. "I'm back," she said to Iris, almost apologetically. "I'm sorry it's taking me so long to make up my mind. . . ."

Iris smiled. She was used to hesitant customers. In the beginning of her career, it had been hard to accept the fact of a potential buyer walking away empty-handed. She had taken it as a personal rejection. But over time she had come to view a walk-away as "just one of those things."

"There's nothing to apologize about," she assured the woman. "Please, take your time."

Iris stepped off a bit to allow the woman space, but she remained close enough to hear Ben speak to her.

"My mother's been buying Iris Karr's work for years," he was saying. "In fact, she asked me to come by today to pick out a new piece for her. The trouble is, I can't decide which piece to buy. I know she'd like just about everything here."

The woman smiled up at Ben. "That's so nice of you, to shop for your mother."

"What piece are you considering?" he asked.

The woman pointed to a slim gold bracelet with a scattering of small inlaid citrines. "Oh, that's definitely my favorite. Citrine is my birthstone. It's just that I don't know if I should spend the money on myself. . . ."

Ben laughed. "I know what my mother would say. God helps those who help themselves."

The woman laughed as well. "You know,

your mother is absolutely right. I've made up my mind. I'm buying the bracelet!"

The woman beckoned to Iris and they completed the sale.

"Thanks," Iris said to Ben when she had gone off. "You didn't have to do that."

"Yes, I did. I believe in your work. And I do want to get something for my mother."

Iris stopped herself from protesting that he needn't. "Only if you accept the friends and family discount," she said.

"If I have to, I will. Thanks. I'm thinking about these earrings." Ben pointed to a pair of gold pendant earrings, each set with a tiny peridot. "They'd look nice with that first necklace Mom bought from you."

"They would," Iris agreed. She wanted to say, "And please thank your mother for not hurling my work into the nearest ditch after what I did to her son." But she didn't. She went about completing the sale and handed the earrings to Bess to wrap.

"Dude, nice turnout."

It was Alec, in his biggest puffy coat and dorkiest hat. Iris felt her cheeks flush as she looked from Ben to Alec and back again.

Bess cleared her throat dramatically. "Since Iris seems to have forgotten her manners, I'll do the honors. Ben Tresch, this is Alec Todd. Alec, this is Ben."

The two men shook hands, said, "Hey," and "Nice to meet you." And then, miraculously, Ben took his leave, claiming an appointment. Alec, looking a little disoriented, wandered off and found Marilyn.

"Well, that was interesting," Bess said, when Alec was out of earshot.

"Oh? In what way?" Iris asked, pretending indifference.

"He didn't have to show up, you know."

"Who? Alec?"

"Iris, don't be deliberately stupid. It's not becoming."

"Sorry," she said. "I know. It was nice of him. He used to come to all of my shows."

"Back when you were a couple."

"Yes."

"Hmmm."

"What does that mean?"

Bess shrugged and walked off to speak with a new customer, leaving Iris to try and answer the question for herself.

CHAPTER 20

Saturday, the seventeenth of December, found Iris and Alec splurging on lunch at Petite Jacqueline at Longfellow Square. Iris had ordered the escargot and Alec had ordered the mussels. It seemed that Tricia had introduced him to the joys of shellfish.

"I guess maybe I should have told you," Iris said when their food had arrived. "That old friend of mine, Ben. The guy you met at the open house yesterday."

Alec frowned. "The ridiculously handsome one beside whom I felt like a troll. Yeah? What about him?"

"Well, he was more than just a friend. We were together for about six years."

Alec put down his fork with a clatter. "Dude, you spent six years of your life with this guy and you didn't even mention him to me once? What's up with that?"

"I don't know," Iris said. It was a lie and it wasn't. "I just . . . I don't know."

"Are you ashamed of him or something?" Alec asked, retrieving his fork. "Is he a nut job? He looked perfectly normal to me. But I might not be the best judge of normalcy."

"God, no! He's eminently sane."

"Well, have you seen him again?" Alec asked. "I mean, after that first dinner Bess told me about? And your open house doesn't count."

Iris shrugged. "Yeah. A little. Well, maybe more than a little. We drove down to Portsmouth one afternoon to see a show at a gallery."

"So you went on a date."

"It wasn't a date," she protested.

"Then what was it?"

Iris thought about her answer. "It was an excursion."

Alec rolled his eyes.

Iris felt annoyed. "Why do you think you know what's best for me?" she demanded.

"Well, someone has to," he countered. "You don't seem to have much of a clue. Just think of me as the older brother you never had."

"The obnoxious older brother."

"I've been called worse. In fact, just this morning my neighbor, that guy in the apartment on my left, told me that I reminded him of —"

"Never mind."

Alec wiped his mouth on his linen napkin. (Tricia seemed to have broken him of the habit of using his sleeve.) "Seriously, Iris," he said. "You say absolutely nothing about someone you were with for six years? You make me look like the warm and fuzzy one. I'm a guy. You're a girl. You're supposed to be all, oooh, let's get married and have babies. I'm supposed to be all, uh, what's the rush and where's the beer at?"

"Hilarious." But Alec is right, Iris thought. Something has gone wrong with me.

"So, should I champion this guy's cause?" Alec asked.

Iris's eyes widened. "How do you know Ben has a cause? I mean, how do you know that he wants . . . that he wants to be with me?"

Alec shook his head in a pitying way. "Iris. Please. A single man doesn't hang around a single woman just to kill time. Men are goal-oriented. They don't do anything randomly. He wants you back."

"First of all," Iris argued, "he's not hanging around me. Like I said, we've met accidentally a few times. And had dinner once. And we saw that show in Portsmouth, but that was work-related. Sort of. Besides, that's ridiculous, that he'd want me back. I dumped him. And not very nicely, either."

"So?" Alec laughed. "We men might not be all that bright in some ways, wanting women who aren't good for us, but we make up for that weakness with persistence."

"Are you saying that I'm not good for Ben?"

"I don't know. Am I? Are you?"

Iris groaned. "You're infuriating. And obnoxious."

"Thank you. My mother tells me it's a gift. She tells me she doesn't remember a time when she didn't want to strangle me."

"How does Tricia feel about this gift?" Iris asked, smiling in spite of herself.

"Interesting — she doesn't seem to find me infuriating at all. Or obnoxious."

"Oh."

Alec's expression brightened. "Did I tell you that her manager told her she was the best employee she had ever worked with?"

"No."

"Well, she did. And Tricia knows the woman's hoping to move to another store before long, one closer to her home, so . . ."

"So you could be dating a manager."

"Dude, talk about hitting the jackpot. Managerial and culinary skills."

They paid the bill soon after and parted outside the restaurant. Alec headed back to his office on Spring Street (computer guys didn't take weekends off) and Iris walked back to her studio (neither did artists). And on the way down Congress Street, she sent up a prayer of thanks to a possible God for her infuriating, obnoxious, and caring friend.

CHAPTER 21

It was Sunday, December eighteenth, and Iris was in her studio, putting the finishing touches on several projects customers would be picking up during the week.

The building seemed peculiarly empty today, though maybe it was her mood that was creating the sense of isolation.

She had spent Saturday night alone in her apartment, trying to read a very good novel by one of her favorite authors, Charles Todd, but unable to focus for more than a page at a time. Her mind kept wandering and her heart kept racing, no matter how many deep and supposedly calming breaths she took. She had hardly slept at all and now, after three cups of black coffee, her nerves felt all jangly.

"Rats!" Her inattentiveness had caused her to knock over the final cardboard cup of coffee. Luckily, there had been only a splash of liquid inside and it had run onto a rag.

"Go away," she whispered to the voice in her head as she dumped the cup into the trash.

It was Alec. "He wants you back," he was saying. "He wants you back."

And in between Alec's refrain, she heard Bess's intense questioning. "Do you still love him?" "Why have you been punishing him?" And God, all those lines of poetry!

Iris moved the wet rag aside. There was no doubt in her mind that Bess and Alec were pushing her toward a renewed romantic relationship with Ben. They might deny that they were actually "pushing" her, but Iris could feel the pressure they were exerting and at moments it made her feel almost breathless.

It wasn't as if the thought of rekindling a romance with Ben wasn't appealing. If she could forget how their relationship had ended, if she could remove all past context, then . . . But of course, that was impossible. Which made a relationship with Ben impossible.

Iris picked up a pair of pliers and put them down again. God, she had been so happy with Ben! She didn't deserve to be so happy ever again. Besides, she didn't think she ever could be. She was almost certain that her capacity for joy had shriveled into a very tiny and possibly very broken vessel.

Anyway, what was she thinking? Ben hadn't said anything about getting back together. There was no possibility of a relationship rising from the ashes of what she had burned, in spite of what Alec and Bess might think. Even if Ben did want her in his life . . . No. When he had touched her shoulder the day he had helped her with the fridge, the sense of fear that had flooded her had been too great.

The fear of his final rejection once he learned of her failure. The fear of his utter disdain. And if for some miraculous reason Ben didn't condemn her for denying her mother her final wish, then there was the fear of her inability to love him the way he deserved to be loved. Not after all she had suffered, not after how she had changed.

Something came to her then, a realization. In a weird way she had been stringing Ben along much as she had strung Alec along, committing to neither of them, giving each man little or none of what was his due. With Alec, her motives had been fully conscious. But with Ben . . . What was she doing to the poor man? The longer she refused to engage with Ben, the longer his opinion of her might remain . . .

Oh, but that was all so crazy! Nothing made any sense!

Too much coffee, Iris thought. Too much stress.

She would turn to a new task, not a project for the Christmas rush, but one she had been putting off for some time. She would force herself to concentrate and maybe the change of project would calm her.

Iris attached a diamond-tipped drill bit to the flex shaft, gathered clamps, and set about to bore a hole in a fine ruby she had bought during the summer. She had in mind fixing a rose gold jump ring to the stone, and then stringing it on an antique rose gold chain she had found at a flea market.

She took a deep breath and began. She worked carefully, with purpose. The process was going well. The stone was lovely. And then — the ruby shattered.

"Damn!" she cried. "Oh, damn, damn, damn!"

The tears began to flow, tears of frustration, tears of self-pity, tears of sheer sadness. She felt so sorry for the poor stone that had shattered, sorry for Ben, and sorry also for herself. She was sorry for her mother, whose loving and creative life had been cut so short.

Iris leaned against the worktable. She was so, so tired of the life she had been living. How much emotional strain could a person endure before she simply gave up the fight to be part of the world? And what then? She would find herself becoming a recluse, someone who had lost all interest in the lives of others, someone so self-focused that she had become abhorrent to society.

"Calm down," Iris murmured. Maybe it was time to give some serious consideration to moving on again. You could never entirely outrun your demons, of course, but a complete change of scene might confuse them enough to slow down their pursuit. She could find a place where Ben would not follow. . . .

Iris stood away from the worktable, dried her eyes, and carefully retrieved the fragments of the ruby. She wrapped them in soft paper, and locked them in the safe. She could probably salvage a bit of the original stone, but she didn't have the energy right then to think of how it could be done.

For now, it would have to remain broken.

CHAPTER 22

It was Tuesday, the twentieth of December, and Iris was in her studio, shivering with more than cold. Ben would be arriving soon.

She had spent Monday in a state of extreme anxiety, especially after running into Ben in the Old Port. He had been coming out of a pottery shop on Fore Street and Iris had not stopped walking as she passed by, calling a half-inarticulate greeting. The sun had been low and blinding, which meant they were both wearing sunglasses. Iris was thankful she couldn't see the look in Ben's eyes as she hurried on. She was grateful he couldn't see the look in hers. By any standard of conduct she had been rude.

Iris found that she was twisting her hands, an entirely atypical gesture. Last December, her life had held some degree of peace and security, but now, nothing felt calm and nothing felt safe, not even her own home. Ben had called her there that morning. He asked if he could come by to talk.

"About what?" Iris had asked, her grip on the phone painfully tight.

"About what we haven't talked about yet," Ben replied patiently.

"I don't think . . ."

"Iris, please. You ran away from me yesterday as if I had the plague. This can't go on."

She had hesitated and Ben had pressed until finally, Iris had agreed to see him at the studio that afternoon.

Iris heard the elevator rumble to a stop, and then footsteps coming slowly down the hall. She moved behind the larger worktable, as if it could somehow be effective protection. And then, Ben was knocking on the open door and walking into the room. He looked tired and uncharacteristically disheveled, his scarf poorly tied, his hair uncombed.

"Maybe I should wait until after Christmas," he said by way of greeting, "but I can't. I've waited too long as it is." He turned and closed the door of the studio. "I need to know what happened back then, after Bonnie's death. I've lived with the uncertainty for three years now, Iris. I'm not sure how much more I can handle."

Iris was robbed of speech. Her hands gripped the edge of the table.

Ben came farther into the room. "I've spent too many hours wondering," he went on, his tone urgent, "trying to figure it all out. And I keep coming up with the assumption that your leaving the way you did had to have something to do with Bonnie's death."

Iris found her voice. "It had nothing to do with my mother's death," she shouted. "I told you that three years ago! Leave her out of this."

"So, what then?" Ben pressed, unfazed by her tone. "Did I do something wrong? Did I say something hurtful? What?"

Iris looked down at her knuckles, white with tension. "I told you then," she said carefully, as if repeating long rehearsed lines. "I just needed a change."

"A change?" Ben laughed unpleasantly. "From what, being loved? I didn't buy it then and I don't buy it now."

"I don't care. It's the truth."

"Your version of it," Ben spat.

Iris raised her head. "You shouldn't have come to Portland," she said. "It was a mistake."

"What? I should have continued to let you dictate the process of my life?"

"How have I been dictating your life?" Iris demanded, angry now. "I walked away. You were a free agent at that point."

Ben rubbed his eyes before answering. "You really think that?" he asked, his tone both weary and darkly amused. "You really believe that the minute you left for Portland all emotional traces, all memories and influences went with you? You really believe you made a clean break? Oh, Iris. Is your memory that short? Is your mind that distorted?"

Iris wanted to answer but she couldn't. She remembered Ben's impassioned pleas, the long letters, the desperate voice mails. Of course she had not left behind a clean slate. Of course she had not forgotten!

"I knew I would be compelled to try one more time to confront you if I moved to Portland," Ben went on. "The fact is, I shouldn't have stopped pursuing you three years ago. But I respected you too much to hound you." Ben laughed bitterly. "You know that old cliché? If you really love someone, let her go. If she comes back to you, she was always yours. If not . . ."

Iris stood, unable to speak, unable to move.

"To think that all along I was trying to protect you," Ben went on. "I knew your mother's death and all those years of her illness had almost destroyed you. And ultimately I let concern for you almost destroy my own future. I even went so far as to get married to someone I barely knew in a hugely misguided effort to — to release you. But I can't keep living this way anymore."

And, Iris thought, neither can I. "You're right," she said, finally finding her voice again. "You should go now. You should live your own life and let me live mine."

Ben looked at her, his bright blue eyes dark with emotion. "Iris," he said, quietly. "Did you ever really love me?"

"No," she answered, as quietly. "I didn't." It was a lie for Ben's sake. . . .

"I don't believe you. But if you need to lie to me and to yourself, then . . ."

"Just go!" she cried. "Please! Stop tormenting me!"

"All right." Ben raised his arms in a gesture of futility and let them fall against his sides. "I can't believe I was naive enough to think that maybe someday we could be together again. I'm sorry, Iris. I won't bother you again."

He turned and strode to the door. He let it slam behind him.

Iris stood at the worktable. She had survived the long-awaited confrontation. She knew that she should feel released. She knew that she should also feel ashamed. But all she felt were the icy chains of calm and denial wrap themselves firmly around her.

CHAPTER 23

Iris sat in Bess's living room on Wednesday afternoon, a big old volume of Grimms' fairy tales on her lap. She stared down at the cover depiction of Rapunzel, prisoner in her tower, and felt weirdly calm. It was a state something like what she had experienced after her mother's death. But unlike three years ago, this time she realized that she was horribly close to exploding.

"I have a confession to make," she said, when Bess had taken a chair.

"Am I the proper confessor?"

"I don't know," Iris answered honestly. "Probably not. But right now you're the only one I feel I can tell without — without completely breaking down."

"You seem decidedly calm," Bess noted.

"It's a facade. And not a very strong one at that."

"All right. Confess."

"Ben came to see me yesterday," Iris said.

"At the studio. He wanted to know the real reason I left him right after my mother passed. I said a bunch of ridiculous things. And then I told him to go away and leave me alone."

Bess considered before speaking. "Okay," she said finally. "There are an awful lot of holes in that brief story. And why do I think I haven't heard the real confession yet?"

Iris took a deep breath. "Because you haven't heard the real confession. Here it is. My mother wanted me to marry Ben before she died. That's all. It wasn't anything outrageous she asked of me. Ben and I were going to be married at some point, anyway. But I denied her request. I knew she was dying but I didn't want to know that. I thought . . . It was ridiculous. I thought that if Ben and I put off getting married she could put off dying. My God, I was an adult but I was thinking like a selfish child! And now I can't get past the guilt."

"Poor Iris." Bess sighed. "And you still haven't told this to Ben?"

"No. I just — I just lied and acted horribly."

" 'Needles of rain pierce the flinching soil
with a lack of mercy that is stunning,
but nothing, oh, nothing

is as cruel as the lack of mercy
a woman affords her self.' "

"Who was that?" Iris asked, though she had no real interest in the answer.

"Lines from a poem I wrote once, all about guilt. If I do say so myself, it's quite good. I suggest you read it in its entirety."

"I could write my own poem about guilt," Iris muttered. "And it would be a long one. Homer and Milton would have nothing on me."

"Be that as it may, I suggest you tell Ben the truth. If he'll see you. If he won't see you, try sending him an old-fashioned letter. Stay away from any public venue like e-mail or for God's sake, Twitter."

"He won't want to see me, not willingly. But we'll run into each other again and we'll nod and look away and . . ." Iris found her grip on the book in her lap had tightened. "God, Bess, what have I done to my life?"

"I wish I knew how to make things all better," Bess said soothingly. "I really do."

"You were right all along, you know."

"About what?" Bess asked.

"About my being unhappy deep down. Marilyn told me that you were worried about me."

"Ah. Well, yes, I was worried. I am worried. Tell me. What do you want to happen now? Between you and Ben, I mean."

Iris thought about that before answering. "I want him to do what I asked him to. I want him to move on with his life. He deserves far, far better than me."

"That's something you might want to let him decide," Bess said.

"I don't understand," Iris said with an exasperated laugh. "How could I possibly be good for him, at this point?"

"Don't try to make other people's decisions for them, Iris," Bess advised. "That's playing God and it's certain to end in disaster. Now, I'm going to make us some tea."

Too late, Iris answered silently, when Bess had gone to the kitchen. Disaster has already struck.

CHAPTER 24

"It's me."

Iris jumped. She hadn't heard his footsteps coming down the hall. "Oh," she said. "Hi."

Alec came into the studio. "No confetti and trumpets? No fanfare at all?"

Iris smiled lamely. "Sorry. It is good to see you."

"Why so glum?"

"Oh, nothing really . . ."

"Iris."

Well, why not tell him, Iris thought. It doesn't matter either way. "It's just that Ben and I had a — a bad conversation. I said things . . ."

Alec frowned. "What sort of things?"

"Stupid things. Things I really didn't mean."

"Why?" Alec asked. "And don't say that you don't know. That excuse doesn't cut it after you're thirty."

He's right, she thought. "Okay. I was

afraid that if I told Ben the truth about —
about what he wanted to know — then . . ."

"What did he want to know?"

"Why I left him right after my mother
died." And Iris told Alec in the clearest possible way all that had happened three years
earlier.

When she had completed her story, Alec
whistled. "You're really a screwed up girl,
you know that?"

"Woman. I'm a screwed up woman."

"Whatever. All I'm saying is that you
might want to do something about that
before it's too late and you find yourself old
and bitter and wearing underwear as a hat."

Iris smiled feebly. "Only drunk frat boys
do that."

Alec didn't smile back. "I wouldn't run
the risk, Iris. Really."

"You're not joking, are you?"

"No. I'm not."

Iris felt a thread of fear snake through her.
Alec was rarely serious for several minutes
on end. His concern touched and worried
her.

"On an entirely different note," he said
suddenly, "I'm here to buy a Christmas
present for Tricia. I don't know why I didn't
buy something at your open house, but I've
been kind of swamped with a new project. I

guess I lost track of time."

"Tricia hasn't been hinting at what she wants you to get her?" Iris asked.

"No." Alec shrugged. "Why would she do that?"

"No reason. Okay. So, what were you thinking of?"

"Well, she's really mad for purple. Got anything purple?"

Iris actually laughed. "You know nothing about gems, do you?"

"Nope."

"I have a lovely amethyst I was going to set in a pendant. But I could set it in a ring if you think Tricia would prefer that."

Alec shrugged again. "I don't know. I think she'd like both. Why don't you decide? But it's got to be fantastic."

"Alec. Have you ever known me to make anything less than fantastic?"

"I don't really get jewelry, Iris. You know that. So, how much is this going to cost me?" he asked.

"Depends. There are materials, time — and there's not a lot of that left — and labor. But there's also the friends and family discount. What's your budget?"

Alec blushed furiously and mumbled a number that caused Iris to slap her hand over her mouth. "I am so in the wrong business!" she said, finally.

"It's just money. Besides, Tricia is worth it."

"Does Tricia have any idea of the kind of money you make?" Iris asked. The girl might seem nice but deep down maybe she was a gold digger and if so, someone had to save Alec from her clutches!

"Of course not," Alec said. "Why would she care? So, can you help me out?"

"I'll have a piece to you on Christmas Eve day. How's that?"

"Thanks, Iris. And do me a favor. Remember what I said earlier. About not winding up a batty old woman all alone in the world due to her own stubbornness or scaredy-catness or whatever it is that's making you miserable."

Iris smiled but tears pricked at her eyes. "Okay," she said. "I promise to try."

Alec waved and loped out of the studio.

Tricia, Iris thought, is one lucky woman to have the love of a man like Alec. And if she hurts him, she added, I am going to have to hurt her back.

CHAPTER 25

Friday was far from over. It was only two forty-five in the afternoon, but already it seemed like the longest day of Iris's life. And one of the worst.

Witness what had happened that morning. She had been walking up Congress Street from the bank when she saw Ben ahead of her, coming out of Yes! Books, a fat volume tucked under one arm. Without thinking she had turned around and run back in the direction of the bank, sliding badly on a patch of black ice and only narrowly escaping a fall. Now her right knee and thigh ached and a bit of the heel of her right boot had come off. She had wrapped the knee in an Ace bandage and taken a few ibuprofen, but the boot situation would have to wait until after Christmas.

Iris was sitting at the pine table in the kitchen, toying with a cup of cooling tea. It had been three weeks since she had first seen Ben across the crowd at the museum's tree lighting. Three weeks during which her heart had begun to reopen and then had snapped violently shut again. Three weeks during which she had struggled both to remember and not to remember. Three weeks of anxiety, punctuated by tiny moments of a glimpsed joy.

Her doorbell rang. Iris got up and looked out the living room window. A mail truck was parked below. With a sigh, Iris headed downstairs. She assumed the mail carrier had a package for one of the other condo owners, Maeve or the guy on the first floor. She couldn't remember the last time anyone had sent her a package at home.

But she was wrong. The mail carrier, a pleasant middle-aged man named Scott, held out a box for her to take. "A Christmas present, I guess," he said. "Hope it's something you've been wishing for."

Iris forced a smile as she accepted the package. It was about the size of a large shoe box, wrapped in brown paper, and tied with twine. Even if she hadn't seen her father's bold writing on the top of the package, she would have known it was from him. Brown paper and twine had been his signature wrapping for as long as Iris could remember, and probably for a long time before that.

After wishing Scott a happy holiday, Iris climbed the stairs back to her apartment, knee aching with each step. She put the box on the kitchen table. She considered letting it remain unopened for a day, maybe more. She considered ignoring it entirely. That could be done. God knew she was an expert at ignoring what should not be ignored.

And then, realizing that whatever was inside couldn't possibly make her feel any more miserable than she already felt, Iris took a scissors from a drawer by the sink and snipped open the string, sliced off the brown paper, and cut open the packing tape beneath. On top of wads of tissue paper was a white business envelope. Iris turned it over and saw her father's business logo and the words Karr Representation.

She hesitated only a moment before opening the envelope to find a handwritten letter. She read it slowly through twice.

Dear Iris:
It occurred to me that the best Christmas present I could give you this year was a small collection of your mother's possessions. They are yours now to do with as you see fit. I only ask that you

treat them with the respect they deserve.

I know that to date you've refused — yes, Iris, I use that word consciously — that you've refused to have any of your mother's works with you in your new life in Portland. I can't pretend that I entirely understand your reasoning or your desire, but I think that I've come closer to accepting that you need to live the way in which you need to live. You're my child but also an adult so I have to believe you know your own mind.

Merry Christmas, Iris. I love you.

Dad

Iris refolded the letter and slipped it back into the envelope. What do I feel, she asked herself. I resent his intrusion. I'm afraid. I'm ashamed. But I'm also curious.

Carefully, she extracted from the box three small tissue paper bundles. Her father — or perhaps Jean — had carefully tied each bundle with a narrow piece of blue ribbon. Iris began to unwrap the first one. She thought of all those years back in Wakefield, sitting cross-legged by the tree on Christmas morning, opening gifts with her parents. What an enormous difference time had wrought.

The first bundle contained a handblown,

nineteenth-century glass Christmas ornament that Bonnie had bought on a trip she and Iris's father had taken to Vienna before their marriage. Iris traced the delicate, rosy-colored form with her finger and remembered how her mother had trusted her to hang it on the tree each year. Gently, she returned the ornament to its wrapping.

The next little package held an elaborate ivory hair comb that had been passed down in Bonnie's family for generations. Iris held the piece in the palm of her hand, feeling how cool and smooth it was. She could remember just about every single occasion on which her mother had worn it, her glossy dark hair swept up for an opening night at a gallery in New York, a New Year's Eve party at the Plaza in Boston, a special concert at the Museum of Fine Arts. Iris carefully rewrapped the comb, wondering if she would ever feel right wearing it.

Iris gasped as her fingers uncovered the item in the third bundle of tissue. It was the ring she had made for her mother — the one Bonnie had worn every day until her fingers became too thin and she risked losing it — the ring Iris wondered if her father had had buried with her mother's body.

The band was eighteen-carat gold, with a prong-set, small but very good brilliant cut ruby. Iris thought of the ruby she had shattered the other day. She hesitated and then slipped the ring on the fourth finger of her right hand. It fit perfectly.

Iris breathed deeply. She felt a pleasant tingle run through her body.

There was one more thing in the box, another sealed white business envelope with a yellow sticky note attached to it. In her father's writing were the words "Iris — Somehow, in the aftermath of your mother's passing, this got lost. I'm sorry. Dad."

Inside was another, smaller envelope. Iris recognized it right away as her mother's signature stationery. And in her mother's precise and graceful handwriting were the words "For Iris."

With trembling fingers she opened the envelope, careful not to tear the flap. Inside was a single sheet of pale dove gray paper.

Her heart was beating rapidly. She feared her mother's anger and more, her disappointment, but she knew that she deserved it all. Slowly, Iris opened the sheet of paper. At the top, printed in purple, was the familiar outline of an iris. The date printed just below was given as less than a month before her mother's passing.

She began to read.

My dear daughter:

I'll be gone when you read this, but, I hope, not forgotten.

How dramatic! That was silly of me. I know you will never forget me, as I will never forget you.

Something has been on my mind since we spoke about your marrying Ben. Well, since I suggested it was something you should do in the not so distant future. I was intensely aware of how uncomfortable my request made you and I've given it all a great deal of thought.

Iris, I am so sorry for making such a selfish request — demand? — of you. Of course I want you to be happy in whatever form that happiness takes. But I also want you to be happy in your own time. I think I understand your response. In fact, I know that I do.

I hope with all my heart that you'll forgive me and do whatever it is you need to do to be blissfully happy when you're ready to accept that happiness.

All my love, from wherever I am in
this fantastical Universe,
Mom

Iris stared down at the single sheet of paper, at her mother's familiar handwriting.

She began to read the letter through again, this time aloud, and as she did she heard her mother's rich voice speaking the words, as if she were standing right there by her side.

When Iris had finished reading she placed the letter on the table. She felt different than she had a moment ago. She felt cleansed, reborn. She felt oddly happy, hugely sad, and very, very tired.

The fact she had known so many years ago and had then so carefully set aside was staring her in the face once again. Grief was loud and messy and almost psychedelic in its intensity. It was hot and obvious and strong. It was a living thing, not to be ignored.

Iris slid into a chair at the old pine table, and laid a protective hand over her mother's letter. She let the tears come, and with them, the joy.

"Oh, Mom," she whispered. "I love you so much."

CHAPTER 26

As she was leaving her building late morning on Christmas Eve day, Iris slipped a card under her second-floor neighbor's door. She felt bad for having waited this long to deliver it. Maeve had told her that she was leaving on the twenty-first to spend the holiday with her family at their home in Bath. Still, Iris thought, there would be a greeting for her upon her return. That was something. Iris felt ashamed that she had never made a real gesture of friendship to her neighbor — it had been selfish of her — and vowed to correct her behavior in the new year. Whether Maeve wanted Iris's friendship was yet to be seen.

Iris tramped down to the first floor, her injured knee throbbing. The guy who owned that condo had been in town for a mere day between business trips before jetting off to spend the holidays in Tortola with some buddies. She knew this because she had run

into him while getting her mail a few da
earlier. He admitted he had forgotten her
first name before loping down the front
steps to his awaiting cab.

So, the building had been entirely empty
but for Iris for the past few days. She had
felt unnerved being the sole occupant, but
why she couldn't say. It was a safe neighborhood, and she hardly ever saw Maeve and
Tom in the first place. She wished she had
kept the few Christmas cards she had
received instead of having tossed them immediately into the recycling bin. The cards
might have been some form of company.

The air was bitterly cold but, except for
occasional flurries, the snow mostly held
off. Iris made her way down Cumberland
Street to one of the city's many homeless
shelters. She had volunteered at this particular shelter since coming to Portland. It was
true that the best way to take your mind off
your own worries was to focus on the needs
of others. But Iris wasn't sure how ef-
fectively she was meeting the needs of
anyone this day. She felt miles removed
from the boisterous conversations around
her.

When the main course had been served
and the guests were relaxing before dessert,
Iris slipped into the hall off the shelter's

room. She sank into a metal folding ﹏t her head in her hands, and let the ﹏e, fast and furious.

﹏ome time later, she couldn't have said how long, she was aware of someone gently patting her back. She looked up. It was one of the guests, a woman somewhere in her seventies perhaps, dressed in a wild assortment of warm clothing.

"What's the matter, honey?" the woman asked.

The woman's gentle touch made Iris's tears flow ever harder. All she managed to choke out were the words, "My mother."

"I had a mother once, too," the woman said. "A long time ago."

Iris wiped her eyes again and looked up at her comforter. "Did you . . . Did you love her?"

The woman's lined and careworn face became beautiful at that moment. "Oh, yes," she said, "very much indeed."

Iris looked down at her mother's ring. "I miss her," she said.

"Of course you do. And I'm sure she knows that up in heaven."

Iris nodded, afraid to venture a reply, and the woman patted her back again.

"A pretty girl like you should have a nice boyfriend," she said.

Iris attempted a smile. It was enough for her companion, who smiled back and went off for the dessert course.

When the meal was over, and cleanup was accomplished, Iris headed out for Alec's apartment. He answered on the first ring of the bell, as if he had been impatiently awaiting her.

"Hey," he said.

"You do have wrapping paper?" Iris asked, holding out a flat, square box she had withdrawn from her bag.

Alec looked puzzled. "What? Oh. I'll find something." He opened the box and whistled. "Whoa. Now that's a necklace. Even I can tell as much. Wow. Thanks, Iris."

Iris nodded. "May she wear it in good health."

Alec put the box aside and handed her an envelope. "It's a gift certificate to Longfellow. I know how you love that bookstore."

"Thank you, Alec. You shouldn't have. But I'm glad that you did."

"And here." Alec took a colorful round tin from a small table beside the door and handed it to her. "Butter cookies from Tricia. They're awesome. She used like three pounds of butter in each batch."

Iris laughed. "I'll break out a backup artery just in case. So, you're going to Tricia's parents' house tomorrow?"

"Yup. I'm meeting them for the first time on Christmas Day. Can you believe it? It's either really good luck or the worst ever."

"I'm betting on the good luck."

"Me, too. Are you going over to Bess's tomorrow?" he asked.

"I was invited."

"You should go, Iris."

"I'll see."

Alec shook his head. "Well, we know what that means. Look, Iris, call me if you need to talk, any time of the day or night. Okay?"

"Okay," she said.

Alec saluted jauntily and Iris left. On the way home, clutching her tin of cookies, Iris sent out an important prayer.

"Mom," she said, whispering the words into the chill air, "if you can hear me, help me. There's something important I need to do tonight. Please, Mom, help me."

And oh, how she hoped her mother had heard.

Chapter 27

Iris whimpered in frustration. The below-freezing temperature and the stiff wind it brought with it did not help to bolster her strength or her mood. She had been on the darkened streets now for close to two hours, in search of Ben Tresch.

Earlier, she had called his cell phone only to get his voice mail. She had left no message because she felt that nothing said to a machine would be adequate. She had then tried his office only to get that voice mail, too. Well, it had been a long shot. She didn't know if he had a landline at home but she did know where he lived so she had gone over to Bowdoin Street, on the way passing a group of carolers, people dressed in their holiday finest, and the winking lights of Christmas trees in windows.

Ben lived in an old building similar to the one in which Iris lived. From what she could tell from the sidewalk, the lights of the second-floor apartment were off and no one came to answer her knocking, loud and insistent though it was.

She had turned away in frustration. She realized Ben could be at a friend's house, or even out of town. She might not see him again for days. She didn't know how she could survive the silence for even moments longer.

Her knee still ached from her near fall on the black ice. The damp cold seeped through the tiniest spaces between her hat and her head, freezing the tips of her ears. Her nose was numb and running and her eyes stung. Her fingers, though encased in gloves inside woolen mittens, were swollen and painful.

Iris struggled not to cry and made her way resolutely into the heart of the city. Not much was open this late on Christmas Eve but she tried what was — the bar at the Regency Hotel, the Grill Room on Exchange Street. But Ben was nowhere to be found.

Iris huddled in the door of a watch repair shop, feeling close to despair. She considered calling Alec — he had told her she could call him night or day — but she rejected the idea. He would be with Tricia and possibly fast asleep, and besides, what could he do but offer her a shoulder to cry on? And that was just not going to be enough, not this time.

Think, Iris, think, she urged herself. He must be here; he has to be here!

And then, something came to her. She didn't know why she hadn't thought of it before. Ben's family was Episcopal, and though Ben himself didn't attend Mass every Sunday, he always celebrated Christmas and Easter. The Cathedral Church of St. Luke was on State Street, mere blocks from both of their homes.

It was a long way back up to State Street but Iris wasn't sure how easily she could get a cab on Christmas Eve, so she made her way on foot, up Congress Street, and then along the buckled brick sidewalks of State, dodging dangerous patches of ice, trying and mostly failing to favor her sore knee. When she reached the cathedral she pulled open the heavy outer door and stepped gratefully into the vestibule.

The sound of organ and voices came to her from behind the closed second set of large wood doors. Iris scanned the table on which were stacked various brochures and saw a sign that told her the Festival Eucharist had begun at ten o'clock. She checked her watch. It was almost eleven thirty. The Mass should soon be over. Quietly, Iris made her way into the church and stood half hidden behind one of the massive marble pillars. In spite of her aching heart, she was moved by the church's beauty. Every pew was packed and it took a long moment before she saw Ben's golden head above the crowd.

A feeling of intense relief swept through her, followed by a feeling of dread. What if Ben walked right by her? What if he refused to acknowledge her? Well, she would deal with that awful possibility if it happened.

Before long the priest was giving the final blessing and then he dismissed the congregation. The cathedral's magnificent organ soared to life again. People began to exit the pews and make their way toward the back of the church. Finally, Iris saw Ben approaching. An old, extremely well-dressed couple walked by his side, chatting quietly.

When the three were only feet away, Iris stepped out from behind the pillar.

"Hello, Ben," she said.

Ben looked startled and not altogether pleased. He said farewell to the couple and stepped out of the way of the crowd behind him.

"Iris," he said evenly, "I didn't see you earlier."

"I wasn't at the Mass. Do you have plans?

I mean, are you going somewhere?"

"I had planned to go home to bed," he said. "Why?"

"There's something I need to tell you. I should have told you a long time ago. I should have told you the other day, when you asked me for the truth. But I . . . I couldn't."

Ben's expression was wary. Iris understood that.

"What's changed since the other day?" he asked.

"My mother talked to me."

Now the wariness became a look of outright concern. "Are you feeling all right, Iris? You're shivering. Did you take anything —"

"No, no. I mean, yes. I'm fine. What I mean is that my mother wrote me a letter right before she died. It somehow got lost. My father found it and sent it to me."

"Oh," Ben said, his look of concern lessening only slightly. "Okay."

"Will you listen to me?"

Ben seemed to think about his answer before saying, "All right."

Iris spoke in a calm, hushed voice. It took every bit of her courage. She told him about her mother's request that they marry before she died, and about her failing to honor that request. She told him about the magical thinking that had caused her to believe she could keep her mother alive by force of will. She told him about the guilt that had driven her away from him. And then, she told him about the contents of her mother's letter.

"Mom understood," she said. "She didn't hate me at the end. She wasn't disappointed in me. She loved me. She still loves me."

Ben shook his head. "So you ran away because . . ."

"I ran away because I thought I had let her down and let you down, too. I believed I didn't deserve to be happy. I . . . I didn't think clearly about what you deserved. I think I must have gone a little mad. I'm so, so sorry, Ben. I know you must be so angry with me."

"I am angry, Iris," he said after a moment. "At least, I was. But mostly I'm sad for you. I'm sorry you've been suffering alone all this time. And I'm sad for me, too. God, it could have been so different. For both of us."

Iris felt tears slipping down her cheeks. "Will you ever forgive me? Can you?"

"All those things you said the other day. About never having really loved me. About wanting me to leave you alone. Did you mean any of it?"

"No. Of course not. Everything was a horrible lie. I was so afraid . . ."

Ben put a hand on her shoulder. "Then of course I forgive you. Of course."

Iris hung her head. "I can't believe you're even talking to me, after all I've done to you."

"I'm talking with you because I love you more than I was ever mad at you," Ben said. "It's pretty simple, really."

"Is it?" Iris managed a smile. "Yes, I guess it is after all."

Ben took her in his arms. "Oh, Iris. What are we going to do?"

She shook her head against his chest.

"Well, we'll figure out something. After all, we are creative sorts."

Iris laughed and held him tighter.

"As pleasant as this is," Ben said after a moment, "we should probably go."

"Yes."

"I'm supposed to be at my parents' house at one o'clock," Ben said when they left the building. "How about I pick you up at eleven."

"But I can't just show up at your parents' house!" Iris cried. "Not after all this time without a word. Not after what I did to them."

"Trust me, they'll be very happy to see

you. Really."

"But you can't just bring in a guest unannounced," Iris protested, somewhat feebly.

"You know my mother always makes room at the table for one more."

"She'll be making room for the stray."

Ben pulled her to him in another strong embrace. "Iris," he said, "you're not a stray. You never were. You always belonged, to all of us."

How wonderful those words sounded!

Together, hand in hand, they began to walk down the path from the cathedral to the sidewalk.

"You're limping," Ben noted.

"Yeah." Iris smiled sheepishly. "I slipped on some ice the other day."

"Are you okay?"

"I will be."

"Good. Merry Christmas, Iris."

"Merry Christmas, Ben." Iris paused for a moment and then said, " 'If ever two were one, then surely we.' "

"That's lovely."

"It's not mine," Iris admitted. "It's a line from a poem by Anne Bradstreet. I read it in one of Bess's books once. I didn't even know it had stayed with me."

"I'm glad it did. Come on," Ben said. "Let's get out of this cold."

"Thank you, Mom," Iris whispered as together she and Ben made their way home.

EPILOGUE

It was mid-March, not quite spring, but the air was warmer than it should be, and on the way to her studio Iris had spotted purple and yellow crocuses in the front yards on Neal Street. Once in the studio she had opened the one window that actually opened and breathed in the fresh air. She touched the gold and ruby ring on her right hand and smiled. So much had changed since last December, and all of it for the better.

Take, for instance, Iris's relationship with her father. In January she had paid him a lengthy and long overdue visit. The time together had benefited them both, especially Iris, who learned some important things about her father, like the fact that he hadn't been able to open the door of Bonnie's studio since the day she had died. Iris had simply never realized how badly her father had grieved. Just because he had married

Jean didn't mean that he had forgotten his first wife.

Together Iris and Robert began the process of cleaning out the studio, deciding what could be donated to an art school, what might be sold, and what should be kept. It was a healing process and Jean and Ben had let them work alone.

Once back in Portland, Iris had begun to design a new line of jewelry. The ideas just seemed to be there for the developing, the designs happening organically. It was, Iris thought, the best work she had done in some time. She had decided to call this new line "Joy," in honor of the joy her mother had brought to everyone she met.

Iris had brought from her father's house not only inspiration but also tangible reminders of her past, like a large packet of family photos, one of her mother's early abstract works in marble, and several of her small sculptures in wood. Iris was creating a life in which her mother was still an important and integral part.

And as for Ben, he had moved into Iris's home until they found a place that suited them both. Iris had retrieved from her father's garage their old soup tureen as well as all the other household items they had collected. The apartment was a little cramped at the moment but cramped felt nice.

A wedding, a marriage, children — it would all happen. There were difficult days — Ben's heart had been badly bruised, his ability to trust, tested — but together, they were healing.

Iris turned away from the window and pulled a sketch of his-and-hers wedding rings from a folder on one of the worktables. She and Ben weren't the only ones contemplating years of marital bliss. Alec had asked Tricia to marry him and unsurprisingly she had said yes — but only if he agreed to shave his head. He looked so much more attractive now. Alec had been right all along. Tricia was smart in the ways that really counted, like the ability to make another person truly happy.

On the topic of happiness, Bess's son, Michael, had moved back East. Southern California no longer agreed with him and it seemed that his interest in becoming a chef was meeting with a lot of resistance from his father. Here, in Portland, Marilyn had given him a job at the restaurant. It was a menial position and meant to test his commitment to the business. So far, washing dishes, mopping floors, and chopping vegetables hadn't deterred him. Bess was very happy to have Michael home with her. Iris thought him a nice guy and Ben thought he was okay, in spite of the huge plug in his left earlobe. Ben didn't care for piercings and internal horns and tattoos, though Michael vigorously argued that they were a legitimate form of art. "They might be art," Ben replied, "but they're ugly art."

"It's me."

Iris looked up from the sketch to find Maeve, her second-floor neighbor, at the door of her studio. Since January Maeve had been working as Iris's part-time assistant and had proved invaluable, not in small part due to her good conversation.

"Hey, you. Isn't it gorgeous out there?"

"Beyond gorgeous," Maeve replied, "in spite of the puddles of muck on our street."

"They don't call it mud season for nothing."

"Who's they?"

Iris shrugged. "No one really knows."

"Well, here are the pencils you wanted. The receipt and your change are in the bag."

"Thanks, Maeve. So, see you later at Snug?"

"Right after my computer class."

With a wave, Maeve left.

Yes, so much had changed since the night Iris had seen Ben across the crowd. And the month of December had been transformational. She would never fear it again, as the countdown to death. She would, instead, regard the month of December as a time in which to celebrate life.

Abandoning the sketch, Iris went back to the open window. The trees were still largely bare so she could see the *Rising Cairn* in all its simple splendor. In her mind's eye she saw the great stone and steel body rise to its full height until it was standing erect, head set to bravely face the future, free to create a new life for itself.

Indeed, Iris had risen.

THE CHRISTMAS
THIEF
LESLIE MEIER

For my editor, John Scognamiglio.
Twenty years and counting!
Thank you, John, for taking such
good care of me and my work.

CHAPTER 1

"That bag is to die for."

As a graduate of the Cavendish Hotel chain's Guests Come First program, Toni Leone was too well trained to point, but Elizabeth Stone followed her colleague's gaze, which was fixed on a Chanel-style handbag made of silver quilted leather with a long, woven leather and chain strap. The woman carrying the bag was dressed in tight black jeans, stiletto heels, and a fluttering silk tunic. Her hair was bleached blond and she was hanging onto the arm of an extremely muscular man.

"It's probably not real," Elizabeth replied, speaking in a whisper. The two young women were wearing matching forest green blazers and standing behind the reception desk at the very posh, very expensive Cavendish Palm Beach Hotel. It was strictly against hotel policy to comment on the guests, but the staff members all did it, especially during the quiet times. The hotel was a historic landmark and attracted the rich and famous from around the world. Located right on the beach, the pink stucco building had eight restaurants, four pools, a spa, and recreational options ranging from tennis courts and an eighteen-hole golf course to paddleboats and shuffleboard. It was also steps away from Worth Avenue, which was lined with designer boutiques such as Gucci, Armani, Ralph Lauren, and Cartier.

"Of course it's real," Toni replied, giving her wavy blond hair a toss. "I saw it in the window at the Chanel store. I can tell the difference between a genuine Chanel bag and a knockoff and I'm surprised you can't."

Elizabeth shrugged and tucked her short, dark hair behind her ears. "If it's real, it's the only genuine thing about her. Her hair's bleached, and I bet she's had quite a bit of work done." She gazed across the vast, luxuriously appointed lobby — where a round gilt and marble table with an enormous display of pink poinsettias was centered beneath a fabulous crystal chandelier — and through the glass doors, where the sun was shining brightly on a flower bed filled with colorful tropical plants. She shook her head. "I've been in Florida for almost six months and I'm still not used to this weather. Eighty-two degrees and sunny — can you believe it's almost Christmas?"

"Uh, yeah," Toni said, winding a lock of hair around her finger. "They put the poinsettias and amaryllis plants in the lobby weeks ago." She'd lived in Florida her entire life and didn't find the climate the least bit odd, unlike Elizabeth, who had grown up in Tinker's Cove, a small town located on the coast of Maine. "Don't tell me you miss the snow — most people come to Florida to get away from the cold winters up north."

Elizabeth hit a few keys on her computer and went to a favorite site. "It's twenty-five and snowing in Tinker's Cove," she said. "Looks like we're going to have a white Christmas."

Toni looked over her shoulder at the live-cam image showing a lighthouse with snow swirling all around it and rough surf crashing on the rugged gray rocks below. "I don't get it," she said. "Why do you want to go *there* for Christmas?"

Elizabeth smiled. "It's home. There'll be tree trimming and carol singing. . . ."

"You can do that here."

"It's not the same," Elizabeth said. "You have to go caroling in the snow and have hot chocolate afterward, in front of a roaring fire."

"I'd rather have a chilled martini on a deck overlooking the ocean, watching the sunset."

Elizabeth laughed. "That's nice, too, but Christmas is about family. I miss my mom and dad and my sisters and my brother and especially my little nephew, Patrick. He's almost three now and he's very excited about Santa Claus."

"Well, you've only got to wait a little more than two weeks and you'll be on your way, flying north." She shivered. "Personally, I think you're crazy to take your vacation in December. The hotel's really busy at Christmas and I'm going to be keeping an eye out for Mr. Right."

"Tell me, again, what makes him Mr. Right?" Elizabeth urged.

"Well, he has to be tall, and good-looking, and sweet, really considerate," said Toni, just as a very ugly, very short man came through the revolving door, dressed head to toe in Ralph Lauren resort wear and sporting an enormous gold watch on a very hairy wrist. "But I'll be willing to overlook all that if he's rich," she added, under her breath as she pasted on a smile. "Welcome to the Cavendish, Mr. Moore. It's so nice to see you again."

"It's nice to be back," he replied. "This place feels like home. I don't know how you do it but I know I'm going to find my bags waiting for me in my room, there'll be an extra-firm pillow on my bed with a sugar-free chocolate, and my favorite low-cal beer is going to be in the minibar."

"That's our little secret," Toni said. "Is it the same Visa account?"

"No, no." Mr. Moore produced an American Express platinum card. "I've got a new one."

"Very well." Toni was clicking away at her keyboard, adding the new information to the extensive database the Cavendish chain maintained about all its customers. That database, envied throughout the entire hospitality industry, allowed Cavendish employees to provide top notch service personally tailored to every guest, and was the reason why Mr. Moore found that extra-firm pillow, sugar-free chocolate, and light beer waiting for him in his room. "Have a pleasant stay," Toni said, handing him the key card. "Room three-oh-five, overlooking the pool."

"See?" he asked Elizabeth, holding up the key card. "My favorite room. You guys take better care of me than my wife does."

"It's our pleasure," she said. "Just give us

a call if there's anything we can do for you."

"Right-o," he said, giving them a little salute with his key card and making his way to the elevator, pausing here and there to admire the blooming orchids and other holiday decorations.

"You know why he likes room three-oh-five, don't you?" Toni asked.

"The view of the pool?" Elizabeth suggested.

"Think again. It's not the pool, it's the women in skimpy swimsuits."

"So Mr. Moore is a bit of a voyeur," said Elizabeth, giggling, just as the hotel manager, Sergei Dimitri, came out of his office, which was located behind the reception desk.

Mr. Dimitri was a neat, middle-aged man with slicked back hair, a small mustache, and a pronounced French accent. Guests adored him, frequently commenting on his warm smile and accommodating nature, but staff members had a somewhat less favorable opinion of him. "Ladies, ladies, how many times must I warn you not to talk about the guests? They pay your salaries, remember that."

"Of course, Mr. Dimitri," Toni said with an innocent expression.

His gaze rested on Elizabeth. "I'm surprised at you, Elizabeth. I don't want to have to place you on probation."

Elizabeth didn't like the sound of that — employees who were on probation could not take vacation time. "Oh, please no, Mr. Dimitri," she said. "I'm terribly sorry."

Mr. Dimitri's eyes were hard, like round black buttons, and his mustache bristled. "You've been warned. Don't let it happen again."

"Oh, it won't," she said. "I promise."

"And don't forget," he told them, "there's a staff meeting this afternoon, when your shift ends."

Elizabeth felt like groaning, but restrained the impulse. Staff meetings were held off the clock, on employees' own time, and she had been planning to spend the evening digging her cold-weather clothes out of storage, in anticipation of her vacation.

"We'll be there," Toni said. "Never fear."

"Good," Mr. Dimitri said, spying an elderly guest exiting the elevator, looking a bit lost. "Mrs. Fahnstock," he cooed, hurrying toward her. "What can I do for you?"

Mrs. Fahnstock's wrinkled face immediately brightened. "Oh, Mr. Dimitri, how lovely to see you."

"Is something the matter, dear lady?"

"Well, this is so silly of me, but I'm supposed to meet my friend, Doris, and I can't seem to find the Victorian Tea Room. Has it been moved?" she asked, furrowing her brow.

"Never fear, these corridors can be confusing." Mr. Dimitri snapped his fingers. "Elizabeth, please escort Mrs. Fahnstock to the Victorian Tea Room."

Elizabeth hurried across the thickly carpeted space and Mrs. Fahnstock's look of befuddlement was replaced with a serene smile. "You're such a darling to help me," she said.

"It's my pleasure, Mrs. Fahnstock," Elizabeth said, taking her arm. "Now if you'll just come this way I'm sure we'll find your friend waiting for you."

Mr. Dimitri stood watching, a thoughtful expression on his face, as Elizabeth escorted the elderly guest through the spacious lobby, which was dotted with numerous luxuriously appointed seating areas. He noticed with approval the way she matched her pace to the old woman's, and kept up a lively conversation as they proceeded along the paneled and carpeted corridor leading to the tea room.

The hotel's largest function room, the Bougainvillea Room, was packed with employees when Elizabeth and Toni arrived, and everybody was talking, expressing different expectations about the staff meeting.

"Bonuses . . . holiday bonuses. I'm sure they're going to announce bonuses," Toni said, taking a seat next to Kieran, one of the doormen.

"Don't be daft," Kieran said gloomily. "Layoffs. It's this recession, don't you see? They're going to cut staff. The hotel's got something like five hundred rooms and more than fifteen hundred employees. Do the math."

"Nonsense," said Ada, one of the housekeepers. She was wearing the lavender shirtwaist dress with a white lace collar that all the housekeepers wore. "The rich are doing just fine, there's no recession for them, and that's who comes to this hotel. The one percent."

"If you ask me, occupancy's been down," Kieran insisted. "I know my tips are."

"Maybe it's something about the health insurance plan," Elizabeth said, following her mother Lucy's oft-expressed advice not to panic until you had to.

"There aren't any charts or books," Toni observed, indicating the single podium in the front of the room. "Wouldn't there be stuff like that if it's only a new health plan?"

Elizabeth suspected her friend was right and her heart gave a little jump when Mr. Dimitri appeared and took his place, tapping the microphone. "Attention, attention," he said. "I promise to be brief."

The room quieted as everyone waited to hear what he had to say; a few fingers were crossed, and a few people were holding their breath.

"I see some anxious faces," he began with a laugh. "Well, you can relax. I have good news."

The employees who were holding their breath exhaled, some even chuckled.

"I have the pleasure of announcing that our hotel has been chosen for a great honor — the entire hotel has been booked by Wall Street financier Jonah Gruber for a Christmas extravaganza for six hundred of his closest friends."

Mr. Dimitri nodded, waiting for the employees to absorb this information. While not exactly ecstatic, everyone seemed interested, wondering what the extravaganza meant for them personally. Elizabeth found herself feeling a bit let down since the event would most likely take place during her vacation and she'd miss it. She almost wished she could stay to see all the famous people who would be attending.

"The highlight of this four-day celebration will be a fantastic black-tie dinner dance, the Blingle Bells Ball, at which Mr. Gruber's wife, the lovely cinema star Noelle Jones, will wear the amazing ruby and emerald Imperial Parure. You may remember that Mr. Gruber bought the parure, which was originally created for Empress Marie Louise, at auction for forty-seven million dollars."

Finally, Mr. Dimitri got the reaction he wanted: there was a collective gasp from the assembled employees.

"That's correct, forty-seven million dollars. Needless to say, security will be a top concern. And that is why I would like to turn this meeting over to our security director, Dan Wrayburn."

Wrayburn, who had been standing to the side of the room, came forward. He was a stocky, muscular man in early middle age with a gray brush cut, and he had the easy, bouncing movement of a former boxer but rumor had it he was actually ex-FBI.

"My top concern — and yours, too — is the safety of our guests," Wrayburn began, his eyes moving restlessly over the group. "This event will bring extra challenges, not only because of the presence of the valuable jewels, but also because the guest list will include European royalty, celebrities, politicians, even the First Lady. All of these high-profile people are potential targets for crimes ranging from simple theft to kidnapping. I am asking you all to remain vigilant — you are the first line against criminal activity. You must keep your eyes and ears open and report anything, anything at all, that appears suspicious to you. If you see something, say something."

Everyone nodded in agreement and Wrayburn cracked a grin. "I'll be issuing more specific instructions in the future, so for now I'll turn things back to Mr. Dimitri. But first let me say I have every confidence that together we can make this a safe and secure celebration for our guests."

Elizabeth nudged Toni. "Sounds like you'll have some prime husband-hunting opportunities."

To her surprise, Toni didn't look pleased. "Don't count on it. We're all going to be under a microscope. And believe me, if anything goes wrong — and something will, count on it — we're the ones who will be blamed."

Mr. Dimitri was again tapping the microphone, demanding silence. "Thank you, Mr. Wrayburn. I know I can count on you all to cooperate with Mr. Wrayburn's plans for security. And now, just one more thing before you go. . . ."

There was suddenly an air of tension in the room; they all knew Mr. Dimitri's habit of delivering bad news just before he ended a meeting.

"All vacations scheduled for the rest of the month are canceled — we need all hands on deck to prepare for this special event."

It hit Elizabeth like a hammer. No vacation! No white Christmas! No little Patrick, squealing with delight at the presents under the tree.

"Too bad," Toni said, sympathizing.

"Yeah," Elizabeth said, remembering another favorite expression of her mother's: be careful what you wish for. For a moment, only a moment, she'd wished she wouldn't be missing seeing all the famous people — and now she'd gotten that wish.

"Cheer up," Toni urged. "We'll have fun. You'll see."

"I guess it could be worse," Elizabeth grumbled, joining the crowd of employees flowing through the doors. Absorbed in disappointment, she didn't notice Mr. Dimitri until he tapped her on the arm.

"A word, please, Elizabeth."

Her eyes met Toni's in a shared look of

dismay, then she followed Mr. Dimitri to his office, certain she was about to be fired, or at the very least, placed on probation. Things weren't going her way today, that was for sure. She never should have made that remark about Mr. Moore.

"Sit down, Elizabeth," he urged, shutting the door after they stepped into the room and seating himself behind his desk.

Elizabeth obeyed, bracing herself for the bad news. No matter what happened, she vowed, she wasn't going to cry. And if she got fired, well, she'd be able to go home for Christmas.

"You've been noticed," he said, smiling.

What a sadist, Elizabeth thought. He was actually enjoying this.

"Your excellent work has been noticed."

Elizabeth sat up straighter. What the heck was going on?

"You may have noticed that our assistant concierge, Annemarie, has been on sick leave. She called today and told me she has Epstein-Barr and won't be able to return for at least four weeks."

"My sister had that once," Elizabeth said. "That's too bad."

"Indeed," Mr. Dimitri said. "And Annemarie's absence at this busy time of year poses a problem for us. I've discussed the matter with the head concierge, Mr. Kronenberg, and he agrees with me that you should take her place."

This wasn't what she'd been expecting and Elizabeth struggled to process this new information. For a moment she pictured herself sitting at Annemarie's curvy little French desk in an alcove off the lobby, impressing guests with her knowledge and expertise. Or not, she thought, assailed by doubt. Did she really have the skills and experience the job required? She was still learning to find her way around Palm Beach. But, she realized, brightening, this might be a genuine opportunity. And Mr. Dimitri wouldn't have suggested it if he didn't have confidence in her abilities.

Finally, she spoke. "I'm very flattered," she said. "I'll do my best."

"Good," he said. "You can start tomorrow."

Elizabeth was seated at Annemarie's desk the next morning, waiting impatiently for Toni's arrival. She couldn't wait to see her friend's reaction, and Toni didn't disappoint when she took her place at the reception desk. Her eyes rounded in astonishment when she spotted Elizabeth and she hurried right over.

"What's this?" she asked. "Did you get a promotion?"

Elizabeth shrugged. "It's temporary. Annemarie's got Epstein-Barr."

"Lucky you."

"We'll see. I feel like a fake. I don't really know what I'm doing."

Toni grinned. "Just pretend," she said in parting, dashing back to her post when she spotted the head concierge, Walter Kronenberg, stepping out of the elevator and heading in Elizabeth's direction. He was a tall man with gray hair brushed straight back; from his stiff, formal manner Elizabeth suspected he might be a retired military officer.

She stood up to greet him, and said, "I'm very honored to take Annemarie's place. I know it's a challenging job but I'm a fast learner and a hard worker."

"Very well, Elizabeth," he said. "Now we must get to work. You have a lot to learn, and we're under pressure with the Gruber event in just two weeks." He sat down in her chair, indicating she should take one of the chairs provided for guests and sit beside him. "First of all, you need the computer password."

Elizabeth knew that concierges had a higher level of access to the Cavendish data bank and was interested to see what information was now available to her.

"I must warn you, all of this information is highly confidential. We don't want to be reading in the *National Enquirer* that one of our guests has a passion for cashew nuts."

Elizabeth was tempted to giggle but stifled the impulse; she didn't think Mr. Kronenberg was joking. "Of course not," she said with a serious nod, watching as he wrote the password on a slip of paper.

"Got it?" he asked, and when she nodded, he tore the paper into tiny bits, which he pocketed.

Elizabeth had a strange sense of dislocation. Was she being trained as an assistant concierge in a posh hotel or was she being briefed for a mission to defend national security?

"Now, Elizabeth," Mr. Kronenberg continued, "on occasion one of our guests will require access to the hotel safe when neither I nor Mr. Dimitri will be available. In that case, you will need the combination."

Elizabeth swallowed hard. This was quite a bit more responsibility than she expected and she remembered Toni's warning that if something went wrong, the staff would be blamed. "Right," she said.

"The combination is in this box," he

continued, producing a small gray metal cash box from a side drawer. "The key to this box is kept with the paper clips."

Elizabeth opened the shallow central drawer and found the compartment filled with paper clips and dug through them, producing a small, silver key.

"Remember," he said, "it is most unlikely that both Mr. Dimitri and I would be unavailable but it does occasionally happen and we don't want our guests to be inconvenienced."

"I understand," Elizabeth said.

"You must tell no one about the combination," he warned in a most serious tone.

"Of course not."

"But I think you will enjoy this job," he said, standing up. "You'll find our guests are most delightful and you'll see that it's a pleasure to help them. Sometimes their requests are challenging, but there's great satisfaction in coming up with the perfect solution." A quick smile flickered across his lips, then he wished her good luck and left Elizabeth on her own.

She had a busy morning, arranging horseback riding for one guest, making dinner reservations for several others, and changing an airplane flight for Mrs. Fahnstock, who had decided to stay a few more days.

Around eleven she caught a breather, but when she glanced across the lobby at the reception desk and gave Toni a little wave, she only got an odd little smirk in response. She was about to go over and ask what the problem was when another guest approached her desk.

"I'm sorry to bother you," said a tall, good-looking guy in his early thirties, removing his Ray-Bans to reveal bright blue eyes. He was dressed casually in a polo shirt and khaki shorts with Teva sandals on his bare feet.

"Not a problem," Elizabeth said, taking in his tousled, sun-bleached hair, broad shoulders, and lean torso and finding him terribly attractive. "I'm here to help."

CHAPTER 2

"Who was the good-looking guy?" Toni asked, seating herself beside Elizabeth at the scuffed Formica-topped table in the employees' break room. The two always had lunch together, usually eating bag lunches they brought from home.

"I don't know," Elizabeth said, prying the lid off a plastic container of salad. "He wanted to know where he could get a flat bike tire fixed and I sent him to the sports center."

Toni's eyebrows shot up. "You should have got his name so you could Google him."

Elizabeth speared a cherry tomato. "He just had a simple question and I was on the phone with Delta, trying to get them to drop the change fee for Mrs. Fahnstock."

"I would have dropped Delta and called back later. He wasn't wearing a wedding ring, you know."

"How do you know that?" Elizabeth asked.

"What have you got, X-ray vision or something?"

"I make a point of checking," Toni replied, licking the last of the yogurt off her spoon. "It saves a lot of trouble later."

"Rings can be removed, you know," Elizabeth said. "They're not permanently attached."

"I know," Toni admitted in a rueful tone, taking a sip of Diet Coke. "Maybe men should be required to get tattoos on their ring fingers when they get married. So tell me, did Dimitri give you access to the supersecret database?"

As all Cavendish employees knew, there were various levels of access to the company's famous database. Desk clerks were among those with the lowest access, mainly to credit card account numbers and personal preferences; concierges inevitably accumulated more data as they maintained records of guest requests; and executives like Mr. Dimitri had the highest level of information, which according to rumor was more complete than data collected by the FBI and CIA. All employees, whatever their level, were required to sign strict confidentiality agreements and anyone caught sharing information was subject to immediate dismissal.

Elizabeth remembered Mr. Kronenberg's warning and shrugged. "So far I haven't seen anything that would interest the *National Enquirer,* if that's what you want to know."

Toni ran her finger around the top of the Coke can. "I was thinking that maybe you could tip me off about rich male guests, say whether they're married or not."

"And their credit limits?" Elizabeth teased.

"Well, yeah, that would be good, too."

Elizabeth wasn't exactly surprised at Toni's request, but she was a little hurt that Toni would ask her to put her job in jeopardy. "No way. I'm not taking any chances. This temporary job could be a big break for me." She paused. "I've already been scolded by Mr. Dimitri for failing to address a guest by name. Apparently the concierge gets an IM alert when a guest checks in, but if I miss it for some reason I'm supposed to politely ask them to introduce themselves. It's a bit awkward — I'm not comfortable doing it."

Toni shrugged. "The guests love hearing their names. It makes them feel like they're the lords of the manor and we're their servants or something."

Elizabeth stood up. "Yeah, well, back in Tinker's Cove, where I come from, people treat everybody the same. It doesn't matter if they're millionaires or garbage collectors."

"Maybe that's fine for you," Toni said, "but personally I'd much rather marry a millionaire than a garbage man."

"I guess I would, too," Elizabeth admitted, laughing.

Elizabeth was ordering a same-day flower delivery for a guest who had forgotten his mother's birthday when the good-looking biker reappeared.

"Hi," he said, grinning and revealing a prominent set of very large, very white teeth.

Elizabeth held up a finger, indicating she was on the phone, and he seated himself in one of the chairs provided for guests. She took the opportunity of looking him over while she completed negotiating the flower order, noting his tanned face and arms, his long, muscular legs, the chunky gold watch on his wrist. Toni was right — there was no wedding ring. Finally ending the call, she smiled and asked, "What can I do for you?"

"I just wanted to thank you for helping me out earlier. They fixed the bike for me at the sports center, no questions asked."

Elizabeth, who had gone to college in Boston, thought she detected a hint of a Boston accent, which she liked. "Guests come first at Cavendish," she said, repeating the company motto in a teasing voice.

"I guess I better fess up," he said. "I'm not actually a guest. I was just biking by when the tire went flat." He bit his lip. "My name's Chris Kennedy, by the way."

"Elizabeth Stone."

"I know," he said, indicating her name tag.

Elizabeth blushed. "Well, maybe you'll be a guest in the future."

"I'd like that. But in the meantime, I was hoping you'd go out to dinner with me. How about tonight?"

The request caught Elizabeth off guard. "Oh!" she exclaimed. "I guess that would be okay."

"Don't sound so enthusiastic," he said sarcastically.

Again, Elizabeth blushed. "It's just . . ."

"I know," he said. "I had you at a disadvantage. So, shall I pick you up here?"

Elizabeth thought of the ratty old shorts and T-shirt she'd worn to work that morning before changing into her uniform in the hotel locker room. It was hardly the outfit she wanted to wear on a first date. "No, I'd like to go home and change out of this uniform," she said.

He tilted his head. "I think it's kind of cute."

Rolling her eyes, she wrote her address and phone number on a slip of paper. "What time?" she asked, giving it to him.

"Seven?"

"See you then."

Chris had no sooner left than Toni dashed across the lobby. "So what was that all about?" she asked.

"He asked me out to dinner."

"That was fast," Toni said. "Who is he?"

"His name's Chris Kennedy."

"Kennedy! He's probably one of *those* Kennedys. They have a place here in Palm Beach, you know."

"He does have a Boston accent," Elizabeth said.

"And those teeth. Those are definitely Kennedy teeth."

Elizabeth was doubtful. "You think?"

"Absolutely. And no wedding ring. That makes him husband material — with money. That's the best kind."

"We'll see," Elizabeth said, not nearly as convinced as her friend. Chris Kennedy was good-looking and she certainly found him attractive, but she didn't really know anything about him. She'd been raised to be cautious in matters of the heart and she wanted to know what kind of person he was before she got too involved.

When her doorbell rang precisely at seven, Elizabeth was ready, dressed in a pastel tunic, a pair of skinny white jeans, and her prized Jack Rogers sandals. She'd figured Chris was a casual sort of guy and didn't want to be too dressed up. She'd used a light hand with her makeup, too, applying only mascara and a slick of lip gloss. When she hurried out of her apartment and down the stairs, meeting him at the door to the apartment block, she was glad she'd worn pants because he had arrived on a motorcycle.

"I hope the bike's okay," he said. "I have a spare helmet."

"Fine with me," Elizabeth said, eager for a bit of an adventure.

"Great," he said, giving her the helmet. "I'll take good care of you."

"You better, 'cause my dad will come roaring into town from Maine and track you down and wring your neck if anything bad happens to me." Setting the helmet on her head, she discovered the straps were too long.

"I can fix that," he said, bending down to adjust them. Feeling his warm hands at her neck and scenting his minty fresh breath, she wondered what it would be like to kiss him. "There," he said, straightening up. "Even your dad would approve."

"I'm not sure of that," she said, climbing on the seat and wrapping her arms around his waist. He was every bit as lean as he looked, she discovered, feeling the firm muscles beneath his polo shirt.

He laughed. "I wouldn't blame him, but I'm really the kind of guy even an overprotective dad can't object to," he said as they rolled off down the driveway.

It was a warm evening and dusk was lingering as they rode over the bridge and along Ocean Boulevard, where moored boats bobbed in the peaceful navy blue water. Some had strings of twinkling lights, a few even had Christmas trees fixed to their masts, and Elizabeth thought of the annual arrival of Santa by boat back home in Tinker's Cove. She had a brief moment of homesickness but Chris took a curve a little bit fast and she tightened her grip around his waist and discovered she was definitely enjoying the present moment, and this ride with this exciting guy.

He pulled up at a tiki bar by the beach, where tables with shaggy grass umbrellas were set up on the sand, and they ordered captain's plates and cold beer. The night air was warm and silky when they seated themselves at one of the tables, waiting for their number to be called. Flaming tiki torches illuminated their faces and Elizabeth thought she was a very long way from home.

"So your family is in Maine?" he asked, taking that first sip of beer.

"Yup," Elizabeth said, meeting his blue eyes. "I grew up in Tinker's Cove, a little town on the coast. My mom's a reporter for a local newspaper and my dad's a restoration carpenter. I went to Chamberlain College in Boston, and this is my first real job, though I worked summers back home." She licked a bit of foam off her lip. "What about you? You sound like you come from Boston."

"Guilty," he said, grinning. "I was supposed to go to Harvard — that's what the family wanted — but I love sailing and biking and I chose the University of Florida instead. I went on to law school and now I'm working with a, uh, conservation trust."

"That must be interesting," Elizabeth said, impressed. "And it's a meaningful job that makes a difference, that makes the world a better place."

He raised his shoulders. "I don't know about that, but it does pay the rent. What about you? Do you like your job at the

Cavendish?"

"I guess it's okay," she replied, "but I don't think I want to do it for the rest of my life. I sort of fell into it because I had a little experience. I worked summers at an inn back home." The sun was long gone and they were enclosed in a flickering circle of light from the tiki torches. Elizabeth slipped off her sandals and curled her toes, feeling the cool sand beneath her feet. "Don't you miss winter?" she asked. "I just can't get used to the idea of Christmas without snow. Instead of balsam wreaths they've got pink and white poinsettias in the hotel — it seems so wrong. I don't mind poinsettias but they ought to be red."

Chris shrugged. "I guess you get used to it. It's Christmas everywhere, after all. When I was a kid I had this book: *Christmas Around the World.* Eskimos sitting around Christmas trees in their igloos and African kids opening presents in grass huts and Japanese kids hanging up stockings in their pagodas."

"I'm not sure that book was culturally correct," Elizabeth said skeptically.

"Now that you mention it," he said, laughing, "I don't think it was." Hearing their number called, Chris got up and returned with a tray loaded with fried fish, French fries, and coleslaw.

"That's enough food for an army," Elizabeth said, taking her plate.

"Eat up," he said. "You'll need some insulation when you go back north for Christmas. You are going, aren't you?"

"No," Elizabeth said, biting into a fry. "All December vacations are canceled for this big party Jonah Gruber is giving. He's some rich Wall Street guy who's booked the entire hotel for four days. Lots of VIPs are coming and everybody's going to have to work extra hours." She popped the rest of the fry into her mouth. "I was really looking forward to seeing my little nephew, Patrick."

"That's too bad," Chris said. "Christmas is all about family. We have this tradition — we all go skiing in New Hampshire. My dad, Joe, he's a great skier, and my cousin, Robbie, he's a fiend on the slopes."

Elizabeth noticed little stars in the sky; the water was a smooth black surface reflecting the lights on the moored boats. Joe and Robbie, she thought, those were names she'd heard in connection with *the* Kennedy family. Joe Kennedy ran a program that provided heating oil to low income people in Massachusetts and Robbie was a nickname for Robert, JFK's brother who was also assassinated. Cousin Robbie might be his son or grandson. Should she come right out and ask him? Would that be pushy? Rude? Too personal for a first date?

"Penny for your thoughts," Chris said.

"Oh, sorry." Elizabeth decided that she certainly didn't want to seem like a celebrity hound or, worse, a gold digger. "I was just looking at the stars. Isn't the sky beautiful tonight?"

"Sure is," he answered, but he wasn't looking at the sky. He was gazing at Elizabeth.

CHAPTER 3

The next morning Elizabeth was still basking in the afterglow of her date with Chris. She'd never been one of those girls like Toni who made up a checklist for the perfect mate, but if she had, Chris would have a check in every box. He was tall and good-looking. He had a good job as a lawyer working in the public interest. Family was important to him. And he'd been a terrific date, fun to be with and considerate. When they'd finally ended the evening, standing in front of her door, he'd given her a long, lingering kiss that made her wish for more. But he didn't press her. He said he wanted to see her again and then he was gone.

Toni, of course, couldn't wait to dissect the date. "So how was it?" she demanded, encountering Elizabeth in the locker room, where she was putting on her Cavendish blazer. "Did you go all the way?"

Elizabeth was shocked. "Not on a first

date! Besides, he was a perfect gentleman."

Toni narrowed her eyes. "Maybe he wasn't that into you."

"He sure seemed interested. We had a great time and he said he wanted to see me again."

"They always say that," Toni warned. "I bet you'll never hear from him again."

That idea bothered Elizabeth more than she cared to let on. "Well, my mother always says never run after a man because they're like streetcars — another one always comes along."

"Well, if that's the way you feel, I guess it's okay then. Too bad you didn't have that spark, that chemistry."

"Yeah," Elizabeth said, thinking their chemistry had been just fine. Every time she thought about Chris, which was pretty much all the time, she felt the stirrings of desire. And once seated at her concierge desk, she found her heart jumped every time the phone rang, in hope that he was calling. He didn't call, however, and she was kept busy by the guests and their endless demands. Busy as she was, she couldn't forget Toni's prophecy that he wasn't that into her, which squatted like some evil toad in the back of her mind.

Then, when he finally did call, she didn't

have time to talk. She'd been conscripted to assist Layla Fine, the professional party planner Jonah Gruber had hired to organize the festive gala. Mr. Kronenberg had minced no words when he gave her the assignment. "You'll find she has a rather forceful personality," he said with a sigh. "Just do whatever she wants and we'll add it to Mr. Gruber's account."

Elizabeth nodded, thinking the bill for the four-day gala was going to be astronomical. Gruber probably wasn't paying the rack rate, which began at over five hundred dollars for a room in season and went up to over five thousand for the top-floor suites; she was sure he'd negotiated a sizable discount. Even so, this was a big deal for the hotel and now, suddenly, she was responsible for making it all go smoothly.

"I just know we're going to get along like a house afire," Layla told her, plunking her tiny little bottom in one of the gilt chairs next to Elizabeth's desk. Up close, Elizabeth could see that Layla wasn't quite as young as she first appeared; long lines ran from her nose to either side of her mouth, and the skin around her eyes was creepy. Nevertheless, she was a bundle of energy and gave a youthful impression, tossing her long blond hair extensions this way and that and dashing about on impossibly high, needle-thin stiletto heels. "So, first let's see what the hotel can offer in the way of activities. These folks are going to be here for four days and we need to provide lots of fun things for them to do."

"We offer lots of options for our guests," Elizabeth said, trying to put Chris out of her mind so she could concentrate on the task at hand. "There's a fitness center, of course, and we're right on the beach. There's boating, golf, tennis, all right here. And I can arrange for horseback riding, helicopter rides, pretty much anything anyone wants."

Layla was shaking her head. "That's all well and good, but these are very special people, the crème de la crème, and they will want unique entertainments, things that ordinary people can't do."

Elizabeth was stumped, painfully aware that she was an ordinary person and didn't have a clue what the extraordinary people did. "What do you have in mind?"

"Well, say a special performance at a theater, or perhaps a private showing in an art museum, things like that. Danny Simpson, the tennis star, is one of the guests. Maybe we could have an exhibition match with Sharapova. That would be fun, wouldn't it? Boy versus girl?"

Elizabeth had a sinking feeling; she knew she was out of her depth here. "I'll do my best," she began.

"Oh, don't worry — I'll help. I'll give you names and numbers. We'll plan four days that they'll never forget." Layla turned her head, giving her wavy extensions yet another toss, and studied the holiday decorations in the lobby, which Elizabeth considered a tasteful assortment of seasonal flowering plants and wreaths, with a few twinkly lights here and there. "You know, these decorations are rather restrained, wouldn't you say?"

"That's intentional," Elizabeth said. "We cater to a wide variety of guests here — Jewish people and Muslims and quite a few Asians and Indians — and they don't celebrate Christmas. It's supposed to be seasonal, not particularly Christmas."

"Well, we'll have to change that," Layla declared. "We need a lot more sparkle, a lot more bling. It's the Blingle Bells Ball!"

When Layla finally left, leaving Elizabeth with several single-spaced pages listing all the things she wanted her to do, Elizabeth tried to return Chris's call. She dialed his cell but only got voice mail, so she left a quick message saying she was sorry they hadn't had time to talk but she'd been busy at work. She half expected him to return her call immediately; she'd called his cell phone, after all, and knew he always carried it. When he didn't call back, she reluctantly concluded it was because he'd decided to ignore her call and blow her off, just like Toni had predicted. She found that thought terribly depressing and threw herself into her work.

It wasn't until she was headed home in her used Corolla, three hours later than usual due to the extra work for the Gruber party, that her cell phone finally rang.

"Hi!" he said, "I missed you. Want to go for a beer or something?"

Elizabeth's heart leaped — he missed her! But she was dead tired. Layla had run her off her feet, trimming dozens of fake white Christmas trees, making calls, packing elaborate gift baskets for Gruber's guests, and fending off reporters who'd gotten wind of the exclusive gala and wanted information. And then there'd been a stressful one-on-one session with Dan Wrayburn, the security director, who had warned her about data breaches and computer viruses and worms. "A beer would be great," she finally said, deciding she didn't want to put him off and risk the chance of letting his ardor cool.

"Great," he said. "Do you want to meet me somewhere? Say Charley's Crab?"

Elizabeth agreed, thinking she was glad she'd worn her Lilly dress to work that morning, instead of her usual workout clothes, just in case Chris called.

He was waiting for her in front of the casually elegant restaurant, dressed in khakis and a pale blue polo shirt, with boat shoes and no socks. She smiled, aware that she was a sucker for the preppy look.

"What are you smiling about?" he asked, when they were seated at a table in a cozy corner of the bar.

"I'm just giddy with relief," she said. "I've been dealing with this awful woman all day. She's the party planner Gruber hired to organize this shindig and she's a piece of work."

"Well, now you can relax," he said. "What will you have?"

"A glass of chardonnay," she said.

He nodded at the waitress and ordered the wine for her and a Sam Adams for himself. "You can take the boy out of Boston but you can't take the Boston out of the boy," he quipped.

"My dad loves their Winter Lager," Elizabeth said. "But you hardly need that down here."

"Sometimes the nights get chilly," he said, with a mischievous grin.

Elizabeth didn't quite know how to take this, so she decided to make a joke. "I know — that's why I wear flannel to bed, even here in Florida."

"I hope you're teasing me," he said, when their drinks arrived. He raised his beer and tapped her glass. "Here's to Yankee girls, or one very special Yankee girl."

Elizabeth laughed. "I don't comb my hair with codfish bones," she said, referring to the silly rhyme she'd learned as a child.

"I like short hair on girls," he said, reaching across the table and smoothing a lock of her hair. "You don't get all tangled up in it."

She took a swallow of wine. "I've got to get an early start tomorrow. I've got a seven o'clock meeting with the security director."

"What does he want with you?" Chris asked, in a casual tone.

"I don't know." Elizabeth shook her head. "Something about the jewels, I think. You know, the whole point of this party is for Gruber to show off these jewels he bought for his wife for millions of dollars. The hotel doesn't want responsibility for them until

379

the last minute, but Layla, the party planner, told me that they've got to come sooner because of some photo shoot for *Town & Country* magazine." She paused, thinking perhaps she was saying too much, and changed the subject from the jewels. "The photographer is only available on one day. His name is Sammie Wong. I never heard of him but Layla says he's famous."

"I've heard of Sammie Wong. He had a show here at Four Arts," said Chris. "It will be interesting to see what he does with the jewels. When are they supposed to arrive?"

Elizabeth was tired and the wine wasn't helping. "I don't know, I guess I'll find out tomorrow," she said, stifling a yawn.

"You're beat," he said, laughing. "What do you say we call it a night? I've got to catch an early flight to Seattle for a conference tomorrow. But save Saturday night for me?"

"Okay." Elizabeth kept her voice cool so as not to reveal her fluttering heart. "It's a date."

But when Saturday finally rolled around, Layla insisted she needed Elizabeth to finalize the seating plan for the Blingle Bells Ball and she had to cancel her date. "I'm so sorry," she told Chris, breaking the bad news on the phone, "but I have to work tonight."

"You're working an awful lot," Chris grumbled.

"Tell me about it. It's temporary, just until this Gruber event is over."

"So what all do you have to do? Fluff the pillows in the Presidential Suite?"

"No, housekeeping does that. It's mostly helping the party planner. She had me trimming awful fake white Christmas trees for days, and wrapping gift baskets and making plans for special events including a celebrity tennis match and a golf tournament and studio visits with artists. You know, I thought I knew how the other half lives, but this isn't the other half, it's the one percent!"

"You must be getting some time off," Chris said. "What about tomorrow? It's Sunday."

"Actually, I am off tomorrow, but I've got to clean house and do laundry and buy some groceries. I've been working ten and eleven hours a day."

"Okay, we'll grocery shop," Chris said. "It'll be fun. Let's say I'll pick you up at one, we'll get a late brunch, and afterward we'll go to Publix, and then I'll cook dinner for you."

Elizabeth couldn't stop smiling; this guy

was too good to be true. "See you tomorrow," she said.

Later that afternoon Elizabeth was surprised when Chris paid her a visit at work. She was at her desk, arranging for limousines to pick up guests at the airport, when she looked up and saw Chris standing there.

"I couldn't wait until tomorrow," he said. "How's it going?"

"Crazy, crazy. I know it's hard to believe, but there's a terrible shortage of limousines in Palm Beach."

"I could offer my services," he said with a grin.

"I don't think a motorcycle will cut it, not with these folks."

He seated himself, propping one ankle on the other knee. "So when is this party starting?"

"The guests are arriving on the sixteenth — that's next Friday — but Jonah and Noelle are coming earlier, to get ready." She sighed. "And then there's those darn jewels."

"Oh, yeah?" Chris's voice was studiedly casual. "What's that got to do with you?" he asked, gazing into her eyes.

"Well, I've got to schedule the delivery and make sure hotel security has the details," Elizabeth said, thinking perhaps she was saying too much. "This thing is turning into a nightmare."

Chris looked concerned. "What do you mean? Problems with Brinks?"

Elizabeth decided she wasn't going to say anything more about the jewels. "It's just all so over the top. Layla — she's the party planner — well, the way she acts you'd think this was life and death and it's really just a rich guy showing off. There are people who are really in terrible situations — dreadful flooding in Indonesia and in Africa they're starving and getting raped and killed by rogue militias. But Layla seems to think the world will end if the vichyssoise isn't chilled correctly or the roses are the wrong color."

Chris looked amused. "So you're a closet revolutionary?"

Elizabeth gave him a crooked grin. "This thing is turning me into one, that's for sure."

"A revolutionary with access to all that supersecret, confidential information about the masters of the universe. You could be dangerous."

Remembering Wrayburn's warnings, Elizabeth grew wary. What did Chris know about the database? And why was he even mentioning it? "Oh, I'm far too insignificant to see much of anything except whether the guests prefer plain or sparkling mineral water."

Chris laughed. "Well, I guess I better let you get back to work." He stood up, then leaned down and whispered in her ear, "See you tomorrow."

His warm lips brushed her ear and she wished for a moment that she could lean against him, like she had on the motorcycle, feeling his body against hers. Then she remembered where she was and gave him a businesslike smile. "See you then," she said.

The moment he was gone, Toni dashed across the lobby. "What was that all about?" she demanded.

"He just stopped by to say hi," Elizabeth said. She knew she was blushing and it was making her furious; she didn't want Toni to know how much she liked Chris.

"He's awfully cute," Toni said, "but I don't think he's really a member of the Kennedy clan. Did you hear about that guy in Boston who was pretending to be a Rockefeller?"

"I did," Elizabeth said. It was all over the news, you really couldn't miss it. But Chris wasn't like that, at least she didn't think he was. For one thing, he'd never actually said he was a member of the Kennedy clan.

"The funny thing is, that guy never claimed to be a rich Rockefeller. He just

384

sort of let people assume it," Toni continued, as if reading her mind.

"Well, I don't care if he's JFK's great-nephew or not," Elizabeth said. "I'm just getting to know him."

"I'm only saying this 'cause I think he might be as fake as that Rolex he wears."

"It's fake? How can you tell?"

"I can tell," Toni said. "And those polo shirts he wears — they're from Target."

"So he's careful with his money. That's not a crime," Elizabeth insisted. But as she said the words, she remembered how uncomfortable she'd felt when Chris mentioned the database. Maybe Toni was on to something and he didn't really like her but was only trying to use her for some purpose of his own.

"I just think you'd better be careful, that's all," Toni said, hurrying back to the reception desk.

Elizabeth went back to her list of limo companies but her thoughts were miles away. Toni had upset her and she figured that was her intention. She was probably just jealous because Elizabeth had a boyfriend. Or did she? They'd only had two dates, actually one and a half, and here she was falling head over heels, struggling to keep her mind on her work when all she wanted to think about was that kiss. That one kiss.

She was being ridiculous, she told herself. It was never good to let a guy know you really liked him. If she kept this up she'd scare him off. It was better to play hard to get, that's what everybody said. She decided she was simply going to put Chris Kennedy completely out of her mind. She'd throw herself into her work and wouldn't give him a single thought until one o'clock tomorrow.

But when Sunday dawned, she was in a state of high anticipation. She quickly tidied her little apartment, showered and dried her hair, and finally confronted the problem of what to wear. Shorts and a tank top? Would that be too revealing? What about a skirt? No good on a motorcycle! Jeans again? Then the phone rang and she learned she didn't have to decide what to wear after all.

"I'm really sorry," he said. "Something's come up and I have to go out of town."

Elizabeth's heart fell to the floor and landed with a thud. "Oh," was all she could say.

"I was really looking forward to being with you," he said.

"It's too bad," she said, determined not to let him know how disappointed she was.

"But I really have a lot to do anyway."

"I'll call you when I get back, okay?"

"If you want," she said, trying to sound as if it didn't matter to her whether he called or not.

"Oh, I want," he said, in a thick voice.

"Have a good trip," she said, hanging up and grabbing a handful of tissues as the tears started to flow. Finally wiping her eyes, she decided she didn't know what was worse: Chris calling off their date or having to admit it to Toni on Monday morning.

As she expected, Toni couldn't wait to ask if she'd had a good time on her date with Chris when they met in the locker room.

Elizabeth opened her locker, took out her makeup bag, and concentrated on applying a fresh coat of lip gloss. "Never happened," she said with a shrug, waving the little wand.

"Why not? What happened?"

Elizabeth pressed her lips together, then examined the effect in the mirror on her locker door. "He had a business trip."

"Or he met somebody else," Toni said.

"Or he met somebody else," Elizabeth repeated with a shrug. Honestly, she thought, she ought to get an Academy Award for acting.

Toni's eyebrows rose in astonishment.

"Aren't you upset?"

"It was just a couple of dates," Elizabeth said. "And frankly, I'm too busy to worry about it. You know, the jewels are coming today. It's going to be a madhouse around here."

The arrival of the Imperial Parure was supposed to be a highly guarded secret. Jonah Gruber had outbid an Arab sheik and a Japanese industrialist for the set, which included an emerald and ruby necklace with a removable pendant featuring the twenty-three-carat Star of Bethlehem diamond that could also be worn as a brooch, plus a tiara, two bracelets, and a ring. His winning bid was many millions above the presale estimate and security was naturally a top concern. Mr. Dimitri had stressed that fact at a special staff meeting, and Dan Wrayburn had bombarded employees with memos threatening immediate dismissal to anyone who leaked information about the jewels. Nevertheless, Elizabeth noticed a handful of reporters and photographers gathering outside the hotel doors shortly before the armored truck was due to arrive.

"How did they find out?" she asked Layla, who was on hand for the delivery.

"Probably Gruber tipped them off himself," she replied.

"Why would he do that?"

"He paid a lot for those baubles and he wants to get his money's worth in publicity. He's got a deal with *Town and Country* magazine; Sammie Wong's going to photograph Noelle wearing the jewels. She's actually here and I need you to help out."

This was news to Elizabeth. "She's here? Now?" Elizabeth asked.

"Yup. We took advantage of the jewelry delivery to sneak her in through the hotel garage. She's waiting up in the Royal Suite, but that's top secret. Don't you breathe a word of it to that crowd out there."

"I wouldn't," Elizabeth said.

"Good." Layla handed her a sheaf of papers. "This is a press release. You can distribute it once the jewels are secured. Then I want you to meet me upstairs in the Royal Suite."

The moment the elevator doors closed behind Layla the armored truck rolled up and the media gang went into action, snapping photos and yelling questions to the guards as they unloaded the metal-clad case containing the jewels. Extra doormen, actually security guards dressed as doormen, blocked access to the lobby, and Dan Wrayburn escorted the armored truck guards to Mr. Dimitri's office, where the hotel safe was located. Once she was sure the recently reinforced office door was tightly closed and the jewels safe inside, Elizabeth stepped through the entrance, distributing the press releases to the crowd of reporters who were clamoring for information outside. They still peppered her with questions: "Did you see the jewels? Are they really worth forty-seven million? Is the hotel worried about jewel thieves?"

"It's all in the press release," she said, ducking back inside and leaving the doormen to handle the crowd. Then she was hurrying upstairs to the Royal Suite, her special knowledge bubbling inside her. She was one of the few who knew that Noelle Jones was actually in the hotel; she was going to see, and perhaps even handle, the incredibly valuable Imperial Parure. If only the folks back home in Tinker's Cove, Maine, could see her now!

When Layla answered her knock and opened the door, Elizabeth had to restrain herself from exclaiming "Wow!" The hotel's four best suites, the Imperial, the Royal, the Majestic, and the Presidential, never failed to impress. Over fifteen hundred square feet apiece, they were bigger than her apartment, and included luxurious bedrooms, a living room complete with wet bar, a dining area, and numerous balconies with ocean views. The decor was elegant and restrained, so as not to compete with the fabulous views.

But even more breathtaking than the view, was the Imperial Parure, which had arrived ahead of her and was displayed in its case on a white lacquered coffee table. Elizabeth couldn't take her eyes off the rubies and emeralds. There must have been hundreds all told. And the huge diamond glittered so brightly in the sunlight that poured through the windows.

Sammie Wong was beside himself with excitement. "This is going to be great," he said, and Elizabeth could almost see the wheels turning in that shaved head, behind those bright, black eyes, imagining the photo possibilities. He was a tiny man, dressed in a black turtleneck and loose pants, bouncing around on bright aqua spring-loaded athletic shoes. "I think we should have the jewels in incongruous settings. . . ."

"Like the bathtub?" Noelle suggested. She was a stunning woman, with a curvy body, luscious red lips, and long black hair that tumbled halfway down her back. She was dressed in a white knit dress that clung to her figure and had discarded a fabulous white fur coat, which lay in a luxurious heap on the carpeted floor.

"We'll see," Sammie said, picking up the emerald and ruby tiara and holding it up to admire it. Then he set it gently on Noelle's head.

"Ohmigod!" she exclaimed. "This thing weighs a ton!"

"Bear up, dearie," Sammie said, disregarding her complaint and hanging the enormous necklace around her neck. The huge Star of Bethlehem diamond nestled just above her breasts, its facets catching the light and splashing the walls and ceiling with patches of shimmering color.

"Look! It's a rainbow!" Sammie exclaimed, pointing at the scraps of vibrant color that danced with Noelle's slightest movements. Then he slipped the ring with its huge emerald on her finger, and wrapped each wrist in a band of alternating rubies and emeralds. Noelle stood perfectly still in front of the pale green silk draperies that screened the room's French doors, and Elizabeth thought she looked like one of those bejeweled royals in an Elizabethan painting. All she was lacking was a lace ruff and a long skirt.

Sammie was already snapping photos, but this was only the beginning. Lugging bags of clothing and props, Elizabeth followed the photographer and his subject through the hotel as Noelle was photographed in the jewels and a swimsuit at the hotel pool, in the jewels and a Chanel suit at a table in the hotel restaurant, in the jewels and an evening gown in the ballroom.

Finally they returned to the Royal Suite, where Noelle started stripping off the jewels and tossing them on the bed. "Whew," she said, "those suckers are heavy, and that necklace poked into my skin. Look!" Pointing with a manicured finger, she indicated a slight, whitened dent on her tanned chest, where the Star of Bethlehem had been.

"You poor thing!" Layla commiserated. "But we're done. You did great and now you can rest."

"No, not done," Sammie said, pulling back the bedcovers and tossing the pillows into a pile, which he covered with the white fur coat.

Noelle smiled slyly. "I think I know what you have in mind."

Sammie winked. "Okay with you? You strip?"

"Sure," Noelle shrugged, slipping out of the terry cloth robe she was wearing and casually arranging her naked body on the fur-covered pillows.

"Beautiful, beautiful," Sammie cooed, lovingly placing the tiara on her head, and once again wrapping her arms in the enormous bracelets.

Elizabeth was stunned, watching the casual way in which Noelle stripped and allowed Sammie to arrange her body in various poses.

"Don't look so surprised," Layla said, amused at her reaction. "She's done this before."

"She has?" Elizabeth whispered, clutching the terry robe.

"Sure. She used to be a porn star. She did it all in front of the camera — and I mean everything."

Elizabeth's jaw dropped. "Really?"

"And she was a centerfold for *Playboy* magazine."

"Where I come from, some people never take their long johns off all winter."

Now it was Layla's turn to be horrified. "Really?"

"Just joking," said Elizabeth, who was growing more comfortable with the situation. If Noelle wasn't bothered, she decided, she shouldn't be either. And she could see why Sammie was so enthusiastic; the contrasting textures of Noelle's flawless caramel skin, the lush white fur, and the glittering jewels made for fabulous visuals.

Finally, the staccato clicking of the camera stopped, and Sammie's assistant handed him a towel, which the exhausted photographer used to wipe his brow.

"About time," his subject declared, yanking the tiara off her head and tossing it on the floor. The necklace, bracelets, and ring soon followed as she stretched, sauntered casually up to Elizabeth and grabbed the robe, then continued on into the bathroom, still entirely nude.

Getting a nod from Layla, Elizabeth scrambled to pick up the jewels and replace them in the case. She could hardly believe she was handling them, actually touching these amazing gems worth millions of dollars. She laid one bracelet across her wrist, examining the effect, imagining what it would be like to wear them all. Then, afraid she would be seen, she tucked the bracelet into its compartment. All the jewelry fit beautifully into the hollows of the velvet-lined case designed to hold each piece. . . . All except the huge emerald ring, which seemed to be missing. It had been there a moment ago, Elizabeth thought, panicking. She'd seen Noelle pull it off. Where was it?

Horrified, Elizabeth began searching through the tumbled bedclothes. How could

Noelle be so careless? she wondered anxiously. The thing was worth a fortune — all the jewels were — and she had thrown them around as if they were nothing to her.

Sammie and his assistant were packing up the photographic equipment, Layla had followed Noelle into the bathroom, so only Elizabeth was concerned about the missing ring. She picked up the pillows and stacked them on the nightstand, she pulled off the sheets and bedspread, she looked under the bed. . . .

And finally found the priceless bauble under the nightstand, where it had rolled into a tangle of wires. Her hand was shaking when she slipped the ring into its groove and snapped the case shut.

"He doesn't really love me," Noelle was telling Layla, as the two emerged from the bathroom. She was wearing the robe now, and her feet were in the floppy terry slippers the hotel provided. "I'm just another acquisition, like these jewels."

So that's why she doesn't care about them, Elizabeth thought with a flash of insight. "Do you have the key?" she asked Layla.

"The key! What did I do with the key?" Layla exclaimed, clutching her head with her hands.

Her panic was contagious and everybody started scrambling, searching for the key to the jewelry case, tossing the contents of the room this way and that. Everybody except Noelle, who drifted out of the bedroom and into the living room, where she settled into a plush upholstered chair and called room service, ordering a turkey club sandwich and a double Scotch.

Finally, when the bedroom had been thoroughly tossed and everybody had searched everywhere, Layla triumphantly proclaimed, "I've found it!" and held up the key. "It was in my pocket the whole time."

CHAPTER 4

Elizabeth let out a huge sigh of relief when the hotel safe clicked shut. She had been entrusted with returning the jewelry case to the safe and was a nervous wreck, hurrying through the carpeted hall to the special elevator that provided access to the exclusive penthouse level with its four luxury suites. That elevator was tucked discreetly away in a corner of the lobby, behind the regular bank of elevators, and only rose to the top floor when a special key card was inserted into a slot.

When the elevator descended and she reached the lobby, Elizabeth dashed across the richly carpeted expanse between the elevator doors and the reception counter and waited impatiently, her heart thudding in her chest, until Toni hit the buzzer and the door to the manager's office opened. She was breathing heavily when she handed the case to Mr. Dimitri.

"Everything's okay?" Mr. Dimitri asked. "All the jewels are inside? And the case is locked?"

"I put the jewels in and Layla locked it," she said. She paused, wondering whether to tell Mr. Dimitri about the frantic search for the key, but noticing a pulsating vein near his eye, decided not to add to his already high level of stress. "After she locked the case Layla gave the key to Ms. Jones."

"Good," Mr. Dimitri said, letting out a big sigh. "That's very good. Now, go and have some lunch. You look a bit pale."

In truth, Elizabeth was dead on her feet, but she was surprised that Mr. Dimitri noticed. Maybe there was more to the old tyrant than she'd realized. Though today he appeared to be more considerate than she'd believed him to be, she still thought she'd been right not to mention the search for the key.

The next few days were a whirlwind of activity as final preparations were made for the guests' expected arrival on Friday. Enola Stitch, the famous fashion designer, came earlier, on Thursday, to make final adjustments to Noelle's gown for the Blingle Bells Ball. There was much speculation about the gown, which had been shrouded in secrecy, much like Kate Middleton's dress before her marriage to Prince William. The secrecy only drove the fashion press wild with anticipation and there were various predictions as to the design, although all agreed it would feature a plunging neckline.

Other notables that reporters would have loved to question included junk bond pioneer Matt Milkweed, hedge fund investor Adrian Robinson, and Goldsmith Shoffner CEO Floyd T. Dewey, but they all dodged the press, arriving through the garage entrance in limos with tinted glass. Aware of the general unpopularity of Wall Street bankers and financiers, they had decided discretion was the better part of valor and were maintaining extremely low profiles.

Others, including Jonah Gruber himself, weren't so shy and gave statements to the reporters gathered outside the hotel doors. Gruber, Elizabeth noted with interest, was a short, slim man with a receding hairline and an odd sense of appropriate leisure wear; he arrived wearing a turtleneck sweater, shiny bike shorts, black socks, and Birkenstock clogs. He kept his comments brief but beamed with pride, standing to the side, as Senator Clark Timson and New York City mayor Samuel Hayes both praised his philanthropic contributions. Guests who were media stars also took advantage of the gathered reporters to add to their luster. Daytime TV diva Norah gushed about her "best friend" Noelle Jones and radio shock jock Howie Storch commented that Noelle was "a real hottie."

The most highly anticipated guest, and the last to arrive, was flamboyant pop star Merton Paul, who was going to sing at the ball. Hundreds of his fans were gathered outside, waiting for a glimpse of the rocker, and their screams heralded the arrival of his white stretch Hummer.

"He's here! He's here!" Toni exclaimed, barely able to contain her excitement. "Can I ask him for an autograph, do you think?"

Spying Mr. Dimitri hurrying to greet the star, Elizabeth shook her head. "Not now, but maybe you'll get a chance later."

"Oh, I love him," Toni cooed. "Look! There he is!"

Elizabeth saw a pudgy middle-aged man wearing a shaggy fur jacket, bell-bottom pants, and a rather obvious wig, but Toni was blinded by Merton Paul's fame. "It's really him," she said, hanging onto Elizabeth's arm. "I think I'm going to faint."

"And who are these lovelies?" Merton Paul asked Mr. Dimitri, approaching the two young women.

Elizabeth took Merton Paul's proffered hand and introduced herself. "I'm the assistant concierge. I'll be happy to help you with anything you need," she said.

When he offered his hand to Toni she apparently found herself unable to speak, hanging on to Merton Paul like a drowning woman.

"This is Toni Leone," Elizabeth said. "She's at the front desk."

"Call anytime," Toni said, finding her voice. "It's marked on the phone: D-E-S-K."

"I'll keep that in mind," Merton Paul said, withdrawing his hand. "Take care, ladies."

"I can't believe I did that," Toni moaned, watching as Mr. Dimitri escorted the rocker to the penthouse elevator. "I mean, I spelled out *desk,* like he doesn't know how to spell."

"You were charming," Elizabeth said, amused at Toni's reaction. "I'm sure he's used to adoring fans."

"I made a fool of myself. Now I'll be so embarrassed every time I see him."

"He's only a person, with a head, two arms, and two legs," Elizabeth said, hearing her phone ringing. "Try to keep that in mind," she said, hurrying to answer it.

Elizabeth spent the rest of the afternoon coping with the demands of the glitterati.

Enola Stitch discovered a crease in her pillowcase and required another — freshly pressed but not starched, and linen, of course. Matt Milkweed wanted a case of Cristal (no problem) and a basket of fresh peaches (a problem, in December). Senator Timson called for a masseuse and Elizabeth got him one, but wasn't convinced that Leon was exactly what he had in mind. Norah wasn't happy with the hairdresser her personal assistant had booked in advance and required someone more in sync with her astral sign. Howie Storch wasn't fussy — any stylist would do, so long as she had a large bust. After Howie's call, Elizabeth thought she'd heard it all, but then she got an e-mail from Sammie Wong asking for a jar of Crème de la Mer, the fabulously expensive skin cream. "I can't believe I forgot to pack it," he moaned.

Elizabeth was on the phone with Neiman Marcus, arranging an emergency delivery for Sammie Wong, when she noticed the lobby was unusually crowded. Suspecting that fans, or even the press, had managed to infiltrate the building, she sent an instant message to Dan Wrayburn. She was aware, as were all the hotel employees, that Jonah Gruber had specified that access to the building was strictly limited to his guests and selected media. Gruber was apparently unable to pass up any profit-making opportunity and had sold exclusive media rights to the event to *People* magazine.

She was keeping a nervous eye on the situation and her fears were confirmed when a bearded guy in a fishing vest approached TV sitcom star Dawn Richards and produced a tiny tape recorder. On the other side of the lobby, behind one of the glittering white Christmas trees that Layla had insisted on adding, she saw a series of camera flashes.

Wrayburn, who was stepping out of the elevator, also saw them and hurried to investigate.

"This is absolutely absurd," Richards protested. She was a curvaceous brunet dressed in a very short skirt and very high heels. "Bobby here is my friend — he's just taking a snapshot."

"Good try," Wrayburn said, "but I know Bobby. In fact, I called him last week and told him the hotel was strictly off-limits."

Bobby started to leave but Dawn grabbed him by the sleeve. "Don't be silly, Bobby. You don't have to leave. This is America. We have free speech here, and I want to put these photos on my Facebook page."

"The hotel is private property," Wrayburn

explained, but his message was undermined by a guy in a fake brown UPS uniform who was photographing the encounter on his cell phone, as was a woman carrying a boxed flower arrangement.

"This is a warning," said Wrayburn, raising his voice. "I'm ordering our hotel security guards to clear the lobby. Only registered guests will be allowed to stay."

"Good luck with that," Howie Storch said, stepping out of the hotel bar with a pair of statuesque, bikini-clad twins hanging on his arms. "You can find me and my friends at the pool." He continued on his way, strolling across the lobby with his companions, and suddenly cameras were everywhere as reporters and photographers trailed the trio.

Wrayburn marched off with a grim expression on his face and Elizabeth realized her phone was ringing — again.

"Concierge, how may I help you?"

"This is Merton," the caller said, unnecessarily identifying himself. It was impossible not to recognize the famous voice.

"What can I do for you, Mr. Paul?"

"It seems I forgot my bubble bath."

"Not a problem. I'm sure we can provide some bubble bath."

"It may be a problem," said Merton. "This is special bubble bath. From Tibet."

Elizabeth wasn't aware that bubble bath was manufactured in Tibet, but she was learning something new every day. "Can you tell me what it's called, and where you usually get it?"

"It's called Lama's Tears; Bono gave it to me. He said it's great and he was right. I'm addicted."

Elizabeth was beginning to suspect this might be more difficult than she thought. "I'll do my best," she said. "But if I can't find Lama's Tears, is there another brand you could use?"

"No way, babe," said Merton. "It's out of my control. I'm hooked. It's gotta be Lama's Tears."

Nordstrom had never heard of Lama's Tears, neither had Saks or Sephora or Neiman Marcus. Elizabeth tried all the drugstores and every bath and body boutique in the Palm Beach area. Batting zero, she finally tried asking Toni, thinking that since she was such a big Merton Paul fan she might have heard of the rocker's favorite bubble bath.

"You haven't heard of Lama's Tears?" Toni was amazed.

"No, and nobody else I've called has either."

"Well, you've been calling the wrong places."

"Obviously," Elizabeth admitted, growing impatient.

"Well, I'll tell you but you're going to have to do something for me."

"What?"

"If I tell you where you can get Lama's Tears, you have to let me take them up to Merton Paul, okay?"

"Okay, okay," Elizabeth promised. "Where do I get it?"

"There's this cool place where all the hip people go. It's kind of a head shop, but they've got some clothes, some vintage. It's called Metaphor."

Elizabeth was on the computer, looking it up, jotting down the phone number. "You're a lifesaver!" she exclaimed, dialing the number.

"Just remember your promise. I get to take it up to Merton's suite."

"I won't forget, I promise," Elizabeth said, placing the order.

When she finished she realized she needed to use a bathroom and decided to break the rules just this once and use the facilities off the lobby, which were a lot closer than those provided for staff. She didn't want to be away from her desk for long, especially since there were so many people milling about in the lobby. The security guards had managed to remove a few paparazzi but others had drifted in, along with dedicated fans of the celebrity guests.

She'd taken a few steps when she encountered Wrayburn, who was looking extremely harried. "I've got to use the ladies' room," she told him. "Can you have somebody keep an eye on my desk?"

"I'll do it myself," he said, seating himself in her chair.

When she returned she saw he had propped both elbows on the desk and was rubbing his forehead. "Thanks," she said.

"No problem," he replied, standing up. Then he gave an abrupt laugh. "No problem. That was wishful thinking."

Elizabeth watched as Enola Stitch was accosted by three very thin women dressed entirely in black, obviously members of the fashion press. Enola greeted them warmly, then shepherded them into the coffee shop. "There isn't much you can do when the guests are the ones breaking the rules," she said.

"You said it," Wrayburn agreed. "I wish I was back in Washington. They take security seriously there."

Elizabeth was about to reply when four

very serious-looking men in suits and wearing earpieces entered the lobby and took up positions; their presence was both imposing and forbidding. Conversation stopped as people became aware of them, everyone suddenly watchful.

"Secret Service," Wrayburn said, using his phone to alert Mr. Dimitri. "The First Lady is arriving."

The atmosphere in the lobby was hushed and expectant, everyone waiting and hoping for a glimpse of the president's wife, and perhaps even a chance to greet her and shake her hand. She was far more popular than her beleaguered husband, who had to cope with the woes of the world, and thanks to her support for disabled veterans, she enjoyed record-high approval ratings from both Democrats and Republicans.

Mr. Dimitri was hurrying into the lobby, straightening his cuffs as he walked to the front entrance. He had taken his place when the door flew open and a uniformed courier barreled in. The Secret Service officers, moving in unison, all reached for their guns.

The courier's hands flew up. "I'm making a delivery," he said. "From Metaphor, attention concierge."

"That's right," Elizabeth said as the agents patted the courier down. "I'm expecting a delivery for a guest."

One of the agents was examining the package closely, finally concluding it was harmless and giving it to Elizabeth. The courier was sent on his way and Elizabeth, rattled by the incident, forgot her promise to Toni and summoned a bellboy to take the package to Merton Paul in the Majestic penthouse suite.

Then the motorcade arrived and Mr. Dimitri rushed out and greeted the First Lady, who was smiling and gracious and insisted on greeting everyone, staff and guests and paparazzi alike. It was a full half hour later that she finally stepped into the penthouse level elevator and the crowd began to disperse.

Elizabeth, wondering why a smile and a handshake from the First Lady could possibly make her feel so good, noticed Chris Kennedy coming through the door. He wasn't out of town at all, she realized. He'd just said that as an excuse for canceling their date. Suddenly, all that warm, good feeling was gone and Elizabeth wished she could disappear, just sink through the floor. At the same time she couldn't take her eyes off him. When he looked at her, straight on, she had to do something so she gave him a little wave. Darn it, she thought, she wasn't going to let him know how upset she was.

By way of response Chris nodded and continued on his way down the hallway that led to the bar and coffee shop. Elizabeth was tempted to follow but knew it was a bad idea. Besides, Toni was at her elbow.

"What a creep," she said. "Coming here like that."

"It's a free country," said Elizabeth, feeling her knees go weak under her and sitting down.

"I wonder what he's doing here."

"I haven't the faintest idea," said Elizabeth. Her phone was ringing and her computer was informing her she had fourteen instant messages.

"Are you going to answer that?" Toni asked.

Elizabeth picked up the receiver and heard Merton Paul's voice, thanking her for the Lama's Tears. That distinctive voice of his carried, and Toni could hear him, too.

"You got the Lama's Tears?" she demanded, when Elizabeth hung up. "And you didn't tell me?"

"I meant to," Elizabeth said lamely.

"You promised!"

"I'm sorry. It was so crazy here. You know how it's been this morning."

Toni's face was tight. "If it wasn't for me,

you'd never have known even where to get the bubble bath!"

"That's true," Elizabeth said, miserably. "I just forgot."

"I thought we were friends." Toni narrowed her eyes. "I'll get you for this, Elizabeth. Don't think I won't."

CHAPTER 5

Toni was as good as her word, giving Elizabeth the silent treatment whenever they met, which wasn't actually that often because they were both insanely busy. At the front desk, Toni's phone rang constantly with demands from the guests for everything from fresh towels to the weather report. When she wasn't answering the phone, Mr. Kronenberg gave her the task of hand-addressing the Christmas cards Cavendish sent to every guest who had stayed at the hotel in the past year. "It's these little personal touches that count," he told her, giving her a box containing one hundred envelopes and telling her there were more in his office when she finished those. "I simply can't manage to do it all myself this year, not with all that's going on."

"I'm happy to help," said Toni, giving the head concierge a big smile. "If there's anything else I can do, just let me know."

She lowered her voice. "I think Elizabeth is in a bit over her head. She was complaining to me, saying some of the guests are terribly demanding."

Kronenberg glanced across the lobby, where Elizabeth had the phone tucked on her shoulder and was scribbling frantically on a notepad. Her hair was mussed and her harassed attitude was a stark contrast to the confident, professional demeanor that Annemarie had always projected. "I'm sure she's doing her best," he said. "It's unfortunate timing that Annemarie got sick just now."

"Epstein-Barr can last for weeks, too," Toni said in a sympathetic voice. Then her tone brightened. "I'll get right to work on those cards — don't give it another thought."

Kronenberg's anxious expression softened. "You're a trooper, Toni."

In truth, Elizabeth was frantically scrambling, without a moment to catch her breath, trying to fulfill guests' special requests while also assisting Layla with the schedule of activities they had planned. Luxury coaches came and went, taking guests on tours of art galleries and museums, shopping expeditions, nature hikes, and golf matches. The golf tournament, in which every foursome included a member

414

of the PGA tour, was a big success. The boy versus girl tennis tournament pitting Simpson against Sharapova became an instant sports legend, and Gruber's guests would be able to fascinate friends and acquaintances with play-by-play accounts for years.

But the main event, the Blingle Bells Ball, was still to come. Every employee was working overtime, preparing for the gala. There were decorations to put up, tables to set, and food to prepare, and the pace grew more frantic as the time drew closer. The doors to the Grand Ballroom would open at nine Sunday evening, and at eight o'clock Layla invited interested staff members in for a sneak peek.

"You've all been working so hard," she told the hundred or so staff members who had accepted the invitation and gathered in the Grand Ballroom's service hallway. "This is what you've done!" She opened the door and they entered reverently, awestruck, almost as if they were visiting a great cathedral, and paraded single file around the perimeter of the room. Even though they had all been involved in the preparations, only a few workers had seen the room in its final glory, complete with dramatic lighting designed for the event by theatrical lighting expert Stefan Ludwig.

Elizabeth found herself awed by the banks of orchids on every table, the swags of silk suspended from the ceiling, and the hand-painted wallpaper panels that had been installed for the occasion. Every table was covered with sparkling crystal and silver, the specially monogrammed porcelain plates sat on silver chargers, and two gilt thrones would be occupied by Noelle and Jonah.

"Every guest will receive a diamond gift," Layla said. "The gentlemen will receive gold and diamond money clips and the ladies will all get one-carat pendants."

"How much are those worth, do you think?" one of the housekeepers, Marketa, whispered, speaking in her lightly accented voice. Elizabeth knew she worked extremely hard, often taking double shifts so she could send money home to her family in Serbia.

"I don't think you can get a one-carat diamond for less than a couple thousand dollars," Angela replied. A bookkeeper for the hotel, she had just gotten engaged. "And that doesn't include the setting. Gold is really high right now."

"You mean, in addition to a ball for four hundred guests, Gruber is giving each a gift worth two thousand dollars? What does that come out to?" Elizabeth asked. "I can't do the math — it's too many zeroes."

"Eight hundred thousand dollars," said Angela, who was a whiz with numbers. "Almost a million."

Elizabeth suddenly felt sick to her stomach. "A million dollars on gifts for people who already have everything they could possibly want."

"I bet some of these women won't even appreciate a single-carat diamond," Marketa sniffed. "It's nothing to them."

"You're right," Elizabeth said, remembering the way Noelle had tossed forty-seven million dollars worth of jewels on the bed, as if they were little more than a ripped pair of panty hose. "So, Angela, what do you think the total bill for this do is going to be?" she asked.

"Millions and millions," Angela said. "But Gruber's got it. I read in the paper that he's worth something like a billion dollars."

"You know," Elizabeth said, "back home in Maine, my mom and her friends have this little charity they call the Hat and Mitten Fund. They have bake sales and beg for contributions so they can give poor kids in our town warm clothes and school supplies. I think their entire budget is maybe a thousand dollars."

"Imagine what they could do with one of these trinkets," Marketa said.

"Yeah, I know what you're thinking," Angela said. "But look at it this way. Gruber's money creates a lot of jobs for folks like us. I heard that Dimitri was considering layoffs because holiday reservations were down. If it wasn't for Gruber some of us would be having a pretty miserable Christmas."

"Ho-ho-ho," said Elizabeth, causing the others to chuckle as they completed their circuit of the glittering ballroom and exited into the dank, fluorescent-lit chill of the concrete-walled service hall.

An hour later, just before nine, Elizabeth was back at her desk. A few early arrivals were drifting about in the lobby, waiting for the doors to the Grand Ballroom to open. Elizabeth recognized several of them, people she'd dealt with in the past few days. There was Katrina Muldaur, a sweet middle-aged woman whose novel about the Spanish-American War was a surprise best seller; she was clearly thrilled to have been invited and was wearing a black lace dress Elizabeth had seen at Macy's for a hundred and forty-nine dollars. The lady author was accompanied by a middle-aged man in a badly fitting tux who tugged on his cummerbund from time to time as he paced about impatiently. Elizabeth suspected he was probably wondering why they couldn't have served dinner at six, which was exactly what her own father would be wondering, if he were here.

Matt Milkweed, the financier, also caught Elizabeth's eye. He was tapping his foot by the elevator, waiting for someone. That someone turned out to be a tiny Asian woman, whose ruffled red evening gown seemed to swallow her up. She had to hold the ruffle encircling her neck down with one hand just so Milkweed could give her a kiss, then she took his arm and they drifted off in the direction of the bar.

Elizabeth was glancing at the clock over the desk and saw it was just five minutes to nine when the office door opened and Mr. Dimitri appeared carrying the metal-clad jewel case. He gave her a nod as he traversed the distance to the penthouse elevator. Then it was nine o'clock and two hotel waiters dressed as footmen complete with white powdered wigs and knee breeches opened the doors to the ballroom and the rush was on.

The band was playing a familiar tune, light and nice for dancing, and the elevator was arriving regularly and discharging guests. Elizabeth found she was enjoying the show, despite her uneasiness with Gruber's display of conspicuous consumption. It was better than a fashion show, she decided, watching Howie Storch's twin dates hobble past in very tight, very low-cut dresses that seemed ready to pop, revealing all. Merton Paul was flamboyant as ever, in a ruby red silk tux that contrasted nicely with the emerald green wig he'd chosen for the occasion. Norah, however, was the very picture of elegance, in white satin and silver sequins. Her insistence on a hairdresser with a compatible astrological sign had resulted in a smooth updo that perfectly framed her heart-shaped face.

Elizabeth was wondering what the First Lady would be wearing when she noticed Dan Wrayburn hurrying across the lobby to the elevators with the look of a man who was very worried about something but trying not to show it. He disappeared behind the elevator doors only to return a few minutes later, deep in conversation with Mr. Dimitri and Mr. Kronenberg. After a brief conference, he left to make an announcement on the hotel's emergency PA system.

"Attention please," Wrayburn began. "This is an official announcement from the hotel management. The Imperial Parure is missing and the hotel is on lockdown, awaiting the arrival of the police. Mr. and Mrs.

Gruber hope that everyone will continue to enjoy the evening, but no one will be able to leave until further notice."

That set off a shocked buzz, with everyone frantically talking, wondering how such a thing could happen. The band, which had stopped playing for the announcement, resumed, but nobody was dancing. Everyone was uneasy, almost as if they were expecting a mob armed with pitchforks to storm the building.

Then, appearing almost magically, as if she'd simply materialized in the ballroom, Noelle was standing on the bandstand. Leaving her desk and standing by the door, Elizabeth had a clear view of the gorgeous woman. Enola Stitch's design more than lived up to the anticipatory hype. She had created a long, strapless sheath of hot pink satin that clung to every curve of Noelle's amazing body, and then gilded the lily by adding a fabulous puffy bustle and train. Every eye in the room was on Noelle, but she unnecessarily tapped the microphone, as if she needed to call the guests to attention.

"I just want to say," she began, in a whispery, little girl voice, "that I hope you will all cooperate with the police and tell them anything you might have seen or consider suspicious. With your help I'm sure we will get the jewels back, and in the meantime, I hope you'll all have a wonderful time. So take your seats because dinner will be served in a few minutes and afterward Merton Paul will entertain with his biggest hits."

She then left the room, clutching Layla Fine's hand, leaving the two extravagant gilt thrones unoccupied.

"You know what this means, don't you?" Toni asked after joining Elizabeth in the doorway.

"It means the party's over," Elizabeth said. The waiters were serving grilled foie gras appetizers but few of the guests appeared to have any appetite. News of the theft had definitely cast a pall over the gala. "They're all going to be scrutinized by the police and they've probably all got something to hide."

"Not just them," said Toni. "The police will start with the staff and I bet quite a few of us have something to hide, too. Mark my words, it's going to be a lot worse for us than it is for them."

Elizabeth knew she was right. The staff members were good, hardworking people but she knew that many of the lowest-paying jobs were filled by illegal immigrants, who feared deportation if their status was discovered. There were also undoubtedly some who had drug or alcohol problems, or a gambling addiction, and they would automatically be suspected of stealing the jewels to feed their habits. Elizabeth was most worried about the handful of employees who had come to the hotel through a program that found jobs for prisoners upon their release. She expected those workers would also face close scrutiny from investigators, so it was quite a shock when she was one of the first called to Wrayburn's office

Of course, she thought, making her way down the hall, she was one of the few employees who had actually seen and handled the jewels. That must be the reason why they wanted to talk to her.

Wrayburn seemed pleasant enough when she arrived, pointing out a chair for her to sit in and introducing Detective Michael Tabak of the Palm Beach Police Department. Tabak, she noticed with some unease, was accompanied by two uniformed officers who had stationed themselves by the door, blocking any escape attempt. As if she would even think of it! She was innocent!

"You are Elizabeth Stone," Tabak began. "Is that right?"

Once she had affirmed her identity she was shocked to hear him deliver the Miranda warning, adding that the entire interview would be recorded by a hidden CCTV camera. "Do you understand?" he asked.

Simply a formality, Elizabeth thought, nodding. They were probably doing this with everyone.

"I would like to show you some video footage taken yesterday," said Tabak, flicking on a small TV.

Elizabeth studied the grainy footage that showed people coming and going in the lobby. She herself appeared as a small figure in the background, seated at her desk.

"Look here," said Tabak, pointing out a male figure carrying a large duffel bag. He seemed to be in a hurry, but there was a moment when he looked in her direction and she waved at him. It was Chris Kennedy, she realized, with a shock.

"Who is this man?" Tabak demanded.

"That's Chris Kennedy," she said reluctantly. "I had a couple of dates with him."

"Why the wave?" Tabak asked, fixing his small, dark eyes on her.

"Just a friendly wave," said Elizabeth. "That's all."

"It looks like a signal to me."

Elizabeth was almost too shocked by this accusation to reply. "That's ridiculous," she finally said. "Why would I do that? What would I be signaling?"

"Letting him know the coast was clear," Tabak said. "That he could get into the office and steal the jewels."

Elizabeth thought she saw a way out of this nightmare. "But even if he got access to the office, and even if I opened the safe for him, which I definitely did not do, the jewels were still in a locked case."

"He could easily substitute a matching case, especially since you'd seen the real case and could describe it to him. Then he could take the case with the jewels, hiding it in that bag of his, and open it later," said Tabak.

Elizabeth felt as if she were in a scene from a very bad movie, but knew it was all really happening. She shook her head. "This is crazy."

"There's no sense protecting him," Wrayburn warned. "We have reason to believe he stole the parure. This is your opportunity to tell everything you know before he has a chance to implicate you. Which he will, believe me."

Elizabeth didn't know what to think. She'd liked Chris a lot, but then he'd broken their date and lied about the reason. Maybe he'd been lying about everything, like Toni said. Maybe he was a fake, like his Rolex. Maybe he hadn't been interested in her at all but had just been using her to get information about the hotel and the jewels.

"Listen, I'm not very happy with Chris Kennedy. In fact I'm not even sure he really is named Chris Kennedy. I have no reason to protect him. If I knew he'd stolen the jewels, I'd tell you, but I don't. I simply don't have anything to tell you," Elizabeth protested.

"You're in serious trouble," Tabak said, fastening that dark stare on her. "Once we catch him — and believe me, we will — he'll do everything he can to put the blame on you."

Elizabeth's head was spinning. She felt like Alice, falling through the rabbit hole into a completely strange and nonsensical world. "I can't believe Chris Kennedy stole the jewels, but if he did, I certainly had nothing to do with it."

"So that's your story," Tabak said.

"It's not a story, it's the truth."

Wrayburn sighed. "That's all for now, Elizabeth."

"I can leave?"

"Yes, but you need to see Mr. Dimitri first."

Tabak had something to add. "And don't

leave town."

Elizabeth stood up, surprised to see that her legs still worked. It was with a sinking feeling, however, that she made her way with heavy steps to the hotel manager's office. She was pretty sure she wasn't going to like what he had to say.

When she reached the lobby, she found it empty, except for a few uniformed police officers. There was a subdued hum of conversation coming from the Grand Ballroom, and the orchestra had been replaced with a pianist, who was providing dinner music. The party must go on, she thought, even if the bling was missing from the Blingle Bells Ball.

Stepping behind the reception desk, she was surprised when the door to Mr. Dimitri's office flew open and Toni popped out.

"Hi!" Elizabeth exclaimed, glad to see a friendly face.

Except the face wasn't all that friendly. "Uh, hi," Toni muttered, ducking past her and rushing off in the direction of the employee's locker room.

What on earth was happening? How could Toni even know that she was suspected of involvement in the theft? And if she did know, why wasn't Toni sticking up for her?

Elizabeth opened the door and saw Mr. Dimitri. He was seated at his desk, looking through a file.

"Elizabeth," he said, a note of disappointment in his voice. "Sit down."

Here we go again, she thought, seating herself.

"I am not one to rush to judgment," he began. "I want you to answer one question, and to tell me the truth."

"Absolutely," Elizabeth said, relieved that somebody seemed willing to believe her.

"Did you have anything to do with the theft of the jewels?"

"No, I did not," she replied.

He sighed. "Are you absolutely sure that the jewels were in the case when you returned it to me after the photo shoot?"

Elizabeth decided it was time to tell the truth. "No, I'm not sure."

"You're not?" Mr. Dimitri looked horrified.

"There was some confusion. Noelle had been throwing the jewels around and —"

"That will be enough, Elizabeth," he said, cutting her off, apparently unable, or unwilling, to hear a Cavendish employee speak ill of a guest. "I'm afraid I'm going to place you on leave pending further developments."

"Leave?" Elizabeth asked. "What does that mean?"

"It means we will hold your job for you until the investigation is complete. If you are exonerated, and I most certainly hope you will be, you will be welcome to return to the Cavendish family."

Elizabeth did a rapid calculation and figured she had eighty-two dollars in her checking account, and only a couple of thousand in her emergency savings account. "Is this a paid leave?" she asked hopefully.

"No," he said, "but you will be paid for the days you worked in this pay period."

That was the first good news she'd had since the theft was announced, she thought, slightly relieved.

"If I were you," Mr. Dimitri said, "I'd hire a good lawyer."

Elizabeth nodded and left the office. At the door she was met by one of the hotel's security guards, who escorted her to the locker room. He stood by, watching as she opened her locker and hung up her green Cavendish jacket, feeling a bit like a disgraced officer being stripped of her military insignia. She turned her back and slipped off the green skirt, then pulled on the shorts she'd worn to work that morning. When she picked up her purse he took it and looked through it carefully; she blushed when he opened the plastic tampon container. "Okay," he said, handing the bag back to her.

She took it and left the building, stepping into the dark night and following the dimly lit path to the employees' parking lot. There, she discovered, the one halogen lamp that lit the lot was out. She unlocked the Corolla and sat behind the driver's wheel, looking back at the golden, glittering hotel and wondering if she would ever be able to return.

Tears sprang to her eyes. Tabak was right. She was in trouble, the worst trouble of her young life, and there was only one thing to do. Call home.

CHAPTER 6

After talking to her mother, Elizabeth followed her advice and took a long bath and went to bed. "Everything will look better in the morning," Lucy Stone told her daughter, but Elizabeth found that hard to believe. Every time she closed her eyes she saw another disturbing vision: Tabak warning her not to leave town or Mr. Dimitri's curt dismissal or Wrayburn's bulldog expression. And then there was Toni, smirking and speculating that Chris wasn't genuine. Was Toni right? Had she been a complete idiot? Or, worst of all, had she actually aided and abetted the thieves without realizing it?

Exhausted at four a.m., she gave up and took the one remaining Ambien in the vial Doc Ryder had prescribed when she'd had a bout of insomnia last summer, anxious about leaving home and beginning her new job. She then fell sound asleep and didn't wake until noon.

Her first impulse upon waking was to call Chris Kennedy, but she couldn't quite make up her mind to do it. Finally, spitting a mouthful of toothpaste into the sink, she gave in, only to get a recording informing her he wasn't available but she could leave a message.

She was about to do so, then remembered the police were most certainly monitoring his calls and snapped the phone shut. Too late, she realized. Her call would be retained by the system as a missed call. In fact, she realized, it was quite probable that she was under surveillance herself. She went to the front window and looked out, wondering if she was being watched.

There was no black sedan parked out front, no unmarked white van on the other side of the street, but she was too paranoid to feel relieved. What was it they said? It wasn't paranoia if they were out to get you. And Elizabeth had the uncomfortable knowledge that she was under suspicion, the police were out to get her and wanted to implicate her in the jewel robbery.

She was making herself a cup of tea — she couldn't face coffee this morning, actually this afternoon — when Toni's face popped into her consciousness. That bitch! There was no other word, she thought, stirring a scant teaspoon of sugar into the mug. It must have been Toni who fingered her, who had told investigators about her and Chris dating. Impulsively, she grabbed the phone, determined to have it out with her.

"Why did you do it? Why did you even mention me to the cops?" she demanded, when Toni answered. "Thanks to you I'm in big trouble."

"I was only trying to help," Toni replied. "I told them you were under the influence of this Chris Kennedy guy, that it wasn't your fault. I told them how he had won you over, using a fake identity."

"How could you know that?" Elizabeth demanded.

"It was obvious. He's a big phony but you were too infatuated with him to realize it. I was only trying to help you, honest."

"Well, you've gotten me in real trouble. They think I conspired with Chris," Elizabeth wailed.

"I didn't realize . . . I was only trying to be a good friend."

Elizabeth doubted that Toni was telling the truth, but didn't want to think badly of her colleague. "I guess it won't matter in the end," she said. "The truth will out and I have nothing to fear because I'm innocent."

"I'm sure that's right," Toni said. "By the

way, they gave me your concierge job. Temporarily."

Something in the way Toni said "temporarily" gave Elizabeth pause. She remembered Toni's threat, after Elizabeth had forgotten to let her deliver the bubble bath to Merton Paul, that she would get back at her. Now, it seemed, Toni had succeeded. Maybe she wasn't really a friend after all.

Suddenly, Elizabeth didn't want to have anything to do with Toni. "I've got to go," she said, tossing the phone on the table as if a spider had crawled out of it.

She picked up her mug of tea and wrapped both hands around it, as if its warmth could somehow console her. Reassure her.

She was a good person, she told herself. It was ridiculous that she should find herself suspected of a crime. She worked hard, she tried to please, and this is what it got her. How could Toni be so mean? She simply didn't understand it. And Chris? Was it possible that Toni was right? Had she been played for a fool?

She sat down on her futon, crossing her legs Indian style, and tasted the tea. It was sweet and spicy, and it seemed to help her clarify her thoughts. She sipped and tried to remember every conversation she'd had with Chris. Had she unwittingly given him valuable information? It was true that he'd mentioned the Cavendish data system, she realized with a start, but she hadn't given him any information. Or had she?

Was it really possible that he wasn't who he'd claimed to be? He looked like a Kennedy, but so did a lot of people. Toni had been suspicious of him right from the start. Was Chris Kennedy as fake as that big Rolex he always wore? And why hadn't he answered her call?

Setting the tea aside, she decided to get dressed and work off her nervous energy in the apartment complex's gym. She threw herself into her workout, starting on the treadmill, then advancing to the Stairmaster and elliptical trainer, then finishing off with a half hour's worth of lazy laps in the pool. When she headed back to her apartment her joints were loose and a bit rubbery, and she was very hungry. She was wondering what she had in the fridge when she saw a strange apparition climbing out of a taxi.

It was a very old woman with a head of curly white hair, carrying a bright red winter coat looped over her arm. There was nothing unusual about seeing an elderly woman in Florida but Elizabeth thought this particular old lady bore an uncanny resemblance to her mother's friend in Tinker's

Cove, Miss Tilley. Christened Julia Ward Howe Tilley many years ago, she was known as Julia to only a few very dear contemporaries, and was Miss Tilley to everyone else.

Elizabeth blinked a few times, staring at this incongruous figure standing on the sidewalk, apparently examining a leathery anthurium blossom. They said everyone had a double — was this Miss Tilley's double?

The apparition turned and smiled at Elizabeth, giving her a wave. Then another figure climbed out of the taxi and began collecting luggage and there was no question at all about her identity. It was her mother, Lucy Stone. There was no mistaking that cap of shining hair or that hideous orange plaid jacket her mother was so fond of.

"What are you doing here?" Elizabeth asked, running up and greeting them both with hugs and smiles. For the first time since she was accused, she was beginning to feel that things might work out for her, that it was going to be all right.

"You're all wet," Miss Tilley observed.

"I was swimming," said Elizabeth, who was still in her swimsuit with a towel draped over her shoulders.

"I was afraid we'd find you in jail," Miss Tilley said. "We took the first flight."

"She insisted," said Lucy, handing Elizabeth one suitcase and taking the other herself.

"I didn't think we'd find you lolling about the pool," Miss Tilley said in a disapproving tone. She patted the snap purse she was carrying. "I brought cash to bail you out."

"If it makes you feel better, prison is still a very real possibility," said Elizabeth. She was pulling a rolling suitcase behind her, leading the way through the apartment complex's landscaped grounds to her building. It was slow going, however, as Miss Tilley and Lucy kept stopping to examine the tropical plants.

"At home, those are houseplants," said Lucy, pointing to a clump of spiky snake plants that were flourishing against a wall.

"Mother-in-law's tongues, that's what my mother used to call them. And look at those poinsettias," said Miss Tilley. "They're as big as my lilac bushes."

"It's amazing," said Lucy, finally shrugging out of her jacket. "It was snowing at home when we left."

"Well, come on in and get settled," Elizabeth invited, unlocking her door and wondering how she was going to accommodate the two women in her tiny apartment, located off the island in the more affordable town of West Palm Beach.

"This is lovely," said Miss Tilley, glancing around at Elizabeth's mix of IKEA and thrift shop furniture. Peeking into the bedroom, she nodded in approval at the queen-size bed. "We'll take the bedroom and you can have the couch. You don't mind sharing, do you, Lucy?"

"Not at all, as long as you don't get fresh," said Lucy, busy hanging up their winter coats in the hall closet. "Now, what's for dinner?"

Lucy opened the refrigerator and examined the contents, Elizabeth went into the bedroom to get dressed, and Miss Tilley settled herself in a sunny spot on the little screened deck off the living room.

"There's nothing to eat," called Lucy. "All you've got is yogurt."

"There are microwave dinners in the freezer," Elizabeth replied.

Opening the compartment, Lucy discovered she was right. "Elizabeth, this is no way to live," she scolded, choosing three of the packaged meals.

Ten minutes later, Lucy had set the table on the deck, thrown some salad in a bowl, and zapped three dinners.

"Warm weather is so nice when you're older," Miss Tilley observed, when Lucy and Elizabeth joined her on the deck and seated themselves on the mismatched chairs at Elizabeth's rickety plastic table. Miss Tilley raised her wrinkled face to the sun, reminding Elizabeth of a tough old lizard.

"With this heat it doesn't seem at all like Christmas," Lucy said, glancing about at the collection of flowering plants that Elizabeth had set on the deck railing. "And you haven't put up any decorations, not even a Christmas tree."

"I haven't had time," Elizabeth said defensively. Her mother's offhand comment had stung. "Most days I've been working from eight in the morning to nine or ten at night."

"Maybe we can find a little tree for you," said Lucy.

"Maybe we should tackle the problem at hand," Miss Tilley snapped. "Now tell me all about it, starting with the young man."

Elizabeth's chin dropped. "How did you know there's a young man?"

Miss Tilley looked at her. "When a young woman finds herself in a predicament, it's always because of a young man. Always."

"I disagree," said Lucy, who had two other daughters besides Elizabeth and often found herself refereeing squabbles and consoling them when mean girls got up to their tricks. "Girls can cause a lot of grief, too."

Elizabeth chewed a bite of chicken parmigiana and swallowed. "In this case," she said, "I think my troubles are due to a woman. Several women, in fact."

"I'm sure there's a man in there somewhere," said Miss Tilley.

"Okay," Elizabeth agreed. "I'll start at the beginning. I'd just been promoted to assistant concierge, it was my first day, and this guy came in with a flat bike tire. I sent him to the hotel's sports center and they fixed it and then he asked me out. We had a great time, and he asked me out a couple more times, but when we were supposed to go out last Sunday — the last day I had off — he canceled at the last minute."

"Does he have a name?" Miss Tilley inquired.

"Chris Kennedy."

"One of *those* Kennedys?" Lucy asked.

"I don't know. Toni, who I work with at the hotel, said she thinks he's an imposter, pretending to be a member of the Kennedy clan, but he never claimed any connection. He told me he was a lawyer and worked for some environmental organization. I thought he was a pretty nice guy. However, the investigators think he stole the jewels and that I was an accomplice."

"I suppose Toni had something to do with

that," Lucy remarked.

"How did you guess? She told the investigators about her suspicions and she told them about me. She told them he was taking advantage of me. She said she did it to help me but I don't believe her. She's got my concierge job now."

"And I imagine she was jealous because you had a boyfriend," said Lucy, spearing a cherry tomato.

"I don't know about that. She was always kind of down on Chris. I think the thing that really got her mad at me was that I promised to let her deliver a package to Merton Paul — he was in the hotel — and I forgot. She was furious, and she said she'd get back at me."

"And she did," said Lucy.

"It certainly sounds that way," Miss Tilley agreed. "You mentioned several women caused you problems. Who are the others?"

"Well, Noelle Jones, Jonah Gruber's wife. I was assigned to help with a photo shoot, pictures of her with the jewels, and she was terribly careless with them. She said they were uncomfortable and threw them on the bed. A ring even rolled under a nightstand and I had to scramble around on my hands and knees to find it." Elizabeth found her frustration was getting the better of her.

"She acted like a spoiled brat."

Lucy clucked her tongue. "She certainly doesn't sound very nice."

"She isn't," Elizabeth said. She was beginning to enjoy dishing about the hotel guests; she'd been working so hard for so long and hadn't been able to vent her frustration with anyone. "A lot of the guests are like that. They think the world revolves around them. If you saw the money Jonah Gruber spent on this Blingle Bells Ball, you'd be horrified. He hired this party planner, Layla Fine, and she spent two weeks ordering everybody around, but mostly me. I had to plan special events for Gruber's guests, 'extraordinary events for extraordinary people,' she said. Like they were better somehow than everybody else, and entitled to the best of everything. Orchids and foie gras and diamond gifts for every guest at the ball. . . ."

"My goodness," Miss Tilley tutted. "Such ostentation. And so unnecessary. My dear father used to say that there was nothing better than sweet water from our well and my mother's home-baked anadama bread, and he was right. That and a clear conscience."

"I don't think anyone at that party had a clear conscience," Elizabeth said. "I don't see how they could. I mean, I kept thinking about people back home who don't have jobs and their houses are in foreclosure and they have to depend on the food pantry to feed their kids."

"This Gruber's priorities certainly seem to be a little skewed," Lucy said, "but I've seen big events like weddings get way out of control in Tinker's Cove, too, especially if there's a professional planner in the picture. What's this Layla person like?"

"I had nightmares about her," Elizabeth admitted. "She was so demanding, she had me running all over the place. Everything had to be perfect, but she was the one deciding what perfect was. I mean, white roses, pink roses, who cares? And they couldn't be just any white roses, they had to be Patience white roses from some outfit in England. Everything was like that. Every day was an impossible quest to find some crazy thing, and if I couldn't find it she'd rip into me, saying I was stupid and lazy."

Lucy gave her daughter's hand a squeeze. "That's terrible," she said. "Nobody should treat you like that."

Miss Tilley, however, wasn't about to be distracted by Elizabeth's complaints. "This has all been very interesting, and therapeutic, I suppose, if you believe in that Freudian nonsense, but we need to focus on the problem, which is that Elizabeth has been falsely accused of being involved in a jewel robbery."

Reminded of the gravity of her situation, Elizabeth's spirits fell. She was in big trouble and she didn't see how these two were going to help her. Her mother was a part-time reporter for a small town newspaper, and had had some success in solving crimes, but Elizabeth suspected that was mostly luck. As for Miss Tilley, she was sharp and had been the town librarian, but she was well over ninety years old. When you got right down to it, they were well intentioned, but that was about all they had going for them.

"So tell me about this young man," Miss Tilley said. "Chris Kennedy. Do you think he stole the jewels?"

"I don't know what to think," Elizabeth said. "I really liked him."

"What do you know about him?"

"Not that much. He was fun to be with, and he was from Boston, so we had a lot in common. He had a motorcycle. . . ."

Lucy was horrified. "A motorcycle!"

"But he had a helmet for me and he made sure that I wore it. He took good care of me."

"And did you —" Lucy began, but she bit her tongue. Some things were personal and Elizabeth was entitled to her privacy.

"He was a gentleman, Mom. We kissed but that was all." Elizabeth's face softened at the memory.

"So if you put everything else aside and just trusted your reaction to him, do you think he is a thief?" Lucy asked.

"Take your time," Miss Tilley urged. "Give it some thought."

"I don't have to," Elizabeth said. "My gut reaction *was* that he's a good guy. I *thought* he was a really, truly good person — but I'm beginning to think I can't trust my instincts. I thought Toni was my friend, for example, and she ratted me out to the police. I've been way too trusting but I'm learning that people are not always who they seem to be, or what they want you to think they are."

"And where is this young man now?" Miss Tilley asked.

"That's the problem," Elizabeth answered glumly. "He hasn't returned my call. I don't know where he is."

CHAPTER 7

"Let's stick to the facts," Lucy said in a brisk tone. "I've been a reporter for a long time, I've interviewed all sorts of people, and I have to say it's almost impossible to tell what people are really like underneath that social veneer. You have to see what they do and how they treat other people, get to know them over a period of time so you can see how they act and not just what they say."

"I agree," Miss Tilley said. "I suppose there's no question that the jewels are really missing. That's the first fact we have to verify."

"You mean, the whole thing could have been staged?" Lucy was definitely intrigued by the possibility. "To defraud an insurance company, for example?"

"I can't imagine why Jonah Gruber, or Noelle, would do that. They're rolling in money. He's the second richest man in the world, something like that. He's got billions," Elizabeth said.

"How do we know that?" Miss Tilley asked. "He has a reputation for being rich, but maybe he isn't. Maybe he's strapped for cash."

"*Forbes* magazine thinks he's rich. They put him right at the top of their list," Elizabeth said. "And he paid forty-seven million dollars for the Imperial Parure. I'm pretty sure Christie's didn't let those jewels go until they got their money."

"That's something we could check," Miss Tilley said. "We could find out their payment policy."

"I'll make a list of questions," Lucy offered, extracting a notebook from her handbag. "First off, we want to know if Jonah Gruber is really as rich as everybody thinks he is, right? And we want to know if Chris Kennedy is really who he says he is."

"Have you actually seen the jewels, Elizabeth?" Miss Tilley asked. "And if you did, do you think they were real?"

"Oh, I saw them. I touched them." Elizabeth remembered laying the bracelet across her arm, how it had felt warm and heavy. "They sure looked real to me, but how would I know? I can't tell real pearls from fakes, or cubic zirconia from a diamond."

"Real pearls feel warm to the skin," Miss

Tilley said, "and you can scratch glass with a genuine diamond."

"I didn't really have a chance to do that," Elizabeth said defensively. "I was too busy chasing after Noelle and that photographer."

Her sarcastic tone got her a sharp look from her mother, but Miss Tilley ignored it. "And you say Noelle was quite careless with the jewels?"

"She acted as if it was all a big chore, all except the last photos they set up. She seemed to enjoy that."

"Because it was the end of the session?" Lucy asked.

Elizabeth remembered Noelle's casual attitude as she arranged herself on the white fur coat, entirely naked except for the jewels. "Because she's an exhibitionist," Elizabeth said. "She stripped completely naked for the last photos. At first I didn't know where to look but Layla told me that Noelle was in porn films and loves to show off her body."

"A week or two in Tinker's Cove would fix that," Lucy said primly. "What was the temperature when we left?"

"Not bad," Miss Tilley said. "It was at least ten degrees, but that doesn't take the wind chill into account. It's the northeast

448

wind off the water that really cools things off."

"That's true," Lucy said with a little shiver. "So after the photo session, what happened?"

"Well, Noelle tossed the jewels on the bed and she drifted off to the bathroom with Layla, carrying a terry cloth robe — one of the robes the hotel provides. There were a lot of costume changes and Layla was wearing it between photos. I gathered up the jewels and put them in the case. Layla came out of the bathroom, wearing the robe, and I told her that the jewels were in the case so she could lock it. She couldn't find the key right away. I sort of lost track of things when I joined in the search, but the key was eventually found — she had it all along — and the case was locked and I carried it down to the manager's office so he could put it in the safe."

"He didn't ask to see the jewels, to check that they were all there?" Lucy wondered.

"He couldn't. The case was locked."

"Did Layla still have the key?" Miss Tilley asked.

"No. She gave it to Noelle after she locked the case."

"And what did Noelle do with the key?"

Elizabeth furrowed her brow, trying to

remember. "I'm pretty sure she put it in the pocket of her robe."

"And probably forgot it," Lucy said, thinking of all the times she'd searched high and low for her reading glasses only to find them in her bathrobe pocket. "Anyone could have taken it. One of the maids, for instance."

"But the case was locked away, in the safe."

"Ah, the safe," Miss Tilley said, sounding like Sherlock Holmes finding an important clue. "Who has the combination to the safe? Do you?"

"Only the manager and the head concierge have the combination," said Elizabeth. "The official hotel policy is quite strict. The safe is only to be opened by Mr. Dimitri or Mr. Kronenberg."

"But what if a guest needs something from the safe when they're not available?" Lucy asked, making eye contact with her daughter. "If I ever heard of a rule that was made to be broken . . ."

Miss Tilley's eyebrows rose to a startling elevation.

"You said it," Elizabeth admitted. "It was the first thing Mr. Kronenberg showed me when I was promoted to assistant concierge. He made me promise to keep it secret, then showed me where he kept the combination."

"So you could get into the safe?"

"I could," Elizabeth admitted, wondering if she'd been set up by the head concierge, or the hotel manager, or both. Wouldn't that be rich? The two most senior employees conspiring to rob a guest!

Miss Tilley broke into her thoughts. "And what if the key to the case was missing for a short while? Would Noelle have noticed?"

"I doubt it," Lucy said. "I suspect she forgot all about the key until she needed it to open the jewel case just before the ball."

Elizabeth suddenly felt very cold, even though it was at least eighty degrees on her sunny, plant-filled deck. Looked at this way, it wasn't at all surprising that she was suspected of being involved with the theft. After all, she was one of the few employees entrusted with the combination to the hotel safe, and she knew how careless Noelle was with the key to the jewel case. "I didn't do it," she said, feeling the need to proclaim her innocence, even to herself.

"Of course not," Lucy said, giving her a hug. "That's why we're here."

Miss Tilley grasped the edge of Elizabeth's wobbly plastic table with her knobby hands and began to raise herself, prompting Lucy to jump up and assist her at the same time Elizabeth steadied the table.

"Really!" Miss Tilley exclaimed. "I'm perfectly able, you know."

"Of course you are." Lucy released her grip on the old woman's arm.

Miss Tilley turned to Elizabeth. "Where is your computer? I presume you have one?"

Lucy tidied up the lunch dishes while Elizabeth settled Miss Tilley at her little café table and showed her how to use her laptop. Then Lucy went off to her storage unit to dig out her small collection of Christmas decorations. When she returned, Miss Tilley had a plan.

"First thing tomorrow I think you should take a look at this Chris Kennedy's apartment and see what you can find out," she said, peering at them over the laptop.

"You mean break in?" Lucy asked, opening the box and examining the contents. "I don't think that's a good idea. It's probably been sealed by the police."

"No way," Elizabeth protested. "I don't want anything to do with him."

"I think you have to," Miss Tilley said. "I fear the police may be right about him after all."

Elizabeth felt sick; she'd been a fool. "What have you found?"

"He lied to you about his job. I've done a computer search checking every environ-

452

mental organization in Florida and he is not employed by any of them as a lawyer or in any other capacity. He's not registered with the Florida bar either."

"So Toni was right about him," Elizabeth said. "But what good will searching his apartment do?"

Miss Tilley scowled and glared at them through her wire-rimmed glasses. "You can find out a lot about a person when you see his home. Take Audrey Wilson, for example. She ran for selectman last spring promising to straighten out town government, but everybody knew she lived in absolute squalor. Even her yard was filled with junk. So nobody believed her and she lost the election."

"That's true," Lucy said thoughtfully, holding up a twig and berry wreath Elizabeth had hung on her dorm room door when she was in college. "I suppose we could at least take a look at the place." She turned to Elizabeth. "Do you know where it is?"

"He pointed it out when we went by," Elizabeth admitted, her curiosity piqued. "But I haven't been inside."

"It's a start," Lucy coaxed. "Have you got any thumbtacks? I want to hang this on the door."

"Right here." Elizabeth opened a kitchen drawer and extracted a plastic box of tacks. "Of course, I don't know if he was telling the truth or not. He might not really live there at all."

"There's only one way to find out," Miss Tilley said.

Lucy hung the wreath, smiling at the effect, then closed the door. "It's better than sitting around here with Miss Marple."

"I'm not deaf, you know," Miss Tilley said, clicking away on the keyboard.

Lucy busied herself unpacking and took a long bath while Elizabeth put fresh sheets on the bed. She only had two sets of sheets, and a few towels, so the arrival of her guests meant she needed to do the laundry if they were going to have fresh linen. When she got back from the apartment complex's laundry room, she found the bedroom door was closed and only one lamp was burning, indicating her mother and Miss Tilley had retired for the night. It was only a little past nine but in Tinker's Cove people went to bed early and got up early.

She put the fresh towels in the bathroom and made up the futon for herself, but she wasn't ready to sleep. She set up the coffeepot for the morning, then settled down with a book. Her eyes followed the printed words and she turned the pages but she couldn't have said what the story was about, as her mind was too busy working on her problems. Her last thought, before she finally turned out the light, was the realization that she had nothing in the house for breakfast.

When she woke next morning she smelled coffee and the unmistakable scent of bacon.

"I popped out and bought some things," Lucy said, waving the fork she was using to turn the bacon. She was washed and dressed, as was Miss Tilley, who was sitting at the table on the deck with a cup of coffee and the morning paper. "Breakfast will be ready in a jif."

When Elizabeth emerged from the bathroom, freshly showered and dressed, she found a plate with bacon, eggs, and toast waiting for her.

"The best thing about Florida is the orange juice," Lucy said, pouring herself a second glass. "So fresh."

"I certainly don't think much of the newspapers here." Miss Tilley folded the big sheets of paper with a snap. "There isn't a word about the jewel theft."

"Be grateful for small mercies," Lucy said. "Imagine if they'd named Elizabeth."

The thought took away Elizabeth's appetite; she put down her fork and picked up her coffee mug.

"The sooner we start investigating, the better," Lucy said. "Besides, they say rain is on the way."

Miss Tilley popped the last bit of toast into her mouth. "And while you're out and about you could pick up a bottle of sherry. Tio Pepe, if you can find it."

"We better go, before she thinks of something else," Lucy said, grabbing her handbag.

Elizabeth gave her mother a tour of the neighborhood, making a stop at a liquor store to buy Miss Tilley's favorite dry sherry. Chris Kennedy's alleged apartment complex was just around the corner, and was similar in layout to Elizabeth's, with a scattering of buildings set in landscaped grounds. A recreation area included a pool, tennis courts, and a fitness center.

"Which is his apartment?" Lucy asked as Elizabeth pulled into a guest parking spot.

"I don't know. We'll just have to check the mailboxes," Elizabeth replied, with a nod toward the gray metal cluster unit where a white postal service truck was parked. They waited and after a few minutes the truck moved off. The two women strolled over and studied the names affixed to each mailbox; Chris Kennedy's name was on the box marked C-4.

"He was telling the truth after all," Lucy said.

Elizabeth scowled, unimpressed. "This doesn't prove anything."

A glance at the neat white brick buildings revealed that each was identified with a large letter. Building C was only a short distance away. When they approached it, they had no problem identifying apartment 4.

It was the one with yellow police tape over the door.

"I expected as much," Lucy said, turning to go.

"Not so fast." Elizabeth found she was suddenly determined to discover as much as she could about the mysterious Chris Kennedy. "This is a ground floor apartment. I bet there's a patio door around back."

They followed the paved path that ran around the building, noting the Christmas decorations that some people had put in their windows. One twinkling snowman winked at them and waved his arm. "I hope he's the only one who sees us," Elizabeth said.

Chris's patio was the only one completely devoid of plants or furniture. "A typical bachelor," Lucy remarked, cupping her hands and peering through the uncurtained sliding door.

Elizabeth studied the patio area, trying to think where Chris might have hidden an extra key. There was no furniture, so that was out. The trim around the door and windows was narrow — no place to tuck a key there — and there was no doormat. Checking out the plantings, she noticed a scattering of conch shells, and when she examined them she discovered one had a key taped inside.

"Good work!" Lucy exclaimed as Elizabeth unlocked the door. "Are you sure you haven't been here before?"

"Never," Elizabeth declared, stepping inside the largely empty living-dining room where a bicycle suspended on large orange hooks screwed into the ceiling provided the only decoration. A saggy old sofa, clearly secondhand, faced a large flat-screen TV that perched on a plank stretched between two concrete blocks. A row of books, mostly paperbacks, was lined up on the floor against a wall.

"Definitely needs a woman's touch," Lucy observed, heading straight for the kitchen and opening the refrigerator. "Very interesting," she said, pointing out a package of fish that was dated the day of the robbery.

"Very smelly," Elizabeth added.

"And from that I deduce that Chris Kennedy was not planning to leave town. Look, there's even a bag of salad in the crisper. You wouldn't buy fish and salad if you were planning to abscond with stolen jewels."

"That's an interesting point," Elizabeth said, peeking into the single bedroom. The comforter on the double bed had been smoothed and there were clothes in the closet as well as a carry-on size suitcase. "It's weird, isn't it?" she said, when Lucy joined her. "It all looks like he just left to go out for a loaf of bread or something."

"If he isn't a lawyer, like he said, I wonder what he does do," Lucy mused.

"Whatever he does, he doesn't keep regular hours." Elizabeth was thoughtful. "Maybe he's unemployed. Or maybe he's a jewel thief."

"There's no computer," Lucy said.

"I guess he took it with him — it could have been in the bag he was carrying in the video."

"There's also no phone," Lucy observed.

"He has a cell phone. Nobody bothers with landlines anymore."

"Right," Lucy said, feeling like a dinosaur, unable to keep up with a changing world. "Check the bathroom. See if his toothbrush is there."

"Good idea. Nobody travels without their toothbrush."

"Unless they forget it," said Lucy.

Elizabeth stepped into the small, utilitarian bathroom that could be a clone of her own. The tiny vanity sink was clean, a neatly folded towel hung on the rail, and a University of Florida mug contained a half-used tube of whitening toothpaste and a very worn toothbrush. "I guess he either forgot it, or he left town suddenly."

"Like somebody on the run," said Lucy.

Elizabeth nodded, wishing she hadn't come. Until now she had believed that Chris was just avoiding her, wary of entanglement and commitment. That was what guys did. The women's magazines were full of advice on how to turn casual love affairs into meaningful relationships. But now it seemed the police were right about him. Why would he leave town so suddenly — unless he had stolen the jewels?

Observing her daughter's crestfallen expression, Lucy tried to offer a positive slant. "Maybe he had to leave in a hurry because his mother was in an accident," she suggested. "Something like that. When people go home, they don't have to take stuff with them. He's probably got plenty of clothes and stuff at his parents' house."

Elizabeth brightened at this idea, but froze when she heard voices on the other side of the apartment door. "Somebody's coming," she whispered.

"Time to go," Lucy said, leading the way. They hurried outside and closed the sliding door behind them, then stepped to the side, where they couldn't be seen from inside the apartment, and waited. A slight breeze stirred the branches of a hibiscus bush, a bird sang, a lizard froze on a rock. Nobody entered the apartment; whoever had been outside had gone on their way.

Lucy exhaled and said, "I could use some of that sherry."

"Me, too."

Lucy studied her daughter's expression, noticing how depressed she seemed. "Cheer up, sweetie," she said. "I know just the thing. We'll stop and get a Christmas tree on the way home. What do you think of that?"

"Whatever," Elizabeth replied with a shrug.

CHAPTER 8

When they got back to the apartment, however, Miss Tilley was waiting for them impatiently. "What took you so long?" she demanded, picking up her purse and slipping on a light jacket.

"We stopped to get a Christmas tree," Lucy said as Elizabeth entered carrying a tabletop-sized balsam.

"It smells so nice," Elizabeth said, sounding almost cheery. "Christmasy."

"Besides, we haven't been gone all that long," Lucy protested. "And what are you up to? Where do you think you're going?"

"I am going out," Miss Tilley said. "Do you have a problem with that?"

"No," Lucy began, putting the bottle of sherry on the kitchen counter, "but I was thinking we could trim this tree. Elizabeth could use a distraction."

"There'll be plenty of time for that later," Miss Tilley said. "You make hay when the sun is shining — that's what my dear mother used to say. Right now is the time for gathering evidence. We need to pick up the pieces of the puzzle. I'm feeling as if I've got a box of pieces but the top of the box, the part with the picture, is missing." She paused for a moment, clicking her dentures. "I need to see the hotel, need to get the big picture."

"That's a good idea," Elizabeth said. "You and Mom should take a look at the place."

"Your mother wants to play Mrs. Santa Claus," Miss Tilley said, pursing her lips. "And besides, I want the behind the scenes tour. I'll need you to be my guide, Elizabeth."

Elizabeth's jaw dropped. "I can't go. I'm on probation. I'm banned from the property."

"That's ridiculous," Miss Tilley said with a sniff.

"It is kind of high school," Elizabeth admitted, "but if I want to get my job back I have to play by the rules."

Miss Tilley's jaw was set and Lucy and Elizabeth could practically hear the wheels grinding away in her grizzled old head. "I've got it," she finally said. "You can wear a disguise."

"It's Christmas, not Halloween," Lucy said.

"And I'm not an elf," Elizabeth added.

"I wasn't suggesting you should dress as an elf," Miss Tilley said. "That would attract too much attention, which is exactly what we don't want. You should go as a maid — nobody looks at the maids."

"She has a point," Lucy said, who had opened Elizabeth's laptop and was soon scrolling through a list of uniform supply companies. "There's a place not far from here that says they provide uniforms for all major local employers."

"Come to think of it, I could use a little rest." Miss Tilley was taking off her jacket. "I think I'll take a short nap while you get your disguise together," she said, with a nod to Elizabeth. "And don't forget a wig. I'd suggest blond. Nothing changes a woman's look as much as a different hair color."

"She's right," Lucy said, writing down the address of the uniform supply store. "And you're in luck. There's a costume shop on the same block."

"Lucky me," Elizabeth said, realizing that resistance was futile. She didn't doubt that Miss Tilley and her mother meant well, but she doubted that their cockamamie efforts would actually help her. In truth, she suspected they would only make things worse and she would probably spend the remainder of her fleeting youth in jail. These were her best years and she would be behind bars, wearing unflattering jumpsuits and a bad haircut.

Her GPS took her into an unfamiliar area of West Palm Beach, where small stores jostled for space with dodgy-looking bars and churches belonging to unfamiliar denominations. When she reached the uniform shop, she was surprised to see it was decorated to the hilt for Christmas. Colored lights were twinkling in the plate glass window, a couple of mannequins in hospital scrubs had wreaths around their necks, and inside a huge Christmas tree took up most of the floor space and Christmas carols were playing. The woman behind the counter, who could have been Mrs. Claus, was plump and twinkly and dressed in a red dress, white apron, and mobcap.

"Merry Christmas!" she exclaimed. "And what can I do for you?"

It suddenly occurred to Elizabeth that she was on a fool's errand. The Cavendish housekeepers all wore lavender shirtwaist dresses that the company supplied, so there was no reason for the store to stock them.

"I know it's unlikely, but do you have anything at all resembling a Cavendish maid's uniform?" she asked.

"I've got the real thing," Mrs. Claus replied. "What size?"

"Four," Elizabeth responded.

"No problem, I'll be back in a tick."

When she reappeared with a neatly folded uniform with lace collar and embroidered Cavendish logo on the breast pocket, Elizabeth could hardly believe her luck. "How on earth did you get this?" she asked. "The hotel supplies them and the girls have to turn them in when they leave. Who needs to buy them?"

"Well, you're buying one." Mrs. Claus raised an inquiring eyebrow. "I bet you spoiled yours and don't want to pay for the replacement, which is the Cavendish policy. My price is a lot cheaper than what Cavendish wants from the girls — a hundred fifty bucks, I think it is. Something like that. They're made in Italy, by nuns or something."

This was news to Elizabeth. "The maids have to pay for the uniforms?"

"Sure they do, if it's torn or stained and becomes unwearable." Mrs. Claus gave her a funny look. "I would've thought you'd

466

know that. What do you want it for, anyway?"

Elizabeth blushed. "My boyfriend has this
fantasy. . . ."

Mrs. Claus grinned naughtily. "Ah! Turn-
down service."

One hurdle cleared, Elizabeth thought
with relief. "But I still don't understand
how you get the uniforms if the girls have
to turn them in when they leave."

Mrs. Claus chuckled. "They're leaving the
country, dearie. They're going back to
Indonesia or Slovenia or wherever and they
want to take as much money with them as
they can, so they sell the uniforms to me.
They know the hotel isn't going to track
them down in Outer Slobovia for a worn-
out uniform."

"Right." Elizabeth realized she'd gotten
more insight about how the Cavendish
chain operated from Mrs. Claus than she
had from hours of training sessions. "So,
what is the price?"

"Twenty-nine ninety five."

Elizabeth paid and left, humming along to
"Frosty the Snowman."

As her mother had informed her, the
costume shop was just a few doors down,
next to the Reformed Chinese-American
Church of the First Light. Inside the shop,

Christmas and Halloween were fighting for space, the Bride of Dracula was sitting on Santa's lap, and a sexy little elf was clearly wild about the Wolf Man. There was no music; the chubby man behind the counter was listening to Rush Limbaugh.

"What can I do for you?" he asked, looking at her through thick glasses and scratching the wispy beard growing on his chin.

"I need a blond wig," she said. "And a pair of fake eyeglasses."

"Going undercover?" he asked, bouncing on the balls of his feet.

"Kind of," Elizabeth said. "It's just a joke, really."

"Like the ACORN thing?" he asked, eagerly.

"Sure," Elizabeth said, unwilling to give him too much information. "So where are the wigs?"

"In the back, behind Rudolph."

The reindeer's red nose was alight, illuminating a rack of variously colored wigs. Elizabeth chose the most realistic-looking blond one, a short, pageboy style, and also chose a pair of tortoiseshell eyeglasses with plain glass. The bill came close to forty dollars, using up most of her cash. On the way home she stopped at a drugstore and bought a bottle of cheap foundation, choosing the darkest shade she thought she could get away with. A display of Christmas tree lights caught her eye at the checkout and she impulsively picked up a box, breaking her last twenty-dollar bill. Going undercover was an expensive proposition.

Returning home with her purchases, she found her mother busy making origami crane Christmas tree ornaments out of colorful pages she'd ripped from Elizabeth's collection of fashion magazines. "Just what we need," Lucy exclaimed happily, when Elizabeth gave her the lights.

"I thought you were a sleuth of sorts, Lucy," Miss Tilley said, her voice dripping with disapproval. "What exactly are you contributing to this investigation?"

"This may look like busywork," Lucy said, waving the scissors, "but I'm actually freeing my subconscious to make connections and solve the theft. You'll see: the solution will pop into my head any moment."

Miss Tilley did not look convinced. "Come on, Elizabeth," she said. "Chop chop. I want to see the scene of the crime."

"Not until you have lunch." Lucy was already spreading tuna fish on huge slabs of whole wheat bread. "I don't know what to do for supper," she muttered. "I refuse to eat one of those microwave meals again."

Thirty minutes later Miss Tilley was seated beside Elizabeth in the Corolla, wearing her usual wool tweed skirt and cashmere sweater set along with thick support stockings on her scrawny legs.

"Aren't you too warm?" Elizabeth asked, sweating in the afternoon heat.

"Not a bit. Now what is our best plan of attack?" she inquired, as they proceeded down the long drive lined with royal palms that led to the hotel.

Elizabeth hesitated before answering, as she came up with a plan. As a pretend maid she had to park in the employee parking lot, but that was some distance from the entrance and she wasn't sure Miss Tilley could walk that far.

"I think it would be best if I dropped you off at the spa entrance," Elizabeth said. "There's no doorman there, so chances are nobody will see you getting out of a car driven by a maid. Once you're inside, you can ask the way to the lobby."

"If anyone sees me I'll just pretend I'm a dotty old lady," Miss Tilley chirped.

Not actually that far from the truth, Elizabeth thought, biting her tongue. "I'll meet you in the lobby. We'll pretend that you're lost and I'm showing you the way back to your room."

"Got it," Miss Tilley said as Elizabeth slowed the car and approached the canopied entrance to the spa. As she predicted, nobody was around and Miss Tilley was able to enter unobserved.

Driving onto the employee parking lot, Elizabeth was strongly tempted to speed off and head for the Mexican border, then remembered that although Florida was in the southern part of the country it was a peninsula surrounded by water and didn't share a border with Mexico. No, she'd have to go to the airport and board a plane to somewhere. Anywhere, as long as it was far away. Australia, maybe. But since she had no money and only had a thousand-dollar limit on her one credit card, that wasn't really an option. And she certainly wasn't dressed for travel in this stupid maid's uniform.

Sliding into a parking spot, she braked and turned off the ignition, then flipped down the visor to check her appearance in the mirror. The blond wig was itchy, but it really did change her appearance. When she slipped on the fake eyeglasses she hardly recognized herself. She took a deep breath to steady her nerves, climbed out of the car, squared her shoulders and, once again, took the familiar route she had followed every working day to the employees' entrance. This time, she feared, would probably be the last.

Suddenly suspicious that she might be observed by a hidden camera, she paused at the time clock and pretended to clock in, snagging a name tag from the adjacent rack and fastening it just above the breast pocket of her uniform. Then she popped into a supply cabinet and got a squeeze bottle of cleaner and a rag; thus armed she was confident she would fade into the background, somebody nobody wanted to see.

Her next problem was getting access to the secure areas of the hotel, which required a key pass. Mr. Dimitri had confiscated hers and without it she wouldn't be able to give Miss Tilley much of a tour. She decided to try the women's locker room on the off chance that somebody had dropped one. When she entered she found she was alone except for one middle-aged woman who was just unbuttoning her lavender shirtwaist.

"Hi!" she said, greeting her. "You haven't seen a key card, have you?"

"Did you lose yours?" the woman asked. She had big brown eyes that expressed concern.

"I must have. I thought it was in my pocket but now it's gone."

"You're in big trouble," the woman said.

"I know," Elizabeth wailed. "I can't afford to lose this job."

The woman's face softened. "Take mine," she said, offering a Cavendish-green rectangle of plastic.

"Are you sure?" Elizabeth was genuinely shocked at the woman's generosity.

"Just slip it through the vent in my locker when you're done — number thirty-four."

"I can't thank you enough," Elizabeth said, impulsively hugging her.

She patted Elizabeth on her back. "Just don't forget to return it."

"I won't," Elizabeth promised, watching the woman pick up her tote bag and leave, walking slowly as if her feet hurt.

Then she herself left the locker room and followed the service hallway, receiving nods and smiles from the few employees she met. So far, so good, but the lobby would be more of a challenge. For one thing, Toni might be on duty, and you never knew when Mr. Dimitri was going to pop out of his office. Reaching the unobtrusive doorway to the lobby, she nudged it open, relieved to see a large party of Asian tourists was checking in at the front desk. Seizing the moment, she slipped into the lobby and began polishing the first thing she saw, which happened to be a lamp. Glancing around, she noticed Miss Tilley, who had seated herself on a plump sofa beneath a twinkling wreath.

Elizabeth made her way around the room, flicking her rag at imaginary bits of dust, until she reached the seating arrangement where Miss Tilley was making a show of admiring a handsome pink and white amaryllis plant that was on the coffee table. Elizabeth bent down and began dusting the table.

"What a beautiful plant," Miss Tilley said. "I believe this variety is called Apple Blossom."

"It's nice," Elizabeth muttered.

"I guess I really ought to go up to my room and get ready for dinner. My son is taking me out," she said, rising with effort and then plunking back down, as if she hadn't enough strength to stand.

"Let me help you." Elizabeth offered, playing along. She took the old woman's arm and helped her to her feet.

"Goodness, I don't feel very steady on my feet," Miss Tilley said with a big wink, just in case Elizabeth didn't realize she was play-acting.

"I'll help you to your room," Elizabeth said, taking her by the arm and intending to lead her to the elevator. She was planning to give Miss Tilley a quick peek of a hallway, maybe a glimpse of an empty room, and then get her out of there. They were almost at the bank of elevators when Elizabeth spotted Mr. Kronenberg crossing the lobby in the same direction, clearly also headed for the elevators. Elizabeth's heart was pounding. She knew that she could kiss her job good-bye if she was discovered. She quickly decided to make a detour to the ballroom, confident they could slip in unnoticed while staff members were occupied with the large group of newly arrived Asian guests.

Much to Elizabeth's surprise, the decorations for the Blingle Bells Ball were still in place, though the patience roses were wilting.

"Goodness me!" Miss Tilley exclaimed. "I didn't expect anything like this!"

"The party favors were diamonds," Elizabeth said. "Money clips for the men, pendants for the women."

"So unnecessary," Miss Tilley said, clucking her tongue. "Such extravagance."

"What next?" Elizabeth asked. "Did you see the pool?"

"I walked through, on my way from the spa," Miss Tilley said. "They have some lovely succulents. So exotic-looking! And birds of paradise."

"Did you see the tea room?" Elizabeth asked.

"I glanced in while I was waiting for you. I took a peek at the gift shop and the bar, too."

Elizabeth thought she might be granted a reprieve. "So do you have the big picture?"

"I'd really like to see the Grubers' suite," she said.

Elizabeth had a vivid mental picture of a jail door banging shut behind her, locking her in a tiny cell. "Really?" she asked, in a small voice.

"Let's go." Miss Tilley sounded like a nursery school teacher rounding up her small charges. "Don't dawdle."

"Take my arm and hobble," Elizabeth ordered, patting her pocket and extracting the key card.

Together they left the ballroom and made their slow way across the lobby to the restricted elevator, which they shared with a swarthy man wearing tennis whites. He ignored them and got off at the junior suite level, leaving them to ascend alone to the penthouse level. They stepped out, into a very white foyer, facing four sets of paneled doors, one for each of the hotel's most luxurious and most expensive suites.

"What now? Do we just go in?" Elizabeth asked. "What if they're here?"

"Knock and say 'housekeeping.' That's what maids do," Miss Tilley urged. "If there's no answer, just go in. You can always say you were checking to make sure they have enough towels."

"And how do I explain your presence?"

"I won't go in unless the suite is empty," Miss Tilley said. "I'll wait here. If anybody comes I'll just pretend I'm one of those foolish old people who go wandering off and get themselves lost."

"Okey-dokey," Elizabeth muttered, tapping on the door and getting no response. "What exactly is the penalty if you're convicted of breaking and entering?" she asked, slipping her key card into the slot.

"In Florida? Probably death by lethal injection."

"Not funny," Elizabeth growled, stepping inside the suite and closing the door behind her. A moment later she came back and admitted Miss Tilley.

It was clear at a glance that the Grubers were still in residence, at least Noelle was, judging from the numerous bags and boxes bearing the logos of exclusive shops that were strewn about the expansive living area with ocean views. The floor was dotted with shoes, and the furniture was piled with heaps of clothing: mountains of white satin and clouds of frothy tulle. The white fur coat was balled up in a heap on the floor outside the bedroom door.

Miss Tilley merely shook her head, clearly horrified at the mess. "Not a very ladylike way to live," she finally said.

Elizabeth was amused at Miss Tilley's old-fashioned word choice. "My women's studies professor insisted that the concept of ladylike behavior is a form of bondage that kept women from expressing their true selves."

Miss Tilley waved an arm at the mess. "Perhaps it's an old-fashioned term, but the concept remains valid, even today. There are still standards of decent behavior," she said, "and this is not any way to live."

Elizabeth was about to agree when she heard voices outside the door and the beep that signaled the door had been unlocked by a key card. "Quick!" she hissed, grabbing Miss Tilley and shoving her into the bedroom. Once inside she glanced around frantically, but the only place to hide was either under the bed or in the roomy closet. There was no way Miss Tilley was going to crawl under the bed, so Elizabeth chose the closet. "Quick, in here," she said, opening the louvered door.

CHAPTER 9

As closets went, it was really top of the line, Elizabeth noted. It was huge, for one thing, amply ventilated and well lit, thanks to the louvered doors that admitted plenty of air and light. Noticing there was a bench to sit on to put on shoes, Elizabeth helped Miss Tilley lower herself onto it. It was really quite a comfortable hiding place, except for the fact that it didn't offer much in the way of concealment. There were only a few pieces of clothing hanging from the rod, probably put there when the maid unpacked. Noelle certainly didn't bother to hang up her clothes after she wore them; she simply pulled them off and dropped them wherever she happened to be when she undressed.

If anyone opened the door, which made the light turn on automatically, Elizabeth and Miss Tilley would be immediately discovered. But what were the chances of that? There was no need for Noelle to open the closet since the larger part of her wardrobe was scattered about the suite, tossed on the furniture and floor. The few garments left in the closet seemed to Elizabeth to be rejects: a simple gray tweed suit, a tan pantsuit, and a couple of conservative knit dresses in muted, solid colors. Not at all the sort of clingy, revealing thing that Noelle usually wore.

Feeling somewhat relieved, she concentrated on listening to what the two women were saying. The closet was located just inside the master bedroom door, only feet away from the wet bar in the living room.

"Jonah is furious with me," Noelle said, plunking some ice into a glass and following with a few splashes of liquid. "He thinks I was careless with the jewels."

He'd be right, Elizabeth thought, remembering the way Noelle ripped off the necklace and tiara after the photo shoot and tossed them on the bed. Elizabeth had actually needed to crawl around on the floor to recover the emerald ring. How could people be so careless? she wondered. Noelle seemed completely oblivious to the jewels' incredible value, didn't have any respect for the money they represented, or the talent and effort that enabled her husband to afford them. Gruber, as everyone knew, was a college dropout from an average, middle-class family who had built his fortune from the bottom up by developing a computer program that spotted developing market trends, which he then applied to build his astonishing fortune.

"What's the big deal?" Layla asked. Her voice was fainter than Noelle's, so Elizabeth figured she must be standing by the door to the terrace. Good idea, she thought, concentrating hard and willing the two women to step outside. If they went out to the terrace, it might give her and Miss Tilley an opportunity to make a quick escape. But no — now Layla's voice was louder, which meant she was coming closer. "They're insured, aren't they?"

"You don't understand," Noelle replied. Elizabeth heard the slight sucking sound that meant the fridge was being opened, and there was more clinking of ice, which undoubtedly meant Noelle was fixing herself another drink. Elizabeth thought it must be alcohol of some kind that she was splashing into the glass.

"So tell me, what don't I understand?" Layla asked. "And since you're pouring, I'll have a Scotch, too, while there's still some left in the bottle."

"Oh, sorry. It's just I'm so distracted," Noelle said. "Jonah's been so mean to me lately. We haven't had sex for two whole days and now he's gone off to Seattle, leaving me to cope with the cops and everything. I know it's because he blames me."

"I still don't get it," Layla said. "If they're insured, what's the big deal? He'll get the money and he can buy more jewels."

"But not those jewels," Noelle said. There was the sound of a glass being set down on a table and Elizabeth winced, thinking of the flawless French polish finish, laboriously applied by hand to all the furniture in the suite. "He was batty about them. Like they made him some sort of emperor. An Internet emperor! He did all this research, and he'd go on and on about the empress, who was Napoleon's second wife. Did you know he divorced Josephine? I thought they were big lovers, like Cleopatra and that Roman guy, or Liz Taylor and Richard Burton."

"They got divorced, too," Layla pointed out.

"You're right!" There was more clinking of ice, and this time the glugging from the bottle went on longer than before; Noelle was pouring herself a generous drink. "You know, Richard Burton gave Liz a lot of jewels. Do you think that jewels are unlucky?

Bad for relationships, I mean?"

"Well, things certainly didn't work out for them, or for Napoleon," Layla said.

"Really? What happened?"

Elizabeth glanced at Miss Tilley, whose wide eyes and pursed lips seemed to express both disbelief and disapproval. She knew how the former librarian detested misinformation.

"He was killed at the Battle of Waterloo," Layla said.

Elizabeth made eye contact with Miss Tilley, who she knew was dying to rush out and correct this false statement. "No, no," she mouthed, and Miss Tilley rolled her eyes and expelled a long sigh.

"That's just tragic," Noelle said. "And he invented champagne, too."

"I don't think that's right," Layla said. Her voice was growing louder, which Elizabeth figured meant she was coming closer to the closet. "I think it was a monk."

"A monk!" Noelle exclaimed, also sounding closer. "That's crazy."

Elizabeth found herself tensing, crossing her fingers and willing the two women to go in the other direction, back to the terrace or the bar. Anywhere except the closet.

"So," Layla asked, "what are you going to wear for dinner tonight?"

When she heard Noelle's reply Elizabeth thought her heart would stop. She instinctively stepped closer to Miss Tilley.

"Jonah wants me to wear that ugly green dress, the one he chose because it set off the jewels. He said I need to watch my image, that I need to appear more conservative now that I'm the focus of so much attention. But if you ask me, I think he's punishing me."

Elizabeth and Miss Tilley both turned to stare at the demure green sheath suspended from a padded satin hanger. It was long-sleeved and high-necked, with a slight gathering of fabric that emphasized the waist.

"So where is it?" Layla asked. "I don't see it anywhere."

"I guess it's in the closet." Noelle's voice rose, as if she'd had a sudden inspiration. "I'm tempted not to wear it. He's not here after all."

Good idea, Elizabeth thought. You don't like it, wear something else. Like those skinny black pants you left on the sofa, and that silky halter top that was draped across a lamp shade.

"I wouldn't do that," Layla advised. "There's bound to be a photo of you on *Page Six* and he's already pretty pissed at you. Why make it worse?"

"Oh, all right." Noelle sounded exasperated.

Darn. This was it, Elizabeth thought, her heart thudding in her chest. The game was up. Miss Tilley stood up and Elizabeth took her hand, as if they were facing a firing squad.

"I'll get it for you," Layla said, opening the door.

You had to hand it to Layla. She was cool as a cucumber when she spotted Elizabeth and Miss Tilley. It was Noelle who was shrieking her head off.

"What are you doing here?" Layla demanded.

"Checking towels?" Elizabeth said. "Just making sure you had enough."

"Very funny," Layla said. "And who's your little wrinkled friend? The towel elf?"

Noelle had quieted down and was staring at Elizabeth. "She's the one who stole the jewels!" she declared, snatching the wig off her head. "I'd recognize you anywhere," she snarled. "I saw you on the video."

"That's utter nonsense," Miss Tilley said. "Elizabeth is completely innocent and, for your information, Napoleon did not die at Waterloo. He died in exile on the island of Saint Helena. The cause is in dispute; some historians believe he was poisoned."

"Big deal," Layla said. "I'm calling security."

"I wouldn't do that if I were you, Lois," Miss Tilley warned, seating herself primly on the foot of the bed. Elizabeth remained standing protectively by her side.

"Lois?" Noelle demanded in a know-it-all voice. "There's no Lois here. You think you're so smart but you haven't even got Layla's name right."

"Oh, I think I have." Miss Tilley turned to Layla. "You're actually Lois Feinstein, aren't you?"

"Don't be ridiculous," Layla declared. "I don't know where you got an idea like that. Everybody knows me, I'm famous. I'm the party planner everybody wants. You can read about me in the *New York Times,* in *Vogue,* even *Vanity Fair.*" She laughed. "And I'm pretty sure you can't afford me."

"Journalism simply isn't what it used to be," Miss Tilley said. "Whatever happened to investigative reporting? It only took me a few clicks of the mouse to discover your true identity." She opened her large purse with a click and extracted a printout of a mug shot picturing a younger but clearly recognizable version of Layla. The name beneath the sullen face was Lois Feinstein. "You were convicted of drunk driving and vehicular manslaughter, for running down three club-goers in Long Island in 2003. One died, one remains in a coma, and the third is confined to a wheelchair."

"Is this true?" Noelle demanded.

"Everybody has a bad day now and then," Layla/Lois said. "It was a long time ago and I've paid my debt to society. I went to jail for five years, and when I came out I started my business and it took off like gangbusters. I think I deserve some credit for making a new start."

"New start!" Miss Tilley scoffed. "Is that what you call stealing your client's jewels?"

"You didn't!" Noelle hissed.

"Of course I didn't," Lois insisted, picking up the Birkin bag she'd left on a chair. "She's all wrong. I didn't have anything to do with the theft."

"I think you did," Elizabeth said, remembering the confusion after the photo shoot. "You pretended to lose the key to the case — that's when the jewels were taken, when we were all scrambling around, looking for the key."

"That's enough!" Lois said, reaching into her bag and producing a small pink handgun. "All of you, get out on the terrace."

"Not me!" Noelle protested.

"You, too," Lois snarled.

"But I thought we were friends," Noelle whined.

"Friends? Is this what you call being a friend? Nattering on endlessly about your problems, about how Jonah doesn't love you? Do you have any idea how self-centered you are? Do you?"

Noelle's face crumpled. "You're the rat! You're the one who stole my jewels!"

"Shut up! Now, out, all of you." She waved the gun, and Noelle darted across the room and out onto the terrace. Elizabeth followed, more slowly, helping Miss Tilley. Once they were outside, Lois slammed the door shut and locked it, leaving them to face the elements.

"We can call for help," Noelle suggested, leaning over the edge. "Yoo-hoo," she screamed. "Help!"

"Save your breath," Miss Tilley advised. "We're too high up, and it's too breezy."

In fact, Elizabeth noted with dismay, the sky had clouded over and the wind was kicking up, signs that a tropical downpour was coming. She was looking for a means of escape, looking for a way to cross the gap to the neighboring terrace, when she heard a shriek from inside the suite. Peering inside, she recognized Dan Wrayburn and — could it be? — Chris Kennedy.

Noelle immediately began banging on the glass and yelling, to get their attention. Wrayburn busied himself cuffing Lois and Chris unlocked the door.

"What are you doing here?" Elizabeth asked, confronting him.

"Yeah!" Lois exclaimed, pointing at Chris. "He's the thief! And they're his accomplices," she added, swinging around to indicate Elizabeth and Miss Tilley. "You've got this all wrong. They broke into the suite! They're the thieves, not me."

Noelle's face was a cold mask of fury. "I'm a thief? I don't think so. This is my suite. You took advantage of me, of my friendship, and you locked me out. Locked me out of my own room, left me to rot on that terrace." She started to move toward Lois, but Chris intervened.

"It's over. The jewels have been recovered," he said. "Your partner in crime, Sammie Wong, was arrested at Teterboro this morning, about to leave for Dubai."

"Sammie had the jewels?" Noelle asked.

"Most of them were hidden in his camera cases, but the Star of Bethlehem was concealed in a jar of Crème de la Mer."

Elizabeth's jaw dropped. "I got that for

him," she said. "Maybe I am a conspirator after all."

CHAPTER 10

Suddenly the suite was filled with uniformed cops. Jonah Gruber had heard the news at the airport just as he was about to board and had returned to embrace a tearful Noelle. Chris Kennedy was explaining the situation to a police detective and Dan Wrayburn was talking on his cell phone, reporting to the hotel manager. Lois, handcuffed and sullen, was seated in a corner of a huge couch; her pink handgun was tagged and bagged and lay on the wet bar's polished pink granite counter.

"I don't think we need to linger," Miss Tilley said. "We're not needed here."

Wasn't that the truth, Elizabeth thought. Chris Kennedy hadn't given her a glance. It was obvious he didn't care a fig for her. He was some sort of investigator and he'd used her to get inside information. And besides, she wasn't eager to explain her presence in a Cavendish maid's uniform to Wrayburn.

"Let's go," she whispered. "I've got to get out of this uniform and return this pass before they figure out I shouldn't have it."

The two women worked their way through the crowded room to the open door, unnoticed in the confusion. The elevator was waiting for them and they descended without incident and made their way to the locker room where Elizabeth slipped the pass into locker thirty-four. They were making their way down the hallway and had almost reached the exit when Mr. Dimitri hailed Elizabeth.

"You know they caught the thieves!" he exclaimed.

"I heard," she said. "It's wonderful news." She stood awkwardly, unreasonably hoping he wouldn't notice the maid's uniform.

"Dan Wrayburn tells me you were instrumental in solving the case," he continued, speaking excitedly. "He said you went undercover, that the maid's uniform was a brilliant disguise and you will be able to testify against that awful party planner the Grubers hired." He shook his head and shuddered. "He said she is a convicted criminal and I don't doubt it. Those absolutely awful fake white Christmas trees were a crime! Talk about tacky."

Elizabeth found herself unable to speak,

but Miss Tilley was only too happy to fill the void. "I'm proud to be Elizabeth's friend," she said. "Let me introduce myself. I'm Miss Julia Tilley, from Tinker's Cove, Maine."

Elizabeth blushed in embarrassment. "I'm so sorry. I should have introduced you. This is Mr. Dimitri, the hotel manager."

"Pleased to meet you." Miss Tilley extended a knobby hand and Mr. Dimitri took it in both of his, then bent down and kissed it. "My goodness," she said. "No one has ever kissed my hand before!"

"It was my privilege," Mr. Dimitri said, oozing the charm he was known for. "And, Elizabeth, I hope you will return to work tomorrow?" His eyes twinkled. "In your green blazer at the concierge desk?"

Elizabeth was suddenly aware that quite a group of employees had gathered around them and were listening to every word. She recognized the faces of Kieran, Ada, Marketa, and so many others who had become her friends.

"Of course," Elizabeth replied.

"I'm not sure that's wise, dear," Miss Tilley said, patting her hand. She turned to Mr. Dimitri. "Elizabeth has been through a great deal lately and she needs some time to recover. Let's say she takes her scheduled vacation and starts her new position on January third."

"A much better idea," Mr. Dimitri agreed. "January third it is."

The group broke into spontaneous applause, causing Elizabeth to turn quite pink with pleasure. Mr. Dimitri leaned close and lowered his voice. "You'll be paid for the days you were on leave and you will find a generous bonus, too."

"Thank you, thank you so much," Elizabeth said.

And then, much to her surprise, Mr. Dimitri took her hand and kissed it, too. Over his sleek, oiled hair she caught sight of Toni, watching with an expression of shocked disbelief, and she smiled.

"*À bientôt,*" Mr. Dimitri said.

"*À bientôt,*" Elizabeth replied, taking Miss Tilley's elbow and walking out the door. It didn't feel like walking on stained and spotty concrete, she realized. She felt as if she were walking on a cloud.

Back at the apartment, they found Lucy putting the finishing touches on the Christmas tree. The origami cranes bobbed on their thread hangers and the little white lights twinkled and Christmas music was playing. "It's about time you got here!" she exclaimed. "I've been frantic with worry."

"We were stuck in a closet," Elizabeth said.

"And then we were discovered and Lois locked us out on the terrace," Miss Tilley added. "She locked Noelle out, too."

"It was scary. Lois had a gun, and the weather was turning nasty. We could have been stuck out there for hours until somebody noticed us."

"Chris Kennedy saved us," Miss Tilley said, seating herself on the futon. "He was on the case all along. They caught Sammie Wong trying to get to Dubai with the jewels."

"My goodness," Lucy said, blinking. "That's quite a tale."

"It was quite an exciting afternoon," Miss Tilley said, looking cool and collected with not a hair out of place. "I think I'd like a glass of that sherry now."

"I got my job back." Elizabeth reported the fact without any expression. "And a bonus, too."

"You don't sound very happy about it," Lucy observed, opening the bottle.

"I should be, shouldn't I?" she asked. "I don't know what's the matter with me. Thanks to Miss T I even got my Christmas vacation."

"That's great!" Lucy exclaimed, filling

three glasses.

"You're probably feeling a bit let down after all the excitement," Miss Tilley speculated, taking the sherry glass from Lucy and tossing back most of the contents in one gulp.

"It's more than that." Elizabeth leaned her elbow on the dining table and rested her chin on her hand. "I feel used. Chris Kennedy didn't really like me, he just wanted to get information from me. And he got me in trouble at work. I was going crazy, worrying about paying the rent. And worse than that, wondering if I'd ever get another job with my reputation ruined."

Lucy gave her daughter a hug. "Well, all's well that ends well," she said, kissing her on the cheek. "Now, it's after six. What shall we do for dinner? There's nothing in the house and I was too anxious to go shopping."

Elizabeth knew that dinner was always at six in the Stone household; her father insisted on it.

Just then the doorbell rang.

"I bet it's Toni, come to apologize." Elizabeth opened the door and gasped, finding Chris standing there. He was holding a huge pizza box and an enormous bouquet of long-stemmed pink roses.

"I'm so sorry," he said. "Will you forgive me?"

Elizabeth thought about the sleepless night she'd spent, and how she'd worried she would never be able to get another job, but that wasn't what had really bothered her. It was the hurt she'd felt when Chris didn't call, when he seemed to lose interest and dropped her. She didn't want to go through that again, not with this guy, she decided, starting to shut the door in his face.

"Elizabeth," her mother said, "he's brought food." Then Lucy was pushing her aside, taking the pizza and flowers. "I think I smell pepperoni, my favorite," she said. "Do come in and have some with us. We're dying to hear all about how you tracked down Sammie Wong."

Chris didn't hesitate. He was inside the apartment and casting sad eyes in Elizabeth's direction. She wasn't moved, however, despite his contrite expression. It reminded her of the looks Libby, the Labrador back home in Maine, would make when she knew she'd done something wrong, like chewing up a favorite pair of shoes. It didn't mean she was actually sorry or that she wouldn't do it again, it was simply a manipulative tactic she used to avoid punishment.

"Put these flowers in water," her mother said, handing her the bouquet.

Elizabeth left Chris standing awkwardly in the living room with Lucy and Miss Tilley and went into the kitchen to get a vase for the roses. She supposed her mother was right and she shouldn't let the flowers die of thirst even if she didn't much like their giver.

When she returned with the vase of flowers she discovered her mother had found the place mats and set the table on the deck, and was opening the pizza box. The rich, spicy aroma filled the air. "Come on, everybody, sit down before it gets cold."

"Elizabeth," she instructed, in her bossy mother tone of voice, "I think there's a bottle of soda in the fridge. Could you get it, please? And some glasses?"

When Elizabeth returned with the soda she discovered the only free seat was opposite Chris, who was waiting politely for the others to serve themselves. She sat down but made a point of not looking at him.

"I assume you were working for the insurance company all along?" Miss Tilley inquired, attacking her piece of pizza with a knife and fork.

"That's right," Chris said, finally taking a piece that was loaded with pepperoni.

"When Gruber took out the policy I was assigned to keep tabs on the jewels. That's company policy when somebody insures an exceptionally valuable item. If it's a painting, we check out the security system, stuff like that. If they're going to loan it to a museum or something, they have to inform us. It's the same with jewelry. They have to agree to keep it in a safe that we've approved and they have to inform us whenever it's taken out of the safe. So when Gruber announced this Blingle Bells Ball I went undercover here at the hotel."

"So you're not a conservation lawyer after all?" Elizabeth asked, narrowing her eyes.

"I lied to you," he said, looking miserable. "I didn't want to but I had to. I was undercover. I couldn't risk being discovered."

Elizabeth, expressionless, chewed her pizza.

"When did you begin to suspect Sammie Wong and Lois Feinstein?" Miss Tilley asked.

"Pretty much right away," Chris replied. "We did background checks on everybody connected with the ball and they stood out like sore thumbs — both had criminal records."

"You'd think Jonah Gruber would have checked, too," Lucy said. "After all, he's supposed to be some sort of computer genius."

"We informed him and he was going to get rid of them but his wife put up a fuss. Noelle insisted on hiring Layla/Lois, said nobody else would do, and Lois insisted on Sammie Wong for the photos."

"And the switch took place at the photo shoot," Miss Tilley said.

"That's right." Chris was reaching for a second slice of pizza. "The jewels were stashed in the photo equipment and Elizabeth took an empty case back to the safe."

"I can't believe I was that stupid," Elizabeth said, nibbling on the crust, her favorite part. "I should have checked the case. I just assumed they were inside when Layla locked it."

"It's a good thing you didn't question her," Chris said. "They might have harmed you." He looked into her eyes and reached across the table, covering her hand with his. "That's when I was most worried, when you were alone with them in that suite after the photo shoot. I was terrified something would happen to you."

Elizabeth snatched her hand away. "You could have told me. You played me for a fool. You even made it look like I was involved in the theft."

"That was for your safety," Chris explained. "We wanted you out of the way, safe at home. But it had the advantage of creating a smoke screen. As long as Sammie and Lois believed the police thought you and I were the thieves, they figured they'd gotten away with it. Sammie was headed off to Dubai with the jewels, on a private jet to avoid screening, and the New Jersey cops were able to nab him. Case closed."

"I guess you're pretty proud of yourself," Elizabeth said with a scowl.

Miss Tilley gave Lucy a significant look and stood up. "Lucy, dear, let me help you with the dishes."

"Oh, right," Lucy said, catching her drift. She picked up her plate and glass and followed Miss Tilley into the tiny kitchen, leaving Elizabeth alone with Chris.

It was warm on the balcony, the moon was rising and the air was fragrant with the sweet scent of Elizabeth's night-blooming nicotiana.

"Please understand," Chris pleaded. "I couldn't risk telling you, telling anybody. I had enough trouble with that friend of yours, that Toni."

"She was on to you right away," Elizabeth said. "She knew you were a Kennedy imposter."

"Imposter! I am a real Kennedy. My dad is Joe Kennedy from Dorchester, proud owner of Kennedy's Transmission Service."

For the first time since he'd arrived, Elizabeth smiled.

"Fake! That's something. Do you know how many Kennedys there are in Massachusetts?" he asked, cracking a grin.

"Quite a lot?"

"Yeah," he said, leaning across the table and taking her chin in his hand. "And I can't wait for you to meet the whole family." Then they were kissing, a hot, spicy, pepperoni-flavored kiss.

When it finally ended, Elizabeth came back for another. "I really, really like pizza," she said.

"Me, too," Chris said.

Dear Reader,

When I was in London a couple of years ago I visited the British Library where I was thrilled to see the page from Charlotte Brontë's manuscript for *Jane Eyre.* It was written in her own clear hand, open to the page that begins, "Reader, I married him." I don't know if Elizabeth will marry Chris, but I have enjoyed spending time with my series heroine Lucy Stone's oldest daughter, Elizabeth, and I hope you did, too.

Elizabeth has been part of the Lucy Stone Mystery Series since the beginning *(Mistletoe Murder)* and we've watched her grow up, go to college, and begin her career. She's always been the most cantankerous of Lucy and her restoration carpenter husband Bill's four children, and I suspect Lucy has a special place in her heart for her. I know that I do.

Of course, Lucy and Bill have three other children, Toby, Sara, and Zoe, and they've all had parts to play in the Lucy Stone Mystery Series, which is set in the entirely fictional coastal town of Tinker's Cove, Maine. Lucy is a part-time reporter for the local newspaper and her job often leads her to uncover crimes. Tinker's Cove is postcard-pretty but is, unfortunately, not immune to present-day problems such as poverty, drug addiction, and organized crime. Individual citizens also wrestle with their consciences, and sometimes succumb to their baser instincts, such as greed, revenge, and jealousy. All of that means there's plenty for Lucy to investigate.

In addition to uncovering crimes, Lucy is a busy mom, deeply involved in town events and holiday celebrations. That is the case in *Easter Bunny Murder,* coming out in February 2013, when she takes her grandson, Patrick, to the annual egg hunt at the Van Vorst estate — a hunt that, I am sorry to say, ends tragically. Lucy's determination to solve a puzzling death leads her into a dynastic drama rife with conflicts and rivalries, jealousies and secrets.

I hope you'll look for *Easter Bunny Murder* and the other books in the series and get to know Lucy and her family. I think you'll discover the Stones are a lot like your family.

Best regards,
Leslie Meier

■ ■ ■ ■

THE CHRISTMAS
COLLECTOR
KRISTINA MCMORRIS

■ ■ ■ ■

Dear Reader,

Only upon completing this novella did it occur to me that my literary journey has indeed come full circle. After all, it was a family Christmas gift that had sparked the idea for my debut novel, *Letters from Home.* The fact I had "borrowed" two characters from that story in order to create *The Christmas Collector,* though now as their elderly versions, seems all the more fitting.

You see, I was in the midst of interviewing my grandmother for the biographical section of a homemade cookbook, intended as a Christmas present for the grandkids, when she revealed a shocking detail: She and my grandfather had dated merely twice during WWII before uniting in a marriage that lasted until his passing, fifty years later. Until then, I had no idea their courtship had blossomed almost entirely through heartfelt letters, each of which Grandma Jean then retrieved from her closet to share.

Captivated by their relationship and a fading era, I soon sat down to pen my first novel, based on the question: How well can you truly know someone through letters alone? What formed as a result was *Letters from Home,* in which a WWII soldier falls deeply in love through a yearlong letter exchange, unaware that the girl he's writing to isn't the one replying. Unique cases of loved ones separated by war have since continued to fascinate me, as proven by my second novel, *Bridge of Scarlet Leaves*. Again inspired by a true account, the story follows a Caucasian woman who, refusing to be separated from her Japanese American husband, moves to an internment camp by choice. In many ways, the struggle of living between worlds, seeking out one's true identity, is a common thread among my books — as are themes of redemption and forgiveness, loss of innocence, the complexities of family, and the importance of memories. I hope you enjoy *The Christmas Collector* for all these reasons and more!

With warm holiday wishes,
Kristina McMorris

For 1940s holiday recipes, special book club features, and excerpts from the letters by Kristina's grandfather, visit www.Kristina McMorris.com.

CHAPTER 1

She tried to ignore him throughout dinner, but the squatty monk held Jenna's focus in a fisted grip. He seemed to be mocking her with a half smile curled into round rosy cheeks, his hand resting on the wide shelf of his belly. Traditionally a symbol of self-sacrifice and frugality, he instead radiated sheer overindulgence.

The fact he was a mere saltshaker didn't lessen Jenna Matthews's anxiety. She shifted in her seat, forced down another bite of instant mashed potatoes. She knew without question the Friar Tuck collectible was new to her mother's house. In a brown robe, his hair forming a silver wreath, he stood amid the Thanksgiving dishes as if staking his claim. A matching pepper shaker and sugar bowl flanked him on the dining room table. Candlelight flickered over the trio, casting shadows across the floral vase and oval doily.

New vase. New doily. New condiment

holders. All signs that Jenna's mother, Rita, had potentially relapsed.

But the woman gave no other indications. Over their holiday meal of turkey TV dinners — her mom's standard menu, now accustomed to cooking for one — she was rattling on about a film she had seen with a friend from her days in group therapy. Jenna feared those sessions might now be needed again.

"I just don't know why they insist on doing that." Her mother used a melodramatic tone for emphasis. "It ruins a perfectly good movie, don't you think?"

At the expectant pause, Jenna reviewed the discussion she had caught in disjointed pieces. "What does?"

"When they have those corny endings."

"Oh. Right."

"I swear, I can't recall the last time I saw a romantic comedy with a realistic ending. Some character always has to give an over-the-top speech in front of a reception hall, or even a whole baseball stadium. As if big revelations only come when you're holding a microphone." She puffed a laugh that jostled her hoop earrings. "Honestly. When have you ever seen that happen in real life?"

Forging a smile, Jenna shrugged, and her mother moved on to the next topic: a

Thanksgiving conspiracy by U.S. turkey farmers, based on her doubts over the pilgrims' actual supper. From a marketing perspective, Jenna hated to admit, the theory was intriguing enough to contemplate. She tried her best to listen, but her surroundings were of greater concern.

What other new purchases lurked in the shadows? She wrestled down the urge to spring from her chair and tear through the china cabinet on a hunt for more evidence. Perhaps she was overreacting.

Then again, she had witnessed firsthand how quickly a handful of knickknacks could multiply until they packed an entire mantel. A wall of bookshelves. Every drawer and cupboard in the house. And before long, you were drowning in a sea of objects no more satisfying than cotton candy: a temporary filler that, for her mother, eventually gave way to the reality of loss. It was this very emptiness that had devoured most of Jenna's high school years.

"Honey?" her mother said.

"Sorry — what?"

"I was wondering what you wanted for Christmas this year."

"Nothing." The reply came stronger than intended. "I mean . . . there really isn't anything I need."

"Well, then. I'll just have to get creative." She flashed a smile, accentuating the Mary Kay lipstick she'd worn since the early nineties. Her shimmery eye shadow matched her irises, a deep sea green like Jenna's, and created arcs beneath brown bangs teased to a frizz. Only once had Jenna tried to update her mom's fashion, citing her cowl neck sweater and stirrup pants, like the ones she wore now, as "Goodwill bound." The half joke didn't fly. Her mother had licked her wounds by buying six new bags of useless "stuff."

Of course, that was back in the midst of her mom's grieving, too soon after their family of three became two. Maybe, at last, she would consider a small change.

"I was thinking," Jenna began, gauging her approach, "I should probably get my hair colored in the next few weeks."

"Oh?" her mother said. "Are you going with a different shade?"

"Just getting rid of the gray." Jenna's stylist would faint from joy if Jenna ever agreed to liven up her shaggy brown bob with red or blond highlights, rather than simply disguising her scatterings of early silver. "Why don't you come along? Maybe try taking off a couple inches. You know, you'd look great with short hair."

Her mother's expression perked for a moment, the idea like a sun rising, then just as swiftly setting. She smoothed the ends of her shoulder-length do. "Maybe some other time."

At thirty-one, Jenna knew that answer well. Through decades of asking permission — hosting a slumber party, buying overpriced jeans — the meaning hadn't changed. *Maybe some other time* equaled *No.*

Jenna returned to her shriveled, gravy-drenched stuffing. The wall clock ticked slowly away. Every swing of its pendulum echoed against the marred wooden floors.

And from the table, that ceramic friar kept right on staring. His painted eyes speared her thoughts, piercing the walls of her past. Despite her efforts, Jenna couldn't hold back. "When did you get the new salt-shaker?"

"Huh? Ahh, that." Her mother brushed her hand clean with a napkin, monogrammed with an *L* for its previous owner — whoever that was — before picking up the item. "I got it back in, gosh, August I suppose. Apparently the creamer broke years ago. I thought I'd shown these to you already."

Jenna shook her head, bracing herself against her mother's nonchalance. Minor cracks and chips on the rims made the set's origin clear. A garage sale. Fliers and posters Jenna had passed on the drive here, each tacked to utility poles in the suburban Oregon neighborhood, now sprang to mind: *Yard sale this way! Clothes and furniture sale one block ahead!* They were like neon tavern signs tempting a recovering alcoholic.

Jenna should have visited more often, to keep better watch. With Christmas around the corner, folks everywhere loved purging their old junk to make room for their new junk. It was the all-American way. As an estate liquidator, Jenna had built a career upon that very principle. But that didn't stop her from despising the holiday that brimmed with manufactured, made-in-Taiwan cheer.

As her mother gazed in admiration at the figurine, Jenna's insides twisted into a braid of fear. "I thought you stopped buying those kinds of things."

"Oh, no, I didn't buy —" Her mother's cheery tone dissolved as she explained, "It was from Aunt Lenore."

Aunt Lenore?

And then Jenna remembered. Over the summer, back in the Midwest, the youngest sister of Jenna's late grandmother had passed away. Lenore used to send them handwritten Christmas cards, among the few people who did that anymore, and create doilies to raise money for the food bank.

Doilies, like the one on the dinner table. The faded floral vase, too, must have belonged to her great aunt.

"So, you just inherited these things," Jenna realized. Relief washed through her until she met her mother's gaze, and a mixture of embarrassment and distrust ricocheted between them.

Jenna sank into her chair, weighted by guilt. She sipped her merlot while her mother set down the shaker. Silence returned, heavy as a damp blanket. It draped the black lacquered chairs, a fake fern in the corner, the framed photo tacked to a pin-striped wall. The black-and-white image caught Jenna's eye. In a grassy field stood a single tulip, almost three-dimensional, airbrushed in vibrant yellow.

"Did you take that one?" she diverted.

Her mom looked over and nodded. "I was driving past a farm over in Damascus when I saw it. Just had to pull over."

"It's a really beautiful picture." A genuine compliment. Her mom's new job at a portrait studio, after a long career with the school district, had recently revived the hobby. "I like the color effect you added."

"Well, I did have some help with that part." A hint of excitement suddenly buoyed her voice. "I used this amazing new editing program. And Doobie's been wonderful, walking me through it. You remember me telling you about him?"

"A little." How could Jenna forget? The name of her mom's coworker sounded like a product of Woodstock. Or at least the remnants of what was smoked by everyone there.

"Anyway, he's also been teaching me about different lenses, and about the shutter speed for action shots — which has actually come in handy lately, with all the families getting their pictures taken for Christmas."

Given the modern rage of posting and sending digital images, Jenna was surprised families still bothered with formal portraits. Especially since, in reality, the majority of those mass-printed cards would receive a two-second glance before being tossed in a box.

Box . . .

Pictures . . .

"Crap."

"What's wrong, honey?"

Jenna groaned. "I forgot to do something."

Terrence, her right-hand man on the current sale, had phoned her yesterday while boarding a plane to see family. "Promise me you'll grab it," he'd said, "so it doesn't land in the trash." He'd meant to set aside a box, which he suspected the client would want to keep.

While Jenna cared little about personal valuables, she did care about promises.

"I'd better get home," she told her mom. "I have to go to work early tomorrow." Early enough to beat Mrs. Porter's garbage truck.

"But it's Thanksgiving. I thought everyone else had the weekend off."

True, each of her four crew members did. Yet Jenna had the most to gain if they met their profit goal. And the most to lose if they failed.

"No rest for the weary, right?" she replied lightly. Feeling a tinge of regret, she averted her eyes while bundling up in her coat. "Thanks for dinner," she said as they walked to the entry.

"Are we still on for this weekend?" her mother pressed.

It took Jenna a moment to identify the reference: the last Sunday of the month, their standing lunch date.

"Absolutely."

They met in a brief hug before Jenna dashed outside and into the rain. Once seated in her car, she looked back at the house. Blue shutters, trimmed lawn, windows aglow. It was an image ideal for a mass-printed card.

Almost.

CHAPTER 2

Drawing a deep breath of night air, Reece Porter rubbed at his right temple. Tension had formed an unbreakable knot. From a patio chair, he watched raindrops puddle on the tarp covering the pool. A drain spout drizzled a stream that bounced off the awning overhead, muted by the din of laughter and chatter and holiday tunes from inside the house.

He'd once considered the stereotypes of huge Italian families as nothing more than myth — pasta and red-sauce obsessed, talking over each other, involved in everyone's business — until he experienced his girlfriend's family, the Graniellos. Even the protectiveness exhibited by Tracy's brothers was fitting of a mob flick. When the accident happened two Decembers back, their distrust of Reece had magnified tenfold. But gradually he had earned their respect. In fact, aided by his dark features, few onlookers would guess he wasn't a natural link in the family circle.

He just wished that circle tonight didn't resemble a tightening vice.

Checking his watch, he blew out a sigh. Ten after nine. Another twenty minutes or so and he could excuse himself without being rude.

"There you are."

Reece turned toward the high yet gentle voice, and found Tracy stepping out of her parents' home. He started to rise, a reflexive habit from months of helping her through doors, up flights of stairs. But she had already closed the sliding glass door on her own.

She held up a pair of steaming coffee mugs. "Hot Apple Pie and a Peppermint Patty. Your pick."

The concoctions from her bartender cousin were always a little too sweet. But if nothing else, Reece enjoyed the tradition of them. He'd come to appreciate predictable comfort.

"I'll take whichever one you don't want," he told her.

After a pause, she shrugged a shoulder and gave him the one that smelled like cider. Then she smoothed her fitted dress and sat next to him. He blew on the surface to cool it off. He took a sip, only confirming his stomach's disinterest. The celebratory champagne was still swishing in his gut.

"You okay?" she asked.

"Yeah. Yeah, I'm fine. Just needed a little break from the noise is all."

She smiled in understanding. The contrast of his own family went without saying.

"You didn't eat much," Tracy remarked, and took a drink from her mug.

"Guess I'm still jet-lagged." It had been only five days since he'd returned from a six-week stint in London, where he'd helped a top account implement a new order-tracking system as part of his global logistics job. On the way back he'd stopped through the San Fran office and had flown back to Portland only this morning.

Perhaps travel weariness was the real root of the evening's claustrophobia. Or at least what was intensifying the pressure.

"You're up next, buddy," one of the uncles had told him over dessert, after Tracy's sister had announced her engagement. Reece had grown well accustomed to the group-wide sentiment. So why did the comment feel more like a threat than an invitation? More importantly, after all he and Tracy had been through together, why were doubts about their future scratching at his mind?

Just look at the girl: perfect posture, as much from Catholic school as from years of riding equestrian; long black hair in a braid, highlighting her narrow features; gorgeous blue eyes, so light they were almost clear. She was no less striking than when they had first met at a charity golf scramble two summers ago. A petite thing, she'd instantly impressed him by nailing the longest drive on the third hole, all to raise funds for a new ward at St. Vincent's.

Little had Reece known how many hours he'd later spend at that very hospital, helping Tracy through physical therapy. The grueling sessions had sealed their bond. Yet that bond was no match for the discomfort now festering between them.

"So . . ." she said as if fishing for a topic. "Did you talk to your parents yet? To wish them a good Thanksgiving?"

"I called Grandma's, but nobody answered. So I left a message on my mom's cell."

"That's strange they weren't there." She was right, though there wasn't anywhere else they'd have spent the day.

"I'm sure they just missed the ring. I'll try again on my way home."

"I hope everything's all right."

Her tone caused Reece a niggling of concern. Elderly couples too often passed in pairs. But it had been five years since losing his grandfather, and still, even at eighty-seven, his grandma was a healthy, feisty little thing.

Detouring from the thought, he mustered enthusiasm over the subject he had no logical reason to avoid. "That's great news, by the way, about Gabby."

Tracy returned his smile. "They make a great couple."

"Do they know where they're getting married?"

"They're talking about Sonoma, at the winery where they met. It's the same place he proposed."

Reece nodded, pushing himself to continue. "Have they set a date?"

"Gabby was hoping for a summer wedding, but Mom wants her to wait till Heidi has her baby, so traveling will be easier."

For a moment, Reece had forgotten Tracy's sister-in-law was expecting a second child. He tried for a casual comment, yet the words wouldn't flow; they snagged on the jagged milestones everyone around them was tackling with gusto.

He forced down another sip of his spiked

cider. Beside him, Tracy fidgeted with the handle on her mug. Noise from the house lightened along with the rain, amplifying their exchange of quiet.

At last, she angled her body toward him. "Reece . . . I think it's time we talked. About our relationship."

He replied with forged levity. "What's on your mind?"

"The thing is, I've been giving my life a lot of thought while you were away. I'm almost thirty, and every time I try to envision us five or ten years down the road, nothing seems clear."

Without her saying it, he knew the source of the haze. It was him. What he didn't know was which obstacle continued to hold him back. From skydiving to bungee jumping, he used to be the type to literally plunge headfirst without a thought.

In a single day, all that had changed.

"I can't help but wonder," she went on, "if you're still with me just because —"

"Tracy!" a voice hollered from behind. Her mother had reopened the sliding glass door. "Heidi and Marco have been looking for you."

"They're not leaving yet, are they?"

"Marco said he wants to get up before dawn. He's already warming up the car."

528

Tracy let out a heavy breath. Apparently, she'd agreed to watch their toddler, freeing the couple for the Black Friday stampede. Not even pregnancy could deter shoppers on a mission.

She looked at Reece, clearly torn.

"Come on, come on," Tracy's mother urged. "They're waiting."

Reece gave Tracy's hand a tender squeeze. "Go ahead," he assured her. "We'll talk later."

Though hesitant, she nodded her agreement. He leaned over and kissed her on the lips, brief enough for a parental audience, and watched Tracy step inside. Her mother sent him an approving wave.

Alone again, he realized he, too, would be free to leave. The idea of settling into his apartment, giving himself a chance to think, to better prepare for the rest of their discussion, sounded awfully appealing.

Before he could stand, his cell phone buzzed in his jacket pocket. He answered and found relief at the absence of urgency in his mother's tone.

"Honey, I'm sorry we didn't call you back earlier. Dinner had me going a bit crazy."

"How'd it turn out?"

"Not the best," she admitted wearily. "I tried to deep fry the turkey this year, and it was a total disaster. While I was dealing with *that* mess, half of the side dishes ended up overcooked."

The kitchen always tended to be this chaotic when, on the alternate years, his grandmother didn't run the show. But usually his sister provided damage control.

"Wasn't Lisa there to help?"

"She got stuck in terrible traffic in Seattle, so she didn't get here till late."

Reece felt a tug of regret for not joining them. Last year, he and Tracy had split time between both families, and ended up not enjoying either one on a tight schedule. Now, at his mother's recap, he was struck by the family traditions he had missed out on, burnt food or not. Thankfully, Tracy had agreed to spend Christmas Eve at his grandmother's house. He could already smell the glazed ham and hot chocolate; could hear Bing Crosby's velvety voice lined with a soft crackle from their record player. No modern CD or iPod. Always a real thirty-three LP, same one since his childhood. Speaking of —

"Do you want me to pick up a tree tomorrow, or is Dad doing that? For Grandma, I mean."

"For Grandma . . ." she repeated in a pondering tone. "Um, well. That's something we haven't had a chance to discuss with you, since you've been gone."

"I don't understand."

A pause fell over the line.

"Mom?"

"Why don't you come over tomorrow and your father can explain."

"Explain what?"

Muffled, she spoke to someone off the handset, then finally returned. "Honey, I've gotta help clean up. We'll see you tomorrow, all right?"

Reece's jaw tightened. He was about to demand she fill him in, but recalled the strain her evening had been. Relenting, he simply said good night. After all, if it was anything critical, his mother would have told him.

Wouldn't she?

CHAPTER 3

Jenna steered through the swampy fog, pulse quickening. Her smearing wipers only worsened the view. Experimenting with the headlights didn't help. Six in the morning, but not a slit of light. Well, except for the blinding beams from passing commuters coasting downward.

She reduced her speed, eyes trained on the solid white line running parallel to the guardrail. In the tree-laden hills overlooking Portland, the Skyline neighborhood was considered one of the most affluent, but come January, their snaking boulevard would turn slick enough for a luge.

It took a little patting to find the defrost button by feel. The second she turned it on she realized her grave mistake. Warm air flooded the windshield and thickened the haze. Resisting panic, she scrambled for the knob to shut it off. In the process she hit the radio button, launching "Carol of the

Bells" through the airwaves.

*Deeeng . . . donnng . . . deeeeng . . .
donnng . . .*

The monotonous loop intensified as she rolled down the window. She poked her head out to see the road. A wall of cold shivered her skin.

*Deeeng . . . donnng . . . deeeeng . . .
donnng . . .*

What the heck was she doing, risking her life to save a measly shoe box? Trading in her nice sedan for this two-door tin can should have reinforced her need to say no. Her first mistake had been to let her old boyfriend talk her into buying a condo together. "A good investment," he'd called it. Of course, she hadn't counted on him losing his job, or the realty bubble bursting. And when they split up, she didn't have much of a choice but to purchase his half.

This, she reminded herself, was the greatest reason for her drive through the misty blackness, her nose threatened by frostbite. Because there just might be a gem in that box Terrence found. He'd mentioned a container inside that appeared to hold jewelry. Clients often didn't realize what they owned. Like exploring a sunken ship, she simply needed to look under the right plank. A single treasure could seal the deal with her boss: "You get me a fifteen percent increase over the last estate, and I'll make you a partner." That's what he'd agreed to after months of Jenna's requests, all posed as a win-win; her boss could focus on other ventures and Jenna, his top employee, would earn them even more if she was personally invested. Her goal finally had clarity, same as the view now through the windshield.

She pulled her head back inside. Teeth chattering, she closed the window and silenced the radio in the midst of "Santa Baby." The lyrics were but a wish list of materialism. Further support that the holiday came once a year too often.

Two turns and a sharp curve later, Jenna parked at the base of the sloped driveway. Its steepness, she'd been told, was part of the rationale behind selling. With Mrs. Porter now living in her son's family home, her large Victorian house loomed dark and still.

At the curb stood a lineup of four garbage bins, each so packed that the lids gapped by a foot. Her crew would be filling many more of those before they were done. The thought made her happy; the idea of scrounging through them made her cringe.

She would check inside the home first.

The keys on her loop were labeled by

house number, organized numerically. A good system in daylight. Prior to dawn, not so much. Judging by the keys' shapes, she went with her first guess. No luck. A second one glided easily into the lock, but wouldn't turn. When she tried to slide it out, the key's metal teeth clenched and held, refusing to budge.

A squeak of brakes spun her around. A van rolled past. She still had time before the trash pickup. But how much?

Just then, the front door flew open. Her keys broke free and dropped to the ground. Fear of an intruder stalled her heart. Then the silhouette gained definition, and Jenna recognized the person she had met briefly in passing.

"Mrs. Porter," she said with a sigh. "I didn't think you'd be here."

"I gathered as much."

Jenna recalled the early hour. "Sorry. I hope I didn't wake you."

"Not at all. I was up doing my Pilates."

At her age? She had to be in her late eighties, and wearing a pink frilly bathrobe, a scarf around her curlers.

"Wow, that's amazing. Really?"

The woman peered over her cat-eye glasses. "No, dear."

At first taken aback, Jenna smiled.

"Well, I suspect you're here to work. So have at it." Mrs. Porter shuffled toward the kitchen, flipping lights on as she went. Word had it, as the widow of a local college president, she was rarely seen in anything but her Sunday best. Predawn clearly afforded an exception.

"I'll be right here in the den," Jenna called out.

Mrs. Porter didn't respond.

Jenna shut the front door and hurried into the study. She yanked the chain of a desk lamp, illuminating the ceiling-high bookshelves. A layer of dust further aged the antique book collection. The room's paisley trim, burgundy curtains, and leather wingbacks were straight out of *Masterpiece Theater* — but surrounded by junk.

When Jenna started a week ago, the stacks of decades-old magazines had been the first to go. Paper grocery bags and used gift wrap, even saved aluminum squares, had filled two whole recycle bins. Typical of Great Depression survivors, the woman "didn't like to waste."

Jenna's mother used to lean on the phrase when her so-called collecting began. She had never gotten as bad as those hoarders on TV; reality programs preyed on extremes. There had been no mold covering her floors. No cause for asthma or scabies. Although maybe, if the woman had continued denying help, that ultimately would have been her. She had certainly accumulated enough for Jenna to keep visitors away. Box after box of unopened items. Many purchases identical. The problem had grown steadily, ignited by Jenna's father. Or rather the day he ran off with a young coworker. As a salesman who'd traveled most of his daughter's life, he rarely reached out afterward. So the morning he called with news, Jenna had steeled herself: He was getting remarried. What she hadn't prepared for was the full impact that hit on Christmas Day, when the presents her mother had bought formed a blockade of half the tree.

Shoving down the memory, Jenna focused on the only boxes that mattered: the moving boxes in Mrs. Porter's study. One after the other she peeked beneath the unsealed flaps.

"Terrence, where'd you put it?" she muttered. She hated to call him this early in the morning.

A packing popcorn crunched beneath her sneaker. She reached down to pick it up, and noticed a shoe box on the floor nearby. She lifted the lid. A small handful of black-and-white snapshots lay in disarray. In the top one, a mix of male and female soldiers posed in a group. Their smiles shone bright, yet their faces appeared as worn as their khaki uniforms. Palm trees framed the backdrop of a pole tent marked with a thick red cross. It was a hospital, based somewhere tropical. World War II, Jenna would guess, though she knew little about the era beyond a few episodes of *Band of Brothers.*

She continued to rummage, and retrieved a hardback copy of *Jane Eyre.* Worn edges, not an early edition. Nothing worth a price tag. Beneath the book was a velvety, hinged container. The last thing in the shoe box, it spurred a flicker of hope. She imagined a diamond bracelet tucked neatly inside. Ten carats. Perfectly cut. Rather, she discovered a Bronze Star.

"Damn."

Plenty of buyers would pay a nice penny for this, reenactors in particular. And technically the piece was fair game, since Mrs. Porter hadn't removed it from inventory. Regardless, not even Jenna could discount the importance it would hold for any client.

She took the shoe box down the hall, toward the whistle of a kettle. By the time she reached the kitchen, the steam was screaming at full volume.

"Excuse me. Mrs. Porter?"

The woman was on a step stool in her slippers. Her pale skin curved gently over thin cheeks. She opened one cupboard, then the next.

"Mrs. Porter," Jenna boomed, to no avail. Was she hard of hearing?

The kettle refused to relent.

"Here, I'll get that for you!" Jenna removed it from the stove and clicked off the burner.

The woman kept on searching.

Maintaining her volume, Jenna asked, "Could I help you with something?"

"You could stop hollering, for one. Gracious, I'm standing right here."

"Sorry, I thought . . ."

"My teapot."

"Pardon?"

Again, Mrs. Porter looked over the glasses perched on the tip of her narrow nose. "I would like to use my little Chinese teapot."

Jenna knew the item immediately. She'd found it in a hodgepodge of tea sets they would soon be displaying for sale. "My friend Sally has that one." At Mrs. Porter's furrowed brow, she explained, "She's a broker of collectibles, so she's just helping appraise some things."

Jenna prided herself on her own assessment skills. However, a unique stamp on the base of the pot, suggesting the possibility of a higher price, called for a second opinion. "I assure you, she'll take very good care of it."

Mrs. Porter took this in, her frown slackening.

This was exactly the reason Jenna hated it when a client remained in the house. How do you handle a person's things — dumping worthless mementos, price tagging their aged furnishings — while the owner hovered in the next room? Chattiness, too, never increased efficiency: *My goodness, was that in there? Where did you find that? Oh, you have to hear the funniest story about the day we bought that.*

Hopefully, Mrs. Porter didn't plan to stay long.

"So, I was wondering . . ." Jenna hid her earnestness. "Since I really hate to be in your way, do you happen to know when you'll be going back to your family's?"

Mrs. Porter snagged a ceramic mug and inspected it for cleanliness. "Not anytime soon from the looks of things."

"I . . . don't understand."

"The bedroom they stuck me in, down in the basement, it flooded in the middle of the night." She descended onto the linoleum. "While they're replacing the carpet, I'm not about to stay in a Holiday Inn when my real home is right here. For the time being, at any rate."

Repairs during the holidays were bad news — for all of them.

Mrs. Porter jerked her chin upward. "What have you got there, dear?"

Jenna suddenly remembered the shoe box tucked against her hip. If the two of them were going to be sharing space for a while, winning the woman over would be wiser than making her an enemy.

Smile in place, Jenna set the box on the nearest counter. "Terrence stumbled across these when he was sorting. We figured you'd like to save them."

Mrs. Porter put down her cup, a question on her face. She raised the lid and picked up a photo. Within seconds, her squinting turned wide-eyed. A small gasp slipped from her wrinkled lips. As her fingertips traced the picture, an invisible shell seemed to melt from her body. Her eyes, brown as bark, turned moist and soft with memories. Even the air in the room seemed to warm.

Jenna couldn't resist a closer look. A serviceman was holding a tiny branch, in the manner of mistletoe, over the nurse's head. His gaze was a combination of mischief and adoration, and despite the snapshot's lack of color, the young woman appeared to be blushing.

"Is that you?" Jenna softly asked, drawn in by the moment. "Is that how you and your husband met, during the war?"

At that, Mrs. Porter's eyes snapped to Jenna. Hand shaking, she dropped the picture. Jenna swiftly reached down for the keepsake, but when she attempted to give it back, Mrs. Porter went steely and cool.

"I'm so sorry," Jenna said. "I didn't mean to upset you."

"Throw them away."

Jenna stared. Mrs. Porter couldn't possibly mean that. She was just rattled, from recollections of the couple's youth. No question, the woman would regret the decision later, when it was too late to reverse.

"You know what," Jenna reasoned, "why don't I set these aside somewhere. I'm sure once you've had a chance to think it over —"

Mrs. Porter broke in loud and firm. "Toss them out, donate them, do as you'd like. But take . . . them . . . away."

Jenna hesitated, still stunned, before returning the picture to the pile. Stoically, Mrs. Porter turned and left the kitchen. A history unspoken trailed her like crumbs.

CHAPTER 4

"I can't believe you're selling her house," Reece spat the moment he entered the garage.

At the greeting, his father slid out from under the antique Ford truck. Dabs of oil tinted his thin charcoal hair and an old T-shirt that outlined his slight paunch. His initial look of surprise hardened as Reece's words set in. He gave his hands a strong wipe with a soiled rag as he rose to his full height of six-two, evening their gazes.

"I take it your mother filled you in."

"She told me enough."

"Then you ought to understand why having your grandma here makes sense. Imagine if I hadn't been there when she tripped and —"

"And she's fine."

"This time, yes," his father pointed out. "But it just proved what I've been saying. She needs people around to help her."

"So hire somebody."

"It's more than that. I told you before, the place is too big to take care of by herself."

"Fine. Then get her a housekeeper."

The man huffed a laugh that clawed at Reece's nerves. It was the same reaction from years ago when Reece asked him to cosign for his first car. Or when he asked for help with his college tuition. Looking back, Reece's decision to drop out might even have been retaliation for that laugh.

His dad hadn't found the choice quite as amusing.

Frustrating thing was, as a longtime security officer for a prestigious bank, his frugal father always had plenty of funds put away. Eventually, Reece had learned not to ask for a single thing. But this was different.

This wasn't about him.

Done with the conversation, his father ducked beneath the Ford's open hood and adjusted plugs on the motor. The expensive toy rarely left the garage. He kept it stored away for fear of the tiniest scratch. Now he wanted to do the same to his own mother.

Over time, since her husband's death, Grandma Estelle's activities of quilting groups and bridge clubs had lessened to none. But she did keep up with her garden and "puttering" in her house. Take those

544

away, and the grandma he adored might fade as well.

"If she doesn't want to move," Reece contended, "she shouldn't have to."

His father responded with a mumble, clearly half listening. Reece decided to say something that would make more of an impact.

"Just because you want to cash in on the sale doesn't mean you have the right to force her out of her own house."

That one worked. His father drew his head back and stood with a glower, tinged with confusion. "Your grandpa left that house to me for a reason. He trusted I'd make sure she was taken care of."

"Yeah," Reece said, "I'm sure staying in my old, flooded bedroom was exactly what Grandpa had in mind." With that, he turned to leave.

He was about to step outside when his father yelled, "Reece!" The tone carried a deep gruffness so seldom used Reece couldn't help but stop. He wheeled back around as his father stepped closer, hands hitched on his hips. "You wanna tell me what the hell this is really about?"

Not until asked the question did Reece realize the core of the issue. It was more than a youthful attachment to a house, more than his recent aversion to major change. What really got to him was that his father was never off duty. Always sizing Reece up, judging him. Policing his acts like a dictator of safety. After the snowmobile crash, Reece had felt enough guilt at the hospital without the guy charging in, shouting, "With all the crazy stunts you pull, how many times have I warned you something like this would happen?"

Reece considered explaining this now. Yet there was no point giving his father the satisfaction of knowing it still bothered him. Besides, what would come of it? His dad was far from the type to acknowledge his own faults.

In the silence, the man took a calming breath through his nose. "Look, son, I don't know what's eating at you. But after talking it through, even your grandmother agreed it was the right decision." At Reece's lack of response, his dad headed back to the engine. "You don't believe me, you go ask her yourself."

An unnecessary suggestion. That's precisely what Reece planned to do.

Jenna parked beside the neighborhood curb, calculating. If she hurried in and out, she'd have plenty of time to grab lunch somewhere before meeting Sally about the appraisals. Fortunately the collectibles broker, with a work ethic rivaling Jenna's, didn't balk at an appointment on Thanksgiving weekend. Otherwise, today would have been chalked up as largely unproductive on Jenna's list.

Cataloging and adding to inventory sheets had been a challenge after her encounter with Mrs. Porter. Unable to concentrate, Jenna had called it a day but followed orders by ridding the house of the shoe box. She could think of three collectors off the top of her head who loved buying World War II memorabilia. For the time being, though, the box would wait in her trunk. Based on the emotion she had witnessed, she'd be surprised if Mrs. Porter didn't have second thoughts.

As Jenna stepped out of the car, a rumble caught her ear. Across the street, a driver was struggling to start an SUV. Reflections of gray clouds shaded the windshield. The possibility of offering to help zipped through Jenna's mind. Then again, thanks to modern communication, who today wasn't fully capable of handling a little car trouble?

She continued toward the Tudor-style house of Mrs. Porter's son and his wife, Sandy. The woman had promised Jenna a key to an upstairs storage closet at the Porter estate. Hopefully, like all the other closets in the home, there would be items of decent monetary value that just needed a dusting or polish. Perhaps while here she could also determine how long before the elderly woman could return to her new residence.

Jenna had almost made it to the driveway when the slam of a car door turned her head. The driver leaned back against the SUV and raked his fingers through his dark brown hair, inadvertently causing his bangs to spike. He blew out a breath that said it was one of those days.

Jenna urged herself to stick with her plan. But something about his expression — a frustration that ran deep and familiar — wouldn't let go. She peeked at her watch. With a grumble, she decided she could always eat after the meeting.

Approaching the guy, she became acutely aware of his athletic build. A navy polo shirt, tucked into belted slacks, showed off his toned biceps, a complement to his square jaw. From his profile, she happened to notice a pink dot on his earlobe from a hole that had been allowed to close. Something about the story there made her smile.

"Is there some way I can help?"

He raised his head with a start. The instant their eyes connected, a tingling invaded Jenna's legs and shot to her chest.

He held her gaze for a long, silent moment, or maybe it only seemed that way, until he replied. "The battery . . . I think it's done for good."

"Do you need to borrow a phone?" She managed a smooth voice.

"I called Triple A already. Guess I was hoping to give it one last shot."

Jenna could relate. She started her own vehicle every morning with the same attitude. Suddenly, she remembered the cables in the hidden compartment of her trunk. "Do you want me to jump you?"

When he went to speak but paused, she reviewed her question. "I meant, in your car." Oh, God. That sounded worse. "Not *in,*" she corrected, "but *on.*"

What was she saying? A burn filled her cheeks.

"I mean *to.* Do you want a jump *to* the car?"

Any trace of earlier angst in his face dissolved. His lips curved into a smile that he appeared to be stifling. "I'd love a jump," he answered. "To my car, that is."

Jenna's insides cringed into a ball. Since when did any guy, let alone a stranger, make her so flustered? Her sole salvation was the subtle blush tinting his olive-toned cheeks.

"I'll drive over." She quickly moved her car to face the SUV before retrieving her cables. Behind the shield of her raised trunk, she closed her eyes and exhaled. Her nerves started to settle as she and the driver focused on their tasks. Popping hoods, connecting batteries, revving motors. She did her best to detour from his gaze. After the mess left from her last boyfriend, she didn't need another complication.

Life was better without the clutter.

Done helping the guy, her shoulders loosened a notch. She leaned into her trunk to put the cables away. Then she turned around and discovered him right behind her. How long had he been standing there? The view of her backside in faded jeans topped with an old sweatshirt couldn't have been rated as sexy.

Not that she wanted it to be.

Because she didn't.

She closed the trunk, hoping to entrap the thought. "So, you're all set."

"I really appreciate your help —" He stopped and shook his head. "Geez, I didn't even ask your name."

"It's Jenna." She stuck out her hand in reflex, and immediately wished she hadn't.

Somehow she knew the touch of his hand would resurrect those damn tingles. And that's just what it did. Only this time around they hit more like a current.

"Well, Jenna, I can't tell you how grateful I am."

"It was nothing. Really."

In the midst of their lingering shake, warm as the deep tone of his voice, Jenna's stomach groaned. A reminder of lunch, and her meeting.

"I'd better get going or I'll be late."

The corners of his eyes crinkled with lines of regret. "I'm sorry to keep you."

She appreciated the excuse to pull her hand away, as much as she hated it.

After an awkward beat, he shrugged and said, "Take care of yourself."

"You too." She hastened off to snag her keys and purse from her car, but then chose to wait in her seat until he drove away, to avoid another exchange.

Once in the clear, she hazarded a look at the dashboard clock. If she left this very minute, she could make it on time. But that would mean having to swing by here again later.

"Oh, crap," she said, making her choice. She dashed outside and up the driveway.

Her second ring of the doorbell succeeded

in summoning Sandy Porter, who was busy listening to someone on a cordless phone. She ushered Jenna inside and motioned her hand like a bird's beak to indicate the caller was a chatterbox.

"I agree," Sandy said into the mouthpiece. "I definitely think you should bring that up at the next committee meeting." Charitable boards and events appeared to fill her schedule. All were likely important enough, but Jenna didn't have time today for patience.

"The key," Jenna whispered, using her own hand motion to illustrate.

Sandy vigorously nodded, bouncing her twisted-up do. Her nails and lips were glossed in pink, perfect matches to her sweater set. Continuing their game of charades, she raised her pointer finger — *Be back in one minute* —and ambled off around the corner.

Jenna flicked at the side seam of her jeans, an anxious countdown. She could hear Sandy rustling through a drawer and commenting cheerily on the phone.

That's when Jenna glimpsed an image in the formal room. On the white fireplace mantel appeared a framed photo of the SUV's driver. A residual flutter drew her into the cream-carpeted room. Was he part of the family?

She picked up the picture to take a better look. A huge waterfall behind him, a backpack on his shoulder, he beamed with a ruggedness that glimmered in his eyes. He was attractive, sure, and had loads of charm. But there was something more than that. . . .

"Oh, here you are!" Sandy entered the room. "Sorry about the phone. Auction season. The thing rings off the hook."

Jenna fumbled with the frame to prop it back in place. "No problem. I was . . . wiping a smudge." She pushed up a smile. "Occupational habit."

Sandy tilted her head at the photo with a prideful glow. "That's our son at Multnomah Falls. Reece and his sister, Lisa, used to go hiking there every summer, before she moved to Washington. You just missed them both, actually."

Jenna strained to absorb anything that followed his name. Reece. Putting that together with the memory of his face returned a simmer to Jenna's cheeks. She needed to switch topics. Now. "By the way, I had a question about . . . Mrs. Porter." It was the first thought her mind could grasp.

"Go on, shoot." Sandy smiled, waiting.

You're a salesperson, Jenna told herself. *Spin this.*

"The thing is, I have some items of hers that seemed pretty important. A box of old pictures from when Mr. and Mrs. Porter served in the military. Even a Bronze Star from World War Two. But when I asked her, she told me to toss it all out."

Sandy didn't ponder this for more than a second. "It couldn't have been them. Probably just some people they knew."

"But, the woman in the photos — her features looked so similar."

"Hmm . . . maybe a cousin, then. I couldn't tell you. But I do know that Bill's father never enlisted. Because of flatfoot, I think. And goodness knows, Estelle isn't the type to have enlisted in the *military*." Sandy laughed softly, making the suggestion seem ludicrous.

When it came to personal items, Jenna welcomed the invitation to do as she pleased. She just wished she could as easily discard Mrs. Porter's reaction.

"So you *don't* think they're worth saving?" Jenna wanted final confirmation.

"From what Estelle told you, doesn't sound like it. Besides, even though she has a great little setup here, with a kitchenette and its own compact washer and dryer, I'm afraid there isn't a lot of storage space."

Jenna nodded. The subject was settled.

"Anyhow, this is for you," Sandy said.

The key. Jenna had nearly forgotten. She accepted the offering, which brought back her other concern: How long until the flooded bedroom was repaired?

Before Jenna could ask, a phone rang in the kitchen.

"Ooh, I need to catch that," Sandy said, stepping away. "Would you mind letting yourself out, sweetie?"

"Um — no. That's fine."

"Thanks a bunch!" Sandy waved and disappeared into the next room.

Releasing a sigh, Jenna headed out.

After sending a text — **On my way!** —she drove toward her meeting. Houses on every block were in the midst of being Christmasized. Neighbors were hanging wreaths, untangling lights. Planting huge plastic candy canes in perfectly good lawns.

Today, though, Jenna barely felt her usual irritation over the scene. Despite her better judgment, her thoughts kept channeling back to the mystery of Estelle Porter's past.

CHAPTER 5

The system had become a clustered mess. Thousands of international shipments continued to arrive at stores with no clear tracking of details. For Reece, this meant an emergency campout at the office, regardless of it being Thanksgiving weekend. Even if the holiday were observed by his biggest London account, it wouldn't matter. Reece and his IT team were ordered to fix the problem before Europe's retailers opened for morning business.

For yet another hour Reece left his techies to their mission. In his office he'd tried calling his grandma, but her house phone had been disconnected. His father hadn't wasted any time. If there was any chance of making it over before she went to bed, he needed the Brit issue solved.

"Making any progress?" he said, peeking into IT's cubicle area.

One of them mumbled "sorta" and the

three continued typing away. They slouched before their computers with four screens each. Why the hell they needed as many screens as the CIA was beyond Reece, but now wasn't the time to raise the question.

He glanced inside the pizza box on the closest desk and found a lone slice. The six-pack of Mountain Dew he'd brought in, bribery for the two caffeine addicts of the bunch, was nearly gone. He wished he could think of something else to speed up the group.

"Anything I can get you guys?"

Instead of responding, over their shoulders the three exchanged codes and technical speak to facilitate their test cases. The mood was sluggish and gray. But then, he couldn't blame them for not being enthused. Working today hadn't been part of Reece's plan either.

After getting his car battery replaced that morning, he had zoomed onto the freeway, headed for his grandma's house. Thoughts of Jenna, the beautiful woman he'd just met, had disengaged his auto-pilot skills. When his cell phone rang, he realized he'd missed the turnoff — by three full exits. His boss's call about the integration disaster had rooted him back in reality.

"I tried to tell them," Reece had insisted,

"rushing the SAP cut-over was a bad idea." Ignoring his warning, some hotshot exec had demanded they implement the complicated system right before a global launch of a winter clothing line. A real genius.

"I know, I know," his boss had said. "But unless we want to lose millions, you'd better round up your guys right away."

Reece had groaned his compliance. In the background, he could hear people talking and laughing, band music blasting from a televised football game.

"Bet you wish you'd taken me up on my offer, huh?" A smirk in the man's tone.

"Hell yeah," Reece had replied, though hadn't actually meant it. Even with the two feet of fresh snow on Mount Hood, rarely seen this early in the year, a snowboarding trip had lost its appeal.

He now grabbed the last slice of pepperoni pizza and called out to his team, "I'll be down the hall if you need me." An ugly mountain of nonurgent e-mails had piled up during his travels. At least that would keep him busy until receiving his cue to help put out the logistical fire.

Reece journeyed through the ghost town of a floor to reach his office. He took a bite of cold pizza and plopped down in his chair. On the corner of his desk was a digital frame he'd grown so accustomed to that he barely noticed its auto slide show anymore. He had forgotten this particular picture, of him and Tracy in a stall beside her horse. He'd never been much of an animal person. Then he'd volunteered to groom Chestnut until Tracy was well enough to do it herself, and the horse gradually grew on him.

Reece smiled at the memory of the first time Chestnut nuzzled his neck, a sign of affection and acceptance, of trust. That was the day Tracy snapped the photo.

The picture faded from the screen, replaced by a shot of the Graniellos. Or "Granolas," as Tracy called them.

"A bunch of fruits and nuts," she liked to joke, "all packed into one big family."

He laughed to himself now, before a realization struck: Tracy was the one he should have been thinking about all morning, not some stranger who'd helped him with his car. And yet somehow, he couldn't shake the buzzing thrill he'd felt from watching Jenna move, from touching her hand. The raw beauty she projected from every pore. The way she seemed embarrassed by anyone flustering her like that —

He stopped there, scrapped the wandering thought.

"Now who's the genius?" he muttered,

and threw his pizza away.

Reece didn't know a thing about the other girl, one he'd never see again. Cold feet. That's all this was. Natural nerves about taking the next step.

He'd learned the hard way not to follow emotions over logic. Snowmobiling at Mount Hood had taught him that. With Tracy on the backseat, they'd been cruising along, having a great old time, when adrenaline lured him into an impromptu race with a guy on the next snowmobile.

"Reece, you're going too fast," he'd vaguely heard her say. Wind and snowflakes blew at his ears, at the mask over his eyes. Tracy clung to his middle as they approached a curve. If he cut the corner around a tree, no doubt they'd take the lead.

Slow down! Maybe her words had come too late. Maybe he'd ignored them, driven by the need to win a no-win contest. There had been no judges. No finish line. Just the rush of hitting a snow-covered rock that launched them into the air, a slow motion flight, rewarding him with a broken arm — and the scare of his life at seeing Tracy's limp form at the base of a tree.

"Oh, God, please . . ." he begged, after crawling over to her. "Please be all right."

Her cloudy breaths kept him from breaking down until they reached the hospital, where a doctor diagnosed her fractured pelvis.

"My horse," she'd said groggily once she was told the news.

At her bedside, Reece gingerly squeezed her hand. "I'll take care of him, don't worry," he told her. "And I swear, Tracy, I'll never hurt you again."

Out of fear now of breaking that promise, something inside him was looking for a way out. That had to be it. That's where all these doubts were coming from. Any fascination with another woman had no place in his life. The time had come to take the leap, to ask the big, looming, inevitable question.

But to do that properly, there was one thing Reece needed: a special heirloom with a history he hoped to repeat.

Chapter 6

Jenna sat up on her white leather couch, reading it once again. Ad copy for the estate sale shouldn't have been this difficult to proof. Terrence had penned a fabulous write-up, as he always did. Wisely, this time he mentioned the family's name. Mr. Porter's former status as the president of a local college could attract more buyers. Even small-celebrity interest helped.

She leafed through her folder, moving on to her task sheet. The meeting with Sally hadn't gone as she'd hoped, most of the items not appraising for more than Jenna guessed. "Let me keep checking on these," Sally had told her, regarding the last two uncertainties.

A slow economy wasn't helping Jenna's cause. The fifteen percent increase she'd promised, and thus her partnership, were slipping from her grasp. Squashing the prospect, she racked her brain for any collectors she'd forgotten to contact. Not a single one emerged. Granted, her resources weren't the problem. It was her thoughts, which kept floating back to Estelle. And her box. And her alluring grandson.

Business and pleasure don't mix, she reminded herself, citing her boss's basic rule. A clichéd concept, but valid nonetheless. In fact, it was one her father had bulldozed right through, leaving Jenna and her mother in his trampled wake.

She shut the file, tossed it aside. From the end table she snagged the remote. She reclined on the couch and flew from one channel to the next. A cheesy talk show. A political debate. An endless slew of reality shows. She kept flipping until she landed on a movie featuring stars she recognized. Cuba Gooding Jr. and Ben Affleck, in *Pearl Harbor.*

The connection to Estelle screamed as loud as the bombs dropping onto the navy ships before her.

Jenna resumed her channel surfing. Eventually she stopped on an infomercial. She treated TV ads and pawning programs like a game, challenging herself to guess the price. Make that two prices: first, the product's worth; second, what it would sell for. She was seldom off by much.

In this one, a bearded man demonstrated a cabinet with a zillion compartments. All silver and glass, it matched everything in Jenna's condo. Of course, she didn't own enough to fill half the thing. Nor did she have anything left to tidy.

The infomercial broke for a commercial — a great irony in that. Black-and-white footage of Nat King Cole filled the screen. He crooned "For Sentimental Reasons" into an oversized microphone. As song titles scrolled upward, the shot changed to another man singing "I'm in the Mood for Love." It was a CD collection of nostalgic songs, ballads from the 1940s.

The war years.

Jenna arched a brow. "You've gotta be kidding me."

She shut the TV off.

From the beginning, Jenna had made a habit of giving clients their space. Anything unrelated to their houses and furnishings was their own business. At the end of the day, it was all about the sale. But . . . never before had she felt stalked by a person's history. By the likes of a shoe box, stored in her car trunk. Something in it kept on prodding.

If only she could identify the source, like locating a pebble in her shoe, she could shake the problem away. A little digging around wouldn't hurt anyone. Not an intrusive investigation, by any means. Just a quick online search. A few public records. Available to anyone.

Before she could change her mind, she dragged her soft briefcase closer and pulled out her laptop. As it warmed up, the rumble of a passing truck rose from three floors below. The motion rattled her large windows. She typed the keywords: *Estelle Porter Oregon.*

An obituary for the woman's husband, Walter, gave a brief summary of his life. No military service, which aligned with Sandy's claim. It mentioned his surviving widow, Estelle Agnes Martin. Besides her maiden name, there was nothing of note.

Jenna skimmed through several other entries, using the name Martin as well. But most of the links pertained to a beer company, specializing in porters, and some PTA president in Oregon, Wisconsin. No info about the right Estelle.

Probably a good thing.

Jenna tried to end the search, yet couldn't. She despised giving up on anything so easily. She stared at the blinking cursor, considering options, and tried: *Estelle Martin military WWII Pacific.*

The page refreshed with all new listings. It took Jenna a mere second to see that the fifth one down contained every one of the keywords. Anticipation flowed through her as she clicked on the link and discovered a site honoring the Women's Army Corps, called WACs, of World War II. She picked up speed, reviewing the pages, searching for Estelle's name.

At last, in an album of photographs, she found it in a caption:

(From left to right) Pvt. Betty Cordell, Pvt. Shirley Davidson, PFC Rosalyn "Roz" Taylor, and Pvt. Estelle Martin.

The corresponding picture appeared to feature the very faces from those in Estelle Porter's box. So why would she have hidden this amazing achievement from her family? At least that's what she seemed to be doing, based on Sandy's comments.

Jenna scanned the next few pages in search of an answer, and froze. Not at the photo in particular, but its caption. For below the image of Estelle with a handsome soldier, the same one who'd fashioned mistletoe from a branch, was the man's name: *Corporal Tom Redding.*

In other words, he wasn't the late Mr. Porter.

Ideas began to whirl. Perhaps the corporal was an old flame who'd never made it home. It would make sense, why Estelle didn't want the box. Especially if no one in the family knew of him. Better to rid yourself of objects that tethered you to the past. Jenna understood that firsthand. Plus, given the sparkle in the man's eyes, the glow in his smile, he would clearly take effort to forget. Almost as difficult as, say . . . Estelle's grandson.

In fact, both men radiated the same type of charm. There couldn't be a connection — could there?

"Oh, stop it," she told herself.

She closed down her computer and set off for bed. Whether possible or not, such theories were none of her business.

CHAPTER 7

"You don't have to do this," Reece insisted.

"What, keep meat on your bones?" his grandma said. "You sure you want to leave that to your mother?" She smirked from her stove, dressed in a pastel yellow sweater and gray woolen pants. Early-afternoon light angled through the window, creating a silvery outline of her soft curls.

Parked in a kitchen chair, Reece folded his arms. "Grandma, you know what I'm talking about."

More stirring of the chowder. More evading his question.

She scooped a ladleful into a bowl. The aroma of comfort food filled the room, just as it had for as long as Reece could remember. He couldn't count how many PB&J sandwiches or bowls of goulash he'd enjoyed at this very table. No one in history could top Grandma Estelle's zucchini bread or strawberry jam, both made of produce grown in her own backyard.

Reece cringed at the idea of a stranger moving in, tromping through her beloved garden. He tried to keep the frustration from his tone. "Regardless of what the paperwork says, this is your home. Dad has no right to make you move if you want to stay."

"Well, he hasn't called in a SWAT team quite yet," she said, delivering his soup and spoon. Per her usual, she would eat only after everyone else was taken care of. "Eat up, now, before you shrivel away."

"Grandma, please. I'm being serious."

She lowered herself into the chair across from him and stifled a cough. With a tissue plucked from her pocket, she dabbed at her nose. Her tired eyes surveyed the room, giving away what she wouldn't verbalize. No doubt, the wooden shelves of Goebel figurines and decorative plates and Amish carvings carried visions of her and her husband purchasing them together. Items that would soon be hawked off to a herd of bargain seekers.

Her gaze settled back on Reece. "Change is rarely easy, dear. Sometimes we just do what needs to be done."

"You know that's not a real answer."

She gestured to his bowl. "Better eat soon,

or I might start feeling insulted."

Given her spunk, a person might take her for the type to speak her piece without pause. Indeed this applied to day-to-day minutiae; though ironically, when it came to the most affecting decisions she remained a traditional housewife and mother who dutifully complied. It would take more nudging to uncover what she really wanted. For the moment, Reece would give her room to ponder.

He blew on a spoonful of soup and swallowed it down. His chest warmed from the hearty, perfectly salted chowder. He wondered how often she cooked for others these days, or did anything social that she used to love.

"Have you seen any of your old friends lately?"

"Which ones?" She dabbed at her nose again. "They're all old."

"I don't know. The ones you used to make quilts with."

"Now, why would I want to spend my Saturdays with blind old biddies, sticking myself with needles?"

"Well, when you put it that way . . ." Reece chuckled.

His grandma then veered to a safer realm, a basic catch-up on his life. Between sips he filled her in about work, and how his team had managed to salvage an account the day before. In the middle of his logistical recap, his thoughts looped back to the photo on his desk. Suddenly he recalled the second reason he'd come here today.

Yet, unsure how to ask, he detoured to highlights of his recent travels. He described the weather, landscape, and culture in London and Seoul. "Did you and Grandpa ever visit Asia together?"

"No, no," she said. "We talked about taking a vacation there, but just never got around to it."

Reece nodded, remembering how he and his sister used to gobble up popcorn while admiring the couple's travel photos, compliments of a white wall and a projector that tended to stick every ten slides.

At the silent lull, his grandmother tilted her head at him. "Dear, is there something else on your mind?"

No reason to stall.

He cleared the nerves from his throat. "I was wondering if . . . well, do you remember my girlfriend, Tracy?"

His grandma scrunched her brow.

Dumb question. As a longtime hospice volunteer, his grandmother had given him plenty of helpful tips about Tracy's daily care — sponge baths around her bandages, helping her out of bed.

"My point is . . . we've been dating for more than two years, and . . . she's amazing. Her family's great and . . ."

"And," his grandmother finished slowly, "you're going to propose."

Embarrassed yet relieved she had said it for him, Reece explained, "You and Grandpa had such a great marriage. Guess I was hoping I could borrow your ring for good luck."

She gazed down at her vacant wedding finger, then rubbed at the loose skin that had prompted her to retire the ring into a jewelry box. "One thing I've learned, you don't need luck for a happy marriage. It's something you work at every day."

Reece didn't know how to respond. Maybe he should have waited. She was already losing so many belongings she valued. "If you'd prefer to keep it, I'd completely understand."

Ignoring the assurance, she continued, "But if you love this girl with all your heart" — a warm smile lifted her cheeks — "I know your grandpa would've been honored to pass it along."

Responsibility pressed onto his shoulders, as if his grandfather's hands were reaching down. Reece came around the table and gave her a hug, taking care not to squeeze too hard. "Thanks, Grandma."

"My pleasure, dear." She patted his back.

As he stood, she added, "I'll have your mother bring the ring here when she stops by tomorrow. Why don't you come over on Monday, and I'll have it all ready for you?"

"That'd be wonderful."

Once they traded good-byes, he threw on his coat and scarf and headed for the front door. His grip was on the handle when he glanced into the formal room. There, items were strewn across a long folding table, prepped to be priced.

Any other year, a fresh-cut tree would already be centered before the large picture window. Its decor never mimicked a store display, color coordinated and too pretty to touch. Instead, the ornaments were a hodge-podge of random shapes and handmade crafts, each holding a special memory. . . .

A noise from upstairs sliced through the thought. Reece strained to hear more. Over the years, thanks to the surrounding forest areas, he'd been credited with ridding the place of a bird, a mouse, and even a bat that had entered through the attic.

He grabbed a newspaper and rolled it as he climbed the stairs. At the top, he waited, listening. Another sound seeped from the guest room on the right, the one he'd used for his overnight stays since childhood. He clutched his weapon and cautiously opened the door. The sight of a person caused him to jump.

With a gasp, the woman spun to face him. Then she released an audible breath, hand over her chest. "God, Reece. You scared me."

His reflexive demand of *Who the hell are you?* died at the recognition of his name. Wait . . . the girl he'd met yesterday. Outside his parents' house.

"Jenna?"

She raised her hand in an awkward wave.

His delight from seeing her again whirled into a mix of surprise and utter confusion. "What are you doing here?"

"When I saw your car outside, I — I thought about coming back later to give you and your grandma privacy. But my crew's off till Monday, and I had some inventory to do, and —" She paused, slowing herself, and smiled. "Sorry if I disturbed you."

The pieces were assembling: the clipboard in her left hand, the moving boxes, the filled trash bags.

"You're the one selling off my family's things."

She opened her mouth, then closed it, as if thrown by his statement. Uncertainty washed over her features. "I've been assigned to this property, yes. But I assure you, we're a professional company."

Reece glimpsed his baseball, setting off an internal alarm. The ball rested on the inside lip of a white trash bag tipped onto the floor. He pulled it out, running his thumb over the seams, ratty from use. "You're throwing this away?"

She shook her head and replied, "No."

He relaxed a fraction, before she added, "The white bags are for donations."

As in, doling them out for free? Dumping them at The Salvation Army?

"You can't do that," he bit out. "My grandfather caught this. It was the first Mariners game he ever took me to."

She straightened her posture and spoke evenly. "You're welcome to keep it if you'd like."

Thanks for your permission, he expressed through a huff.

What else of value was she planning to toss out? Reece sifted through an open box on the bed and picked out a pennant flag from his Notre Dame years. His mother always cleared out memorabilia with every passing stage of his life. But his grandparents were different. His room here was like a precious time capsule.

At least it had been — until now.

Jenna gripped her clipboard with both hands. "If the flag is special to you, please, take it. But my work here is under contract. Everything of significant sales value is considered frozen inventory."

"Inventory? This isn't a store."

"I'm sorry if this is hard for you," she offered. "But it's a job my company takes great pride in —"

"Yeah. The pride of a vulture." The reply flew from his mouth. Her lips flattened into hard lines before he registered the full harshness of his remark. Jenna, specifically, wasn't the villain here.

"Listen," he tried to explain, "this wouldn't be happening if it was up to me. There are things here that are really special."

"Yes," she burst out, "I know. *Everything* is special to *everyone*." She stopped abruptly. Lowering her gaze, she wheeled around.

Reece sought appropriate words, all of which eluded him — as did the true core of his anger. He wanted to halt time. Or, better yet, to go back to a period when life made sense. He glanced down at his hands, desperate for an answer. Between his fingers, emotion hummed, trembling the cracked letters of his pennant, his grandpa's weathered ball. Finally, at a loss, he dropped them into the box and walked away.

CHAPTER 8

Jenna hurried through the doors and scanned the chattering crowd. Decorative saddles and rodeo posters adorned the walls. She located her mother in a far booth; the profile of her bangs were tough to miss.

As Jenna threaded through the restaurant, empty peanut shells cracked underfoot. The scent of barbecue ribs and the sizzling of steaks made her light-headed, or perhaps it was simply the good news. And good news was definitely what she needed after yesterday's run-in with Reece Porter. The arrogant, self-righteous twit. If she had known better, she never would have helped that deadbeat with his dead battery.

The single upside of their last exchange was the amount of work she had plowed through after he'd left. Some people eat when they're upset, some opt to exercise, some like to bake. Jenna organized. Toss, repair, sell, sell. Toss, repair, sell, sell.

Still, she'd been unable to fully purge her frustrations, most of which were at herself, for letting him get under her skin. It wasn't like Reece had said or done anything worse than a handful of other clients' emotionally charged relatives. Yet from him, the words and glares came with tentacles. They'd latched on and kept her reeling half the night. Pondering. Justifying. Far more people were grateful for her services, simplifying an overwhelming chore after a loved one's passing or when downsizing to a retirement home.

Fortunately, today's announcement had pried away Reece's hold.

"Sorry I'm late." Jenna scooted into the seat across from her mother. She plopped down her purse beside the minibucket of peanuts. "I was about to leave when I got some fun news."

"Did you get my message?" Her mom religiously phoned the day of their monthly luncheons to confirm their date.

"Oh, I forgot to check it," Jenna confessed. "I was on the other line with Sally — which is what I have to tell you about. Apparently, the director of the Portland History Museum was scheduled to be a guest on *Morning Portland*. You know, the TV show?" Reliving her earlier excitement, Jenna didn't wait for affirmation. "The lady was slated to promote a Jackie O exhibit. But since they're in-between curators, things slipped through and they didn't get proper clearance from the family trust. So now there's no new exhibit, and . . . anyway . . ." Back to the point.

"Since Sally's the one who helped arrange the TV spot through her producer friend, she was trying to help find another guest. And turns out, they liked the idea of me doing a segment about appraising used jewelry. As part of a budgetwise series for the holidays."

"Wow, that's fantastic." Her mother's eyes shone bright with anticipation, her makeup remarkably toned down. "But, honey, about my message . . ."

"Gosh, sorry. I'm rambling." Jenna laughed at herself, wondering if she'd taken a single breath since arriving. "Why, what were you calling about?"

The conversation broke off as a man approached their table. He was decked out in cowboy boots and a western shirt, like the rest of the themed staff, but with the added touch of a bolo tie. Maybe it denoted employee of the month.

"You must be Jenna," he said.

He knew her name? Oh, boy. Ten minutes

late, and her mother had already loaded the waiter up with too many details. Jenna hoped to God it wasn't meant as a setup, since the guy had to be in his fifties.

She was about to ask for a minute to peek at the menu, when he slid into the booth beside her mother.

"Great to meet you finally." He offered Jenna his hand for a shake. "Your mother has raved on and on about you."

"Honey, this is Doobie," her mom chimed in. "The friend I've told you about. From the studio, remember?"

This was what Doobie looked like? A cowboy — in downtown Portland?

Her mother fidgeted with the end of her fork, and said, "Jenna . . ."

That's when it dawned on Jenna that she hadn't provided him with her hand in return. "Hi," she said, reaching out.

His palm was rough and his shoulders a bit thick, as if he'd been a football lineman back in the day. A crew cut appeared where Jenna had envisioned dreadlocks or a salt-and-pepper ponytail. Everything about his appearance surprised her — although nothing shocked her more than watching him now, draping an arm over her mom's shoulders. His blatant coziness eliminated any possibility of mere friendship.

"I hope you don't mind me joining you. Your mom and I were supposed to grab lunch tomorrow. But plans changed, and I need to meet my daughter, Cee Cee, to do a gift exchange."

"I see." Jenna tried to say more, but her lips had gone numb.

"Besides, I told Rita, here, it's about time the two of us got introduced." He slanted a smile at Jenna's mom, making her giggle.

Jenna flashed back to her own reaction of first meeting Reece, and how foolish that now seemed. Meaningless. A passing attraction. No different than this, she assured herself. Since the divorce, her mother had occasionally mentioned dates that never developed into anything. Just because Doobie was the first to make Jenna's acquaintance didn't mean it was serious. After all, the guy already had his own family. No doubt that entailed enough emotional baggage to fill a whole pickup truck.

The thought sobered Jenna's mind. "So, you have kids."

"Just one daughter. About your age, actually."

"Were you married before?"

"Sure was."

"How long?" Jenna pressed on.

"Oh, a smidge over ten years."

"What broke the two of you up?"

Her mother snapped, "Jenna."

Maybe a business mode of appraising wasn't appropriate. Jenna hated to dull her mom's enthusiasm, just as she didn't enjoy informing clients that their perceived "treasure" was worth less than a jelly roll. But in their best interest, someone had to be objective.

"It's okay, I don't mind," Doobie said, smiling. "When Cee Cee's mom started dating Gary — that's her husband now — I hear my daughter grilled him for hours." He laughed, visibly relaxing Jenna's mother, before he addressed the question.

"My ex and I were friends all through high school. Probably should've kept it that way. Good news is, we get along better nowadays than when we were married."

Jenna grappled with his answer. What was he saying? They might reunite as a couple one day? She was tempted to ask, but her mom intervened.

"Speaking of good news." Her segue came off forced and awkward, a direct reflection of this surprise meeting. "Jenna, tell him about the morning show."

The guest spot. A deflated topic.

None too soon, a waitress arrived with three mason jars of water. "Sorry for the wait, folks." She produced an order pad from the half apron over her jean skirt. "Are y'all ready?"

Jenna didn't know what she was ready for. But she did know she needed space to organize her thoughts. "You two go ahead and order."

Worry creased her mom's features. "Honey, you aren't leaving, are you?"

An empty raft on the *Titanic* couldn't have been more appealing.

Doobie gently patted her mom's hand. The gesture, to Jenna, was equally sweet and terrifying.

"Of course not," Jenna replied, pasting on a smile. "I just need to go to the restroom."

The server moved aside as Jenna slid out.

Relief spread across her mom's face and lowered the shoulder pads of her sweater.

Jenna wove her way toward the bathroom, enticingly close to the exit. Again, shells crunched beneath her soles, the sounds like glass — like the memory of her life, her mother — shattering.

This man could be the nicest guy on the planet, but if things didn't work out, what would happen to her mom? One more rejection, one wrong step, and *crack!* Would there be enough pieces to put back together?

CHAPTER 9

"Hello?" Reece hollered again from the base of the staircase.

No answer. No creaking on the floor above. Had he misremembered? He was sure his grandmother had said to stop by on his way to work, that her ring would be ready for him by then.

It's not as if he was on a deadline to propose. All the same, it was better not to lose momentum. "Grandma, are you home?"

She had to be around here somewhere. He strode through the dining room and on to the kitchen. Maybe she'd moved back into his parents' house already. But why leave the front door unlocked?

Oh, yeah — Monday. Jenna and her crew would be here soon. It was something he didn't like to think about. A call to his mom would confirm his grandma's whereabouts. With no working landline, he'd have to use his cell. Then he remembered: He'd forgotten his mobile at home.

Great.

He turned for the hallway before he heard a voice, faint and strained. It came from the laundry room. A whisper of fear brushed over the back of his neck. He rushed in and found his grandmother slouched on the floor in her bathrobe, leaning up against the dryer. A load of damp laundry lay across her lap.

He knelt beside her, his pulse pounding in his head. "What happened? Are you all right?"

"It hurts . . . in my chest." Her breaths came sharp and choppy. "My arm, I can't feel it."

Oh, God, a heart attack. Like his grandpa. "I'll get some help. You're gonna be fine."

No phone. There was no phone to call. Damn his father! And damn himself for forgetting his cell!

The hospital. It was less than ten minutes away.

"I've got you now." He fought the tremble in his tone as he picked her up. One of her hands gripped his shirt. "I'm taking you to the hospital."

Carrying her toward the entry, he kept a cautious pace, all the while wanting to break into a run. He was nearly at his SUV when two cars pulled up and parked along the curb. Jenna Matthews jumped out and raced over in a panic.

"What happened?"

"She needs a doctor."

"Is there something I can do?"

He glanced into his passenger window. Work files and empty water bottles littered the front seat. "Open the back door," he told her, which she did in a blink.

"Here, I'll help you." Jenna hopped inside and guided Mrs. Porter onto the backseat. "Go on and drive. I'll stay with her."

Reece agreed and closed the door.

The instant he started the engine, he reversed out of the driveway, past Jenna's stunned coworkers. He shifted gears and took off as fast as he could.

"Slow down," he heard from the back. The same warning Tracy had given on the mountain. This time he would heed it.

"That's it, just slow your breathing," Jenna soothed, and Reece realized she hadn't been talking to him. "There you go, Mrs. Porter, that's better."

In the rearview mirror he connected with Jenna's eyes. *Everything's going to be fine,* she seemed to tell him, her arm around his grandma's shoulders.

He hardly knew this person. Two days ago, he'd treated her like the enemy. Yet here she was, once more, coming to his rescue.

Back and forth, back and forth. Seated in the waiting area of the emergency room, Jenna watched Reece pace the tiled floor. He'd paused solely to phone his family, right after a nurse wheeled his grandmother off for examination.

"Why don't you sit down for a while," Jenna encouraged, as much for her own sake as his.

He stopped and glanced up at the wall clock. Relenting, he perched on the chair beside her. There were only two other people in the room, relatives of a man who had fallen from a ladder while stringing Christmas lights.

"I should've listened," Reece murmured.

He didn't elaborate. Was that her cue to prod?

Eyes unseeing, he shook his head. "My dad said she needed someone around to watch her, but I wouldn't listen. And here I've been acting like a kid. How stupid is that? It's just a damn house."

Jenna thought of his baseball and pennant, displayed in a room he'd probably known since birth. All those objects tied to positive memories. "It's not stupid," she insisted. "That house is part of who you are."

Her words were merely meant for assurance, but once out there, to Jenna's surprise, it dawned on her that she actually believed them.

Reece answered with a marginal nod, and began a nervous tapping on his knee. The sound turned the heads of the other couple, who already appeared to be on edge. Jenna gently touched Reece's hand to calm the movement. Although it worked, she hadn't planned on his fingers wrapping around hers in response. He looked at her with genuine warmth.

"Thanks for staying," he said.

Jenna had no real ties to Estelle Porter, yet here at Reece's side, she felt as though they were facing this crisis together.

Of course, in actuality they weren't. They were business acquaintances, which he too seemed to recall before he drew his hand away and broke from her gaze.

For several minutes they sat in quiet, save for occasional noises from the hallway. The squeaking of shoes, the rolling of a hospital bed. In spite of her desire to stay, perhaps it was appropriate she leave.

As Jenna debated on how to slip out politely, a tall man in blue scrubs entered the room. Her chest tightened as he walked closer. Reece bristled in his seat, right before the doctor passed them to reach the people in the corner. The three spoke quietly, then left to go visit their patient.

Reece sank forward, elbows on his knees, intense with worry.

Jenna clasped her hands on her lap, resisting the urge to reach out again. "Your grandmother's a strong person. I'm sure she'll be fine."

He released a breath, resonant with doubt. "Ever since my grandpa died, she's needed someone to take care of her. I should've seen that and been around more."

At that moment, Jenna suspected he too had no idea of the woman's secret. A confession rose inside, fueled by a need to alleviate Reece's guilt. Or perhaps, more than that, to defend Estelle, a woman much too capable for pity.

"Did you know she was in the army?" Jenna blurted.

Lines formed on Reece's forehead. He stared as though she'd spoken in gibberish. "Who?"

"Your grandma. She served in World War Two. At some kind of field hospital." Right or wrong, Jenna's business or not, the truth was out there now.

"A hospital? She's never said anything —"

"I found a box, Reece. Inside it was a Bronze Star and pictures of her in uniform, from serving in the Pacific."

"But — that can't be right," he said, processing. "The other day, she even told me, she's never been to that area."

Jenna suddenly remembered the corporal in the photos, and a slew of deep-reaching theories returned. But that's all they were. Conjecture. And this certainly wasn't the time to detract from the situation.

"I only brought it up so that you know she's a fighter. I imagine she's survived a lot worse."

Taking this in, Reece nodded slowly, then again with more surety. His eyes gained a mark of hope.

"Mr. Porter?" Another man in scrubs entered the room, spurring Reece to stand. Jenna also rose, praying Estelle's bravery had seen her through.

"Is my grandmother all right?"

The doctor's expression gave away nothing. "We've done an EKG and a chest X-ray. We're still waiting on test results to rule everything out."

"What kind of tests? Are they for her heart?"

"Some standard blood work. We want to

be extra sure, but she appears to have simply suffered an inflammation of the lining of her lungs. Usually brought on by the flu, or even a common cold."

"So — not a heart attack?"

"That's right."

"But she was having problems breathing."

"From what I can tell," the doctor said, "it was just anxiety from what was happening. That's not uncommon." His mouth curved upward, a kind smile Jenna wished he had worn as he first approached. "At this point, she's been monitored. All her vitals are stable. We've given her a little something for the pain, so she's resting easy now."

Reece blew out a breath, a slight sheen in his eyes. A wave of relief flooded the air and washed over Jenna.

"A nurse will come see you in a few minutes. She'll take you over to your grandmother."

As the doctor departed, Reece looked as though he might burst from joy. Instead, he swung in Jenna's direction and wrapped her in a snug embrace.

"Reece, I'm so relieved."

"Me too," he whispered against her neck. The heat of his breath traveled over her skin. Her body tingled, as if every nerve had risen to the surface. She savored the feel of his heart beating, the faint scent of his earthy cologne, and found herself hoping the moment would last.

But then his grip loosened. He drew his head back and stared into her eyes. Mere inches separated their lips.

At the sound of voices in the hall, Reece stepped away. His parents had arrived. A glimpse at Mr. Porter's face indicated he was questioning the scene. Given the situation, Jenna imagined how terrible this had to look. She edged backward, wishing she could disappear into the tan walls.

"Honey, is there any news yet?" Sandy asked Reece. Before he could relay the update, a nurse came to lead them off. Sandy, noticing Jenna's presence, perked with surprise, then seemed to understand what had brought her here. She gave Jenna's arm a grateful squeeze on her way out, her husband leading the way.

Reece turned back with an awkward glance. "Thanks for your help."

"Sure," she replied.

Left alone in the waiting area, Jenna picked up her coat from a chair. Every movement took conscious effort as she gathered her bearings.

"Excuse me," a woman said. Beneath the bangs of her braided black hair, her striking blue eyes shone with concern. "The receptionist told me a family was waiting in here — the Porters. Did you happen to see anyone come by?"

She had to be Reece's sister. The resemblance was clear. "They just went to Estelle's room. She's doing great, by the way."

The woman sighed, hand over her chest. "I'm so glad."

In the beat that followed, her blue eyes clouded with confusion. "I hope this doesn't sound rude, but — who are you?"

It was a reasonable question, considering the family update Jenna had supplied.

"Sorry about that, I'm Jenna Matthews." She thought better of describing her professional role, this not being an ideal time to discuss an estate sale. "I take it you must be Lisa," she said, flipping the spotlight.

"Me?" A small laugh. "Oh, no. I'm Tracy Graniello."

Jenna accepted a handshake before Tracy added, "I'm Reece's girlfriend."

It took every bit of strength in Jenna to uphold her smile. Through the instant drought of her throat, she managed to push out, "Of course."

They released hands and Jenna went straight to gripping her coat. She averted her eyes, feeling as transparent as glass. "I should get out of the way. I'm sure if you ask somebody, they can help you find the Porters."

As Jenna started to leave, Tracy asked, "Would you like me to tell them anything for you?"

Jenna shook her head. What more could she possibly say?

CHAPTER 10

With every step, Reece grew more leery of the scene waiting in Room 303. The beeping of monitors and scent of medications revived a painfully clear vision. He could still see his grandfather, lying in a hospital bed, the family gathered around to bid farewell.

Now at his grandma's door, Reece welcomed the contrast. She was fully awake and propped upright in an automated bed. His worries melted away as he kissed her on the cheek. On his grandma's other side stood his mom. His dad gave a brief greeting, verging on gruff, then went to consult a doctor, not one to trust Reece's recount. What else was new?

Reece shut out the thought and asked, "Are you feeling better?"

"Oh, I'm fine," his grandma said. "Nothing to get riled up about." She waved her hand dismissively, a contradiction to the IV cord attached to it. A trace of pain meds seeped into her manner. "How soon can we leave? Place is chockful of germs."

His mom asserted, "They need to confirm everything's okay first."

"I already told the doc, I'm fit as a fiddle."

After the episode in the car, Reece wasn't about to let her think she could jet out of here without final clearance. "That's what you say now, Grandma. But you weren't that way an hour ago."

"Jeez, Louise. Can't a grown woman have a little scare without creating a fuss? When your daddy was little, someone would yell 'boo' and he'd wet his pants. It didn't mean I'd hold him hostage."

"You're not being held hostage," his mom argued. "You're in a hospital."

"Yeah, well. They both poke and prod ya, force you to eat tasteless slop, and charge you a ransom." She turned to Reece. "You be the judge."

He couldn't help but laugh.

Though his mother's mouth twitched from a near smile, she arched a brow at him: *Don't encourage her.* From a plastic pitcher she poured a cup of water and handed it to his grandma.

Having people around to help the elderly woman, Reece acknowledged, could prove

597

healthy rather than hindering. Unfortunately, the trade-off of that change would be another *I told you so* from his father. Reece's mood declined at the notion. "Do you want me to take Grandma home after they discharge her?"

"Your dad and I can do that, sweetheart. Her room at our place is ready for her to move back in." She brushed a piece of lint from the edge of the blanket and asked his grandma, "How about something to eat?"

"So long as it's not bread pudding. No sense wasting my teeth while I still have them."

His mom rolled her eyes, yet gave in to a smile. "Be right back."

Once she'd left the room, Reece heard a release in his grandma's breath. Her shoulders sank into the pillow, as though tired from keeping up a show.

He took a seat on the edge of the bed and leaned toward her. "How are you really feeling, Grandma?"

Her lips tightened. The morning seemed to replay in her mind, adding a subtle hoarseness to her voice. "I'll be all right, dear," she said. Then she lifted her chin and tenderly pinched his cheek. A gesture of love, and thanks. She had remarkable strength at her core.

Reflecting on Jenna's claims, Reece wanted to probe, to learn how far that strength extended. But now wasn't the time.

"Is there anything I can do for you?" he asked.

"Besides breaking me out of here?"

"Besides that."

She considered this. "You can give me the clicker, I suppose. If I have to sit around doing nothing, might as well watch *Wheel of Fortune*."

He grabbed the remote from a nearby chair and passed it along. "I didn't realize that show was still on."

"Just the reruns."

"Isn't that cheating? To already know the answers?"

"Not if you're too senile to remember." She gave him a wink and started flipping through the channels. "Dear, would you go see what your mother's scrounging up? Last thing I need is a bowl of mashed peas. Some Jell-O would be nice."

"I think I can handle that."

He offered a smile he managed to wear until he made it around the corner, just out of her sight line. Leaning against a wall, beneath a swoop of red and green garland, he felt the exhaustion of a roller coaster, a steep drop of *what ifs*. The emotional jostling of another near loss slammed against his chest.

He blew out a breath, regrouping. About to resume his mission, he heard his name being called from the side.

His father.

"Nurse said Tracy's looking for you," he told Reece.

Tracy was here? Then Reece remembered. He'd sent her a text message. "Where is she?"

"In the waiting area, where I found you," he said, "with the estate gal." Disapproval edged his voice.

"Look. Nothing happened with us."

"If you say so."

"Jenna was just there, at the house, and —" He stopped, threw up his palms. "You know what? Doesn't matter. You're gonna sit in judgment no matter what I say." He turned for the hallway.

"Reece," he snapped.

If Reece ignored the order and left, would it be worth it? What story would his father pass on to Tracy?

He wheeled back around to face a silent glower. It was obvious what the guy wanted to hear. After all this time, might as well get it over with. "Fine. You were right. You've won, okay?"

His father cocked his head. "Won?"

"About Grandma living alone, about my crazy stunts. You wanted me to play it safe, that's what I'm doing. Anything that involves a risk, it's gone. I'm living the way you've always wanted. So, yeah. You've won."

"Now, you hold on," he said. "I don't tell you how to live your life."

"Oh, really?" A prime example rushed into Reece's mind. "How about after the accident?"

His dad shook his head, as if straining to reassemble the memories. Reece, on the other hand, could recall every word, every syllable his father had spewed at that hospital. With the recollection came guilt and shame and resentment from that day.

"After we crashed, I thought I'd killed Tracy. Did you know that?"

The knot on his father's forehead tightened.

"At the hospital, her family hated me, and they had every right to. But when *you* got there, more than anything I needed your support. Not a lecture about how badly I'd screwed up. That's something I was well aware of."

His father opened his mouth but, to Reece's surprise, stalled on any retort.

"Excuse me, gentlemen." The nurse who had guided them from the waiting room suddenly appeared. "We have to keep the volume down in here."

Neither of them replied.

"You're welcome to take this conversation elsewhere." It was a command, not a suggestion.

"That's all right," Reece answered quietly, tearing his gaze from his father. "We're finished."

CHAPTER 11

The house was empty.

Scanning the family room, Jenna stared at the half-filled boxes, the countless items needing to be inventoried and tagged. According to Terrence's voice mail, he'd taken the crew home, uncomfortable working today with the client's health in jeopardy.

In the industry, he was one of the compassionate ones. Plenty of liquidators would have charged through without a thought. The longer you're in the business, the more hardened you're supposed to get. It's about sales, not people. Simplifying, not complicating. Purging, not collecting. It's about getting the job done — which clearly wasn't happening. Two weeks from the estate sale, and thanks to the holidays, they were barely making a dent.

No question, Terrence had made the right decision. But that didn't stop Jenna's frustration from mounting. She snagged a dried-up potted plant she'd meant to toss earlier and dropped it into a black trash bag. From a nearby cabinet she yanked out a stack of games. Their cardboard containers were disintegrating from use. No point checking for missing pieces. Parcheesi, Hangman, Battleship, chess. One after the other, she dumped them all. A deck of Skip-Bo cards spilled over the floor.

She groaned. "Perfect."

On her knees, she snatched them by the handful. She pitched them into the bag, faster and harder with each scoop. This was her own fault; she'd let the job get too personal. Estelle's shoe box, which she'd brought in from her trunk, would be next on the list. She'd sell what she could and toss the rest.

Out with the clutter, she reminded herself. Life was easier without it. Her exchange today with Reece Porter had only confirmed that.

The guy had sent her emotions into a jumbled spiral, and why? Fact was, she barely knew him. He'd certainly never denied having a girlfriend. Nonetheless, a feeling of betrayal swelled inside. Worse yet, of being no better than her father's mistress.

The thought was irrational. Just like the tears building behind her eyes. Pushing them down, she reached under the sofa to gather the stray cards. A 9 was just beyond her reach, like so many other things these days.

Lying on her side, she stretched out her arm. Almost . . . had it . . .

The doorbell chimed. Reflexively, her finger flicked the card away. Jenna fumed as the bell rang again. Her parked van likely boosted the caller's hope in summoning a person. Soon, persistence would lead to an annoying series of knocks.

Jenna marched toward the entry and swung open the door. "Yes?"

An elderly man stood under the portico, out of the rain. He wore a damp trench coat over his suit and navy bow tie, a fedora hat shielding his eyes. His silver mustache was narrow and neatly trimmed.

"Pardon me, miss. I hope I'm not bothering you." He spoke with such tenderness Jenna swiftly reined in her emotions.

"Not at all. What can I do for you?"

"I saw an ad for the estate sale with this address. Said it was for the Porters."

She should have guessed. Estates with well-known owners tended to attract sneak peeks.

"I'm sorry, but we're not having a preview on this house. If you'd like to come back on

December seventeenth —"

"I'm not here for the sale. I . . ." The man grabbed the hat off his head and squeezed it to the medium frame of his chest. "I just need to know if Stella . . ." He inhaled a breath before the rest tumbled out coarsely. "Has she passed?"

Stella?

"Do you mean Estelle Porter?" Considering the topic, clarity was essential.

He mustered a nod as Jenna realized the implication that had drawn him here. Estate sales for elderly residents commonly followed a death. From the stranger's intensity, Jenna was grateful the day's emergency had ended the way it did.

"Mrs. Porter is alive and well," she told him. "She's simply moving in with her family."

A gasp shot from the man's lips, which suddenly quivered. Same for his hands. "Thank you," he breathed. "That's . . . thank you."

Dazed, he fumbled in replacing his hat and started to leave. An old Chevy sat empty in the driveway, streaked with raindrops. The last thing Jenna needed was another distraction, but she couldn't let him operate a car in his unsettled state, especially with the slick, winding roads in the area.

One hospital run was enough for the day.

"Sir," she called out, "why don't you come inside?"

He angled a quarter of the way back, then raised a hand. "I'd better not. I wouldn't want to intrude."

"It's just me here, and I'd love the company."

The man hesitated, contemplating.

"Please," she said, growing weary. "Just until the rain lets up."

He glanced at the road, his car, the house. With a small nod, he agreed.

"Do you live around here?" Jenna asked, padding the silence as she waited for the microwave to beep.

The man sat in his chair, fingering the brim of his hat on the Formica table. "Summerville Center."

"Oh, sure. Over in Tigard." Two of Jenna's past clients had moved into the retirement home. "Seems like a nice place to live."

He smiled softly.

At last, she delivered the mug. He steeped his tea bag by lifting and dropping it several times.

"So," Jenna said, "you've known Estelle — or Stella, for a long time?"

He took a sip before replying. "It was

quite some years ago."

Silence again.

She debated on excusing herself and returning to task, but intrigue, her greatest enemy lately, baited her to stay. "I'm Jenna, by the way," she began. "And your name is . . . ?"

Inclining his head, he accepted her handshake. His light blue eyes held a charming if worn twinkle. "Tom," he said.

As she watched him take another sip, his look of discomfort growing, the connection sank in. Still, there had to be a million Toms out there.

"I really ought to be going," he said suddenly.

When it came to Jenna's work, there had always been lines, invisible but clear. Yet after a week with the Porters, those lines were blurring. And now, with the man's departure imminent, any rules ceased to exist.

Rising, he donned his hat.

"Are you Corporal Redding?" she blurted.

He froze, his eyes downcast. An infinite pause stretched the air taut until he spoke. "Stella told you about me?"

"Well . . . she . . ." Jenna had to confess, "No. Not exactly."

His gaze lifted, swirling with disappointment, confusion. He wanted to know if he'd been forgotten. Jenna understood the feeling, from her father. And she refused to let this kindhearted man believe the memory of him was lost.

"Mr. Redding," she said, coming to her feet, "I have something to show you."

In the den, Jenna led Tom around an obstacle of hand trucks and moving supplies. She guided him to sit in the cushioned swivel chair. Forbidding herself a second thought, she presented the infamous shoe box.

Slowly, he pulled out the photographs and laid them on the desk. His expression lightened by degrees until, as with Estelle, the decades since the war vanished from his face.

"It was just yesterday," he murmured.

"This is you, then, with the mistletoe." It wasn't a question, just an observance of a mystery being solved.

He touched that particular picture and sported a boyish grin. "Had to get creative. I was bound and determined to get a smooch out of that girl."

Jenna smiled along with him, feeling as if she had been there. "And did it work?"

Tom shook his head. "Only on the cheek.

Consorting like that was against the rules."
He let out a soft laugh. " 'Course, she found
me later behind the supply tent and gave
me a kiss I'll never forget. Blew my army
socks clear off."

"So . . . you two started dating?"

"Well. Not officially."

No elaboration. Perhaps he preferred a
less intimate topic.

Jenna retrieved from the box another piece
of the puzzle. The Bronze Star. As she
flipped open the case, he tilted his head.
"Ahh, yeah," he sighed.

"Do you happen to know how she got
this?"

He hummed in affirmation, running his
thumb over the grooves of the medal. "We
were stationed in Dutch New Guinea at the
time. MacArthur was leapfrogging toward
Tokyo. Docs and nurses were being rotated
up to the front. Stella volunteered to help,
which I didn't like one bit. And I sure as
heck told her so."

"But she went anyway," Jenna guessed.

Tom glanced up, brow raised. "One thing
about Stella. She was the sweetest girl you
ever met. But make no mistake, few people
were better at holding their ground." A mix
of frustration and admiration seeped into
his voice. "Turned out to be a good thing,

610

anyhow. Saved a whole lot of soldiers out there."

After a moment, Tom set down the award. He straightened, prompting Jenna to do the same. He was going to leave. But he couldn't. Not yet. A buried tale was surfacing. All that was left in the box, however, was a tattered book.

A last ditch effort, she hastened to hold up *Jane Eyre*. "Any idea if this was special to her?"

Tom stared for several seconds. His skin paled. As he sank into his chair, any remnants of nostalgic warmth drained away. He handled the book as though poison soaked its pages. On the inside cover was an inscription Jenna could make out from her view.

My dearest darling,
Merry Christmas!

Tom

Shoulders hunched, he shut his eyes. "That's all I could come up with," he said before forcing another look.

Jenna simply waited, not pushing.

"It was her favorite novel," he finally added. "I spent a good half hour trying to write a thoughtful note, and that was it. No mention of love. No gratitude for taking care of me." He shook his head as tears welled. "I was so angry at the world. It was never her, of course, but that's who I took it out on."

Jenna was struggling to keep up. Yet he gazed at her intently, a plea for understanding.

"We were being shipped home, from the Philippines. War was over. People were celebrating for days. With all the commotion it took me a minute to even realize I'd been hit."

The way he spoke the word, Jenna gathered the meaning. "You were shot?"

"Some drunken GI had fired off a pistol. Got me right in the kneecap. That's why we held off marrying. I told Stella I wouldn't go down that aisle till I could walk nice and smooth. That's how dumb and stubborn I was."

The tragic irony was staggering to Jenna. Serving in a world war, only to be wounded by your own side. And all while celebrating America's victory.

"Did you break up because of your injury?" she dared to ask.

"If it weren't for an infection, things might've been different. But you see, I couldn't work for some time. And alcohol helped dull the pain." He clutched the book as he continued. "Back then, being a man meant earning a paycheck. You couldn't have a woman doing it for you. Wartime was one thing, but back at home, life was supposed to be normal. Besides, Stella was too good for that. I promised I'd take care of her, and somehow it all got turned around. I actually had myself convinced it'd be a relief for us both when we went our separate ways."

Estelle's efforts to break from the past began to make sense. Jenna's soap-opera theories fizzled on the spot.

Tom released the book. He attempted to flatten the edges he'd bent. "Important thing is, when I happened across her husband's obituary, listing their kids and grandkids, I knew she'd had a good life. Just like I had with Noreen — God rest her. So really, it all worked out for the best."

"Had you ever thought about contacting Stella? To tell her all of this?"

He stifled a small laugh. "Wrote at least six versions of a letter over the years. In the end, always felt like nudging a beehive. Didn't seem right to disturb her life."

Jenna nodded, relating to the intent. The couple's circumstances, though, had changed. "Maybe it's time to mail one of those letters."

His gaze dropped to the photos. He shrugged a shoulder and said, "Oh . . . I don't know. . . ."

"Mr. Redding, you came here today, worrying it was too late. But now you know it's not."

"Yeah, well. We'll see." His tone didn't sound promising.

He patted the book, a farewell motion, and rose to his feet. "I'd really best get going."

"Are you sure? There's really no reason to rush."

"Nah, nah. I've taken up enough of your time."

She yielded with reluctance and walked him to the door, where they traded holiday tidings. He was a few steps outside when he pivoted back. "Miss," he said, "I want to thank you for that."

Thanks for what? For allowing Jenna to pry open old wounds?

"I really didn't do anything you should be grateful for."

His lips curved into a wistful smile that argued otherwise.

CHAPTER 12

Although part of him still resisted the change, Reece had to admit the setup was better than he'd expected. In the basement of his parents' house, the walls of his old bedroom had always been the color of stone. Fitting for a teenager, it had provided a brooding backdrop for posters of rock groups and rebel athletes. The feeling of being separate from the house had made it an ideal spot during high school.

He rotated slowly now, hardly recognizing the space. A fresh coat of buttery yellow paint had transformed the dungeon into a cozy cove. A miniature kitchen appeared where a storage closet once stood. Best of all, elements of his grandma's home were sprinkled throughout: a mounted shelf of porcelain figurines; down bedding and a claw-footed hope chest; floral curtains that virtually matched her own.

Below the two windows, his grandma sat

in her rocking chair, sifting through Christmas cards forwarded from her old house. A tasseled lamp glowed on the nightstand, brightening her pallor. She looked remarkably better than she did in the hospital. Hard to believe that was only four days ago.

Reece held up the poinsettias, the pot wrapped in a silver bow. "A little housewarming gift for you."

She merely flicked them a glance. "Lovely, dear."

In the wedge of quiet, he set the plant on her dresser, another furnishing from her house.

"Why didn't Dad ever say he was going to fix it up like this?" Reece said this more to himself than her.

"Could be that you never asked."

True. Although he couldn't imagine asking his father much of anything at the moment. Thankfully, the guy was holed up in his garage, making it easy for Reece to slip in and out before dinner.

Just then, the aroma of baked crescent rolls wafted from upstairs. The slight trace of burnt dough delivered an idea.

"You know, with you being here now," Reece suggested, "Mom can finally pick up some cooking tips."

After a halfhearted smile, his grandma

continued to study her cards in an absent manner. Adjusting to a new way of life was never easy. Quiet time to dwell often made things worse.

"Hey, how about some music?" He turned the knob of her antique RCA radio. He'd forgotten how touchy those dials were to find a station without static. At last, an FM channel projected a clear tune, "Grandma Got Run Over by a Reindeer." The repetitive chorus tended to grind at his nerves, but he hoped the lyrics might give her a giggle. Which they didn't.

He was grateful the song ended, until he registered the next one: "I'll Be Home for Christmas." He clicked the radio off.

"Mom says she's set aside an area in the backyard so you can garden in the spring."

His grandma murmured her acknowledgment.

"Also, I hear some of your friends have been calling to check on you. I think they've been hoping you'll join their quilting group again."

He waited for a wisecrack about hanging out with blind old biddies. But nothing came.

Reece couldn't stand seeing her this way. He understood where she was; he'd been there before himself. And it was his grandma's no-nonsense advice that had ultimately yanked him out of his cave. Serving up that same tidbit to her now, about throwing a solo pity party, was tempting. Unfortunately, he doubted his own ability to deliver the words with his grandma's charm.

He perched on the end of her hope chest, wishing he possessed a magic formula to revive the strong grandmother he knew.

He'd done his best to stamp out thoughts of Jenna the last several days — the powdery fragrance of her skin, how close he'd come to kissing her and, once again, screwing up his life — but at this moment, her assurances returned with unavoidable clarity. She'd seemed certain of his grandmother's courage, all based on a past Reece knew nothing about. It could be helpful, reminding his grandma of her younger days, when her military service required independence and bravery.

Surely it was worth a try.

He clasped his hands, elbows on his knees, and leaned closer. "Jenna Matthews — the girl working at your house — she told me about a box she found. Things you saved from the war."

His grandma's hands went still. Her gaze remained on her lap.

"Is it true you served in an army hospital?"

Her silence served as confirmation, along with the sense that she'd hoped to keep that nugget under wraps. But why? Why the cover-up, the lies?

"At first, I told Jenna she had to be mistaken. That you'd even said you'd never been to Asia before."

"Vacationed," she corrected boldly, and raised her head. "I said that I never *vacationed* there. Aside from a few coconut cocktails, it wasn't exactly Club Med."

One could argue it a technicality, but at least she wasn't denying the claim.

"I just don't get it," he said. "Being an army nurse is something you should be proud of. Why didn't you ever mention it?" Reece could see vets not wanting to share details, given how gruesome he imagined the war had been, but not hiding their service altogether.

"Please, Grandma," he insisted gently. "You can tell me about it."

Following a lengthy pause, she looked into his eyes and appeared to recognize her own stubbornness — meaning Reece wasn't about to let the subject go.

She sat back in her chair and set her cards aside. Then she sighed, as if dusting off stored-up words. "We weren't nurses," she clarified. "That would have taken a lot more training than enlisting in the WAC, and I was too eager to do my bit. Once there, of course, we took to their duties all the same."

"So you *were* stationed in the jungle?"

"It was nothing like *Gilligan's Island,* I can tell you that much. After a few days in Hollandia, we sure didn't resemble Ginger or Mary Ann." She let out a small laugh. "You should have seen my parents' faces. About had a conniption over my appearance when I got home. It just supported why they were against me joining up in the first place."

"And that's why you never talked about it," Reece concluded, still trying to understand.

"It wasn't just them. Society's never been a fan of change, dear. Once we came back, I learned real fast that putting WAC on a résumé was a surefire way *not* to get hired. The soldiers we'd helped, they knew the truth, but most people at home preferred to believe we'd helped boost morale in . . . well, other ways."

Reece got the point, along with her motivation for secrecy. Shame dictated she close that chapter of her life as though it had never happened.

"Then, years later," she said, eyes glimmering behind her glasses, "I met your grandfather. Together we created a family I couldn't be prouder of." She paused before reaching over to pat Reece's forearm. "Way I see it, better to focus on the path ahead, rather than hanging on to what's already done."

Her pointed remark wasn't lost on him. Clearly, she had overheard him and his father bickering at the hospital. Considering their volume, how could she have avoided it? Maybe Reece was long overdue to drop the weights of his own past. "I hear what you're saying, Grandma," he conceded.

But then, recalling where this conversation began, he sent the lesson right back at her. "Who knows, I might even get the itch to join a quilting group. Visit old friends, start cooking, gardening. That kind of thing."

She pursed her lips, fighting a smile that ultimately won out. "Who on earth taught you to be such a smart aleck?"

"Must be hereditary."

"Must be."

As they laughed together, the room gained an even cozier feel. That's precisely how it remained throughout the rest of their chat, which shifted to lighter topics. It went unspoken that their thoughts and emotions needed a break. And so, they engaged in the usual discussions of books and weather and *Wheel of Fortune.*

At a natural lull, their talk having run its course, Reece prepared to leave. He stood and gave her a soft peck on the cheek.

"Oh, wait, before you go," she said, gesturing toward her jewelry box. "Got something for you in the bottom drawer."

It didn't dawn on him what that something would be until he grabbed the knob. A velvet ring box stared back at him.

"You still wanted that, didn't you, dear?"

He creaked open the case. Inside, a small marquise diamond topped a beautiful silver band. Amazing how a whole future could rest on such a small object.

Reece turned to his grandma, replying with a smile.

Time to live without regrets.

CHAPTER 13

Jenna shifted in her director's chair, fending off the urge to fidget. Lightbulbs framing the mirror compounded the heat generated by her nerves. She should have skipped her morning latte. The caffeine was proving anything but soothing.

Mia, the makeup artist, pulled a comb from the apron tied around her hefty middle. Her almond-shaped eyes and corn-rows lent her an exotic look. Candy cane earrings shimmered against her chocolate skin. "Okay if I touch up your hair?" she asked, aerosol already in hand.

"Spray away." Jenna pinned on a smile, which she dropped once she felt her cheeks tremble. A guest spot on a talk show had sounded so exciting. But after arriving early at the station, the producer had put such stress on the live-air aspect of *Morning Portland,* Jenna now feared a tongue-tied disaster. It didn't help that her mother had told everyone on the planet about the program.

"Been on the show before?" Mia asked while launching a shower of hairspray.

Jenna coughed on a mouthful and shook her head.

"Well then, I'll make sure your debut looks fabulous. You're talking about used jewelry, right?"

"Right," she squeezed out.

The woman deshined Jenna's face with a brush full of powder. "Buying or selling it?"

Once the air cleared enough, Jenna said, "Both."

Their fractured conversation resembled visits with her dental hygienist, who never failed to ask a question when Jenna's mouth was stuffed with cotton, cardboard, or bubble gum fluoride. As the current exchange trudged along, she tried not to grimace at the heavy application of red lipstick and rosy blush — although her mother would be thrilled. Jenna repeatedly reminded herself that the studio lights washed out color.

"Don't know about you," Mia remarked, "but I couldn't do it."

A pointed pause hauled Jenna back to the discussion. "I'm sorry . . . ?"

"Wear a divorced person's ring. Or even a hawked engagement band, for that matter.

Just so much sadness and turmoil tied to those kinda things."

Jenna countered with her usual: "Yes, but they could bring a lot of happiness to the new buyer."

"I don't know, maybe . . ." Mia worked at taming a lock of Jenna's shag. "Then again, I'm more of the sentimental type. Every spring I vow to clean out my daughter's art projects from school, now with her off at college, but just can't bring myself to do it."

Jenna easily visualized the boxes, crammed with wrinkled handprint paintings and glitter-shedding snowflakes — none of which would be viewed more than twice.

"What about you?" Mia asked with another spritz. If she was perpetuating conversation to ease a nervous guest, the attempt was failing.

"I don't have kids."

"No, I meant is there anything you collect?"

That word again. "There's nothing."

"Oh, surely there's something you cherish enough to hang on to."

Jenna shook her head against the disbelief that blared in the woman's tone. Why was the concept so hard to get? "I am *not* a collector."

Mia paused the primping, fist on her hip.

The woman was only making small talk. When had Jenna become so neurotic?

In the stiffening silence, the woman sharpened an eyebrow pencil.

Jenna searched for a way to backpedal before Mia added, "Way I see it, we're all collectors in one way or another. Keepers of memories, if nothing else. Some aren't as pretty as others, but wipe out one half and you'd lose the other. . . ."

As her words trailed off, Tom Redding's face appeared in Jenna's mind. Wrinkles at the corners of his eyes, as well as his mouth, bespoke smiles and frowns, happy and sad moments, like the memories in Estelle's box.

That darn haunting box.

Jenna still couldn't bring herself to throw the thing away, yet she should have. Life had been easier before its complicating ties. Disposing of others' items had always brought relief — at least until the craving returned. Which it always did. Like an addiction, some might say. Like cigarettes or alcohol, or . . . hoarding.

"Miss Matthews?" The intern who'd initially greeted Jenna poked her head in from the greenroom. "We're ready for you."

Jenna sprang from her chair, thankful for the interruption.

"Not just yet," Mia ordered, filling Jenna

with dread. Had the woman somehow read her thoughts?

Mia merely removed the protective tissues she'd tucked into the collar of Jenna's sweater, which the producer had borrowed from wardrobe for a festive look.

Jenna reviewed herself in the mirror. Between the bright red garment and matching lipstick, she felt like a Rudolph the Red-lipped Reindeer.

"Right this way," the intern said. She led Jenna down the same hall she'd traversed earlier to set up her display.

Again, they wove through the station's maze, past editing rooms with walls of monitors and enough buttons and switches for a NASA control center. With a wave of the girl's badge over a security pad, an alarm beeped once and the door opened.

"Watch your step," she said as they approached an obstacle course of thick black cords. Each was connected to one of several mounted cameras facing the empty news anchors' desk. A solid green wall denoted the meteorologist's area. Reporting the weather in Portland — rain, drizzle, downpour — had to be as thrilling as reporting sunshine in Hawaii.

The intern held a finger to her lips, a warning to Jenna that the microphones were

hot. In the studio kitchen, the host, whose former role as a sportscaster befit his appearance, was sampling a Cajun twist on Christmas turkey. Judging from the sweat beading on his forehead, the meat had fully absorbed the chef's Southern spice.

When the show broke for a commercial, a floor director clipped Jenna's mike in place, then rushed her to the table of jewelry. Jenna had borrowed some from her boss, some from coworkers; others she'd snagged from a pawnshop. The host threw her a quick hello before guzzling water from a glass and flipping through a script. The female floor director launched a countdown. A cameraman gripped his handles as he spoke into his headset while the other camera moved on its own.

Amid the chaos of the room, Jenna's ears turned hot. She smoothed her hair over both lobes, praying they weren't the same shade as her sweater.

Focus on the table, she told herself. She would work her way from left to right, just as she'd practiced, starting with a gemmed bracelet that only needed a few minor repairs to double its value.

"We're live in five, four . . ." The floor director continued silently with three fingers. Two. One. Then a red light glowed on

the camera as she pointed to the host.

"Welcome back to *Morning Portland*," he said, standing beside Jenna. " 'Tis the season of gift giving. If your pocketbook is a little light this year, not to worry. Used jewelry could save the day. Here to tell us how is Jenna Matthews, an estate liquidator who's built a career on pricing and selling off other people's treasures."

Jenna winced at the introduction. Yeah, it was true, technically, but it sounded so pilfering stated that way.

"Thanks for being on the show." He smiled at her, but she could see in his eyes that he'd rather be talking about touchdowns than trinkets.

"Thanks for having me."

"To start off, why don't you tell our viewers how determining the value of jewelry can come in handy at Christmastime?"

"Well," she said, recalling her rehearsed speech, "if you understand how to appraise a piece acquired at an estate sale or a flea market, for example, you'll know what you're actually giving someone. It's also helpful when you're selling jewelry you already own."

"And those proceeds can be used to buy other gifts," he finished.

"That's right."

"Sounds dollar-smart to me. I bet there's lots of collectors out there who have a drawerful gathering dust. My wife, for one." He winked at the camera.

The vision of a drawer invaded Jenna's thoughts. If she were given even half of one to fill, what would she put inside? All she had collected was empty space. A preventative measure, it created a barrier against anything that might hurt her. The flip side being that nothing meaningful could get through.

"So, let's get started," the host went on. He gestured to the brooch on the right side of the table. "How about this pin? What would that go for?"

Pin? He was supposed to start with the left. The bracelet! At home, over and over she had practiced in that order. Pores of perspiration opened on her scalp as her mind reeled in search of the value.

Think, think . . .

The Victorian brooch was an heirloom. Terrence's mother had given it to him the Christmas before she passed. Not to wear himself, of course, but to keep in the family. He let Jenna borrow it, claiming his mom would have loved showing it off. He said that as a kid he used to believe the ivory profile was fashioned after his mom.

"Just a ballpark figure," the host prompted, alerting Jenna that she hadn't responded.

"I would say . . ." she began. "The value would be . . ."

The guy flickered an intense glance at the floor director, a plea for help with his stage-frightened guest.

Jenna hastened to calculate, to estimate anything close. Then another image came to her: Estelle's Bronze Star. From it, a sudden peacefulness flowed, for there was only one true answer.

"It's priceless."

Covering with a smile, the host flashed another side glance. "I'm sure to the owner it is. But, what do you think the dollar range would be?"

"Really . . . there isn't one."

"Excuse me?"

The revelation struck like electricity, humming through her veins. How could anyone put a price tag on a woman's final gift to her son? It could be a rock or a blade of grass, and no dollar amount would do it justice. The same applied, she realized, to a kid's baseball caught with his grandpa.

Confidence growing, Jenna explained, "Perception is what dictates price — whether it's paintings and furnishings or antiques and jewelry. That's a basic standard for any type of retail. It's what says a store can charge eight dollars, or eight hundred, for a pair of shoes. All that said though," she confessed, "what I didn't understand, for a long time now, was the major role memories play in that perception."

"Uh, yes," the host interjected, "I see what you mean." His uncertainty over the segment's direction tolled as loud as bells.

Jenna, on the other hand, knew precisely where her message was headed. She turned to the camera and spoke directly to her mother.

"In different ways, we all have voids to fill. Holidays, for a lot of people, can bring those feelings out even more. The best thing we can do is to fill our lives with things that matter, like . . . turning a favorite hobby into a job, or finding a person you're crazy about. Even if none of those things come with guarantees."

The story of Tom and Estelle, despite their relationship's end, exemplified the need to take a risk.

"Allowing people you care about into your life," she continued, "and letting them know how important they are, that's the best present you can give them." In the brief lull, Jenna glimpsed the wide-eyed host, spurring her to veer back on course. "Which is . . . why a gift of jewelry . . . carries more value, in every aspect, when it's personal and tied to a memory."

At the floor director's cue, the host angled toward the teleprompter. "Definitely a great message for the holidays. Speaking of holidays, after the break Mimi the Elf will teach us how to make ornaments out of plastic toys from fast-food meals, sure to become the talk of the neighborhood." He pushed up a grin. "Don't go away."

The instant the red light turned off, the host's expression made clear his last line wasn't meant for Jenna. Instead, his eyes told her: *Go. Away. Now.*

Swept off by the intern, who stole back the mike, Jenna wound through the station, pausing only to reclaim her shirt. She signed out at the front desk, where a television was now airing Mimi the Elf.

"That was quite a segment," the receptionist said.

"Yeah," Jenna breathed, and handed over her visitor's badge.

"Best one I've seen in a while."

Jenna would have taken the phrase for sarcasm if not for the tone, pulled from a deep well of sincerity. "Thanks."

In the parking lot, Jenna inhaled the crisp

morning air. Clouds had given way to a clear winter sky. Everything about the day felt different.

As she retrieved her keys from her purse, she noticed a message on her phone, a text from her mom: Loved the show. Loved your sweater. Love you.

Jenna smiled at the note, guiding her thoughts to a memory. A conversation from Thanksgiving. Indeed, like a character in a romantic comedy, with a microphone on and the world tuned in, Jenna had been seized by a revelation. There was a good reason, she decided, to declare your stand in public. Because then you couldn't go backward.

Her career would be the next step.

While she still believed in the job's value — helping families, transitioning residents — the idea of price tagging Estelle's effects wrung Jenna's stomach. How could she pay her mortgage with another person's memories? No partnership would be worth the trade. If she had to sell her condo, even at a loss, that's what she had to do.

The prospect, though scary, thrilled and liberated her — thanks, in part, to Terrence. Of any coworker she knew, he would treat the Porter estate with compassion. She floated on this certainty as she sat in her car, before the buzz of her phone jostled her. She expected to see her mom's number, not Sally's.

"Oh, boy." Jenna braced herself for an earful about her behavior on the show. Needless to say, she didn't foresee another invitation.

"Can you talk?" Sally greeted with urgency.

Jenna wavered. How long did her friend plan on commenting? The segment itself didn't last more than five minutes.

"Um . . . sure."

"I didn't want to get your hopes up, in case I was wrong. But I just heard back from an old professor of mine in Chicago."

"Wait. What are we talking about?" Obviously, Sally had missed the broadcast.

"The teapot from the Porter estate," she explained. "I knew it denoted the Qing dynasty, and that the stamp was rare. But I've been fooled by something similar before."

Jenna's thoughts spun as she pictured the little Chinese teapot.

"Jenna, are you still there?"

"So .... are you saying . . . ?"

Sally replied with a smile in her voice. "Merry Christmas, sweetie. You hit the jackpot."

CHAPTER 14

Reece squeezed the side handle, more out of frustration than for safety. Beside him, bundled in winter sporting wear, Tracy steered their golf cart toward the green.

"Uh-oh," she sang out, nose scrunched. She brought them to a stop by the sixth flag. "I think it's in the water."

Big surprise. So far today, his shots had landed him in several sand traps and in knee-high rough. Once on another fairway. His thoughts were a jumble, his muscles the furthest thing from loose. When he'd arranged their golf outing, he hadn't actually planned on them playing a round.

But then, he hadn't banked on Tracy running late to the clubhouse, near frantic they'd miss their tee time. Nor had he foreseen the ranger who'd glowered at them for stalling the game on his watch.

"Hon, I need to talk to you," Reece had told her as they approached the first tee box.

"After this hole, okay?" She'd dashed off to set up with her pitching wedge, ponytail swinging through the back of her Pinnacle cap. Rushing had slightly hooked her drive, causing her to mutter a few choice words. Not an ideal moment to pop the question.

Still, he'd wanted to follow through. This was, after all, where they had first met — an idea he'd borrowed from her sister's proposal. Plus, for an outdoor girl like Tracy, the mountain backdrop, towering trees, and open air fit her perfectly. The rarity of blue sky on a December day in Oregon, just as forecasted, had seemed a telling sign.

Yet before he could retrieve the ring, tucked into his golf bag, a foursome from the Hit 'n' Giggle club had pulled up for their turn. Armed with visors and Bloody Marys, the boisterous ladies had, unknowingly, stomped out Reece's attempt.

Hole two had become his next option, then three, then four. But no moment had felt right. Reece had sped through his putting, to gain privacy from the group. This only worsened his shots, aggravating him more. An ugly cycle. With Christmas just two weeks away, the window of opportunity was narrowing; he refused to attend another

Graniello holiday without making things official.

New plan of attack, he told himself, striding toward the water to the left of the green. Pitching wedge and putter in his grip, he surveyed the area, desperate for an idea.

The clubhouse.

Three more holes and they'd be at the halfway mark, a good chance for a lunch break fireside. Whoever said proposing over a Payne Stewart Burger wasn't romantic? Points for uniqueness. They could look back at it one day and laugh.

"Yesss," Tracy exclaimed. Her chip onto the green had placed her ball in an ideal spot. From there it rolled in a gentle curve, almost in slow motion, and ended — *plonk* — in the cup. Her lips stretched with elation before she glanced at Reece. In an instant, she dropped her smile, stifling her celebration.

Compassionate. He mentally added the trait to the list, a compilation of all the reasons he'd be a moron not to marry the girl.

"Any sign of your ball?" she called out.

He rotated in a circle and shook his head.

Lofty chatter projected from the foursome gaining on them.

"Why don't you just call it a nine?" Tracy

suggested. As in, a mercy score so they could skip this hole and move on. Surely, that's how the Bloody Mary gang was playing. With twice as many people, how else were they progressing so fast?

Or were his skills today even more pathetic than he'd gathered?

Reece straightened, pulling back his shoulders. Today, of all days, he needed his ego intact.

"I'll take the drop." He reached into his right pants pocket. Nothing but plastic markers and wooden tees. He patted the other front pocket, then those of his Windbreaker. Empty. He'd blown through them all. At this rate, he couldn't even qualify for the Hit 'n' Giggle league.

He spoke through a clenched jaw. "Can you give me an extra?"

"Sure thing." Tracy offered an overly cheery smile. "I'll bring it over."

As he waited for a spare, he studied the murky water that had swallowed his ball. In the reflection was a guy who, not so long ago, would have shucked off his spiked shoes, rolled up his pant legs, and waded into that icy water without hesitation.

He rubbed at his temple with his gloved hand, pushing down the thought, and noted Tracy's delay. He raised his head. Rather than mere steps away, she had gone over to their cart. She was searching for a ball in her golf bag.

No, not hers — his. *His bag!*

"Tracy, wait! I'll get it!" He meant to speed-walk in a seminatural manner but instead burst into a sprint.

Fortunately, his warning worked. She halted any movement until he reached her, at which point she slowly lifted her eyes. The source of their intensity lay in her palm. His grandmother's box. Open. The ring exposed.

"Is this . . ." she said, a wisp of a voice. She didn't finish; she already understood.

Reece took a breath. He saw himself kneel, hold up the ring, and take her hand. He heard his own speech, saw tears fill her eyes, right before she accepted.

This was it. The grandiose moment.

But at the recollection of his grandma's phrase, a condition of using the ring — "If you love this girl with all your heart" — his world froze. His legs wouldn't bend and hands wouldn't rise. His speech had crumbled, and the syllables wouldn't adhere.

"Yoo-hoo!" a woman hollered. Her singsong tone broke through his paralysis, turning his head toward her. "Mind if we play through?" she asked.

Reece managed to motion his hand in agreement. The ladies flitted their fingers in thanks, then stood there. Waiting. It dawned on him that he and Tracy should move aside if they didn't want a golf ball to the skull. He angled back toward Tracy, to guide her away, but she had disappeared. His heart pounded like a fist to the chest.

He scanned the area until catching sight of her. She'd found a park bench off to the side, an empty space often used for the snack cart. She was staring down at the ring that glinted in the sunlight, but her expression wasn't the kind that preceded happy tears.

Reece forced down a swallow of confusion, offense, relief. Hands balled at his sides, he made his way over and lowered himself beside her.

Not looking up, she said, "Reece, you don't want to propose to me."

His lips parted, an effort to craft a denial — that refused to come. She was right. And hearing the sentiment aloud confirmed it all the more. Nevertheless, he cared for her deeply and hated that his behavior might have hurt her.

"I think it's obvious what's been going on," she told him. "It's finally time we talked about it."

A million thoughts entered his mind. Cautious, he said, "Okay . . ."

She set down the ring box and peered into his eyes. "After I went to the hospital and met that girl you were with, that's when I knew for sure."

Jenna Matthews . . . that's what this was about?

He'd had a feeling his father was going to blab for no good reason. "Nothing's going on between us. You have to believe me —"

"I do believe you." Tracy's reply, firm and calm, stopped the revving of his defenses.

"Then . . . what?"

She shook her head and gazed toward the passing carts. "When Jenna and I met in the waiting room, I introduced myself as your girlfriend. She tried to hide it, but it was obvious she was disappointed."

Given the chaos of that day, Reece hadn't considered the two of them crossing paths. God, Jenna must have taken him for a —

He snipped off the thought. His history with Tracy took precedence, everything they had endured as a team.

"That doesn't matter," he insisted. He reached out and held her hand, regaining her attention.

"It does if you're not sure about us," Tracy stated.

"What? No, but I am."

"But if you weren't —"

"Sweetheart, you don't have to worry. Remember, I promised I'd take care of you."

"Yes, I know that." Her voice gained a graveled edge. "But that's not a reason to stay together."

"What are you talking about? There are other things —"

"Reece," she burst out, "I was planning to break up with you."

His mind did a double take. He pulled his hand away. Like the ring, he'd become open, exposed.

At last, she shifted her body to face him, softening. "I liked you, Reece, from the minute we met. You were unpredictable and loads of fun. But we were really different." She quickened her pace, sounding tense from effort. "We'd only been dating a few months. I was going to move on, but then the accident happened. You were so wonderful, sticking by me. . . ."

The reality of their past snapped together and crashed into Reece's head. It rattled his core before gradually settling in. "And guilt's kept us together," he finished.

After a heavy pause, Tracy nodded. "I

think you're a great guy, I really do. We're just not meant to be together like this," she said. "Honestly, I think we've both been pretending to be something we're not."

The scenario was certainly a familiar one. His grandmother, all from a shame of her own, had spent decades hiding part of herself, playing things safe to please others. Even now, she deserved to live her life, not watch it pass by.

The same could be said about him, he supposed.

"So . . ." Reece sighed.

"So," Tracy echoed.

"What do you say we call it a day?" His reference addressed much more than the game, which naturally went without saying.

She smiled in thoughtful agreement. Her eyes misted over as they relaxed into the quiet.

"Still friends?" she asked.

Whether they would be or not, he didn't know for sure. But he did know they would always share a piece of each other's past.

"Get over here," he encouraged, motioning with his chin. When she scooted closer, he layered his arm over her shoulders and rested his cheek on her head.

On the bench beside them remained his

grandma's ring. Light bounced off the diamond, as if sending him a wink.

CHAPTER 15

Anticipation thrummed as Jenna waited for the big unveiling. Seated in the reception area, she glimpsed her reflection in a window. On the daring scale, her fresh, cherry Coke highlights were nothing compared to the transformation taking place across the salon.

Once again, she flipped through the magazine featuring the new look her mother had chosen. The hairstylist was so eager to get started, intent on sending the frizzy bangs back to the eighties, that she barely glanced at the example.

"It'll look fabulous," Jenna had said, detecting second thoughts in her mother's eyes. Jenna was still astounded her mom had initiated the appointment, a tough yet much-needed decision. Just like Jenna's career.

According to Sally, the teapot boasted a value upward of forty grand. The single antique piece would have ensured Jenna's partnership — at the cost of her conscience. *I'm not being stupid, I'm not being stupid,* she'd told herself, entering her boss's office. Quitting anything went against Jenna's nature, let alone a job with an enticing payday. But when she walked away, a burden she hadn't known existed lifted from her life.

"You can come see her now," the receptionist announced.

Jenna tossed the magazine aside and followed with the anxiousness of a father about to view his newborn.

"She's over there." The receptionist pointed toward the farthest hair station before skittering away. Jenna hoped that wasn't a sign the lady was taking cover.

Past wafts of styling sprays and chemical dyes, Jenna threaded through the room. Hair dryers boomed, mimicking a 747 at takeoff. In the corner, a row of hunched manicurists tended to ladies with fancy updos. Sparkly hair clips and berry red polish screamed of holiday parties.

Finally, Jenna hooked gazes with the stylist. If her mom hated the results, there would be no second attempt.

In a magician's move, the stylist yanked off her customer's cape and swiveled the chair one-eighty, presenting her creation.

Jenna gasped. She just . . . couldn't believe . . .

Her mother's brow knotted in fear. "You don't like it."

On a solid note of honesty, Jenna shook her head. "Nope," she told her. "I *love* it."

Her mom giggled in relief. Like a little girl wobbling in heels, an air of excitement outweighed her uncertainty. She touched the shortened sides that ran just below her jawline, sloping longer toward the front. All frizz and gray had been banished from her sleek, straightened hair.

"And Doobie's going to love it even more," Jenna added.

Her mom brushed off the comment, betrayed by her reddening cheeks. Already, Jenna could see the awe in his face while picking her mother up for their weekly lesson. Personally, Jenna wasn't a fan of country-western dancing, but she'd recently joined them anyhow, and was glad she had. Witnessing the devotion in every look he sent her mom was well worth the boot scoots and grapevines. Most of all, her mother's returning confidence continued to swell Jenna's heart. New jeans to replace the woman's stretch pants were a mere bonus.

"How about some lunch to celebrate?" Jenna asked. "I say we show off our new looks."

Her mother fingered her flattened bangs, as if deciding. Then she smiled with a youthful giddiness and nodded. "My treat this time."

Reluctant, Jenna agreed. Until she found a job, and could afford more than her own TV dinners, she wasn't in the position to argue.

"I just need to freshen up first," her mother said.

"I'll meet you in front." Jenna headed to the reception area. While waiting, she glanced out the window. She spied a familiar face in the store across the street.

Could it be . . . ?

Antique stores traditionally ranked as her least favorite hubs. She dreaded the musty air, cramped spaces, and clash of displays. For the potential reward, however, she was willing to endure.

She turned to the receptionist. "Please tell my mom I'll be right back."

At the window display, her nose an inch from the pane, Jenna delighted in her find. Once more, it was the squatty monk. Make that *lots* of squatty monks.

Side by side they stood, like a village of holy men. Varied in size, they wore wreaths of gray hair, brown robes, and rosy cheeks. She scanned the queue with hope. A large water pitcher and gravy boat. Salt and pepper shakers. A sugar cup and . . . there it was! A fully intact creamer, handle and all. It was a perfect replacement for the set inherited from Aunt Lenore. Silly or not, Jenna felt like it completed the memory of the sweet old woman. She couldn't imagine a more meaningful gift for her mother.

If she wanted to keep the surprise, she had to hurry.

A bell on the door jangled as she entered. She prepared for a dusty waft. Instead, the lemony scent of polished wood welcomed her. At the sales counter, she joined the line of two other customers. The cashier's gentle eyes matched his Santa beard, and his knit snowman pullover could sweep a national contest. For ugly Christmas sweaters, that is.

Cha-ching, cha-ching.

The antique register, while pretty to look at, wasn't the fastest way to do business.

She started tapping her toes, hoping to subliminally rush the guy along. Soon she realized she was keeping time with the tune playing on the speaker. "Jingle Bell Rock" had a pretty catchy beat —

She stopped mid-thought and rolled her eyes. Yet she couldn't help smiling. Aliens must have replaced her grinch-like heart while she slept.

The first customer finished and the line moved up.

Cha-ching, cha-ching.

Tamping her impatience, Jenna glanced around the store. A baby buggy was parked nearby, its oversized wheels weathered from walks. On the maple vanity lay a silver shaving kit, beside it a mother-of-pearl hairbrush. How often had they been used to primp for a special occasion?

As if transformed by a wand, the old, worn items surrounding Jenna became anything but "junk." They were storytellers. Rather than price tags, she now saw their tales. A wedding knife and server had shared a couple's first cake. A jukebox had played records for a patron-filled diner. An army jacket had witnessed triumphs and tragedies. Come to think of it, the chocolate-hued uniform, fit for a woman, was used during World War II.

Topped with a cap, the mannequin enticed Jenna over. She touched the stripes sewn onto the sleeve. Her heart cinched at the thought of Estelle and not seeing the family again. The sale was only two days away.

"She's a beauty, isn't she?" The clerk gestured toward the uniform, eliminating the possibility that he was speaking of Estelle. "Hard to find a 'Hobby hat' in such good condition. Are you a fan of memorabilia from World War Two?"

"I guess you could say I've become one."

His face lit up. "Got lots of stuff sprinkled around. More things from the Women's Army Corps, too, if you're interested. Most are priced well below value. People just don't realize what they're worth."

"No," she said sadly, "I bet they don't."

"You know, my mother-in-law served with them over in Europe. Never spoke about it much, though." As he rubbed his beard, Jenna perked.

Was there more to Estelle's secrecy than Tom Redding? The mystery continued to nag at Jenna. She hoped she wasn't prying by asking, "Do you happen to know why she didn't talk about it?"

"Oh, I dunno," he said. "I imagine it wasn't the most acceptable job at the time. Taking care of the kids, having dinner on the table by five — back then, that was the role women were proud of. Or were supposed to be, at any rate."

As a modern woman, independent and

career-driven, Jenna hadn't thought of it that way. It seemed almost too simple, and yet made absolute sense.

The man jerked his thumb to the side. "Would you like to see more stuff like this?"

Yes prepared to spill from her mouth when she remembered her mother. "Another day would be great." Jenna would definitely be back. "For now, I'll only need the monk creamer from the front window."

"Oh, sure, sure. Even got the original box for it in the back room. Be back in a jiffy."

Jenna watched him scoot off, rounding a table of porcelain dolls. As he reached into the display, her cell phone rang. She expected to see the salon's number, calling on behalf of a concerned mom. To her surprise, again it was Sally.

"Tell me you didn't do it," she demanded, obviously about Jenna's career.

"Afraid so," Jenna replied.

"So what's next?"

"I'm figuring it'll come to me, hopefully sooner rather than later."

The clerk, creamer in hand, pointed toward the back room. Jenna lifted her hand in acknowledgment as he traveled through the store, neatly displayed and packed with enough valuables for a museum.

A museum . . .

A display . . .

Valuables . . .

The idea materialized, a scattering of threads being woven. With all of Jenna's connections to brokers and collectors, why hadn't she thought of it before?

"Hey, Sally. Is the history museum still trying to replace that exhibit? The one that was going to be on Jackie O."

"Um — yeah. Why's that?"

Jenna's excitement bubbled up like champagne, a celebration in the making. She prayed Terrence hadn't donated that shoe box.

"Hold on," she said, and held the phone to her chest. She called out to the clerk now emerging from storage.

"Sir, how much would you charge for the Women's Army Corps items?"

"From World War Two?"

"That's right."

"Depends." He scratched his head. "Which ones?"

Jenna smiled. "All of them."

CHAPTER 16

Christmas Eve had arrived, and Reece still couldn't decide whether or not to go. In the shadows of his car, parked downtown, he remained a block away. He rolled his key over and over in his palm. According to his mom, the museum had made a point of confirming the family's attendance. A variety of his grandma's estate items had been added to their permanent collection. As a holiday treat, they'd all been invited to the premier showing.

Well, not Reece necessarily. With Jenna Matthews somehow involved, he doubted the invitation was meant for him.

Since parting ways with Tracy, he'd once gotten up the nerve to give Jenna a call. The message he'd left her, a belated thanks for her help at the hospital, felt pathetically transparent. How do you slip into a casual voice mail that you're no longer in a relationship? Answer: you don't.

Not surprisingly she didn't call back.

What a jerk he must seem. Reece was probably a major reason she had cut ties to the estate, to prevent crossing paths. By now, she'd surely moved on to another sale and left thoughts of him behind. And yet, the possibility of seeing her again had been powerful enough to draw him here.

Though maybe not to the front door.

He envisioned his family just now walking in: his sister with her husband, his mother and grandma. And his dad. Since their hospital run-in, his breakup with Tracy must have provided even more ammo. The awaiting lecture was as appealing as tonight's show — personal elements of his grandparents' lives, laid out for gawking strangers. Despite the honor of a museum's acquisition, a public display made him uneasy.

Again, Reece flipped over his car key. The ignition slot like a magnet, it urged him to start the engine. He could face his dad in the morning, before the family gathered for Christmas. . . .

He vanquished the thought. Too often, where his dad was concerned, Reece found himself acting like a kid.

Enough. Now more than ever, his grandma deserved the family's support. If he'd learned nothing else — from the accident, from her secret past — it was how to put the needs of others first. Tonight was a perfect opportunity to act on that lesson.

Reece straightened the necktie of his suit and exited the car. Within minutes, he was climbing the concrete steps toward the pillared entry.

"Welcome," a woman said at the door. "Your name, please?"

"Reece Porter."

"Ah, yes. The rest of your party's already checked in." She ran a yellow highlighter through his name, listed alphabetically on the sheet. "I hope you enjoy your evening."

So did he.

"Thank you."

Inside, behind a USO banner, three ladies in vintage uniforms stood on a low, miniature stage. They harmonized about yuletide carols being sung by a choir. Red, white, and blue bunting decorated the walls. A waiter with a tray of champagne offered Reece a glass. Microbrews were more his style.

"No thanks," he said, a moment before he spotted his dad alone, depositing an armful of jackets at the coat check. "On second thought."

The server handed over a half-filled flute that Reece finished in two gulps. Through a scattering of guests, his father glanced over. The look on his face confirmed he had plenty to say.

Reece set aside his glass and waited, steeling himself. He suddenly wished he'd swallowed his pride and reached out before now, so their confrontation would already be done.

"Reece," his father greeted evenly.

"Dad."

A tense beat passed, the unspoken like shards, clear and sharp.

"So where is everybody?" Reece asked.

"In the other room there." His father gave a nod toward the end of the hall, where murmured discussions floated out over the tiled floor. Then he peered at Reece and spoke firmly. "But, I'd like to have a word with you first. . . ."

Here it came.

"It's in regard to what you said, about me not supporting you."

"Dad, please. I know where this is going." To have peace in the family, especially at Christmas, Reece was willing to apologize. Certainly there were things he, too, could have handled better.

Yet his father charged on. "I've pondered

it a whole lot, and the thing you need to hear is —"

Strangers strolled past, hopefully out of earshot.

"— I've been wrong."

Reece blinked. He reviewed the words, a shock to his senses.

"Fact is, in my line of work, I've been trained to prepare for the worst. And I guess that's made me a little . . . overprotective."

Baffled, Reece continued to stare.

"I hope you can at least see why I acted like I did. After getting that call to come to the hospital . . ." His dad shook his head, trailing off. Color rose in his neck, and his eyes gained a sheen.

No question, for both of them, his grandma's recent collapse had ratcheted up their last confrontation.

"It's okay," Reece offered, barely audible. He cleared the emotion from his throat. "I think we were both on edge, worrying about Grandma."

"No, Reece. I meant when I got the call for *your* trip to the ER."

The second twist again took Reece off guard.

His dad released a breath, hands on his hips. "I know I've been tougher on you since then. But you have to understand, that drive to get there . . ." He finished in a near mumble. "Well, it was about the longest of my life."

Reece had been so terrified over Tracy's condition, he hadn't thought of how strongly his parents, namely his father, had been affected by the scare. How much his father must have always been unnerved by Reece's reckless stunts, for fear of a phone call no parent wanted to receive.

The stress of waiting for word on his grandma's episode had given Reece a taste of that fear. He didn't see until now how alike he and his dad were. Both had been trying so hard to control things they couldn't.

"For what it's worth," Reece admitted, "I've been wrong too. About a lot of things."

After a thoughtful pause, his father nodded. "Guess we're not always as brilliant as we give ourselves credit for."

Reece's mouth curved into a smile. He placed a hand on his dad's shoulder. "Don't worry," he assured him, "I won't tell Mom you said that."

They shared a laugh, slicing through the remnants of tension. Clearly, many more discussions would be needed to strengthen their relationship. But for now, Reece

couldn't think of a more promising beginning.

Chapter 17

Almost showtime, but still no sign of him.

A good thing, Jenna reminded herself as she surveyed the reception hall. She needed to stay alert in case of any snags. Families of elderly guests and major donors congregated about her. The ribbon cutting would commence at any minute.

She lifted her posture, savoring the confidence of her burgundy cocktail dress and pumps. Utmost professionalism was essential to her new boss, the director of the private museum. Jenna still couldn't believe her good fortune. She wasn't about to let Reece Porter indirectly ruin it. In his presence, she never failed to revert to a teenager — full of blushes and giggles and too easily tempted to cross the line of morality.

"They're such nice people," Jenna's mom exclaimed, returning with Doobie, whose western sports coat dressed up his jeans and boots. "That Estelle woman, she's just so charming."

"She's definitely an amazing woman," Jenna agreed.

"And Sandy and her daughter, Lisa? Just fabulous."

Jenna had no idea introducing her mom to the three Porter women would have surpassed basic, cordial greetings. Rather, it became a fifteen-minute exchange from which Jenna had to excuse herself, for fear Reece would join them when he arrived.

Skirting the notion, she again admired her mom's black pantsuit, as modern as her hairdo. She'd never looked lovelier, or happier. Granted, a gaudy peacock brooch glimmered from her collar, an accessory that oddly put Jenna at ease. An improved mom was great — not an altogether new one.

"Rita, tell her the news," Doobie encouraged, sweetly touching her chin.

"Oh, yes! I almost forgot." She angled toward Jenna. "Apparently" — an inserted pause to build suspense — "since Sandy's on the auction committee for the Children's Cancer Association, she's going to call me next week about their gala. They're not happy with their photographer, so she wants to talk about working together."

"Mom, that's wonderful."

"I really have Doobie to thank for talking me up, even though *he*'s actually the one they should be hiring."

"Ah, bologna," Doobie said. "You're gonna do such a good job, you'll be gettin' calls from all over town. Won't she, Jenna?"

"Absolutely."

Doobie was right. A prestigious event like that had the potential to rapidly boost her mother's career.

"I say we toast to the both of you," he declared. "How 'bout some bubbly?"

The flutters in Jenna's stomach wouldn't mix well with alcohol. "Maybe later."

"I'll take a glass," her mom replied.

"Be back in two shakes." With a wink, Doobie disappeared into the crowd, just as a museum docent approached. She appeared on the verge of panic.

"Jenna, have you seen the big scissors for the ribbon?"

Pressure to impress their patrons, to smooth over the Jackie O mishap, magnified the importance of every detail.

"Last I saw," Jenna said, "they were at the front desk. Bottom drawer, I think."

"Phew. Thank you!"

When the woman sped away, Jenna's mom gazed around the room. She spoke in amazement. "I can't believe you put this together so fast."

"Mom, I didn't exactly do it on my own."

Her mother waved this off and met her eyes. "The point is, I'm very, very proud of you."

Jenna felt a glow from inside. She recognized it as a deep, genuine pride, not only for the person she was becoming — more of herself, if that made any sense — but for the woman standing before her.

"Ooh, I almost forgot." Her mom reached into her purse and retrieved a wrapped, palm-sized box. "I brought along your Christmas present."

Jenna hesitated, though not because of a resistance to gift giving. The buzz of the teeming space, and weaving of waiters with passed hors d'oeuvres, didn't make the moment ideal. What's more, she'd left her mother's collectible creamer, wrapped with a few other goodies, back at her condo — the home she thankfully wouldn't have to give up.

"Wouldn't it be better if I open this tomorrow?" Jenna suggested.

"You could, but I thought it might bring you luck for tonight." The sparkle in her mom's eyes made it impossible to decline.

Jenna removed the paper, and out of the rectangular jewelry box she pulled a beautiful silver bracelet made of Cheerio-sized links. A shiny heart, engraved with her initials, dangled from the middle: *For J. M.*

She ran her finger over the letters, fully understanding what she held. A mother's symbol of love. Many decades from now, maybe a stranger would find it in a flea market or an antique mall. And maybe, if fortunate enough, that person would sense its story.

"Thank you," Jenna whispered. "I love it." Tears welling, they traded a long heartfelt hug.

Then stepping back, her mom relieved her of the box and wrapping. "I'll go throw these away for you."

Jenna nodded at the simple but meaning-ful offer; her mother was now taking care of others. So captivated by the change, Jenna almost forgot about her bracelet. She placed it around her wrist and secured the clasp. Luck tonight might come in handy.

"Merry Christmas, Jenna," said a man's voice. She knew that smooth timbre.

Against the weight of dread, she straight-ened.

Reece Porter. A sleek, charcoal suit and black shirt accentuated the broadness of his shoulders. Splitting the width of his chest was a burgundy tie. Beside her dress of a near-identical shade, a person could mistake them for a date.

"I didn't think you were going to be here." Her greeting tumbled out, sounding more of hope than observance.

His smile tentatively lowered as he motioned behind him. "Guess I could catch a movie down the street instead."

"No, I didn't mean — I meant — when I didn't see you with your family, I thought . . ." Once again, he'd made her a flustered mess. "Do you need help finding them?"

"Nah, I already did, thanks. Just wanted to come over and say hi."

"Well. Hi." She glanced away, mentally scraping for an excuse to escape. But her mind was too busy scolding her pulse. Why did it insist on quickening at the sight of those dark brown eyes?

"So," he drew out. "How goes life in the estate world?"

The question threw her off. She thought he would have heard the news from Sandy. Although why would he ask about her? He had a gorgeous, raven-haired, blue-eyed girlfriend to occupy his thoughts.

"I'm not in the business anymore," Jenna replied.

"Wow. I didn't realize."

She lifted a shoulder and said pointedly, "Turns out, it wasn't a good fit."

"You find something better?"

Had he missed her message? Or was he challenging her?

"I'm working at the museum now, as an assistant with acquisitions."

"So life is good, then."

"Life is good."

She meant to smirk at him, but his return smile melted the smugness right out of her. And those damn eyes. Once more, they caused her cheeks to flame.

To her relief, a question came to mind, a cool splash of water. "Will your girlfriend be joining you tonight?"

At that, his gaze fell away. Thank God. But then he shook his head and said, "We're not together anymore."

"I see."

Wait — what?

"I guess you could say we weren't a good fit. Just took us a while to see that."

The echoed sentiment reverberated between them. She tried to resist, but her defenses, flimsy as they were, couldn't compete against his undeniable sincerity. "I'm sorry it didn't work out."

"Actually, it did — is," he amended. "Everything is working out. Just not the way

I'd pictured, maybe."

Although cautious, Jenna allowed herself another look in his eyes. In them she found mutual understanding, a commonality of unexpected paths. Whose life ever turned out the way they planned?

"Ladies and gentlemen, your attention, please."

The female voice abruptly reminded Jenna of her surroundings, the task at hand. Her boss, Deanne, appeared at the arched entrance of the main hall. A wide red ribbon, tied into a Christmas bow, created a horizontal barricade. Behind her, a closed velvety curtain blocked early peeks.

Jenna projected a look of attentiveness.

Deanne raised both arms, palms to the back in an Evita-like pose. The signal worked, and the USO singers concluded their song in a few quick bars. The room fell to a hush. It was all a tad dramatic, but so was Deanne. And Jenna liked her that way. During the past two weeks of preparations, Jenna had come to adore the woman and her boundless passion for history.

"We are extremely pleased to have so many esteemed guests with us this evening," Deanne resumed, inadvertently gesticulating. Not the safest of habits with the oversize scissors in her hands. "While we had originally planned to showcase the life of Jacqueline Kennedy Onassis, I firmly believe the collection we've prepared is equally impressive. Maybe more so, as it spotlights significant heroes in our nation's history who all too often go unrecognized."

As Jenna strove to listen, she could feel Reece stealing side glances in her direction. She hoped to God the heat crawling up her neck wasn't betraying her with a beet red hue.

In what seemed a hundred hours later, Deanne wrapped up her speech, cut the ribbon, and on cue, two docents slid open the curtains. The crowd murmured as they traveled forward. Over the heads of the herd Jenna located her mother and Doobie. She gestured for them to go on in, that she'd catch up with them soon. Wafts of perfumes and colognes, plenty of Old Spice, mingled in the air.

"Here they come," Reece reported as his family drew closer.

Estelle stood at the helm in an emerald green dress and pearls, her expression distraught. "I really don't see how anything of mine would've been important enough to be here."

"Well," Jenna said, "why don't we find out?"

Estelle eyed her at length, then yielded by shuffling into the stream of people. Jenna followed, batting away doubts that this was a mistake. She again told herself: Once Estelle viewed her achievements in a revered display, and with family at her side, she would fully embrace her due credit.

On the right, they came across the uniform that had kicked all of this off. It now hung sleek and pressed on an elegant mannequin. Yellowed wartime letters filled the case to its side.

Estelle paused for only a second before continuing onward.

Military recruitment posters, enlarged and mounted, zigzagged down the wall. They featured colorful drawings of women in every branch: the WACs and WAVES, WAFS and WASPs, ANCs and SPARS, and more.

What began as an idea to honor the members of the Women's Army Corps had expanded to include thousands of others. Jenna still had trouble keeping all of their acronyms straight, but not her gratitude for what they had sacrificed.

She hoped that message was coming through, but Estelle's face remained unreadable. A glimpse of her family's confusion generated little assurance.

The rectangular display case awaited on the left. Jenna debated over pointing it out, but then Estelle halted. Her eyes squinted behind her glasses as she angled her walk. Her Bronze Star, labeled with her name, was propped beside a collage of photos. Though they all featured her unit in the Pacific, only a few of the pictures had belonged to Estelle.

She stood there, staring at the case. Not saying a thing. No smile, no happy surprise. Just a quiver in her hands.

"Toss them out, donate them, do as you'd like."

Those were the words she'd used when Jenna had first presented the keepsakes. Could she have truly meant she wanted them destroyed?

"Mom, are these of you?" Sandy asked, confounded.

Still, nothing in response.

The family closed in on the case, studying the items intently.

Jenna felt the angst of an incompetent conductor. She was orchestrating a performance headed rapidly for disaster.

"How did you . . ." Estelle began in a rasp. Her gaze remained on the pictures. "Where did you find all of these?"

An honest answer might only make things worse.

"Mrs. Porter, if you're not comfortable with this, I could certainly let the director know."

They could remove at least the Porters' belongings — Jenna hoped.

Estelle's ragged breaths suggested she was starting to cry. Jenna moved closer, flashing back to the woman's health scare. But then Estelle glanced up to reveal a growing smile. The puffs of exhales came from quiet laughter, not tears.

"Hard to believe it," she said, motioning downward, "but that's how we did our laundry in a bind."

Moisture sprang to Jenna's eyes out of sheer relief. Amid the collage, she located the photo of Estelle and a stunning light-haired woman. They were wringing out garments over upturned helmets.

Estelle gained a reminiscent tone as she went on. "Gracious, everything we owned molded in that humidity. And the mosquitoes?" She blew out a sigh. "All bigger and deadlier than Sasquatch."

Jenna grinned as Estelle's focus went on to the next picture. Three ladies sat in a jeep while Estelle leaned against the hood. Palm trees in the background dotted the scene.

"Would you look at that," she said.
"Roz . . . and Betty. You know they used to call us the SOS girls, Shirley and me, on account of our names."

"I'd heard that," Jenna replied in truth, then diverted from an inquiry about her secret source. "You must have worked hard to take care of the patients there."

With a calmed hand, Estelle touched the glass, hovering over a snapshot. A WAC was serving a food tray to a bedded soldier. "Met some real good fellas in that ward, that's for sure. Her response carried a current of bittersweet memories. Something in it confirmed that the reference wasn't limited to patients.

Reece's father turned from the collection. "But — this is the Bronze Star," he said, a near whisper. "Mom, why didn't you ever tell us you served in the war?"

When Estelle fumbled for an answer, Reece interjected, "Because she thought her past was something to be ashamed of. And she was wrong."

The warmth and meaning of his words seemed to resonate with his grandma, as well as his father. In fact, they had the same effect on Jenna.

"What a cute puppy," Lisa commented,

admiring the photo of Estelle with a York-shire.

"Ahh, yeah," Estelle said. "She used to ride with a flight crew. Called her . . . oh, what was it? Smoky, I think. Her tricks were great for cheering up patients. The staff too." Estelle shook her head with an air of remembering, and asked Jenna, "Wherever did you find these?"

As if summoning the answer, in the most literal sense, Jenna spotted his face. Tom Redding stood across the thinning room, dapper in his bow tie and gray suit. He'd claimed he was too busy to come, a blatant excuse. Yet he had gathered the nerve after all.

"To be honest," Jenna replied, "I had a little help."

Estelle wrinkled her brow. Her gaze proceeded to trace where Jenna had been looking and discovered the elderly gentleman. As he made his way over, he removed his fedora and smoothed his silver hair.

Recognition captured Estelle's face, punctuated by her hand to her lips.

They stood only a few feet apart.

"How are you, Stella?"

Again, she had fallen silent and still.

The tension palpable, Tom tried again, "You're looking lovely."

Reece touched Jenna's elbow. *Who is this?* he mouthed. The rest of his family appeared just as bewildered.

Tears mounted in Estelle's eyes, mixed with questions. Beneath those arose a history of romance and heartbreak. Had Estelle harbored too much of the latter to even return a greeting? Maybe Tom should have mailed the letter he'd mentioned, to test the waters first.

A metal tinkling entered the air. At the end of the room, adjacent to the next hallway, Deanne jiggled a bell over her head. "Pardon me, everyone. But we have a special performance about to begin in the next hall. If you'll kindly follow me."

The USO girls were scheduled to sing a tribute. Jenna had helped assemble the small stage between the Rosie the Riveters area and that of the All American Women's Baseball League. It was a highlight that now mattered little, for Jenna's heart ached for Tom — who now angled sideways, as if to leave.

But he didn't. He was simply offering his elbow. "Shall we, Stella?" he hazarded to ask.

She glanced down, then back to his face. The whole family was watching, waiting.

After a long beat, she slowly raised her

arm and hooked it through his. Although inquiries in her eyes persisted, the smile stretching her lips mirrored the one now lighting Tom's face. Evidently, he had no need for a letter. He'd delivered himself instead, which was a hundred times better.

Together, the couple walked out of the emptying hall. Reece's dad and mom exchanged looks of pleasant interest, and the rest of the family followed behind.

Except for one.

Reece gave Jenna's sleeve a soft tug, turning her around. "You mind filling me in?"

To best explain, she guided him to the last photo. Tom was holding a small branch above Estelle's head. "That's them."

Reece leaned down for a closer view. "What's he got there?"

"Some makeshift mistletoe."

He grinned. "Smart guy."

When Reece stood up, the distance between them shrank to inches. From the warmth of his breath and realization of being alone, Jenna fought off a shiver. Tenderly, he ran the back of his fingers across her cheek.

"So, tell me," he said. "Did it work?"

"What's that?"

"The mistletoe."

She shook her head *no*.

"That's too bad."

Through the fog of Jenna's thoughts came the rest of the story. "After their holiday party, though, she found him behind the supply tent."

"Then what happened?"

Before she could say more, he demonstrated a guess by pressing his lips to hers. She hedged for a second, merely from surprise, then wrapped her arms around his neck. She could feel his heart against her chest, and lost herself in the beat. His hands, strong and safe, rounded her waist and pulled her close. As he kissed her deeper, her skin prickled and knees went soft. Indescribable desire surged through her body.

Never had her emotions clashed like this. Newness battled the familiar in the scent of his skin, the taste of his lips. His touch wove a web of comfort and fear. A tangle of thoughts. A collection of feelings.

Jenna never wanted it to end.

ABOUT THE AUTHORS

Fern Michaels is the *USA Today* and *New York Times* bestselling author of *Tuesday's Child, Late Edition, Betrayal, Home Free, Southern Comfort,* and dozens of other novels and novellas. There are over seventy-five million copies of her books in print.

Fern Michaels has built and funded several large daycare centers in her hometown, and is a passionate animal lover who has outfitted police dogs across the country with special bulletproof vests. She shares her home in South Carolina with her five dogs and a resident ghost named Mary Margaret. Visit her website at www.fernmichaels.com.

Holly Chamberlin is a native New Yorker, but she now lives in Boston — the aftermath of stumbling across Mr. Right at the one moment she wasn't watching the terrain. She's been writing and editing — poetry, children's fantasies, a romance novel or two, among many other genres and projects, her entire life. She has two cats, Jack and Betty, and when she's not writing her hobbies include reading, shopping and cocktails at six.

Leslie Meier is the acclaimed author of sixteen Lucy Stone mysteries and has also written for *Ellery Queen's Mystery Magazine*. She lives in Harwich, Massachusetts, where she is currently at work on the next Lucy Stone mystery.

Kristina McMorris is an award-winning author and graduate of Pepperdine University. She lives in the Pacific Northwest with her husband and two sons. Her first novel is *Letters from Home*.